Praise for *Blackberry Beach*

"Both series fans and newcomers will delight in the tender romance and comforting atmosphere."

Publishers Weekly

"Hannon's town of second chances continues to inspire sweet love stories like those in Debbie Macomber's Blossom Street books."

Booklist

"*Blackberry Beach* clearly showcases author Irene Hannon's complete mastery of the Christian romance genre with its deftly crafted characters and memorable, narrative-driven storyline."

Midwest Book Review

"Two charming romances, a lovely small-town setting near the ocean, gentle inspirational messages, and well-drawn characters. A wonderful gem."

All About Romance

"Delivers all the heart and hope and second chances that have become trademark with the series."

Best Reads

Praise for *Starfish Pier*

"With its nicely interwoven faith elements, Hannon's multifaceted return to Hope Harbor focuses on how forgiving oneself is as important for healing as forgiveness from others. Series fans will be overjoyed by this complex, stirring tale."

Publishers Weekly

"The restful location and quirky townsfolk are sure to be soothing to those who enjoy Christian romances set in small towns."

Library Journal

"A pitch-perfect contemporary romance novel by a gifted author who is a complete master of the genre."

Midwest Book Review

Praise for *Driftwood Bay*

"Readers will delight in this pleasant romance. Hannon's take on loss and survival is simpatico with Debbie Macomber's Blossom Street series."

Booklist

"Full of faith and characters that readers will want to root for until the end."

Publishers Weekly

"Character-driven, thought-provoking, and highly recommended for connoisseurs of the genre."

Midwest Book Review

HOPE HARBOR
1 Bayview Lavender Farm and Tearoom/Driftwood Bay
2 Harbor Point Cranberries
3 Seabird Inn
4 Gull Motel
5 Marci's house
6 Sea Glass cottage
7 Pelican Point lighthouse
8 Sea Haven Apartments
W
N
S
E
Gull Island
Little Gull Island
Pelican Point
Starfish Pier
Dockside Drive
Main Street
Bluff Avenue
Harbor Street
Highway 101
Pelican Point Road
Starfish Pier Road
Sandpiper Cove
Charley's house and studio
Blackberry Beach

DOWNTOWN
HOPE HARBOR
1 Foghorn
2 Grace Christian Church
3 Eric's law office
4 Hope Harbor Herald office
5 Lou's Bait & Tackle
6 Sweet Dreams Bakery
7 Charley's taco stand
8 Pocket park and gazebo
9 Urgent care center
10 Eye of the Beholder
11 The Myrtle Café
12 Budding Blooms
13 Chocolate Harbor
14 The Perfect Blend
15 St. Francis Church
Gull Island
Little Gull Island
N
S
E
W
Sea Rose Lane
River
Dockside Drive
Bluff Avenue
Main Street
Harbor Street
Charley's

Sea Glass Cottage

A Hope Harbor Novel

IRENE HANNON

Published by Revell
a division of Baker Publishing Group
PO Box 6287, Grand Rapids, MI 49516-6287
www.revellbooks.com

Printed in the United States of America

Library of Congress Cataloging-in-Publication Data
Names: Hannon, Irene, author.
Title: Sea glass cottage : a Hope Harbor novel / Irene Hannon.
Description: Grand Rapids, MI : Revell, a division of Baker Publishing Group, [2022] | Series: Hope Harbor
Identifiers: LCCN 2021042939 | ISBN 9780800736163 (paperback) | ISBN 9780800741044 (casebound) | ISBN 9781493434145 (ebook)
Subjects: LCGFT: Novels.
Classification: LCC PS3558.A4793 S415 2022 | DDC 813/.54—dc23
LC record available at https://lccn.loc.gov/2021042939

This book is a work of fiction. Names, characters, places, and incidents are the product of the author's imagination or are used fictitiously. Any resemblance to actual events, locales, or persons, living or dead, is coincidental.

Baker Publishing Group publications use paper produced from sustainable forestry practices and post-consumer waste whenever possible.

21 22 23 24 25 26 27 7 6 5 4 3 2 1

To Monsignor John Leykam
(aka Father Sean Murphy Lynch Leykam)—
Thank you for all your kindness to my father
through the years.
Your esteem and affection warmed his heart—
and it was mutual.

And to Margie Meyers—
With gratitude for your many
thoughtful gestures and the gracious hospitality
that fed not only his body but his soul.

Dad was blessed by the gift of both your friendships—
as am I.

1

Asking for help from a man who hated you was hard.

Really hard.

But she was out of options.

Jack Colby was her last resort.

Despite the cool Oregon breeze tripping along Dockside Drive, a bead of sweat trickled down Christi Reece's temple as Jack completed his purchase at the stand on the wharf. Prying one white-knuckled hand off the steering wheel, she inhaled a lungful of the briny Hope Harbor air and swiped away the external evidence of her nervousness. Thankfully she alone was privy to the pretzel twist in her stomach and the erratic lurch of her heart.

A savory aroma wafted toward her from the white truck that had been Jack's destination on this sunny end-of-April afternoon, setting off a rumble in her stomach. But eating was low priority—even if her last meal hours ago had consisted of a stale bagel and gas station coffee.

The man she'd driven thirty-plus hours to see lingered to exchange a few words with the cook, who adjusted the baseball cap over his long gray ponytail as the two shared a laugh.

Still smiling, Jack lifted a hand in farewell, picked up the brown bag containing his order, and strolled her direction.

Unless time had softened his heart, however, he wouldn't be smiling for long.

Pulse pounding, Christi fumbled with the handle on the older-model Nissan that had carried her more than two thousand miles. Pushed the door open. Swung her shaky legs to the pavement, praying they wouldn't fold.

Jack gave her a casual glance as she slid from behind the wheel and stood. The kind you bestowed on a stranger who happened to catch your momentary attention.

No hint of recognition flickered in his eyes.

A twinge of disappointment nipped at her—but that was foolish. Eleven years had passed. Her once-long hair had been cropped to shoulder length, and she didn't lighten the dark blond hue anymore. Oversized sunglasses hid most of her face. And life had taken a toll. The frothy twenty-year-old college student he'd known—and loved—was long gone.

Jack's pace slowed, as if he'd realized there was more to this encounter than chance.

Her cue to move forward.

Squeezing her fingers into tight fists, she approached him. Unlike her, he'd benefitted from the passage of time. The handsome twenty-three-year-old who'd brightened that carefree summer had filled out. Matured. Acquired an intriguing aura of worldliness that enhanced the considerable appeal she'd once found difficult to resist.

Christi stopped a few feet away and tried to fill her uncooperative lungs. "Hello, Jack." The greeting came out a bit husky, thanks to the tail end of the cold she'd been fighting for the past week.

His smile evaporated, and a pair of crevices creased his brow. "I'm sorry. Have we met?"

Still no glimmer of recognition.

"It's been a while." She drew a shaky breath and removed her sunglasses. "Christi Reece."

As the name of the woman who'd once stolen his heart—then trampled on it—reverberated in the quiet, peaceful air of the town he now called home, Jack's lungs locked.

Christi Reece, here?

Impossible.

Yet as he scrutinized her, reality smacked him in the face. Her hair was shorter and not as blond, and a decade of living had snuffed some of the youthful glow from her complexion, added a smudge of shadow beneath her lush lower lashes. But the brilliant cornflower blue of her eyes remained undimmed, and those full lips that had caressed his with eager abandon looked as soft as ever despite a slight droop at the corners.

It was her, even if her voice was deeper than he remembered.

His stomach bottomed out, and he swallowed past the sudden bitter taste in his mouth.

Why, after all these years, had she invaded his turf? Tainted the new life he'd created far from his Midwest roots? Resurrected the memories he'd banished of the day his world had crumbled?

He gritted his teeth, his appetite vanishing despite the savory aroma of Charley's tacos wafting up from the bag clenched in his fingers.

"What are you doing here?" If the question came out harsher and more resentful than he intended, so be it. The sentiment was spot-on.

She tucked a lank strand of hair behind one ear. "I came to see you. To t-talk to you."

He frowned at the subtle stammer. Christi Reece, nervous?

Major disconnect.

With her wealth and privileged upbringing, she'd always possessed an overabundance of confidence and composure. What was going on?

But curiosity wasn't sufficient motive to extend this conversation or probe for particulars.

"I have nothing to say to you." He pulled out his shades, slid them on, and prepared to make a fast exit.

As if sensing his intent, she took a step closer, palms extended in a placating gesture. "Look, I know I hurt you. I know what I did was wrong. Worse than wrong. It was unconscionable. Not a day has gone by that I haven't regretted my behavior. If I could fix the damage, I would."

He steeled himself against the trace of tears in her voice. "What happened between us is ancient history. If you came here for closure, consider it done." He turned on his heel and walked away.

"Wait! Please!"

Please?

He faltered midstride.

That word hadn't been in her vocabulary eleven years ago. Christi Reece had known how to cajole and sweet-talk her way into getting whatever she wanted, but she'd never resorted to pleading.

Keep walking, Colby. You know she's a master manipulator. Don't be fooled again.

He resumed his retreat.

"Please, Jack. I need help, and I-I don't have anywhere else to t-turn."

He hesitated again—and bit back a term that would have shocked his mother.

How could this woman who'd used him and hurt him still have the power to get under his skin?

But he'd always been a sucker for people in trouble—especially desperate ones.

And Christi sounded desperate.

Bracing, he slowly angled back.

Big mistake.

She'd followed him, stopping touching distance away. A brimming tear was poised to spill down her cheek.

A knot formed in his gut, and he took a quick step back.

Didn't help.

Seeing this once-poised, self-assured woman reduced to tears activated a potent—and unwanted—protective instinct.

"What kind of help?" He shifted into the intimidating, wide-legged stance that served him well as a cop, shoring up his resolve to keep his distance.

"I need money. A loan. I'll pay it back as fast as I can. With interest."

Silence fell between them as he tried to process her request. Failed.

Why would a woman from her wealthy background need money?

"You'll have to explain that to me."

"I just did. I need money."

"Why don't you ask your father?"

Her throat worked. "He died six years ago."

Hard as he tried to quash it, a brief surge of sympathy swept over him. Losing her father would have been tough. Hard-nosed and snooty as the man had been, he'd doted on Christi. They'd been as tight as father and daughter could be. As she'd told him during that golden summer, it had been the two of them against the world after her mother died when she was ten.

Good as David Reece's intentions may have been, however, giving his daughter everything she wanted had been a mistake. All he'd done was create a spoiled little rich girl—and a spoiled *big* rich girl.

Water under the bridge now. What was done was done.

But in light of her father's generosity to his only offspring, why was she having money problems? As his sole heir, she should have inherited his estate.

"Are you telling me your father didn't leave you well fixed?"

She moistened her lips. "His businesses weren't as successful near the end."

He cocked his head. "As I recall, you had a penchant for designer clothes, first-class trips to Europe, and high-end resorts. Did you squander the inheritance?"

A shaft of pain darted through her eyes, and she dropped her gaze. Picked at a piece of lint on her jacket. "No."

"Then why do you need money?"

"Like I said, he didn't leave me as much as you may think."

"But he left you what he had."

"Yes."

"What happened to the money?"

"It's a long story."

And not one she intended to share.

Message received.

He switched gears. "Why come to me of all people?" He at least deserved an answer to *that* question.

She watched two seagulls flutter down and snuggle up together ten feet away. "Because you cared for me, once."

He wasn't going to fall for the hint of wistfulness in her inflection that suggested she'd harbored feelings for him too, back then. He knew better.

"Like I said, that's ancient history. Over and forgotten." He used his most dismissive tone.

She searched his face, her voice soft but certain as she responded. "If that were true, you wouldn't still be angry with me."

Checkmate.

But no way was he going to admit she had the power to rouse emotions in him—of any kind—after more than a decade.

"I'm not angry." *Liar, liar.* "But I *am* in a hurry." Also not true. His night shift didn't start for hours. "How much money are you talking about?" Not that it mattered. Of course he wasn't giving her a loan. But refocusing the conversation on her request would deflect attention away from the sudden, simmering anger she'd detected. Anger he thought he'd long ago put to rest.

She transferred her weight from one foot to the other and gave him the amount.

Not paltry—but not a fortune either. Well under six figures. Less than the amount her father had dropped on her each year as he indulged her every whim.

Strange how their situations had reversed. He could write a check for that total and never miss it.

But she didn't know that.

Or did she?

He narrowed his eyes. "That's a chunk of change. What makes you think I have that kind of money?"

"I saw your debut book in the library two weeks ago, on the bestseller rack." Her gaze didn't waver, suggesting she was telling the truth. "I picked it up because the title intrigued me, and when I flipped it over, I saw your photo on the back. The name didn't match, but I knew it was you. I remembered you telling me you wanted to write a book someday. Finding it on that shelf was like a sign from above. An answer to my prayers for guidance."

He didn't attempt to hide his skepticism. "Since when did you get religion?"

"I've learned a few things through the years."

"Like what?" The question spilled out before he could stop it, and he threw up a hand. "Never mind. Not interested. How did you track me down?"

"It wasn't hard. The author bio said you lived in the Pacific Northwest. That narrowed the search—and the internet is an amazing tool. I didn't find any mention of a wife who might object to a loan, and I know your family is gone. I figured a *New York Times* bestseller would have the financial resources to help me."

A common misperception. She may have researched *him*, but she hadn't done her homework on author income.

"A bestselling book sounds more impressive than it is. In general, you have to write them consistently to get rich. Most authors have day jobs."

"Do you?"

"Yes." However, the stellar performance of his first novel had led to significant income far beyond his advance. And the lucrative three-book contract that had followed would provide a cozy cushion for his future unless he decided to live the high life—which was *not* in his plans.

But he didn't have to share any of that with Christi.

Some of the color leeched from her cheeks. "I knew you might refuse because you didn't *want* to help me, but I never thought it would be because you *couldn't*." She rubbed her temple, her tension almost palpable.

"I didn't say that."

"You implied it."

Yeah, he had—and a man in his profession shouldn't shade the truth.

"My book's done well—and more are coming." He left it at that. "Why do you need such a large sum of money?"

"I have an obligation to fulfill."

The two seagulls stood and waddled closer, watching the human drama with their unblinking avian eyes.

Weird.

Why weren't they heckling tourists for handouts or hanging around the fishing boats in the harbor like normal gulls?

"I'm sorry you have financial issues." The comment was perfunctory at best. Her mess wasn't his problem. "But you were always adept at getting what you wanted. I imagine that skill will see you through this crisis."

Her lips quivered. "I don't have anywhere else to turn, Jack. If I did, I wouldn't be here. You were my last hope."

Were.

Past tense.

He didn't much like the sound of that. Desperate people could take desperate actions.

But again—not his problem.

He took another step back. "I'm sure you'll come up with something."

One of the gulls at his feet fluttered its wings, gave him a beady-eyed stare, and emitted a raucous squawk that sounded like a rebuke.

He stifled a snort. As if seagulls were capable of such a reaction. No doubt the bird was hoping for a scrap from his fish tacos. A handout.

Kind of like what the woman across from him was after.

They were both out of luck.

Christi's shoulders slumped, and dejection radiated from her. "I knew the odds were against me, but I didn't have anything to lose by asking except gas money."

A few beats passed. There was nothing else to say—unless he offered her the loan she'd asked for.

Not happening.

Tightening his grip on the cooling tacos, he spun away and strode toward his Jeep. He was *not* going to look back. Literally or figuratively.

Christi Reece was part of his past, and that's where she'd stay. He'd moved on, built a life he enjoyed, achieved his dream to write a bestselling crime thriller. He was exactly where he wanted to be.

And he wasn't about to let the woman it had taken him years to expunge from his dreams barge in and disrupt his peace of mind and placid existence.

Even if the dormant emotions she'd awakened were already messing with both.

2

The man she'd pinned her hopes on didn't look back at her. Not once. He slid behind the wheel of his Jeep, started the engine, and drove away.

Vision blurring, Christi swiped off the tear trailing down her cheek as the tiny flame of hope in her heart flickered and went out. But what else had she expected, really? The image of the hurt and disillusionment in his eyes the day she'd betrayed him was seared into her brain, as clear as if the incident had happened yesterday. And while time could dull pain, wounds often lingered in memory—as his obviously had. It was clear forgive and forget weren't in his vocabulary. At least not for her.

The two seagulls who'd witnessed their exchange inched closer, and she sighed. It was hard not to envy them their uncomplicated life. Birds didn't have to worry about paying bills or guilt or complicated relationships. And if life got tough, they could soar into the sky and fly far away from their problems.

Christi angled back toward the road and watched the taillights of Jack's Jeep disappear around a corner. In hindsight, it had been foolish to let the discovery of his novel send her on a cross-country wild-goose chase. The book hadn't been a sign from above to track him down. It had been a fluke. Hope Harbor wasn't going to live up to its name for *her*.

So what was she supposed to do now?

She glanced up at the late-afternoon sky, where billowy white clouds were scuttling across the blue expanse.

Lord, please show me what to do next. The clock is ticking for Tasha. If I can't come up with a solution, she'll—

"Good afternoon."

Christi jerked and swung around.

The guy from the taco stand ambled toward her, smiling. "Sorry. I didn't mean to startle you. I saw you talking to Jack and wanted to welcome you to our charming town. I'm Charley Lopez—better known in Hope Harbor as the taco man." He extended a hand as he inclined his head toward the white food trailer, where his first name was emblazoned in colorful letters above the now-closed serving window.

She rubbed her palm on her jeans and returned his warm clasp. "Thanks, but I'm just passing through."

"Sorry to hear that. This is a wonderful, welcoming community. How long are you planning to stay?"

Excellent question.

If she could, she'd leave this minute. But fatigue was turning her mind—and her muscles—to mush after her marathon drive from Dallas. Before she hit the road again, she needed a cheap place to crash and a decent meal. Perhaps sleep and food would clear the muddle from her brain.

"I guess I'll be here until tomorrow."

"If you don't have accommodations lined up yet, may I suggest the Gull Motel?" He motioned up the hill above the harbor. "Nothing fancy but clean and easy on the pocketbook. And if you want to take in a fantastic view while you're here, I'd recommend Pelican Point lighthouse." He swept a hand the other direction, toward the sea. "You can't miss the road to the point. It's a few minutes up Highway 101. On a clear day like this, you should be able to see for miles. It's a terrific spot for thinking . . . or sorting through problems."

Christi scrutinized him. His tone was conversational, but warmth and caring radiated from his insightful dark brown eyes. Almost as if he was aware she was searching for guidance.

Get a grip, Christi. You're reading far too much into this exchange. The man is being friendly, nothing more.

She forced up the corners of her mouth. "Thanks for the recommendations."

"My pleasure." He lifted a brown bag like the kind Jack had been toting. This one was also emitting a heavenly aroma. "I have an extra order of tacos that could use a home. Can I convince you to take them off my hands?"

Her nose twitched as he swung the bag back and forth. Tempting—but the peanut butter crackers in the car would have to suffice for dinner. The balance in her bank account was in the danger zone, and takeout food could be expensive.

"Um . . . I have snacks in my car."

A fan of lines appeared in the weathered skin at the corners of the man's eyes. "Not as tasty as my tacos, I bet."

No question about it, given the delectable aroma that had jump-started her salivary glands.

"How much are they?"

"First order is always on the house."

She did a double take. "You give free tacos to everyone who passes through?"

"Not as a rule. Mostly to newcomers who plan to stick around. But these are extra, and they're either going to you or to Floyd and Gladys." He nodded toward the seagull couple hovering nearby.

She inspected the duo, a touch of amusement tickling her funny bone despite her glum mood. "The birds have names?"

"All of God's creatures have names."

O-kay. This guy was a character. But he seemed genuine—and harmless.

"I wouldn't want to deprive your friends of a treat."

"Floyd and Gladys won't mind. They know I'll make it up to them tomorrow. Right, you two?" He directed his question to the birds.

One of them gave a laugh-like cackle, and the other ruffled its feathers. A moment later, in a flutter of wings, they were airborne and flying toward the harbor.

Charley held the bag out to her.

As her stomach rumbled, she caved. For once she'd accept a handout. After the disappointing results of her long trek to Oregon, this stranger's kindness was a balm to her soul.

"Thank you." She took the offering.

"If you're not in a hurry, you may want to mosey up to Pelican Point to enjoy them. It's a world-class view, and at this hour on a weekday you should have the vista all to yourself. The tacos will stay warm for the short drive."

"I may do that." If she could convince her growling stomach to wait five or ten more minutes for nourishment.

Charley adjusted his Ducks baseball cap. "I hope you have a pleasant stay, however long you're in our fair town. And I'll be cooking again tomorrow if you get another hankering for my tacos—or want any more information about Hope Harbor."

"I appreciate that. But I expect I'll be on my way early."

"If your plans change, you know where to find me." He touched the brim of his cap and wandered down the wharf.

She watched him leave, a tiny smile hovering at her lips. What a pleasant man. Much more agreeable than the other occupant of the town she'd encountered.

Too bad Charley the taco man wasn't in a position to offer her a loan. He seemed like the type who'd give someone the benefit of the doubt—and a second chance.

The type Jack had once been.

But she'd been a fool to expect miracles—and that's what it would take to soften his heart.

Banishing those depressing thoughts, she considered Charley's suggestion. She could chow down here rather than drive up to the lighthouse. The benches spaced along the wharf, flanked by overflowing flower boxes, were inviting—and the scene was restful.

Yet solitude and a panoramic view were appealing. Perhaps up at the lighthouse, with nothing but sky and sea around her, she'd find direction—and clarity.

Less than ten minutes later, after traversing the two-lane road that wound past an occasional house tucked among the trees, she emerged at the headland.

The vista, as Charley had promised, was stunning.

Bag of tacos in hand, she struck out down the path from the parking lot to the lighthouse. After choosing one of the benches that offered a sweeping view of the sea, she slid her arms into the sleeves of her jacket and opened Charley's bag. Inside she found three packets wrapped in white butcher paper, along with a bottle of water.

Her throat tightened, and she blinked to clear her vision. The timing of the unexpected gift—and the man's kindness—couldn't have been more providential. Maybe she didn't know where she was going from here, or what tomorrow held, but for this moment she would be thankful for the small blessing that had graced her day.

One bite into her first fish taco, Christi's eyes widened. This wasn't an ordinary taco. It was a gourmet delight, filled with rich goodness, capped off with a zing from whatever spices and sauce the man had used.

Scratch small blessing. This taco was magic.

She savored the delicious trio, stretching out her dinner as long as she could. Even after the last morsel was gone, she lingered on the bench, letting the peace of the setting seep into her soul.

Only when fog began to roll in, obscuring the blue sky and dimming the light from the setting sun, did she stand. It was time to find the motel Charley had mentioned—and pray the price was as reasonable as he'd implied. After spending last night in the car at a rest stop while she caught a few hours of sleep in the midst of her marathon drive, a shower and a real bed would be heaven.

Crimping the top of the bag in her fingers, she turned and—

Oh. My.

Fog was descending around her. Fast. Already the gravel path to the parking lot was half obscured.

A sinuous swirl of cool vapor enveloped her, and she set off at a fast jog, tossing her trash into a receptacle as she passed.

Once behind the wheel, she put the car in gear, flicked on the lights, and pointed her Nissan back toward 101.

The fog worsened as she crept down the narrow road, reducing visibility to a handful of yards. Hunching forward, she squinted into the murkiness and clutched the wheel. Driving in this kind of weather was beyond dangerous.

Christi peered at the shoulder as she crawled forward. The safest plan was to find a driveway and pull off, wait out the fog. She could finish the trek back to the highway after it lifted.

Less than a minute later, a gravel lane appeared to her right.

Thank you, God!

She swung in and inched down the one-lane drive, scanning both sides for a wide spot where she could maneuver her car around to face the road and be ready to head out the instant visibility improved.

As she crunched along, two hazy, ethereal orbs of light appeared through the mist.

A house?

She cut her headlights and continued forward. The residents might not appreciate a stranger appearing on their doorstep in this remote spot. What if they called the police? That's what she'd do if it were *her* house. In today's crazy world, it was reckless to take chances.

And a trip to the police station in the back of a cruiser was not on her itinerary for this already disastrous trip.

She continued to roll along on the gravel until the fog thickened so much she couldn't see three feet in front of her. If there was somewhere to turn around, it was cloaked in mist. There was nothing to do but stop where she was and hope the gray shroud lifted before darkness fell.

Christi cut the engine—and utter quiet descended. If the twin lights up ahead *were* from a house, not a sound seeped through the walls. It was possible the owners weren't home. Or they could be hunkered down inside beside a cozy fire, enjoying a cup of hot chocolate.

A most appealing prospect, since the temperature had plummeted as fog cloaked the landscape. Her bare-bones car didn't boast the luxury of a thermometer, but the sixtyish temperature earlier at the wharf must have dropped fifteen degrees.

Suppressing a shiver, she checked the gas tank gauge. The Nissan was running on fumes. One more item to add to her to-do list as soon as the mist dissipated. In the meantime, wasting fuel by turning the engine on and off to activate the heater wouldn't be smart. If she ran out of gas, she'd have to hoof it back to town.

Christi reached behind her, snagged one of the blankets she'd cuddled up in at the rest stop last night, and lowered her seat. There was no reason to be nervous, despite the isolation and dense fog. If she couldn't see to get out of here, no one else could see to get in. Might as well try to catch a few z's while she waited, shake off a bit of the bone-deep fatigue that had plagued her for most of this trip.

Tucking the blanket around her, she let her eyelids drift closed . . . and the world around her faded away.

It took the chattering of her teeth—and the relentless shivers racking her body—to finally jar her awake.

After shaking off her grogginess in the darkness, she worked her arm free from the blanket and twisted her wrist to see the face of her watch. Nine o'clock? She'd slept two full hours without moving a muscle?

The crick in her neck provided the answer.

She adjusted her seat back to an upright position, rotating her neck as she surveyed her surroundings. It was impossible to see much in the dark, but it was clear the fog was thicker than ever. And it felt as if the temperature had dropped another ten degrees.

Staying in the car was no longer viable. Not unless she wanted her head cold to turn into pneumonia.

Like it or not, she'd have to knock on the door of the house—if it *was* a house—and hope the occupants were trusting and compassionate souls who would take pity on her and provide a warm haven to wait out the weather.

She shoved her fingers through the tangles in her hair, pulled a flashlight out of the glove compartment, and pushed the door open.

The dampness burrowed into her at once, and she hunkered deeper into her inadequate jacket as she hurried toward the fuzzy twin beacons, keeping the beam of the flashlight aimed at the ground in front of her.

After a few yards, the outlines of a cottage emerged from the mist.

Yes! The lights *were* from a house.

Only faint illumination shone from behind the drawn shade in the window on the right, but the matching electric lanterns that flanked the front door radiated welcome—and warmth.

She ascended the single step at the entry, took cover under the peaked roof above the small porch, and searched for a doorbell.

Nada.

But the brass knocker on the front door would do the job.

Christi lifted it and gave a light tap as she rehearsed a brief explanation for her presence.

Thirty seconds passed without a response.

Well, shoot. Maybe no one was home after all.

Or was it possible they hadn't heard her timid summons?

A harder knock was in order before she gave up and resigned herself to hours of shivering discomfort in her car.

She lifted the knocker again and gave three loud raps.

The door creaked open on the last thump.

Whoops.

She released the knocker and scuttled back. Didn't people in Oregon believe in locks? What if the owners thought she was breaking in? How was she going to explain her—

A gust of wind whipped past, and the door creaked open several more inches.

Uh-oh.

Christi braced. Surely someone would hear the door and come to investigate. She'd just have to explain as best she could and hope they believed she wasn't a thief—or worse.

Another half minute ticked by.

No sound emerged from within.

She took a deep breath. There were two options. She could close the door, retreat to her car, and spend the next few hours shivering—or she could suck it up, try to rouse the owner, and explain her predicament.

Another cold whorl of fog spiraled around her.

Decision made.

She edged closer to the door again and called through the opening. "Hello? Is anyone home?"

No response.

Wiping her hands on her jeans, she leaned forward and peeked through the crack in the door.

The light she'd seen through the shades was dim, but it was sufficient to illuminate the large room.

The large *empty* room.

There wasn't a lick of furniture in the place. No carpet or rugs broke the expanse of empty floor. The walls were bare.

The cottage was unoccupied.

But if that was the case, why hadn't the owners locked the door?

A question without an answer, so no sense dwelling on it.

The more pressing issue was what to do next—retreat to the car or explore?

A blast of chilly air whooshed past.

No contest. If nothing else, this structure would offer more shelter and warmth than her car until the fog lifted.

She pushed the door wider and gave the inside a once-over. The glow she'd noticed came from a nightlight plugged into an outlet on the wall. Meaning the cottage had electricity.

Why, if it wasn't occupied?

One more question without an answer.

She tiptoed into the large room to the right of the small foyer, where the light was. Hardwood floors covered the whole expanse, from the front of the house to the back. A large stone fireplace and mantel dominated the far wall, and logs were piled next to the hearth.

Odd.

After sweeping the beam of her flashlight around the room to confirm she was alone, Christi crossed to the fireplace. Logs were also laid on the grate, kindling tucked underneath, and a box of long matches rested on the hearth.

Logs that could provide warmth on this cold, damp night.

Dare she light them? Cuddle up in her blanket in front of the fire?

As she mulled over that bold move, she crept around the rest of the cottage. The small room on the other side of the foyer was also empty. Down the hall beside the stairway, and opening to the larger room with the fireplace, was a simple but adequate kitchen.

After returning to the foyer, she climbed the stairs to the second floor, which featured three dormer rooms—also empty. The largest one was finished and boasted another fireplace, but the two smaller ones lacked drywall taping, painting, and other finishing touches. Two full bathrooms complemented the half bath on the first floor, one of those also only partially finished.

The house appeared to be a work in progress—yet it didn't feel as if the construction was recent. It was more like someone had started to build this cottage but never finished.

If the structure was abandoned, though, why were there logs in the grate, waiting to be set alight with the flick of a match?

She doubled back to the living room and flashed her light into the fireplace. The inside was pristine, suggesting no fire had ever touched it. Nor did the fireplace implements beside the logs show any sign of use.

Strange.

Stranger still? Despite all the weirdness, she wasn't freaked out. Nor did she feel any urge to flee.

Instead, all she wanted to do was light the fire, curl up in her blanket, and go to sleep.

And that was exactly what she was going to do.

In the morning, after the fog lifted, she'd clean out the grate and stop at the city offices in town. Someone there would know—or could find out—who owned this place, and she'd leave enough cash to cover the cost of the logs, plus a little more. In the end, it would be cheaper than a motel room.

Mind made up, Christi returned to the door. There was a bolt on the inside, so once she made a fast trip to the car for pillow, blankets, and purse, she could shut herself in for the night.

Four minutes later, all those items in hand, she locked the cottage door behind her, opened the damper on the fireplace, and lit a match. The kindling flamed at once, and within minutes the logs were crackling and sending warmth into the room.

Bliss.

Christi stretched out on one blanket in front of the fire, pulled the other one over her, and scrunched the pillow under her head. It wasn't the softest bed she'd ever slept on, but it was cozy.

And as she drifted off to sleep, halfway between consciousness and slumber, the oddest thing happened.

She'd never been to Hope Harbor before. She didn't know a soul here except Jack. She'd stumbled onto this cottage by chance.

Yet for the first time in years, she felt at peace—and at home.

3

Why was there a car in the driveway of Sea Glass Cottage?

And why had he discovered it near the end of his eleven-to-seven shift, on his last patrol circuit?

Jack slowed the cruiser on Pelican Point Road, in front of the gravel drive that wound through the trees toward the cottage. While the sun wouldn't crest the hills to the east for another fifteen minutes, the dawn light was sufficient to dispel a few of the shadows.

But dawn, dusk, or midday, that car didn't belong there.

So much for clocking out fast and heading home to write for a few hours before he crashed. Depending on what he found at the cottage, his plans for the morning could be toast.

He swung into the driveway, called in his location to dispatch, and ran the Texas plates.

The car was registered to a Christine Powers from Dallas.

Brow puckered, he scanned the Nissan again.

Christine—as in Christi?

Too bad he hadn't paid more attention to her vehicle yesterday at the wharf. Not very observant for a police officer—but he hadn't been in law enforcement mode during their brief conversation.

He did a second database search for Christine Powers's driver's license. Not his typical protocol in situations like this—but he didn't usually run into old girlfriends sporting an air of desperation either.

There were no suspensions on the plate, nor any active warrants on the license. The description and date of birth on the license, however, matched what he knew about Christi.

This car belonged to her—and in light of her different last name, she must be married.

A jolt that felt a lot like disappointment shot through him, and he expelled an annoyed breath. So what if she'd given her heart to someone else? Who cared? As he'd told her yesterday, their relationship was ancient history.

But if she *was* married, why was she here alone? Why did she need money? And what was she doing at an unoccupied cottage?

Much as he'd like to avoid another encounter with her, he was stuck. It was his job to follow through if a trespassing law was being broken.

Resigned, he left the patrol car behind and approached the cottage.

As he got closer, he sniffed. Was that a lingering hint of woodsmoke in the air? Like the kind from a fireplace?

What was going on in there?

He stepped up onto the front porch. Frowned. Where was the sturdy padlock that always secured the door?

After crossing the porch, he clasped the knob and twisted. It turned—but the door refused to open.

The windows were shaded, so he cupped his hands around his eyes and peered through the sea-glass-studded sidelights that bookended the front door.

Nothing. It was too dim inside to see anything, and the colorful sea glass mosaic obscured the view, providing privacy for occupants.

Could he gain access through the back door?

He left the porch and circled the cottage to check the rear door.

No luck there either. The padlock on that door was in place.

He retraced his route to the front. Whatever Christi was up to—trespassing, breaking and entering, squatting—he'd have to deal with it.

But he didn't relish another face-off with her on this otherwise beautiful Friday morning.

Bang! Bang! Bang!

Christi jerked her eyelids open at the rude awakening from one of the best night's sleep she'd had in months. Maybe years.

"Police. Open up!"

Police?

Pulse pounding, she leaped to her feet as the hard, authoritative voice breached the walls of her impromptu motel. Pale light filtered around the edges of the drawn shades as she stumbled toward the door and tried to fight off the lingering sluggishness of her deep slumber. Had she slept all night?

More pounding.

"I said open up! I'm not going to wait all morning."

Question answered. She'd been dead to the world for hours.

And now she'd attracted the attention of law enforcement.

Wonderful.

"I'm coming. Give me a m-minute." She picked up her pace, fumbled with the lock on the door, and pulled it open.

The glowering, uniformed officer on the porch, mouth set in a grim line, eyes cold as they swept over her, was . . . Jack?

Her jaw dropped.

The caring, kindhearted man she'd once known, who'd read philosophy and dreamed of writing a novel, had chosen a career in law enforcement? *That* was his day job?

As she tried to wrap her mind around that unexpected piece of news, Christi shoved her rat's-nest hair back. Smoothed a hand down her wrinkled jacket. Too bad she'd kicked off her shoes last night. Another inch of height would give her more stature and self-confidence—and the hole in her sock wouldn't be as obvious.

Jack's gaze fixated on her exposed toe for a moment, then rose to her face. "You want to explain what you're doing here?"

"I got stuck in the fog." She gave him an abbreviated version of the story. "I was afraid to drive, and it was too cold to spend the night in my car." She pulled out a tissue and swiped at her nose.

"How did you get in?"

"The door opened when I rapped with that." She indicated the brass knocker.

"What happened to the padlock?"

"What padlock?"

"This door is always padlocked."

"It wasn't last night."

He let a few beats pass. "I want to do a walk-through."

She stepped aside. "Be my guest."

"Is anyone else with you?"

"No."

"Wait here."

He left her to do a quick circuit of the house, stopping by the hearth after he finished. "Where did you get the logs for the fire?"

"They were here. Along with the matches. The fire was ready to be lit. For the record, I was planning to stop at the city offices and let someone know I'd stayed here. I was also going to offer to pay for the logs."

Twin furrows creased his brow. "Why would all the material for a fire be here?"

"I have no idea."

He fisted his hands on his hips and scrutinized her. "Are you in the habit of entering strange houses and spending the night?"

A spark of anger sprang to life deep inside her, and she slammed her arms across her chest. Tipped up her chin. "No, I am not. I was tired and cold and spooked about driving in the fog. I found an empty, unlocked house that offered shelter and warmth. I'm not going to apologize for taking advantage of that—especially since I planned to make it right this morning."

"So you say."

"I'm not lying."

His lips twisted. "In light of our history, you'll forgive me if I'm skeptical."

She deserved that.

Her shoulders slumped, and she let her arms drop back to her sides. "Are you going to arrest me?"

"Even if you didn't break the lock to get in, you *are* trespassing. I'll have to contact the owner, see if they want to press charges." He pulled out his cell.

"Fine. I'll clean up while you do that. Remember to tell them I was going to pay for the logs."

She crossed to the hearth as he exited. After sweeping up the still-warm ashes from last night's fire, she deposited them in the can beside the fireplace, put on her shoes, folded up her blankets—and waited for the verdict.

One thing for sure.

Given his hostile attitude, if Jack had any say about it, she'd end up behind bars for the duration of her stay in town.

So much for Charley Lopez's claim that Hope Harbor was a welcoming community.

Jack kept the phone to his ear as he walked several yards away from Sea Glass Cottage, even though there was no one on the other end of the line. Pretending to place a call had been the first excuse he could think of to buy himself a few minutes to mull over next steps.

There was no need to have the city manager track down contact information on the owner. He'd had that since he'd sold his book and could afford to buy a house of his own instead of rent an apartment. And this place had been on his radar from the day he'd spotted it three years ago, during his first patrol circuit.

Every inquiry he'd sent to the management company that handled the property had been rebuffed, however. The owner wasn't interested in selling. Yet the cottage, while well maintained, remained empty.

It didn't make sense.

As for how the anonymous owner would feel about a stranger taking refuge on the premises—impossible to know until the management company offices opened in an hour or two and the department called to ask.

In the meantime, what was he supposed to do with Christi?

He raked his fingers through his hair as two seagulls circled overhead, the rising sun gilding their wings.

Taking her to the station would be extreme—but could he trust her to stay in town until the property owner weighed in?

Impossible to say.

While she seemed sincere about wanting to compensate the owner for her uninvited stay, that could be an illusion. An act. She'd been a master at pretending, once.

A knot formed in his stomach, and he gritted his teeth. Rehashing the past was *not* productive. He should rebury the painful memories her appearance had resurrected and focus on the present.

Forcibly engaging the left side of his brain, he shifted into analytical mode. Why not get her contact information, ask her to stick close for a few hours, and take down her credit card number to cover the cost of the logs? There wasn't much risk in that—unless the owner wanted to prosecute for trespassing and Christi bailed rather than deal with the consequences. That could complicate his life.

Taking into account the missing lock and the logs in the fireplace, however, it didn't appear she'd been the sole trespasser. While vagrants were few and far between in Hope Harbor, evidence suggested someone besides her had been making himself or herself at home here. Rather than take legal action against Christi, the owner would be wiser to beef up security on the premises.

Pocketing his phone, Jack pushed through the front door and returned to the living room. She was sitting cross-legged on the floor beside her folded blankets, hugging her pillow.

"What's the verdict?" Her tone was impassive, but a hint of trepidation lurked in her irises.

"We won't be able to contact the owner for a couple of hours. I'd like you to stay in town until we get a reading from them. If you'll give me your cell number, I can have someone call you as soon as we hear back." He pulled out his notebook. "A credit card number would also be helpful if the owner wants you to pay for the logs."

She reached for her purse, unzipped it, and withdrew the sort of pay-by-the-minute burner cell favored by the criminal element. "I don't have a smartphone anymore. This is for emergencies, and I haven't memorized the number." She turned it on. Pushed a few buttons. Recited a number. Then she pulled out her wallet, extracted a credit card, and read off that number too.

He jotted both down. "Which name is on the card—Reece or Powers?"

Her eyebrows rose. "You ran my plates."

"Normal protocol."

"Reece—but I haven't switched it on all my ID yet." She dipped her head and tucked the phone and wallet back into her purse.

If she was reverting to her maiden name, did that mean she was divorced? And was a messy breakup the cause of her money problems?

The questions hovered on the tip of his tongue—but they weren't relevant to the trespassing incident. Nor was she likely to answer them, in light of her previous reticence about personal subjects. So he settled for a query on a different topic.

"Why don't you have a smartphone?"

"It's an unnecessary expense." She stood and gathered up her purse, pillow, and blankets, keeping her back to him.

She couldn't afford a real cell phone? An item no longer considered a luxury but a necessity by the majority of people in the US?

Just how strapped was she for cash?

"This is a cozy house—with a spectacular view." She gave the space an appreciative sweep, her gaze lingering on the vista of the sea through the large bay window that took up much of the back wall. "I wonder why no one lives here?"

He wasn't obligated to respond to her rhetorical question. But he found himself answering anyway.

"The story I heard is that a husband and wife from Kansas were building it as a retirement home. When she died suddenly during the construction, he didn't have the heart to finish it—or sell it. It fell into disrepair, and after he passed away, the property was tied up in probate for a long while. Someone bought it from the heirs several years ago, cleaned it up—but never moved in."

"Why not?" She pivoted back to him, forehead wrinkled.

Jack shrugged. "Whoever owns it may be holding it as an investment. The property will only go up in value."

"It's such a shame to leave it sitting here empty." Her features softened as she took another look around. "This is the kind of house that should be filled with love and laughter."

He agreed—but he didn't have to tell her about his futile attempt to buy the place, or his rebuffed proposal to rent with first dibs to purchase if it ever *was* for sale.

"The owner—or owners—can do what they want."

"Are they local?"

"I have no idea. No one does. The property is handled by a management firm."

Her brow crinkled again. "Why would the owner be secretive?"

"Like I said, it may be someone who views this as an investment and prefers to remain anonymous. Assuming they live in the area, it would be less awkward to negotiate a higher price if personalities are left out of the equation." He motioned toward the door. "Shall we?"

She toted her belongings past him, stopping to examine the sea glass sidelights illuminated by the rising sun. "These are beautiful."

"They're why this place is called Sea Glass Cottage." He didn't have to say anything more—but he seemed to have a case of motor mouth today. "According to the story I heard, the original owner created these for his wife using pieces of sea glass they gathered during their walks on the beaches here. Apparently they vacationed in Hope Harbor for years before they bought this land."

She juggled the bedding in her arms to trace around one of the opaque aquamarine-colored pieces with her fingertip. "What a thoughtful gift."

He steeled himself against the sweet smile curving her supple lips. "Not in the same league as a piece of Tiffany jewelry, though."

"No. It's better."

Was she kidding? Tiffany's had always been her go-to store for bling.

He watched her as she examined the sidelights. There wasn't a trace of artifice in her demeanor. Only appreciation for the workmanship—and the sentiment.

Curious.

The Christi he'd known in St. Louis wouldn't have wasted a nanosecond on the sidelights.

He gave her a more thorough inspection. Fashion wasn't his forte, but her attire didn't seem high-end. The jeans were practical and well-worn, not those skinny high-priced ones she used to prefer. Her sport shoes were scuffed. Her jacket showed signs of wear. Not to mention the sock with the gaping hole.

She was also thin. Too thin. And she'd made no attempt to mask the shadows under her lower lashes or her gauntness with makeup. In fact, the woman who'd once placed a high priority on grooming wasn't wearing any cosmetics as far as he could see. Nor did her hair reflect the cut of a pricey salon. It was hard to tell what style it was under all the tangles, but it appeared to be a simple, straightforward cut.

As if sensing his perusal, she glanced toward him. A faint flush crept over her cheeks, and she dropped her hand from the glass. "Sorry. I didn't mean to hold you up." Hefting the bedding higher, she walked out the door.

He followed more slowly. "Are you going back to town?"

"Yes." She continued to the older-model Nissan that was a far cry from the sporty Jaguar convertible she'd driven eleven years ago. "I'll stick close until I hear back from you." She stowed the bedding in the back seat.

"It won't be me. My shift is over. The chief herself may call—or another officer."

"Okay." She straightened up, her expression neutral, and motioned toward his cruiser. "You're blocking the drive."

"I have to secure the door, but I'll back onto the road to let you out first." He surveyed the cottage. "The owner will want to replace the padlock—and consider installing a security system if vagrants are using this place."

"I don't think they are. I didn't get the feeling anyone had ever spent a night here."

"The supply of wood and missing lock would indicate otherwise."

"I can't speak to the lock, but the fireplace had never been used." She fished out a tissue and wiped her nose. "The bricks inside were pristine. Even one fire would have left scorch marks."

That was true.

Which made the whole setup she'd found all the more strange.

But this wasn't his mystery to solve. All he had to do was secure the door, have someone contact the owner, and write up a brief report. After that, he could wash his hands of the whole matter—and of Christi.

The sooner the better.

"I'll move my vehicle."

"Thanks." She zipped her jacket against the morning chill but remained standing by her car. As if she wanted to continue their conversation.

But just because he was more bothered than he wanted to admit by her obvious dire financial straits—and the fact she'd spent last night sleeping in an empty house on a bare floor—didn't mean he should say anything he could come to regret.

Especially since the odds of them seeing each other again were slim to none.

The prudent plan would be to walk away with a simple goodbye.

In case she was hungry, though . . .

"If you want to get breakfast, the Myrtle Café in town has an early bird special until eight."

"Thanks, but I have peanut butter crackers in the car."

"That's not a meal." Especially with the case of sniffles she was nursing. She ought to have real food and a large glass of OJ.

"I'm not a big breakfast eater. Is there a grocery store nearby?"

He should let this go. Her eating habits were none of his concern—even if she'd once liked big breakfasts and was no doubt skipping today to save money.

"Yes. We have a small market." He gave her the name and location.

"Thanks." Still she lingered by the car door, chewing on her lower lip, fingers clamped around her keys as a few beads of perspiration broke out on her upper lip despite the chilly morning air. "Look, I know you said no to a loan yesterday. But I *would* pay you back. And I could give you this as collateral." She pulled out the chain that hung around her neck to display a ring with a large diamond in the center, flanked by several smaller stones.

A shock wave rippled through him as he examined the treasured piece of jewelry she'd often worn on her right hand during that fateful summer.

"That's your mother's engagement ring."

"I know." She swallowed. "It's worth a lot. I have the appraisal."

She quoted him the figure. "I thought about taking it to a pawn shop, but they wouldn't give me anything close to its actual value. Besides, I wasn't confident they'd keep it for me until I could reclaim it. Would you at least think about the loan? As a business transaction, not a personal favor. I don't have to have an answer this minute. The money isn't due for thirty days. Please?"

The sun crested the hill, highlighting the taut lines of her face and the urgent entreaty in her eyes. Both chipped away at the formidable wall he'd constructed around his heart—as did her willingness to give him her mother's ring as collateral.

A danger alert began to flash in his mind, and his pulse spiked. He had to get away from her. Fast. Before his wall crumbled further.

But hard as he tried to voice it, the "no" stuck in his throat.

Fine. He'd go with plan B.

"I'll think about it—but don't hold your breath." Fair warning. Because he was *not* giving her the money. He might not be able to refuse her request while she was standing a few feet away, but he could text it.

Her irises began to glisten. "You have no idea how much that means to me. Thank you."

Blast.

If she started crying, he was in big trouble.

He retreated a few steps. "I'll move my car."

Without waiting for a reply, he strode toward his cruiser. Once inside, he backed onto the road, guilt pricking his conscience.

It had been wrong to take the coward's way out—and unkind to create false hope. He should have sucked it up and told her no rather than delay the inevitable.

As she pulled out of the driveway, she lifted a hand in farewell.

His conscience jabbed him again.

Letting her drive away without fixing this was wrong.

He unwrapped his fingers from around the wheel and motioned for her to stop—but she turned onto the road and picked up speed.

She must have thought he was returning her wave.

Short of following her and breaking the bad news on the side of the road, he'd have to go with a call or text.

But he wouldn't leave her in limbo for long. By the end of the day, he'd give her his decision.

The Nissan disappeared around a curve in the road, and he swung back into the driveway. After parking by the cottage, he fished a padlock out of his trunk. As soon as he secured the premises, he could be on his way.

It took mere seconds to attach the lock to the door, but he lingered to examine the sidelights. They *were* beautiful. Yet their history was sad. Neither the man who'd made them nor the woman he'd loved had realized their dream of a life here together. The house had stood locked and empty all these years, nothing but a hollow echo of what might have been filling the rooms.

Like the hollow echo in his heart after Christi had rejected him.

But the lock on this house had disappeared . . . and now Christi had rattled the lock on his heart.

Not good.

Locks performed a valuable function. They kept unwanted visitors out—and unwanted emotions in.

Fortunately, she'd be gone soon. Why linger if the loan was a no go? She could return to Dallas and get on with her life, and *his* life would return to normal.

All he had to do was bury the memories of their two brief and unsettling encounters deep in a closet in the darkest corner of his heart.

And hope the lock he put on them was more reliable than the one on the door of Sea Glass Cottage.

4

Package of peanut butter crackers in one hand, bottle of water she'd refilled at the service station drinking fountain in the other, Christi strolled down Main Street during the Hope Harbor morning rush hour—such as it was.

There wasn't any bumper-to-bumper traffic, but the Myrtle Café Jack had mentioned was doing a brisk business. The savory aroma of bacon and biscuits was almost as hard to resist as the enticing scent of cinnamon wafting from the aptly named Sweet Dreams Bakery she'd passed on Dockside Drive a few minutes ago.

The crackers would have to do until the market Jack had told her about opened, though. Her food dollars would stretch much farther there than at a restaurant.

But the coffee shop across the street? *That* was tempting.

She stopped at the corner and perused The Perfect Blend—also a popular spot, as evidenced by the steady stream of customers. A caramel latte would taste s-o-o-o-o good about now.

Keep walking, Christi. Think about how much food you could buy at the market for the price of a froufrou drink.

Right.

She forced herself to continue across the intersection and start down the next block.

Her phone rang as she passed the second storefront, and her pulse stumbled.

Was this the verdict on her trespassing offense?

She moved out of the traffic path on the sidewalk, set her water on a bench, and groped for her cell.

A pleasant female voice responded to her greeting. "Good morning. This is Chief Graham-Stone from the Hope Harbor police department. Am I speaking with Christi Reece?"

"Yes." She squeezed the phone. *Please, Lord, let this not be more bad news.*

"I'm following up on your discussion with Officer Colby this morning. We contacted the management firm that handles Sea Glass Cottage. They've advised us it may take a day or two to connect with the owner. How long were you planning to stay in town?"

Nowhere near *that* long. Springing for a motel room for two nights would put a large dent in her dwindling finances.

"I was hoping to leave sometime today." And sleep at a rest stop again en route to Dallas.

The sound of shuffling papers came over the line. "I see you left a credit card number to cover the cost of the logs you used at the cottage. And according to Officer Colby's report, there wasn't any damage. I don't expect this will be difficult to sort out. If you have to leave, we can contact you after the owner weighs in."

Relief stole the stiffening from her legs, and she sank onto the bench. "Thank you."

"Not a problem. I hope you'll have an opportunity to enjoy a quick sample of our town before you head out. Hope Harbor is a very welcoming community."

The same phrase Charley the taco man had used to describe the place.

"I wish I could, but I have to get home." Such as it was.

"I understand. We all have schedules to keep. Safe travels."

Christi thanked the chief, slid the phone back in her purse, and appraised the classic small-town Main Street. Hope Harbor did have a warm, friendly vibe—and under other circumstances, it would be pleasant to linger. Let the soothing ambiance infiltrate her soul and dispel the tension that had become her permanent companion.

But she had to get back to Dallas. Find another waitress job to pay the bills while she continued her search for a position that offered a decent salary and more career potential—no small challenge with her limited résumé and impractical art history degree.

Christi scrubbed her forehead. What had she been thinking, to choose such an unmarketable major?

That your daddy was going to take care of you all your life and you'd never have to worry about finding a real job.

She winced at the hard truth and leaned back against the storefront behind her. How shallow she'd been back in those days. The world had revolved around her, fun had been her main goal, and her sole ambition had been to squeeze as many social activities as possible into her schedule.

Pathetic—and empty.

But you grew up fast when life imploded.

Either that, or you caved.

A chilly breeze swept past, and she zipped her jacket higher.

If nothing else positive had come out of all her recent disasters, at least she'd learned she wasn't a quitter. Without those hardships, she might never have discovered her inner core of strength, nor taken a hard look at herself and realigned her priorities.

A patrol car turned the corner, and she straightened up, heart lurching into a gallop. But that was foolish. Jack wasn't in that car. He'd be off duty by now.

Nevertheless, as the vehicle rolled down the street, her fingers began to tingle. Same as in the old days, when the handsome, buff young man from the landscaping company had smiled at her across the manicured lawn, tempting her to spice up her summer with someone from outside her well-heeled circle.

And what a summer it had been, filled with flirting and stolen kisses and clandestine rendezvous.

Yet despite her superficiality and party girl mentality, Jack's quiet strength had resonated with her. Life may have dealt him a succession of hard blows, but he'd carried on, searching for his path, taking responsibility for his future instead of adopting a victim mentality.

An example she'd followed during her own trials.

One more debt she owed the young man who'd wooed her and won her that long-ago summer.

The patrol car neared, and Christi gripped her purse tighter—but the officer behind the wheel who lifted a hand in greeting had a couple of decades on Jack.

She responded to his wave, battling equal parts relief and disappointment—which was silly. She'd done what she'd come to do, and she'd hear from Jack again. He'd said he'd get back to her with an answer, and he always kept his promises.

In the meantime, she had much to be thankful for. Clearance from the police chief to leave. An impromptu taco feast yesterday, courtesy of Charley. A memorable place to spend last night. And a soothing stay, however brief, in a town where the very air brimmed with hope.

But it was time to move on. The market Jack had told her about ought to be open by now. She should find it, stock up on provisions, and begin the long trek back to Dallas.

Except she didn't want to. Not quite yet.

Why not let the peace of this place seep into her pores for another ten or fifteen minutes while she ate her crackers and drank her water?

Because once she reentered the real world, with all its stress and heartache and guilt, a generous reserve of serenity would come in handy.

That young woman looked like she could use a friend.

Beth Adams leaned sideways inside the window of The Perfect Blend to get a clearer view of the blond sitting on the bench across the street, eyes closed, head tipped back against the wall. Fatigue radiated from her. As if mustering up the energy to stand and struggle through another day, one weary step at a time, was beyond her.

Pressure built in Beth's throat.

Been there, done that, still doing that many days—and it was a hard, discouraging place to be.

"Morning, Beth. You want the usual?"

Swallowing past the tightness, she turned toward the owner of The Perfect Blend. "Hi, Zach. Yes, I'm a creature of habit."

"Nothing wrong with knowing what you like. How're things?" He set to work concocting the cinnamon-topped, two-shot mocha she favored.

"Business could be better." She gave the young woman another once-over and joined him at the counter.

"Tell me about it. If wildfires continue to plague the area come summer, tourism will take a huge hit. We'll all be hurting."

"I know—and I was counting on the seasonal visitors to help me recoup the start-up costs of my shop."

"I hear you. I was in the same boat when I launched this place a few years ago. The first twelve months are critical. You opened in October, right?"

"Yes."

"Let's hope the fire scourge is over by summer." He snapped the lid on her to-go drink and set it on the counter. "Anything else?"

Beth edged toward the front window again. The woman continued to sit on the bench. Alone. Possibly hurting—and desperate for a touch of kindness.

"Beth?"

At Zach's prompt, she rejoined him at the counter. "I think I *will* add to my order." She perused the contents of the glass pastry case. "I'll take a piece of cranberry nut cake and a lavender shortbread cookie."

He grinned and reached behind him for a waxed bag. "You must be in a splurge mood today."

"They're not both for me."

"I wouldn't hold it against you if they were. Everyone deserves to indulge once in a while." He deposited the goodies in the bag and set it on the counter too. "Anything else?"

"What's your most popular drink?"

"The caramel latte and classic Americano are neck and neck."

"Give me a caramel latte." Perhaps a sugary drink would help sweeten up that young woman's life.

"You got it." Zach set about preparing the drink while Beth retreated to the window again.

The woman hadn't budged, thank heaven. Otherwise this impetuous act of kindness would be a bust.

As Zach fitted the cups into a carrying tray and deposited the bag in the middle, Beth returned to the counter and extracted her credit card. She tried to keep the bench in sight, but several people queued up behind her, blocking the view.

"You're all set." Zach tapped the chip reader.

She inserted the card, waited for the prompt to remove it, and picked up her order. "Thanks. I hope you have a great day."

"You too. I know for a fact that the caramel latte and sweet treats you ordered will give *some* lucky person's day a boost." He motioned toward the tray.

"I hope so."

She edged past the crowd and pushed through the door, fighting off a sudden attack of doubts as she hurried across Main Street. Yes, her intentions were benevolent—but she wasn't the impulsive type. Nor was she in the habit of initiating contact with strangers.

Unlike her husband, Steve, who chatted up anyone who crossed his path, she tended to wait for other people to initiate conversation. She and her husband were on opposite ends of the introvert/extrovert scale.

Which made today's behavior totally against type. What in the world had prompted her to venture outside her comfort zone?

Beth stepped up onto the curb and gave the woman another assessment. No one else passing by was paying any special attention to her. Nor did they appear to feel any compulsion to let her know someone cared.

So why did *she*?

The answer eluded her.

Besides, any normal person would have every right to be suspicious if a stranger approached bearing coffee and sweets. The world today was filled with craziness. What if she—

"Morning, Beth."

She swung toward Harbor Street. Charley lifted a hand in greeting as he strolled toward her from the direction of the wharf.

"Good morning."

"I see you've already visited The Perfect Blend. My next stop. Zach whips up the best Mexican coffee this side of the border." He inspected her tray, lips curving up as amusement glinted in his irises. "Are you double-dipping this morning?"

"No." She shot a quick peek at the young woman. "I, uh, bought a drink for someone else."

Charley glanced toward the bench. "That was thoughtful of you. The world could use more random acts of kindness. And one simple, caring gesture can make all the difference to someone who's hit a hard stretch."

"I suppose that's true."

"Count on it." Charley shifted his attention back to her. "I saw your help-wanted sign in the window yesterday. I wonder if that young woman is waiting to apply?"

No, she wasn't. Beth was certain of that.

The sign did give her a legitimate excuse for initiating a conversation, however—and it should mitigate any concerns the woman might have about being approached by a stranger.

"I don't know. I'll ask before I go in."

"Sounds like a plan." Charley examined the sky as a drop of rain left a dark splotch on her cardboard carrier. "And none too soon. I believe we're about to get a shower. Have a wonderful day, Beth."

"Thanks. You too."

He touched the brim of his Ducks cap and ambled across the street as if the intensifying rain was of no consequence.

She, on the other hand, picked up her pace. Maybe Charley didn't mind getting wet, but the thought of spending the next hour or two waiting for her damp clothes to dry while she tended the shop was *not* appealing.

The bench-sitter didn't stir as Beth approached. Didn't she realize it was beginning to rain? That the skies could open any minute? That she should seek shelter?

Or perhaps she didn't care enough about herself to worry that getting wet and chilled could lead to a bad cold—or worse.

A pang of compassion echoed in Beth's heart, stirring up the embers of long-dormant emotions, and she halted.

Softer emotions were dangerous—and best left undisturbed. They opened you to hurt and loss and mind-numbing, debilitating grief.

Harder emotions, like anger, were much safer. They insulated. Fueled. Helped you cope. It was best to cling to them.

She eyed the door to the shop. It wasn't too late to change her mind, go inside instead of detouring to the bench.

But walking away from those in need was wrong—and this woman was emitting strong distress signals, even if no one else was picking them up.

Beth gripped the tray tighter. She could do this. It wasn't as if she had to enmesh herself in the woman's life, after all. As Charley had said, sometimes a small act of kindness was all it took to lift someone's spirits.

So she'd offer coffee and bakery items, along with a place to wait out the rain—then send the woman on her way, hopefully encouraged and better able to face whatever challenges were disrupting her life.

Pasting on a smile, Beth forced her legs to carry her to the bench—and prepared to do her good deed for the day.

"Excuse me, miss. Miss?"

As someone touched her shoulder, Christi stiffened and jerked her eyelids open.

A slender, midfortyish woman stood three feet away, holding a cardboard carryout container. She was well dressed, and her mouth had a slight upward tilt—but the tension radiating from her set off alarm bells.

Christi eased farther away on the bench. "Yes?"

"Were you waiting for me?"

The red alert intensified, and her big-city self-defense mechanisms kicked in.

"No. I wasn't." She stood, prepared to bolt if this conversation got weirder.

"Oh. I thought that might be why you're here." The stranger motioned toward the window of the shop beside them.

Christi shifted sideways. A "part-time help wanted" sign was taped on the inside of the glass.

Ah. That explained the woman's question.

Her wariness subsided.

"No. To tell you the truth, I hadn't even noticed it."

"Too bad." The woman's words didn't match her tone—but it was hard to fault her lack of disappointment at not finding a job candidate on her doorstep. No one who wanted that position should show up for an interview in worn jeans and sneakers. "I saw you while I was at the coffee shop across the street and hoped we could chat about the job over a drink and a bite to eat." She lifted the cardboard tray.

A whiff of coffee drifted toward her as the rain intensified, and Christi inspected the cups and the bag containing who-knew-what delights.

So tempting.

But she couldn't take either under false pretenses.

"Like I said, the bench is what drew me here—not the sign."

"Sorry for the misunderstanding." The woman gave the sky a sweep. "I believe we're in for a bit of weather. If you'd like to come in until it passes, you're welcome to share my goodies. I don't want all these calories."

Did everyone in this town give away free food and drink?

But much as she'd like to accept the woman's hospitality, it didn't seem fair to take refreshments intended for a job applicant. Except the peanut butter crackers hadn't put a dent in her hunger—and the plain tap water she'd washed them down with wasn't in the same league as a rich cup of coffee.

Plus, a jolt of caffeine would give her an energy infusion as she began her drive back to Dallas.

All at once, the skies opened, and the woman hustled to take shelter under the small awning above the door. "Would you hold this for me?" She extended the tray.

Christi joined her under the protective cover and took the cardboard carrier.

The woman extracted her key from her purse, slid it into the lock, and pushed the door open. "Give me a minute to flip on the lights."

Rather than stand in the doorway, Christi followed her in, stopping a few feet inside to survey the eclectic but tasteful interior. The shop appeared to be a combination art gallery and high-end handcraft boutique. A number of paintings were displayed on the walls, and shelves and cases contained jewelry, art glass, ceramics, leather goods, dried flower arrangements, woven items, candles, handmade greeting cards—and much more.

The owner rejoined her and took the tray. "I should have introduced myself sooner. Pardon my etiquette blunder, but I was more interested in getting out of the rain. Beth Adams. I'd shake your hand, but mine are occupied. We haven't met, have we?"

"No. I only arrived last night. Christi Reece."

"A pleasure to meet you. I know you aren't interested in the job, but I have a caramel latte that will go to waste if you don't drink it." Beth touched the lid on one of the cups.

Caramel latte? Her favorite?

Strange coincidence—and doubly hard to resist.

"I have to admit that's my favorite splurge coffee drink."

"Then my order was inspired. I'll have to thank Zach at The Perfect Blend for his suggestion." Beth tilted her head toward the counter. "There are two stools back there. Shall we sit?" Without waiting for a reply, she toted the tray that direction.

Christi followed a few paces behind, slowing to scan the business cards in the holder beside the register. Clever name for a shop—and Eye of the Beholder fit. With its wide array of artsy merchandise, anyone should be able to find an object of beauty here to suit their taste.

"I like your shop." She slid onto one of the stools behind the counter while Beth passed her a napkin.

"Thank you." The owner split the paper bag to reveal two delicious-looking treats and fished a plastic knife from a drawer. After cutting the loaf cake into fourths, she broke the heart-shaped cookie in half. "All of the products are from Oregon, many of them local—like our pastries here. The cranberry nut cake is a Harbor Point Cranberry Farm specialty, and the shortbread is from Bayview Lavender Farm. Help yourself." Beth sat and picked up a piece of the cranberry cake.

Since rain continued to pummel the sidewalk out front, her car was parked two blocks away on the wharf, and she did *not* want her cold to relapse, she might as well enjoy this brief delay in tackling the long drive south.

Christi took a sip of the latte. Sampled the cake. "Mmm. These are both delicious."

"Wait until you try the shortbread. It's infused with lavender. So what brings you to our fair town?"

Not a subject she wanted to discuss.

"I, uh, had some personal business to take care of." She swept a hand over the shop and redirected the conversation. "I like the idea of featuring local goods."

Beth took the hint. "I do too. I had an online business for years before I opened this place last fall. The bulk of my orders still come through my website."

Understandable. Hope Harbor seemed too small to support an establishment like this.

"What prompted you to open a physical shop?" Christi picked up half the shortbread cookie and sipped her latte.

The woman's cup hesitated halfway to her lips for a split second, and a flicker of . . . anguish? . . . darkened her irises.

It appeared more than one person in this shop had dark secrets in her past.

Beth set the cup back down. "Hope Harbor is a popular seasonal tourist destination. I decided there was more business to be had. Having a physical space also let me expand my inventory to items that don't lend themselves to shipping, like those dried flowers." She waved a hand toward the display, then picked up the other half of the cookie heart and ran a finger over the broken edge. "I also had more time on my hands than was healthy, and I thought the challenge of opening and running a shop would keep me busy." She offered a smile that seemed forced. "It did—and how."

"Do you have other employees?"

"No—and a one-person show has its downsides. That's why I'm hiring a part-time helper. Full-time, actually, for two or three weeks while I have a knee replaced. If I don't line someone up soon, I'll have to shut down until I'm back on my feet. That will put a major dent in the balance sheet." She grimaced.

"I hear you." Christi bit into the shortbread. It melted in her mouth, leaving behind a subtle hint of lemon, lavender, and . . . mint? Man, the people in this town knew how to bake—and cook.

"I haven't given up hope that someone will come along. Do you work full-time?"

"I did, but I'm between jobs." Enough on *that* subject. "I wish I could help you out until you find someone more permanent, but I'm planning to head back to Dallas today."

"That *would* be a daunting commute for this job." A brief twinkle sparked in Beth's eyes. "What's your field?"

"My degree is in art history." She finished her cookie and peeked at the two remaining pieces of cranberry nut cake.

"Go ahead and eat those. I had a big breakfast this morning, and I don't usually indulge in sweets this early in the day—even if I do keep a stash of chocolate-covered almonds in that drawer for a midafternoon snack." She indicated one farther down the counter.

"If you're certain you don't want them . . ."

"They're yours." Beth sipped her coffee. "It's too bad you aren't from the area. With your background, you'd be an asset to the shop even in a temporary capacity."

It *was* too bad. Working in a place like this would beat waitressing while she searched for a permanent position that tapped into *some* of the expensive education her father had paid for.

"I do like the vibe here."

"Well, if you want to relocate, I'd love to have an art history major on the staff. Unless you have family commitments, or a significant other, in Texas."

"No. It's just me."

The bell over the door jingled, and Beth gathered up the remnants of their snack. "Duty calls." She swiveled toward the customers, a couple brandishing a dripping umbrella. "Morning, folks. I'll be right with you. There's an umbrella stand by the door."

"No worries." The man dispensed with the umbrella. "We'd like to browse for a few minutes anyway."

Reluctant as she was to end this pleasant interlude, Christi finished the cranberry cake, washed it down with the last of the latte, and stood. "I should let you get to work. Thank you for your kindness this morning. It meant a lot."

Beth took her hand and cocooned it between her own. "It was my pleasure. I enjoyed meeting you. And I hope you find a job that brings you happiness back in Dallas."

"Thank you. Good luck with the knee replacement."

"I'll manage. You learn to cope when you're on your own."

Christi gave the platinum band and diamond ring on the fourth finger of the woman's left hand a surreptitious peek. Was Beth a widow? If so, was the recent loss of her husband why she'd had too much time on her hands and had sought distraction in this shop?

Beth added nothing more, however, and asking personal questions would be out of line.

"I agree that self-reliance is a handy skill." Although facing knee surgery without a support system would be a challenge. Far more difficult than searching for a new job.

Too bad she didn't have a place to stay here—like a friend's spare room. If she did, she'd hang around and help Beth out at the shop until after the knee surgery.

But her only acquaintance in town didn't come close to qualifying as a friend. Even if Jack relented and gave her the loan, it wouldn't be due to any tender feelings on his part. It would be a straightforward business deal.

The customers signaled for help, and after a moment's hesitation Beth leaned over and gave her a hug. "Safe travels. And take this." She pulled a collapsible umbrella from under the counter. "Otherwise, you'll be soaked in thirty seconds."

"I can't take your umbrella."

"I have another one down there—and more at home. I live on the Oregon coast, after all." She squeezed her arm and went to assist the couple.

Christi's vision misted as she crossed to the door. If only she could linger here. This town fit her perfectly, like the designer gowns that had once filled her closet. Except Hope Harbor was tailored more to her heart and soul than to her body.

She paused at the exit and lifted a hand in farewell to Beth. Then she opened the door, put up the umbrella, and plunged into the cold April shower that the old adage promised would bring May flowers.

But barring divine intervention, she wouldn't be here to see them.

5

The writing wasn't going well.

No, scratch that.

The writing wasn't going, period.

Jack glared at the blinking cursor on his computer screen, blew out a breath, and picked up his mug emblazoned with the words "I'm in the zone."

If only.

He downed the lukewarm dregs of his third caffeine infusion of the morning and leaned back in his swivel chair.

May as well face it.

The writing session was a bust—thanks to Christi.

It would have been smarter to crash after his shift like he usually did instead of trying to channel his tension into writing.

He pushed back from the desk in the spare bedroom that served as his office and stood. With nothing to show after three hours planted in front of his laptop, he ought to throw in the towel and try to get a few hours of shut-eye. That would be a more productive use of his time—unless sleep was as elusive as words.

A distinct possibility.

Because the woman he'd once loved had dominated his thoughts from the moment her identity registered on the wharf—and seeing her again this morning had further ratcheted up his agitation.

Which was nuts. He was over her, for crying out loud. Had long ago recognized his so-called love for what it was—infatuation, pure and simple. The truth was, he'd been nothing more than another dazzled victim who'd fallen prey to her superficial charms. As a result, her unexpected reappearance in his life should have had zero impact. Created nothing more than a brief blip.

Instead, it had caused a tremor that registered in the danger zone on his Richter scale.

And the implications of that weren't sitting well.

He forked his fingers through his hair and stalked over to the front window of the apartment. Letting her drive away from Sea Glass Cottage this morning had been a mistake. He should have taken off after her, told her the loan wasn't happening, and been done with it.

Now he owed her a follow-up.

But a text would have to suffice—*after* she left town and there was no possibility of another disruptive face-to-face encounter. Hopefully the chief would have an answer from the property management company by this afternoon and the trespassing issue could be resolved. At that point, she'd be free to leave.

In the meantime, sleep was top priority. Otherwise he'd be running on fumes during his shift tonight—and while Hope Harbor wasn't a hotbed of intrigue or crime, no police officer could afford to be less than alert while on duty. Crazy stuff happened everywhere these days.

A postal service truck passed by the window, continued to the end of the Sea Haven apartment complex, and made a U-turn. Meaning mail had been delivered early today. And in light of the solid gray expanse overhead, it would behoove him to collect it before Mother Nature decided to wave her sprinkling can over town again.

He exited the apartment, returned the carrier's wave, and strode toward the mail alcove. Sixty seconds later, he fitted his key in the lock on his box and pulled open the door.

A bulky manila envelope took up most of the space, and he worked it out, along with assorted bills and ads.

As he retraced his steps to the apartment, he flipped the envelope over and scanned the front. His name and address were handwritten, but the script was unfamiliar.

The top left corner was bent back, so he straightened it out—and picked up his pace when a few drops of rain splattered on the walk in front of him.

Squinting, he tried to read the smudged return address. Did it say Chicago?

Odd. He didn't have any acquaintances there.

Could this be junk mail?

Unlikely. Junk mail didn't come with handwritten addresses.

Perhaps a reader had tracked down his home address.

He stepped onto the small porch on his unit, weighing the envelope in his hand.

That was possible. Despite the efforts he'd made to keep his private life private, fans could be persistent—and the internet was a trove of personal information for anyone willing to dig deep.

As Christi had.

An image of her standing in the deserted cottage this morning, toe sticking through the hole in her sock, flashed through his mind—but he quashed it at once. He was done thinking about her.

After setting the rest of his mail on the patio chair he'd never used, he pulled out his pocketknife. Slit and bowed the envelope.

A smaller, opaque plastic sleeve was inside, a pink envelope taped to it. There was also a short typed note.

Curious.

He pulled out the note first and checked the signature.

Huh. Not a reader after all, but a vague name from the past.

He returned to the top of the sheet and began to read.

Jack:

We've never met, but my sister Natalie asked me to contact you and pass on the enclosed in the event of her death. Three weeks ago, she was killed by a hit-and-run driver while crossing the street to her car after a late-night shift at the restaurant where she worked. The perpetrator hasn't been caught.

The enclosed should be self-explanatory. I've jotted my contact information at the bottom of this note. I'll wait to hear from you.

Erica West

The woman had provided an email and phone number.

Jack called up a fuzzy image of Natalie. He and the waitress at the diner he'd frequented for a handful of months had been nothing more than casual acquaintances, but still. To die that young was tragic. She'd have been . . . what? Forty?

Strange that she'd wanted her sister to contact him after all these years.

He pulled the pink envelope off the plastic sleeve, extracted the much longer note, and began to read.

Three sentences in, his heart lurched, and he groped for the edge of the chair. Lowered himself into it as he skimmed the rest of the letter.

Could this be legit?

A low growl of thunder rumbled in the distance, suggesting unsettled weather was ahead.

No kidding—especially if this note was for real.

And it could be, despite the slim odds. After all, he'd thought the chances of ever running into Christi again were low too—and look how that had turned out.

As for the odds that two events from his past would come back to haunt him within the same twenty-four hours? They had to be minuscule.

All at once, the skies opened and a gust of wind whipped past, flicking raindrops his direction.

He stood, let himself into the apartment, and leaned back against the closed door, envelope clutched in one hand, letter in the other, waves of shock rolling through him.

This could change his life.

This *would* change his life if it was true.

And that would be easy to determine. All he had to do was open the opaque sleeve and take the appropriate steps.

Another boom of thunder rolled through the air, vibrating the walls of the apartment.

A squall was definitely brewing in Hope Harbor.

But no matter how fierce the approaching gale, it would never come close to matching the intensity of the storm already raging within.

Peanut butter, an apple, an orange, beef jerky, several protein bars, crackers, tuna fish, and a bag of nuts.

Christi completed her quick inventory of the provisions in her small cart and started toward the checkout line. She should be set for the long drive home.

As she wound through the aisles, the muffled sound of her ringtone came from deep within her purse, and she halted. Jack—or the police chief?

Didn't matter. Either one of them could be bearing news that would change her plans.

She pulled out her phone, wedged herself beside a display of breakfast cereal, and greeted the caller.

"Ms. Reece? Chief Graham-Stone again. Have you left town yet?"

"No—but I'm about to head out."

"I'm glad I caught you. I heard back from the property management company in Coos Bay faster than I expected. The owner isn't going to press charges for trespassing."

Christi closed her eyes and exhaled. *Thank you, God.* "That's great news. Do they want me to pay for the logs?"

"No. But the management company did ask that you call them before you leave."

Christi frowned. "Did they say why?"

"The owner wants them to pass along a message. I can give you the number and contact name, if you have a pen handy."

"Yes. Hang on a sec." She dug through her purse and extracted a ballpoint and slip of paper. "Ready whenever you are." She jotted the name and numerals as the chief recited them. "Did they drop any hints about the message?"

"No—and I didn't probe. My sole concern was the potential trespassing charge."

"I understand. I'll make the call as soon as we hang up."

"Perfect. Have a safe journey."

"Thank you." Brow still pleated, Christi pressed the end button. Did the owner want to question her further about how she'd gained access to the cottage? Ask if she'd seen anything suspicious during the night she'd spent there? Try to glean a few more clues about the logs and the missing lock beyond what Jack had covered in his report?

If so, they'd be disappointed.

But a call wouldn't delay her departure more than a few minutes. It was the least she could do after they'd been so gracious.

She tapped in the number of the management company and asked for the man whose name the chief had provided.

The call was transferred immediately, and he got straight to business. "Thank you for your prompt response, Ms. Reece. The owner of the cottage where you spent last night has asked that we pass along an offer to you."

Offer?

She moved her cart aside as another shopper stopped at the cereal display. "What kind of offer?"

"The cottage has been vacant for a while, and in light of what you found, the owner believes it would be prudent to have someone on-site who could watch over the property. I was instructed to ask if you'd like to live in the cottage and fill that role. There would be no duties other than your presence. While there's no financial compensation involved, no rent would be charged and all utilities and other expenses would be covered. The offer is for six months, with the possibility of renewal."

Christi focused on a box of Lucky Charms cereal that was front and center in her field of vision as she tried to digest the proposal.

Instead of prosecuting her for trespassing, the owner wanted her to occupy the cottage and protect it from *other* trespassers—all expenses paid?

"Ms. Reece?"

"Yes. I'm here. I'm just . . . flummoxed, I guess."

"I agree it's a most unusual proposition."

No kidding.

"But why would the owner ask *me* to do this? I mean, he or she doesn't know me, and I don't know them."

"I can't answer that. I don't know them either. All of our communication goes through their attorney—who is a partner in a prestigious Portland law firm, by the way. So this offer is on the up-and-up, in case you're concerned."

Christi stared at the stack of cereal boxes.

Maybe the offer was legit, but what kind of person—or persons—gave a stranger a free place to live? And not some falling-down dump, but a charming cottage with a touching history and a world-class view.

Compared to her tiny studio apartment in Dallas, it was a palace.

Intriguing as the prospect was, however, she couldn't just up and leave Texas. Relocate to a place she'd never set foot in until yesterday.

Could she?

"I was told to give you twenty-four hours to think about the proposal." The sound of shuffling papers came over the line, as if the man had grown impatient with the long stretches of silence from her end. "Do you want to consider it, or would you like to give me an answer now?"

Tell him no, Christi. Reputable law firm or not, this whole setup is bizarre. Why would the owner go to such extremes to protect their anonymity? Why would they trust a stranger with their property? Go back to Dallas.

Sensible advice.

Yet Texas held nothing but bad memories—Tasha being the one exception.

"Ms. Reece?" A definite nip of impatience had crept into the man's tone.

"I'll take the twenty-four hours." The words spilled out before she could stop them.

"I'll let the owner know. You can reach me at this number anytime tomorrow morning. If you decide to stay, there will be a small amount of paperwork to complete. Enjoy the rest of your day."

The line went dead.

Slowly Christi lowered the phone and tapped the end button. What on earth had come over her? She should have said no outright. There were too many unanswered questions connected with the odd offer.

No harm had been done, though. All she had to lose by staying one more day was the cost of a night at the Gull Motel—and she'd planned to find an inexpensive place to spend last night anyway. She could use those funds for tonight.

Besides, delaying her answer gave her an excuse to linger in Hope Harbor.

So she'd pay for her provisions, find the motel, take a long shower—and think. Perhaps call Tasha and get her take. Her friend would give her an honest opinion and sound counsel, as she had through the whole sordid mess of the past two years.

Christi glanced again at the display of Lucky Charms beside her cart. Ironic, since good fortune had long been absent from her life.

But maybe . . . just maybe . . . her luck was beginning to change.

6

The ring was in his pocket.

Tonight was the night.

Jack grinned as he clipped the top of the boxwood hedge that rimmed the large circular drive in front of the house Christi and her father called home.

"How can you look happy in ninety-five-degree weather?"

At the disgruntled question, Jack glanced at his coworker. "I'm not feeling the heat much today."

"Yeah?" Bill wiped his brow on the sleeve of the uniform shirt provided by the landscaping company. "What's your secret?"

"I'm thinking pleasant thoughts."

Bill snickered and went back to work. "Would that pleasant thought be blond and blue-eyed?"

"Maybe." No sense denying it, since Bill had caught him and Christi in a stolen clinch under the rose arbor not long ago. Besides, after tonight their couple status would be public knowledge.

"She's by the pool—in case you want to say a quick hello. She came out while I was back there blowing the grass clippings. You're due for a break anyway."

Yeah, he was. And tonight's date felt like an eternity away.

"I wouldn't mind grabbing a water to cool me down."

"It'll take more than a bottle of water to do that." Bill snorted and went back to trimming.

Ignoring the jibe, Jack set his clippers beside the hedge, ran his fingers through his hair, and jogged toward the back of the house.

As he rounded the corner of the imposing, southern-style mansion, he paused beside a fern-topped stand. Christi was reclining in a lounge chair, an open book in her lap—as if she'd set it aside to soak up a few rays or enjoy the view of the manicured lawn.

His view wasn't too shabby either.

Man, she was good-looking. And so much fun. The air around her always crackled with energy and joy and carefree abandon, easing the heaviness in his heart. In her presence, life was happy again.

As it would be forever if she said yes.

He started forward—but halted as a tall, sandy-haired dude emerged onto the terrace from the house.

Scowling, Jack retreated behind the fern. Dirk Mason had been hanging around all summer, taking Christi to the multitude of charity and social events she attended. A convenient escort, nothing more, according to her—and an excellent smoke screen for their relationship while she softened up her dad, who might not approve of her dating someone with a less-than-stellar pedigree.

But if all went well, Mason was about to become history—and Christi's father would have to accept that he couldn't control his daughter's choice of men.

"Good morning, beautiful." Mason descended the steps to the pool.

Christi angled toward him with a smile. "Morning. Did Angie let you in?"

"Yes. You have a most agreeable housekeeper." He dropped onto the edge of the chaise lounge beside hers. "I was passing by and thought I'd see if you were free for dinner tonight."

Jack folded his arms, lips curving up. This ought to be interesting.

"Sorry, no. I already have plans."

"Another hot date?"

"You know better."

"Do I?" He leaned forward, hands clasped between his knees, a hint of anger in his question. "I've heard rumors you've been seeing a gardener *on the sly."*

Jack's mouth flattened. The man wasn't making any secret of his derision for manual labor.

"Where did you hear that?" Christi removed her sunglasses.

"From a reputable source who spotted the two of you getting cozy."

"Dirk!" She sat up straighter. "Are you jealous?" Christi's chiding tone suggested that notion was absurd.

A wave of unease swept through Jack.

"Should I be?"

In answer, she swung her legs to the ground, rose, and sat close beside Mason.

Thigh-to-thigh close.

Jack fisted his hands at his sides.

Instead of responding with words, she draped her arms around Mason's neck, tugged his head down, and kissed him.

Thoroughly.

After they came up for air, Christi gave a throaty laugh. "Does that answer your question?"

Despite the heat, an arctic chill blasted through Jack's heart. That intimate, you're-the-only-one-for-me inflection should have been reserved for him.

"I don't know." Mason played with a few strands of her hair. "My source was trustworthy."

Christi tossed her wavy mane, as she often did when a situation wasn't to her liking. "Fine. I'll admit the truth. You've been busy prepping for the LSAT, and I've been bored. So I found a way to amuse myself. Have some harmless fun. End of story. Do you really think I'd ever get serious about a gardener? *He doesn't mean a thing to me. Didn't that kiss prove it?"*

"I don't know. Let's try it again."

He reached for her—and Christi didn't object.

The ground shifted beneath Jack's feet as they renewed their clinch, and he groped for the edge of the pedestal. Missed. Knocked the fern to the ground. The ceramic pot shattered on the stone pavers, the sound echoing in the quiet community of residential estates.

Christi jerked back from Mason's embrace, and their gazes collided, a cavalcade of emotions parading through her eyes. Shock. Horror. Dismay. Embarrassment. She started to rise, as if she wanted to speak to him.

Too late. He'd seen—and heard—enough.

Jack spun on his heel and sprinted toward the front of the house. Toward his car.

But no matter how fast he ran, he'd never be able to escape the gut-twisting truth.

The woman who'd cajoled her way into his hurting heart had used him. Played him for her own amusement. Because she was bored.

It had all been a game with her.

A cry of anguish rose in his throat, wrenched from the depths of his soul. He opened his mouth to let it out, and—

Beep. Beep. Beep. Beep.

At the staccato summons, Jack jerked awake. Shoved aside the tangle of sheets. Fumbled for the cell on the nightstand. After he muted the alarm, he wiped a shaky hand down his face. Squinted at his watch.

He'd actually fallen asleep for an hour.

But given the nightmare-day replay that had strobed through his slumbering mind, staying awake would have been preferable. He could have dealt with mind-numbing fatigue far easier on his shift tonight than the tension now thrumming through his veins.

Thrusting the nightmare into a dark corner of his mind, he swung his feet to the floor, rested his elbows on his knees, and massaged his forehead. It was stupid to waste time regurgitating the distant past. He had pressing matters to deal with, and they required his full attention.

Like reporting for duty in four hours. Following up on the letter that had arrived earlier in the day. Getting in at least sixty productive minutes of writing. Dispensing with Christi's loan request.

The latter could wait, however, in light of his latest crisis. She'd said she didn't have to have an immediate answer, mentioned a due date thirty days away. The other issue was more urgent. He had to call Erica before he reported for his eleven-to-seven shift.

Ten minutes later, a cup of coffee in hand, he picked up the pink sheet of stationery and reread the letter from Natalie.

Jack—

I'm certain you never expected to hear from me again, but now that I'm gone, you need to know the secret I've kept all these years.

You have a daughter. Her name is Hannah.

I thought about trying to find you when I discovered I was pregnant, but we both understood the one night we spent together was more about comfort than commitment. I also knew fatherhood wasn't in your plans back then. Nor did I want to subject Hannah to a life traveling back and forth between two parents.

I've made many mistakes in my life, and perhaps my silence about this was one of them, but I did intend to contact you when Hannah was older. If you're reading this letter, death has preempted that plan.

My sister is prepared to raise Hannah, and I've named her legal guardian in the event you don't want to take her. Please discuss this with Erica—and between the two of you, make the best choice for the daughter I cherished, who filled all the empty places in my life with joy and love.

Jack drew in a shaky breath. Set down the letter.

Of all the ways to find out you were a father, this came nowhere close to making the short list.

Fortified with a swig of coffee, he tapped in Erica's number.

She answered two rings in, though it was difficult to hear her with all the background noise.

After he identified himself, he got straight to the reason for his call. "Your package arrived today."

"Let me try to find a quieter spot. I'm at O'Hare. Hold for a minute." A muffled boarding announcement came over the line, along with other noises that faded away before she spoke again. "Sorry. Airports aren't the best place to hold phone conversations—especially not this kind. I imagine you're in shock."

"At the very least."

"Are you going to take the test?"

This was not a woman who beat around the bush.

He surveyed the prepaid, mail-in DNA kit that had been inside the opaque plastic sleeve along with a photo of a ten-year-old girl who had his dark eyes, aquiline nose, and slightly asymmetrical lips. "Yes—but I'm 99 percent certain Hannah's my daughter." The family resemblance was remarkable.

"I'm 100 percent certain. I remember the summer Natalie met you. I was living in New York, and I heard quite a bit about you during our infrequent phone chats. First name only, though. She was quite taken with you, you know."

No, he didn't. Until that last night, Natalie had been nothing more than a friendly, sympathetic ear to him.

He transferred his weight from one foot to the other and jammed his free hand in his pocket. "I had no idea. We never dated."

"I know. I also know she wasn't seeing anyone else that summer. That's why I always assumed the Jack she'd mentioned was the father. She confirmed that in a letter she left for me, along with the package for you, in care of her attorney. From a legal standpoint, she dotted all the i's and crossed all the t's in terms of her wishes for guardianship."

"Is Hannah with you at the airport?"

"No. My pastor and his wife agreed to let her stay with them last night. I've been able to stick close since Natalie died, but I had an overnight business trip to New York I couldn't cancel. Normally I'd have spent tonight there too, but I didn't want to impose on my pastor any longer than necessary. I just got back to Chicago." A sigh came over the line. "My job requires significant travel, and dealing with the logistics has been challenging."

Another incentive to step up to the plate, beyond the overriding fact that any man who fathered a child owed that child a full-time dad.

Even if he was a late-in-the-game entry.

He picked up the small cardboard container. "The supplier of the kit uses rapid DNA technology. That means results will be available in two to three days. I'll do the cheek swab and overnight it tomorrow. By midweek we should have confirmation."

"Then what?"

She was asking what he intended to do if the paternity test came back positive.

He set the box back down, tightened his grip on the cell, and stared out the window. Rain pummeled the earth, and the world was dark and inscrutable beyond the pool of illumination cast by his porch light.

Like his future.

"What's your relationship with Hannah?" He ought to factor that into his decision.

"Sad to say, we're practically strangers. I've never married, and my job keeps me on the move. I've also spent a number of years overseas. Natalie and I rarely saw each other. I've been as much a stranger to Hannah as you are until Natalie . . . until these past three weeks." Her voice caught.

"I'm sorry for your loss." His expression of sympathy was tardy, but his brain wasn't firing on all cylinders.

"Thank you. We weren't that close, thanks to the gap in our ages and the different paths our lives took, but it's hard to lose your sole family connection. Other than Hannah, of course."

"How would you feel about me taking her?"

"May I be honest?"

"Please."

"At the risk of sounding self-centered, I'd be relieved. I'll honor my promise to Natalie if you don't want her, but it will upend my life—and no doubt disrupt hers as well at a time when she needs stability." A beat ticked by. "I'm also only the aunt."

And you're the father.

She didn't have to say that for the message to come through loud and clear.

Much as he'd like to deny it, her point was valid.

He had to do the right thing. Take responsibility for the consequences of his mistake—like his father had taught him.

A flash of lightning lit up the sky. Masses of roiling black clouds agitated the heavens, and disquiet hung over the landscape—along with a sense of looming catastrophe . . . and inevitability.

The weather outside was a perfect mirror for the turmoil within.

Because bottom line, if he wanted to be able to live with himself, he had but one choice.

He turned away from the window, toward the light-filled apartment, and took a deep breath. Said what had to be said. "I'll take her, Erica. Once we get the test results back, I'll call and we can work out the details."

"From what Natalie told me about you, I'm not surprised by your decision. I won't say anything to Hannah until I hear from you."

"Thanks. I'll be back in touch soon."

They ended the call, and Jack slid the cell back in his pocket. He had to switch gears, try to get into writing mode for a while, then report in for his shift. If he was lucky, it would be a quiet, routine night.

But unless he woke up tomorrow and discovered the events of the past thirty-six hours were just a bad dream, nothing else about his life was going to be quiet or routine again for the foreseeable future.

7

"It's about time you called me, girlfriend. Texts are *not* cutting it!"

Christi folded her legs and leaned back against the headboard in the Gull Motel as dawn light filtered through the canted slats in the blinds. After last night's raging storm, it appeared the sun was attempting to regain the upper hand.

"Sorry, Tasha. It's been kind of wild here."

"Define wild."

"Well . . . I spent the night in a deserted cottage and got cited by the police. I was offered a job. Two jobs, actually. I have a free place to live, if I want it—no strings attached. I've also enjoyed a couple of gratis meals."

Silence.

A smile tugged at the corners of Christi's lips. It wasn't hard to picture her friend. She'd be twirling one of her cornrow braids, forehead knitted, suspicion lurking in the depths of her dark irises while her mind processed at warp speed.

Christi waited her out.

"I have questions."

"Why am I not surprised? Fire away."

Tasha didn't hesitate, and Christi answered them all. Or all the ones she could.

"That's quite a story." Her friend exhaled. "I get taking refuge in the cottage and the job at the shop and the free food. I don't get the caretaker thing or this anonymous owner."

"Me, neither. But it doesn't matter. I mean, no sane person would take such an offer, right? Or decide on the spur-of-the-moment to leave a town they've lived in for five years to move to a place they've never set foot in before."

"Unless there's nothing to leave behind and the new place is filled with kind people who throw free food, free rent, and job offers at you."

Leave it to Tasha to cut to the chase.

Christi focused on the cross hanging on the wall across from the bed in the cozy motel room that felt more like home than her bare-bones studio in Dallas. Charley had promised clean and affordable, but he hadn't mentioned charming. "Are you saying I should do this?"

"Nope. That's your call. All I'll say is that Hope Harbor sounds like a little piece of heaven."

"I won't argue with that. Except giving up our weekly coffee-and-gabfest sessions would be hard."

"Gabfests are why phones were invented—and I can sip coffee on my end while you sip on yours. Plus, it's not like either of us has roots in Dallas. If I ever get that restaurant back in KC, I'll be moving home anyway."

The very reason Christi had made this trip.

"It'll happen, Tasha. I know it. Don't give up on this opportunity yet."

"I haven't. I'm bending the good Lord's ear every day. Speaking of that . . . I've been praying your trip was a success. Did you finish whatever business took you halfway across the country? The business you wouldn't share with me?" Tasha's tone was teasing, yet there was a hint of hurt underneath.

"I haven't finished it, but I got the ball rolling." No way was she going to tell her friend about the loan request—or raise her hopes—unless she got more receptive vibes from Jack.

"Your marathon drive doesn't have anything to do with me and my restaurant, does it?"

Christi caught her lower lip between her teeth. Of course, a friend who'd listened to all her dark secrets and angst would be suspicious about her reticence regarding this trip.

That's why confining their communication to texts rather than calls had been safer.

"Why would you think that?" Lame—but she had to play dodgeball until Jack gave her an answer.

Tasha snorted. "Girl, I know you. Better than I know my own sister. And that guilt complex of yours is world-class. You have to stop blaming yourself for the accident. It wasn't your fault."

But it was.

And because of her carelessness, Tasha's dream was in ashes.

No matter how much her friend tried to reassure her, that was the truth of it—and until she exhausted every possible means to help restore that dream, she wasn't giving up.

Christi massaged her temple, where a headache was beginning to throb. "You're being kind."

"Nope. Honest. If I'm supposed to get the restaurant, I will. It's in God's hands."

True.

Though sometimes God enlisted humans to intervene to ensure his will was done.

"I'll keep praying."

"Me too. So you want my opinion about these offers? Don't walk away without giving them serious consideration. You can job hunt from anywhere, you know. And you wouldn't have to trek back here if you decide to relocate. I could pack up your place and oversee the movers. You don't own much stuff. All you have to do is say the word."

The room grew fuzzy, and Christi plucked a tissue from the box on the bedside table. Swiped at her nose. What had she done to deserve such a friend? Especially since she wouldn't have given

Tasha a second look in her younger days, when status and wealth and pedigree were everything.

Thank God she'd come to recognize that the measure of a person wasn't in their bank account or social standing but in the treasures of their heart. And in that regard, Tash was the richest woman she'd ever met. Generous to a fault, nonjudgmental, kind, smart, faith-filled, loving—she was the real deal.

How she'd miss her if she decided to change addresses.

"I appreciate your willingness to coordinate the logistics of a move for me—but it's a huge step. And it's not like I have any friends here."

"You'll make some."

"I won't find anyone like you."

"What? There aren't any cornrows up there?"

Leave it to Tasha to inject humor if a conversation trended too emotional. "You know what I mean."

"Yeah, I do—but we won't lose touch. That's a promise. I'll call you so much, you'll be sick of me."

"Never."

"Wait and see. Listen, I gotta run. We have a high-profile event tonight, and the head honcho chef wants all hands on board super early. Will you call me tomorrow with an update?"

"Yes. Thanks for listening—and for the advice."

"Just call me Dear Abby. Ta-ta."

As Tasha ended the connection, Christi swung her feet to the floor. A beam of sunlight peeked through the blinds, suggesting the fog and rain had finally lifted. And wonder of wonders, her cold seemed to be gone after her sound night's sleep, and her energy had rebounded.

Why not take a walk through town? Or go back to Pelican Point? Or find a beach to stroll on? Perhaps in one of those places she'd find the answer to the question that was front and center in her mind.

Stay—or go?

"Hey, Jack—everything okay?"

A hand clapped him on the back, and Jack turned. Sergeant Steve Adams of the Oregon State Police cocked an eyebrow at him.

Jack coaxed up the corners of his mouth. "Fine. Just ready to call it a night. Or should I say morning?" He was already an hour late checking out, but a three-car pileup—with injuries—in the closing minutes of a shift took time to sort out.

"I hear you. This was a messy one." Steve surveyed the scene, where troopers were directing traffic while tow trucks jockeyed into position to haul away the damaged vehicles.

"Thanks for sending in reinforcements. This one was more than I could manage alone."

"Not a problem. You and the Hope Harbor police have covered for us with calls that required a faster response than we could manage. Any plans for the weekend?"

Jack rested one hand on his holster. "The usual, for the most part." Other than mailing in a mouth swab to confirm he was a father and following up on a loan request from the woman who'd broken his heart. "How about you?"

"I have to work on a talk I'm putting together for a middle school next week. Superintendent wants to enhance law enforcement visibility—and image—among our youth. Can't fault the intent, but I'm not that great with kids." A flash of pain echoed in his eyes.

Jack studied him. What was that about? After all, Steve was a father. Or had been, until tragedy took his only son. And based on conversations he'd had with his state police colleague over the past three years, there hadn't been anything obviously amiss with that relationship.

However, he'd thought the same about Steve's marriage until the man and his wife separated last summer. That had been a surprise. From what he'd seen, the state police sergeant was kind, considerate, and conscientious.

But who knew what went on behind closed doors?

Despite the placid, in-control image people presented to the world, their private lives could be a mess—as the events of the past two days demonstrated in his own life.

Jack went with a generic response. "I agree the image of law enforcement could use bolstering—and kids can be a receptive audience. I'm sure it'll go fine."

"Yeah." Steve fiddled with a clip on his belt. "This is the first one I've done since . . . that Beth won't be reviewing, though. She used to read all my presentations and always had excellent suggestions." The man cleared his throat and watched a tow truck separate two interlocked bumpers with a loud wrench. "You see her much?"

Jack grimaced at the too-casual inquiry.

He should never have told Steve that he and Beth lived in the same apartment complex. It prompted awkward questions like this. And it wasn't as if he knew her all that well. Her unit was at the far end, and other than their brief exchange at the funeral last June and a few casual encounters in town since she'd opened her shop, they'd had little contact.

But it was clear that despite whatever had happened to break up their marriage, Steve loved his wife. Wanted to stay connected, even if it was through a third party.

"No. You know how police work can be. I come and go at odd hours."

"I hear you." Steve motioned toward the street as a Hope Harbor cruiser pulled up. "Your reinforcement is here."

End of conversation about Beth.

Jack expelled a relieved breath. It wasn't that he lacked sympathy, but what could you say to a man who was grieving his son and missed his wife?

Officer Jim Gleason parked and joined them. "Sorry I was delayed. Emergency run with Methuselah to the vet in Coos Bay for

Eleanor Cooper. The life of a small-town police officer." He gave a good-natured shrug.

"How old is that cat anyway?" Jack pulled out his keys.

"Not as old as Eleanor. I hope I'm as spry if I make it to ninety-four. I'm happy to report Methuselah should be fine—and I got a piece of Eleanor's legendary fudge cake as a thank-you." Jim grinned.

"Lucky you. Where was Luis?" Her housemate usually took care of such matters.

"Working." Jim surveyed the scene. "What have you got here?"

Jack gave him a quick briefing, said goodbye to Steve, then headed for his patrol car and slid behind the wheel. On any normal Saturday, he'd go straight home and sleep. But today was far from normal—and he wasn't tired.

Besides, if he did manage to fall asleep, he could have another replay of yesterday's dream.

The mere prospect of that sent a shudder through him.

Why not swing by The Perfect Blend, treat himself to a large cup of the decadent Mexican coffee Charley had gotten him hooked on? After the turmoil of the past two days, a pick-me-up was in order—and a caffeine infusion would help fortify him as he tackled the logistics of how to accommodate a ten-year-old girl in his life.

A surge of panic swept over him at the enormity of that task, and he picked up speed toward The Perfect Blend. Yes, he was delaying the inevitable—but a brief respite in the pleasant oasis of the coffee shop before chaos descended again wasn't too much to ask, was it?

Forty-five minutes later, the subtle but comforting taste of cinnamon lingering on his tongue, he leaned back in his seat by the window. Exhaled. This had been an inspired idea. Here, among the laughing, chatting Saturday crowd enjoying the weekend, his nerves had calmed. He could almost pretend, for this brief interlude, that life was normal and—

His heart stumbled, and he lurched forward. Peered at the woman in the fringe of his vision, on the other side of the street.

Was that Christi?

Yes.

The coffee he'd ingested began to gurgle.

Why on earth was she still in town? According to the chief, the owner of Sea Glass Cottage hadn't pressed charges, and Christi had said she was leaving yesterday. What had changed?

Didn't matter. He had to get out of here.

He straightened up and swiveled away from the window.

"Morning, Jack." Charley ambled over, a lidded cup in hand, his usual smile in place. "I don't often see you here on Saturday."

"The Perfect Blend isn't part of my usual weekend routine." He groped for his keys. "But I thought a caffeine fix would set me up to tackle the day."

"Couldn't hurt. Did you order my favorite?" He indicated Jack's cup.

"Yes."

"Ought to do the trick." He sipped his own café de olla, clearly in no hurry to cut their conversation short.

Jack sent a surreptitious glance out the window. Christi had paused several storefronts down to rummage through her shoulder bag.

Thankfully he'd parked around the corner and could slip out the back door undetected—as soon as he escaped from Charley.

"I had a chat with your friend Thursday."

He shifted his attention back to the taco-making artist. "What?"

Charley motioned across the street with his cup. "Christi. I saw you two talking on the wharf and introduced myself after I shut down the stand. I wanted to welcome her to town."

A muscle clenched in Jack's jaw. "She's not my friend."

"No?" Charley's eyebrows rose.

"No. And she won't be here long."

"She did say her visit would be short." Charley sipped his coffee and perused her again. "I wonder if she fell in love with Hope Harbor and decided to stay. It's been known to happen."

Jack's pulse lost its rhythm again.

Now *that* was a disturbing possibility.

But it was also unrealistic. No one relocated on a whim. Especially to a tiny town where you were apt to run into a man who'd made it clear he wanted nothing to do with you.

Her departure must have been delayed. Car trouble, perhaps. A worsening cold that would render the long drive untenable. A forecast of bad weather en route.

Still, he couldn't quell the flickers of unease sparking in his nerve endings.

She started walking again, and he straightened up. "I doubt she'd want to live here."

"Why not?" Charley's tone remained conversational, but his penetrating gaze delved deep.

Too deep.

Jack slipped out of his chair and picked up his empty coffee cup. "This isn't her kind of place."

"No?" Charley looked toward Christi again. "What kind of place would she like?"

"A big city, with lots of glitzy, high-end stores and gourmet restaurants."

"Funny. That wasn't at all the impression I got of her. She came across as low-key and down-to-earth. Also a bit discouraged, to be honest—and in need of a friend."

He'd gotten the same vibes.

But she'd fooled him once, and despite the down-and-out image she now projected to the world . . . despite the fact that Charley's insights were typically spot-on . . . he wasn't taking anything about Christi Reece at face value.

"Be careful with her if she hangs around, Charley."

The man tipped his head. "You have a history?"

"Yes—and not a happy one." That was more than he'd planned to reveal, but the town sage had a knack for eliciting confidences. However, he also kept them. So at least the revelation would go no further.

"I'm sorry to hear that. But history doesn't have to define us. As Thomas Jefferson said, 'I like the dreams of the future better than the history of the past.'"

"I'm more of a Santayana fan myself."

A fan of wrinkles appeared at the corners of Charley's eyes. "He was also a wise man. Remembering the past *does* help us avoid repeating mistakes. At the same time, it's important to recognize that people—and circumstances—can change . . . and positive changes can bring a plethora of possibilities. And now, with that eloquent example of alliteration, I'll let you get on with your day." He winked, touched the brim of his Ducks cap, and wandered over to speak with Marci from the *Hope Harbor Herald*.

Jack frowned after him. Was Charley suggesting he give Christi another chance? But why would the man do that when he had no idea of their history? No clue how she'd used him—or how devastated he'd been? How broken?

Or perhaps he was reading too much into Charley's comment. The resident philosopher was prone to erudite musings. Always thought-provoking but often general rather than specific.

Except this one had hit close to home.

Jack angled back toward the window. Christi had resumed her stroll down Main Street—and toward The Perfect Blend.

His cue to exit.

Maybe she'd changed. Maybe she hadn't.

But despite Charley's inference, there were no possibilities between them.

Because he wasn't putting his heart at risk ever again. Whatever affection or love he had to spare from this day forward was going to be directed to the daughter he hadn't known existed—and who deserved it far more than Christi.

8

The help-wanted sign was still in the window.

Christi stopped outside Eye of the Beholder, beside the bench where Beth had approached her yesterday offering goodies, shelter from the rain—and a job that could tide her over while she continued to seek employment in her field. A quest that could be done from anywhere, as Tasha had pointed out.

She also had a free place to stay, if she wanted it. A *charming* free place.

Should she take a risk? Leave Dallas—and all her unhappy memories—behind? Or was it foolish to hope this little seaside town would offer greener pastures?

She sank onto the bench and closed her eyes.

Lord, I could use your help here. I'm not asking for writing in the sky, but a clue would be welcome. Anything that would give me direction and—

A scraping sound came from across the street, and she straightened up. A tall, dark-haired guy about her age was positioning an A-frame sign, filled with writing, near the entrance of The Perfect Blend.

As he retreated inside, she squinted at the quote that was attributed to Einstein.

"In the middle of difficulty lies opportunity."

O-kay. That was weird timing.

Could this be the answer to her prayer for guidance? Or was it mere coincidence?

Impossible to say—but the message was apropos.

The door of the shop behind her opened, and Beth stuck her head out. "Christi! I thought it was you—but I got the impression you were leaving yesterday."

"That was the plan, until a few unexpected opportunities came along." She flicked a glance at the sign across the street again. Maybe she ought to take the message to heart—and *follow* her heart. She gripped the edge of the bench and went for it. "Your job was one of them."

Beth's eyebrows peaked. "You mean you're considering it?"

"I wasn't at first—but a place to live kind of dropped into my lap yesterday, and I have no real ties to Dallas. I also like Hope Harbor. There's something special about this place." *Plus, if I stay, I may be able to convince Jack he can trust me to repay a loan.*

"I agree. I lived in Coos Bay for twenty years, but this has always been my favorite getaway spot. When I needed to relocate—and decided to open a shop—this was my first choice." Her tone remained conversational, but a dark shadow passed over her face. Again.

Further proof that Beth's decision to open Eye of the Beholder had been motivated by more than business reasons. Especially since she'd also moved here, despite the ring on her left hand.

Perhaps the shop owner was as much in need of a friend in town as she was, and the position would benefit both of them beyond a mere employer/employee arrangement.

"If you have a few minutes, would you like to talk specifics about the job?" Christi stood.

"Absolutely." She waved her inside.

Their discussion, held at the same counter where they'd shared sweets and drinks yesterday, didn't take long. The pay was more than sufficient to cover her expenses, since she'd have no housing or utility bills, and the hours were reasonable. In fact, with evenings free, she could wait tables at night to earn a few extra bucks.

And every dime she saved would go into her Tasha fund, in case Jack didn't come through with the loan. She couldn't put aside enough in thirty days to keep her friend from losing the current opportunity, but it would help when the next one came along.

Beth extended her hand as they wrapped up their discussion. "Welcome aboard. I have to admit, I was beginning to think a part-time employee wasn't in the cards. It's almost like a miracle."

"It kind of feels like that to me too." Christi squeezed her fingers. "I'll be here bright and early Tuesday morning to fill out all the paperwork and begin learning the ropes—unless you want me to come in Monday for a training session while you're closed."

"No, Tuesday will be perfect. My knee surgery isn't until a week from Monday, so we'll have five days to work out any kinks." Beth stood and smoothed a hand down her pristine black slacks, giving Christi's worn jeans, faded T-shirt, and scuffed sneakers a discreet scan. "If you'd, uh, like an advance on salary, that's no problem. There's a wonderful resale boutique in Coos Bay with vintage and designer clothing. The prices are incredible."

No surprise the woman was concerned about her attire—the same outfit she'd worn yesterday. She'd dressed for comfort rather than style on this trip, and her ensemble did *not* fit the ambiance of this upscale shop.

"Thank you for the offer. I can manage until my first paycheck—but I'd love the name of that shop." Not that she'd frequent it much in the future, but a few versatile pieces could come in handy while she waited for Tasha to pack up her apartment and send the contents north. There weren't many items left after her wardrobe purge over the past twenty-four months, but the few designer pieces she hadn't sold via luxury clothing resale sites should be sufficient.

"If you change your mind, let me know." Beth jotted on the

back of one of the business cards and handed it over. "Here's the name of the shop, plus my home address and cell number. Don't hesitate to call anytime."

"Thank you." Christi tucked it in her purse as a customer entered. "I'll see you Tuesday."

"Enjoy the weekend in the meantime."

As Beth greeted the new arrival, Christi stepped out into the sunshine. Amazing how light could transform places—and perspectives.

She drew in a lungful of the tangy salt air.

Maybe staying in Hope Harbor was imprudent.

Maybe taking a spur-of-the-moment job and agreeing to occupy a house owned by a secretive landlord was foolish.

Maybe driving all the way from Texas to Oregon to ask for a loan from a man who hated her had been crazy.

But being here felt right.

So before she got cold feet, she'd call the management company and arrange to sign whatever papers were necessary to lock down a six-month stay in the cozy cottage she'd stumbled across in the fog.

And she'd also pray her impulsive decision to upend her life wasn't going to be another mistake that would add to the burden of regrets already weighing down her soul.

Not again.

As the first rays of sun crept over the hills behind Hope Harbor on Tuesday, Jack slowed the cruiser and stared down the drive that led to Sea Glass Cottage.

Christi's Nissan was parked in front.

Fingers clenched around the wheel, he glared at the older-model car. Why would she come back here—especially after being given a pass once for trespassing? And how had she gotten past the padlock he'd put on the door? As far as he knew, the key had been sent to the management company, along with a bill from the city for the lock.

Even more important, why was she still in town? If she'd left Saturday after he spotted her through the window of The Perfect Blend, she should already be back in Texas.

But she wasn't—and now he'd have to investigate.

Muttering a word his mother wouldn't have liked, he swung into the drive and drove slowly toward the cottage.

Whatever her excuse for being on the premises again, he ought to use this opportunity to deal with the loan issue once and for all. Tell her to her face it was a no go and be done with it, rather than resorting to a text. Much as he disliked her, it was wrong to build up her hopes. Had he not been busy reconciling himself to the fact that he was a father, he'd have dealt with the issue three days ago.

He set the brake, slid from behind the wheel, and locked the vehicle. She couldn't use fog as a justification for trespassing this go-round. The weather had been clear all night. But whatever excuse she came up with, he wasn't cutting her any slack. And neither would the owners, if they were smart.

People who took advantage of you didn't deserve your sympathy or consideration.

Squaring his shoulders, he strode to the front door. Once again, the padlock was missing.

He tried the handle. As on his previous visit, it turned but didn't open. Nothing to do but resort to loud knocking.

"Hope Harbor police. Open up!"

Twenty seconds later, a lock was flipped and the door swung back.

Whoa.

It was Christi, no question about it, but she looked different. More polished and put-together. She'd restyled her hair and enhanced her features with makeup. Her black slacks and soft blue sweater were a major step up from the worn jeans and T-shirt she'd been wearing during each of their previous encounters. And the shadows beneath her lower lashes had either diminished or been camouflaged.

She gripped the side of the door as he completed his once-over. "Good morning."

Her greeting refocused him—but he didn't return it. "What's going on?"

"What do you mean?"

He waved a hand over the cottage. "Why are you back?"

"I live here." A glint of amusement sparked in her irises.

A muscle in his cheek ticced. As far as he was concerned, there was no humor in this situation. "Explain that."

"The owner wanted a pseudo caretaker and offered me the job."

He stared at her. "What?"

"The owner invited me to live here. Do you want to see the paperwork I signed Saturday?"

"Yes." At the very least.

"Come in while I get it." She left the door open and retreated into the house.

He crossed the threshold into the small foyer and gave the interior a sweep. Empty, as on his last visit—though a savory aroma filled the air, suggesting someone had cooked breakfast.

And that someone had to be Christi. A woman who hadn't known how to boil an egg eleven years ago, when her father's household staff took care of such mundane chores.

One more disconnect between the Christi in Hope Harbor and the one he'd known in St. Louis.

She reappeared and handed him several sheets of paper clipped together.

Legalese wasn't his forte, but as he sped through the document, two things jumped out.

Not only was the owner giving Christi the place rent-free, they were covering all expenses. And she was staying six months—at least.

He tried to sort through the avalanche of thoughts that was muddling his brain.

Why was she extending her stay? Last he'd heard, she was heading back to Texas ASAP.

How was he going to deal with having her underfoot? In a town the size of Hope Harbor, they were bound to see each other on a regular basis.

Why would the owner ask a stranger to live here and watch over the place but refuse an offer by a police officer to not only fill the same function but pay his own rent and expenses? He was a far more qualified candidate for the caretaker role.

An alert began clanging in his mind, and he flipped to the last page. Skimmed the signature line. The document had been signed by a representative from the management company, not the owner.

He scrutinized Christi. "Doesn't this arrangement strike you as odd?"

"Yes." No hesitation in her agreement—and the subtle tightening of her features was telling. "But as a dear friend told me, don't look a gift horse in the mouth. I did check out the legal firm in Portland that handles the owner's business. It has a stellar reputation. I also had the locks rekeyed."

"Do you have any clue who owns this place?"

"No."

Neither did he. None of his queries into renting or buying the cottage had revealed the owner's identity, and he'd had no legal justification—or right—to probe deeper. Still didn't.

He handed her the papers. "Everything appears to be in order." Even if her presence was going to add exponentially to the chaos in his life.

"Good."

Official business finished, he shifted gears. "I have another question."

"Okay." Caution underscored her tentative agreement.

"Why are you moving here?"

"I was offered a job—beyond watching over this place."

"Where?"

"A shop called Eye of the Beholder, on Main Street."

"Beth Adams's place."

"You know her?"

"It's a small town. Don't you have a job in Dallas?"

She played with the edge of the document, and when she continued, her voice was softer. Sadder. "Not anymore. The place where I worked went out of business, and there was nothing holding me there except one close friend."

His jaw tightened. "The same friend who gave you the gift horse advice?"

"Yes. Leaving her will be hard."

Her.

The tension in his shoulders dissipated—for reasons he refused to consider.

"But she's the only one there I care about—or who cares about me." As Christi continued, she fingered the corner of the agreement she'd signed. "I felt more at home here in the first twenty-four hours than I ever felt in Dallas. People have gone above and beyond to be gracious and welcoming. Most people, anyway." She gave him a quick peek, then dropped her gaze again.

Guilt jabbed at his conscience—which was ridiculous. He owed Christi nothing. Not welcome. Not graciousness. And not a loan.

Next order of business.

She lifted her head as he opened his mouth to give her the bad news—but at the deep-seated weariness and defeat in the depths of her eyes, he snapped it closed again.

Gone was the frivolous, flirty, self-centered party girl he'd once known, whose shallow quest for constant fun he'd mistaken for exuberant joie de vivre.

This was a woman who'd been through the wringer. Who'd been knocked down and was struggling to regain her footing. Who'd lost the life she'd once known and been thrust into a strange, new world where no one waited on her, money was in short supply, and holey socks were the norm.

How could he strike one more blow that might knock her off-balance permanently? Who knew how close she was to a precipice?

"What happened to you, Christi?" As the blunt question spilled out, he winced. So much for subtlety and discretion.

Her lips twisted into a humorless smile. "Life."

"That's not an answer."

She shrugged but offered nothing more.

Let it go, Colby. If she doesn't want to talk, you can't make her.

"Are you divorced? Is that why you have money issues?" Again, the questions tumbled out—suggesting his diplomacy skills needed a major overhaul.

She took a tiny step back, and despite her makeup, her complexion lost a few shades of color. "No. I never got divorced."

Then where was her husband?

"You use your maiden name."

"Yes." She moistened her lips. "I intended to get divorced. He died before I could set that in motion."

She was a widow?

Jack let out a slow breath. Losing a fortune would be traumatic. Losing a spouse as well would be devastating. No wonder she was reeling.

"I'm sorry."

"Don't be." Her features hardened. "Say a prayer for his soul if you like. That's what I do. But don't feel sorry for me. My life is better without him."

As Jack digested that, a disturbing suspicion began to niggle at him. "Was he abusive?"

"He never hit me, if that's what you're asking." She twisted her wrist to display her watch. A plain, vanilla timepiece. Nothing like the diamond-encrusted piece of fine jewelry she used to wear that also happened to display the hour. "I have to finish getting ready for work. I don't want to be late on my first day."

Their discussion was over—and she hadn't mentioned the loan. But it had to be on her mind, as it was on his.

"You said the loan you asked me for can wait thirty days."

A brief flare of hope sparked in her irises. "Yes. A few less now."

"I'll give you an answer in the next three weeks." Telling her no today would be like kicking someone while they were down, and he wouldn't do that to his worst enemy. After a couple of weeks in Hope Harbor, she might be less stressed—and more able to take bad news.

"Thanks. I *will* pay you back. You can keep my mom's ring until I do." She touched the chain at her neck.

No way was he taking her mother's ring. If he gave her a loan, it would be because he trusted her word that she'd repay him, not because he had physical collateral or—

He frowned.

Wait.

If he gave her a loan?

There was no if about it. The answer was no. He just wasn't quite ready to lay that on her yet.

"I don't want your mother's ring." He summoned up his sternest expression. "You've never told me why you need the money, other than a vague reference to an obligation to fulfill."

She caught her lower lip between her teeth. "It's for someone I owe a great deal to. Someone who was there for me when I hit bottom."

He frowned. "You'd go into major debt for this someone else when you obviously have money issues of your own?"

"It's a long story." She edged past him and waited by the door. "You're on duty, and I have to go to work."

He was being dismissed.

While a dozen more questions clamored for answers, he'd overstayed his welcome.

Putting his feet in gear, he walked past her as a faint, fresh fragrance enveloped him. Sweet and simple. Far different from the exotic, jasmine-infused scent she used to use that cost hundreds of dollars an ounce.

So who was the real Christi?

Yes, the woman who'd taken up residence in Sea Glass Cottage appeared to be down-and-out, but if her fortunes revived, would she revert to her former ways? Was she still selfish and shallow underneath? Or were the changes that seemed to have occurred more permanent?

Impossible to know.

But as he left the cottage behind, the questions followed him.

Searching for answers, however, could be dangerous. He should heed the old adage about burned once, twice shy. Refuse to let her suck him under her spell again.

Besides, even if positive changes in people and circumstances brought new possibilities, as Charley had suggested, this was the wrong time in his life to contemplate launching—or relaunching—a romance.

Because Christi didn't have a corner on mistakes.

And in the weeks and months—and years—ahead, his number one priority had to be the little girl who'd gone far too long without a dad.

9

The school presentation was over.

Thank heaven.

Steve flipped off the faucet in the restroom and pulled two paper towels from the dispenser. Being around kids had been every bit as hard as he'd expected—even if these middle-schoolers were at minimum five years younger than Jonathan had been when he'd . . . when they'd lost him.

Pressure built in his throat, and he wadded up the towels. Flung them into the trash can. Rotated his taut shoulders.

To make matters worse, the kids in the audience had picked up on his tension. They'd been as fidgety as a beached seal desperate to escape to a more agreeable environment. Like the cafeteria—the next item on their Thursday schedule.

The one good outcome of today's presentation? Since he wasn't likely to get a stellar review from the administration, the odds were low he'd be tapped for another such assignment in the future.

He smoothed a hand over his hair and pushed through the door, into the hall. The closest exit was on the other side of the lunchroom, so he detoured through there.

The ear-splitting noise level didn't help the ache in his temples that had appeared halfway through the presentation, and he picked up his pace, scanning the room.

Typical school cafeteria.

Harsh overhead lights. Long rows of tables with attached bench seats. Neutral colors. Food on the floor.

He dodged a smashed French fry.

As soon as he got out of here, he'd swing by Starbucks and get a venti dark roast. That ought to reduce the throbbing in—

His step slowed as a solitary kid caught his eye.

The boy, one of the younger students in the room, was sitting at the far end of a long table. Four older kids were grouped together at the other end, paying no attention to him. A sandwich rested in front of him on top of plastic wrap, a couple of bites gone.

Steve stopped and pulled out his cell. Pretended to check messages as he watched the boy push his food aside and pull a notebook and pencil out of the backpack beside him. He flipped the spiral-bound pad open, bent his head, and began to draw.

Like Jonathan used to, whenever he had a few spare minutes. His son had been an excellent artist.

Too bad he hadn't had a father who told him that more often. Praised his talent. Encouraged it.

Steve clenched his teeth. His twenty-twenty hindsight was useless at this point. The past was past, and there was nothing he could do to change it.

Pocketing his phone, he prepared to continue toward the door as two kids passing the table stopped behind the boy.

"Hey, look. Noah's drawing pretty pictures again." The taller of the two elbowed his companion, a sneer in his voice.

"Yeah. What're you drawing today, Walsh? Butterflies?" He leaned down for a closer inspection.

Both boys chortled as Noah tucked into himself and closed his notebook.

The other two kids walked on, leaving him in peace.

After waiting until they were a safe distance away, Noah rewrapped his sandwich and put it into his backpack.

Man, kids could be mean.

Steve remained where he was, watching the boy prepare to beat a hasty retreat, lunch uneaten.

Had Jonathan's classmates ribbed him about his artistic bent? If so, he'd never mentioned it.

But his son hadn't been a complainer. All he'd ever wanted to do was make his parents proud—and happy. Whatever it took.

And that had been his downfall.

The boy at the end of the table rose, notebook under his arm—and without any conscious decision to approach him, Steve began walking that direction.

When Noah noticed him, he paused, brow rumpled.

Forcing up the corners of his lips, Steve held out his hand. "Hi. I'm Sergeant Adams with the State Police. I gave a talk here today."

The boy set down the notebook and took his hand. "I know. I heard you."

"I bet you were bored."

"No. I like hearing about different careers. Last month a marine biologist talked."

"It's hard to compete with someone like that." He motioned to the table. "Could I sit with you while you finish your lunch? If I leave, I'll have to go back to work." He hung on to his smile, but it would have been easier to maintain if he'd had a shot of caffeine.

"Uh, yeah, I 'spose that would be okay." He slid back onto the bench seat, leaving room for his unexpected lunch companion.

Steve sat and folded his hands on the table. "You're Noah Walsh, right?"

The boy squinted at him. "Yeah. How'd you know that?"

"I overheard those two kids who were talking to you."

A faint flush crept across Noah's cheeks, and he hung his head. "They think I'm a sissy."

"Because of this?" Steve tapped the notebook.

"Yeah."

"My son used to carry one like that. He liked to draw."

"Me too." Noah pulled out his sandwich and peeled back the plastic wrap.

"May I look?"

The boy shrugged. "Sure. I guess."

Steve opened it. Page after page was covered with sketches. Most were living creatures—animals, birds, fish . . . and yes, a butterfly. A few were inanimate objects. All the drawings were exceptional for a child this age.

"I'm impressed." He studied an intricate rendering of a dragonfly. "Do you take art lessons?"

"No." The sandwich was disappearing fast.

"You should." The kid had real talent. "Have you ever talked to your parents about that?"

Noah tore off a piece of crust and rolled it into a ball between his fingers, forehead crinkling again. "No. I don't know who my dad is. My mom died when I was eight. I just got a new foster family."

Tough life.

"Have you ever showed your foster parents your drawings?"

"Once." He smashed the ball against the tabletop with his thumb. "But my foster dad's more into sports, you know?"

Steve took a long, slow breath.

Yeah, he did.

But that was just one of Noah's problems. Absent parents and peer ridicule were two more strikes on top of a sports-oriented foster father who didn't appreciate—or encourage—other talents.

And three strikes could put you out.

This was the type of kid who all too often ended up on the street—unless someone cared enough to encourage their interests and help them develop their talents and self-esteem.

"Do they have an art program at school?" Steve pushed the notebook back toward Noah.

"We have art class once a week. I don't know if there's anything else. I've only been here three months."

Ouch.

Changing schools near the end of the academic year would be hard on even the most self-confident kid.

"What grade are you in?"

"Sixth. I'm eleven." He shoved the last of his sandwich in his mouth and washed it down with a swig of water from his bottle. "How old is your son?"

A bell rang, and chaos erupted in the cafeteria as kids scrambled to gather up the remnants of their lunch and heft their backpacks into position.

"Older than you." Steve pulled out a card and handed it to Noah as the boy slid the notebook into his backpack and stood. "If you ever want to talk about drawing—or anything else—my cell number is on there. I always answer, day or night."

The boy fingered the card as if it were made of gold. "You mean I could call you? Anytime?"

"Yes."

"Epic." Noah stowed the card inside the pocket of his jeans and hefted his backpack. "I gotta get to class."

"And I have to go back to work." He stood too.

"Thanks for liking my sketches."

"Thank *you* for letting me see them."

The boy flashed him a quick grin and trotted over to join the throng of students funneling out the cafeteria door.

Steve watched until Noah was out of sight, his heart a tad lighter. He may not have impressed most of the students today with his talk, but his presence had had an impact on at least one of them.

Too bad he couldn't do more for the boy than offer him a friendly ear. Like find a way to get him involved in an art-related activity.

As he should have done for his son.

A wave of grief and regret rolled over him, and he grasped the back of the chair Noah had vacated until the room steadied.

Beth had always been the one who searched out opportunities for Jonathan to develop his talent, while he tried to push him into sports.

And now the boy whose sunny smiles and innate kindness had graced his days with joy and love was gone, leaving an aching void behind that could never be filled.

As the cafeteria emptied, Steve trekked toward the exit, the smell of greasy fries sending a wave of nausea through him.

Or maybe his queasiness came from all the guilt and self-recriminations that knotted his gut day and night.

If only he'd listened to Beth through the years. Stopped trying to mold his son into someone he wasn't and could never be—no matter how hard he tried.

And he'd tried.

Too hard.

Steve pushed through the door and continued to the cruiser, resting a hand on the roof as he lifted his face to the deep blue heavens.

Lord, please let Jonathan know how sorry I am, and that I'm proud of him. Forgive my mistakes. And show me how to reach Beth, convince her I've recognized my faults and that my contrition is real. Help her forgive me—even if I don't deserve it. I need her, Lord. Now more than ever.

It was the same prayer he'd been uttering for months, but it had brought little comfort—or results.

Shoulders drooping, he slid behind the wheel. God was listening. Of that he was certain. But the loneliness was oppressive. Without Jonathan and Beth, the house the three of them had shared was silent as a tomb—and as empty of life.

He put the car in drive and pulled away from the school, casting one last look in the rearview mirror as he drove away.

Funny.

For a few brief minutes during his impromptu visit with Noah, the loneliness and grief had receded. Maybe because for the first time in months, he'd given someone else's pain more attention than his own.

Had God put Noah in his path for that very purpose? To show him that the way forward wasn't to dwell on past mistakes, but perhaps to make a difference now—today—in someone's life?

Could that someone be Noah?

But it was hard to see how he could be there for a little boy he'd met only today when he'd failed to be there for the people he'd known—and loved—for longer than Noah had been alive.

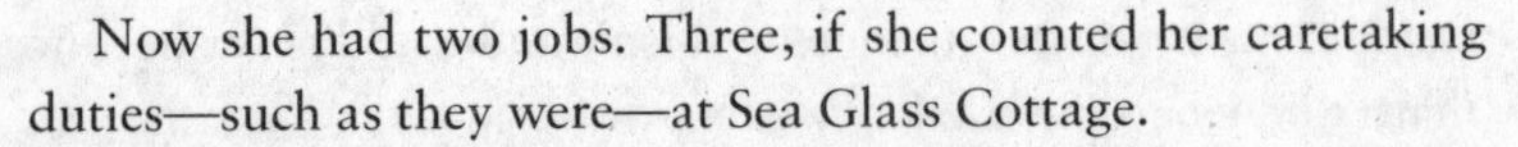

Now she had two jobs. Three, if she counted her caretaking duties—such as they were—at Sea Glass Cottage.

Christi exited the sports bar and restaurant in Coos Bay modeled after a popular chain that catered to a largely male clientele. She had the experience for the server gig, and the tips were excellent, according to the stylist who'd shaped up her tresses. Information the woman had imparted after Christi mentioned she was in the market for an evening job. The woman moonlighted here and had been happy to give her the name of the manager.

But the uniform was off-putting.

Short shorts and a figure-hugging tank top weren't part of her regular wardrobe.

The stylist had said the place was aboveboard, though—and what else did she have to do with her evenings? Besides, any extra money she could squirrel away for her Tasha fund would be welcome.

As if on cue, her cell began to vibrate and Tasha's name flashed in caller ID. Christi stopped beside her car in the parking lot and put the phone to her ear. "Are you reading my mind? I was just thinking about you."

"Were you wondering if I got your place packed up?"

"No. I told you I don't expect you to do that. The movers can take care of it tomorrow."

"Girl, you really want a bunch of strange guys pawing through your underwear? It was no big deal. All I had to do was empty the drawers and closets into boxes. Didn't take long. Everything's ready for the moving crew. I'm in your apartment now, as a matter of fact. I swung by on my way to work to do one more walk-through. Trust me, this is more zen-like than the chaos waiting for me at the restaurant."

A soft mist began to fall, and Christi felt around in her purse for her keys. "I sink deeper in your debt every day."

"No, you do not. Put that out of your mind. This is what friends do. So tell me how it's going up there. You like the job?"

"Yes. The woman who owns the shop couldn't be nicer. I hope I can manage the place for two weeks on my own, until she's able to come back part-time."

"Piece of cake."

"Easy for you to say." She pulled out the keys.

"And easy for you to do. You have an excellent mind, even if you didn't have much opportunity to demonstrate that in your prior position."

"Like none."

"That will change. I predict your days of waiting tables are over."

Christi glanced at the restaurant behind her.

If only.

"I don't know. I could pick up a few extra bucks if I got a part-time serving gig."

"You want my two cents? Focus on the job at the shop and devote the rest of your energy to finding a position that taps into your brain."

"I'll think about that." She unlocked her door and angled away from her new place of employment.

Several beats ticked by.

"You're gonna go back to waiting tables, aren't you?"

"Not full time—but a few hours a week would help fill the coffers. And I can't spend every waking minute hunting for a permanent job."

"Promise me you'll think about it before you heft another tray."

Christi slid behind the wheel. "I can think about it." And she would. But that wasn't going to change the facts. The job was a done deal. The paperwork was filled out, and her first shift was Saturday night. Two days away. "How's everything with you?"

She listened while Tasha regaled her with a hilarious story about one of the sous chefs in the restaurant, and as they said goodbye, her spirits were lighter.

But as she put the car in gear and drove past two young guys in the parking lot who were likely getting a jump on happy hour, she had to fight back a rush of nerves.

Waiting tables in a family diner in Dallas wearing jeans and a T-shirt was one thing.

Waiting tables in a male-oriented sports bar in this restaurant's uniform was another.

The money would be welcome, however—and worth whatever hassles she encountered, if they helped Tasha achieve her dream.

Even if she'd rather spend her off hours snuggled up in front of the fire in Sea Glass Cottage with a cup of tea and a feel-good novel.

Or pleading her case to a certain police officer who could make Tasha's dream come true with the stroke of a pen—if he relented.

But as she drove away, the reality was hard to ignore.

While she'd continue to pray Jack's heart would soften, the evidence to date suggested that would take a miracle—which was as hard to come by as finding a happily-ever-after ending in real life like the ones in her favorite novels.

And despite the upbeat vibe in the town she now called home, it would be foolish to hold out much hope that that would change.

10

Hannah was his.

Jack let out a slow breath as he reread the results posted on the DNA firm's secure online portal.

The confirmation wasn't a surprise—but it did slam home the reality that his life was about to change.

Forever.

He logged off the site and gave the packed parking lot a sweep, fighting the temptation to restart the engine, go home, and spend Saturday night adjusting to his new reality.

Too bad he hadn't ignored the text alert that the results were ready. Waited until later to check them out. Because now he was in no mood to attend Greg's retirement party.

But after the stellar letter of recommendation his captain had written for him when a slot opened in Hope Harbor three years into his tenure with the Coos Bay PD, it would be rude not to show up.

He didn't have to stay long, though. An appearance would suffice. There would be a large contingent of officers here to keep the party rolling—and loud bars weren't his scene, anyway.

After that, he'd head home, finalize the plans he'd been formulating all week based on the expected test outcome, contact Erica to ensure they were in sync with all the legalities that had to be handled, and book a flight to Chicago.

He slid out of the Jeep, locked it, and crossed the lot toward the building.

As he drew close, the doors opened to disgorge a group of partiers.

Cringing at the blunt force trauma to his eardrums from the din that spewed out, he hesitated on the threshold. The decibel level in there was dangerously high.

Yet another reason to leave fast.

Bracing for further auditory assault, he plunged into the rowdy horde.

It didn't take long to find the retirement celebration. Cops worked hard, but they also played hard—and their boisterous revelry was definitely amping up the volume in the place.

"Jack! Glad you could come!" Greg called out and waved at him above the crowd.

He lifted a hand in response and began burrowing through the bodies blocking his path to the honoree.

It was slow going.

As he paused to come up for air and get his bearings, someone jostled him from behind.

"Sorry. It's tight in here."

At the familiar female voice, he stiffened. Slowly turned.

Despite her heavy makeup and the meticulously mussed hairdo that screamed flashy blond, there was no doubt about the identity of the woman standing inches away.

It was Christi.

Someone else bumped into him, and as he shifted aside, she elevated the tray in her hands, keeping it between them.

Tray?

He frowned.

In the crush of people, and with the tray acting as a visual barrier, it was hard to get a clear view of her from the neck down—but as the crowd continued to ebb and flow around him, he managed to catch a glimpse of her attire.

She was dressed like the waitress he'd noticed as he wove through the throng, her shorts and tank top leaving little to the imagination.

Major disconnect.

The Christi Reece he'd known in St. Louis had worn subtly sexy outfits—but they'd reeked of class and elegance.

This one didn't.

Nor did the woman he remembered belong in a place like this as a *customer*, let alone an employee.

"What's going on?" He locked onto her gaze.

She moistened her heavily rouged lips. "What do you mean?"

"What are you doing here?"

"Isn't it obvious?"

"Let me rephrase." He leaned closer. Otherwise, he'd have to shout to be heard over the racket. "*Why* are you here?"

"I need money. You know that."

"You already have a job."

"Not in the evening."

"Why would you moonlight *here*? Wearing *that*?" He swept a hand over her attire, struggling to maintain his cool.

"Why not here?" Her chin lifted. "This is a respectable business. The outfit may be skimpy, but the tips are generous."

"Hey, babe." A tall guy muscled in and gave her a leer that set Jack's teeth on edge. "My buddies were wondering what happened to our drinks. I was sent to do reconnaissance."

The corners of Christi's mouth lifted, but her return smile was a sham—even if the recipient was oblivious to her lack of enthusiasm. "Getting through this crowd is a challenge."

"Then let me lead the way." He shouldered ahead, leaving her to follow.

She started after him—until Jack took her arm.

"I thought you said you didn't need the money for thirty days."

"I don't." She tossed the reply back at him. "But since my funding source is uncertain, I have to do what I can on my own."

"You aren't going to earn that amount in your timeframe by working here."

"I know. But every dollar helps." She tugged free and followed in the jock's wake.

Jack had to muster up every ounce of his willpower to hold his ground. This was none of his business. If Christi wanted to work here, that was up to her.

But she doesn't. You know that, Colby.

Yeah, he did. This scene didn't fit the St. Louis Christi, nor did it fit the Christi who'd shown up in Hope Harbor a week ago.

She was here for the money. Period. No matter how uncomfortable it made her.

And she didn't have to be. All he had to do was give her the loan she'd driven two thousand miles to request in a desperate bid to repay an obligation.

But if he caved, a business deal would link them together for the foreseeable future—and how much interaction did he want to have with the woman who'd made mincemeat of his heart?

The truth?

Too much.

He exhaled and scraped a hand down his face.

Like it or not, that was the reality. There was something intriguing—and appealing—about this new version of Christi. And the temptation to find out how much of that elusive something was real versus feigned was strong.

Given the package that had arrived in his mail mere days ago, however—and the ensuing complications—getting tangled up with Christi in either a business or personal capacity would be a mistake. He had a finite amount of time and energy, and between his police work, his writing commitments, and a surprise daughter, his plate was full.

Christi would have to fend for herself.

Yet as he tracked down Greg, passed on his best wishes, and retraced his route to the front door, he found himself scanning the room for one last glimpse of her.

No luck. She'd vanished.

Was she busy in another part of the bar—or doing her best to walk a wide circle around him?

Impossible to know.

A chilly wind whipped past as he stepped out into the night air, and he flipped up the collar of his jacket. Strode toward his Jeep. In forty minutes, he'd be home and getting ready for his night shift.

Once behind the wheel, he surveyed the parking lot, where several groups of young studs had congregated.

Scowled.

As far as he knew, there'd never been any serious incidents at this place. But would these guys—or others like them—be hanging around when Christi got off work? Would she have to run the gauntlet—alone—to get to her car? What if she encountered trouble?

But that wasn't his problem. Not unless he *made* it his problem. And he had plenty of his own without taking on someone else's.

He twisted the key in the ignition. Backed out of his spot. Pointed the Jeep south. And drove a tad too fast toward Hope Harbor.

Yet no matter how hard he pressed on the accelerator, he couldn't escape the image of that guy leering at Christi. It was burned into his brain . . . and making him hot under the collar.

If she was determined to earn as much money as possible toward her goal, however, there wasn't anything he could do to persuade her to nix the sports bar gig—unless he was willing to fork over the cash she'd asked for.

What a conundrum.

One that plagued him for the entire drive through the dark night.

Only on the outskirts of Hope Harbor did he ease back on the accelerator.

And maybe that was the best plan to follow with Christi too. Slow down. Wait and see how he felt about her situation in the next couple of weeks. Once he got over the shock of her being in town—and finding her in that bar—it was possible his curiosity and concerns would subside. Especially after Hannah was in his custody and demanding his full and undivided attention.

He hung a right onto Starfish Pier Road, toward his apartment. Perhaps, with all the balls he'd soon be juggling—not to mention all the legalities he was dealing with through the attorney he'd contacted to ensure there were no glitches in securing his paternal rights—thoughts of Christi would fade into the background.

But as he'd learned the hard way, few emotion-laden situations were resolved that easily.

Nor were the resolutions without consequences.

Maintaining a firm grip on the small vase of flowers she'd picked up at Budding Blooms back in Hope Harbor, Christi read the hospital room numbers as she passed.

There. That was Beth's.

She crossed to it and gave a soft knock on the half-closed door. "Beth? It's Christi. Are you awake?"

"Yes. Come in." Her employer's voice sounded strong, despite the surgery that had taken place in the early hours of this Monday.

Christi pushed open the door—and found a tall, white-coated man at the foot of Beth's bed. She halted. "I can come back later if—"

"Don't leave. I'm finished." He pulled back the curtain that had blocked her view of Beth. "She's all yours."

Despite the major operation her employer had undergone, her color was excellent and her eyes were alert.

"If there wasn't a bunch of medical equipment in this room, I'd never know you had a knee replaced this morning." Christi circled the bed to stand on the opposite side from the doctor.

"I have a great surgeon. Meet Ben Garrison. I already told him about you."

The man, who appeared to be in his late thirties, smiled and extended his hand across the sheet. "A pleasure."

Christi took it and returned the sentiment.

"Ben and his wife live in Hope Harbor." Beth shifted her position slightly. "Marci's the editor of the *Hope Harbor Herald* and heads up the chamber of commerce. I got to know her after I agreed to fill a vacancy on the chamber board—and she led me to Ben."

"I'm sure you'll meet her soon." The doctor grinned. "My wife's a dynamo, with her finger on the pulse of everything that happens in town. She knows almost as much about what's going on as Charley does—which is saying a lot, if you haven't figured that out yet. And now I'll leave you two to visit. Barring any complications, expect to be discharged late tomorrow afternoon, Beth."

"Thanks. I want to sleep in my own bed ASAP."

"I hear you. Nice to meet you, Christi. Welcome to Hope Harbor."

"Thank you." She waited until he left the room before setting the flowers on the wheeled bedside table. "I hoped these would brighten up your day."

"What a thoughtful gesture." Beth touched a petal, features softening. "I didn't expect this—nor did I expect you to drive back to Coos Bay after getting up at the crack of dawn to chauffeur me here this morning. I could have taken a cab."

"I was happy to do it." Letting someone travel solo to a hospital for surgery would be a major lapse of charity. "Besides, I, uh, had to be in this area tonight anyway."

In fact, she was due at work in an hour. Not that she intended to tell anyone in Hope Harbor about her sports bar gig, though. It was unfortunate she'd run into Jack there—on her first night, of all things—but why would he spread the news?

"Were you able to swing by my mailbox?"

"Yes. I took care of that en route. I put all of your mail on your kitchen table, like you asked—except for this." She pulled an envelope with a handwritten address from her purse and held it out. "I thought it might be a personal note you'd want to read."

Beth hesitated for a moment, conflict registering in her eyes, then took it. Set it on the sheet. "Thank you. Now I have one more favor to ask. There's a special chamber of commerce meeting Wednesday night for all members, and I'm not going to be up to attending. Could I impose on you to represent me and take notes? I'd like to stay in the loop. Of course I'd pay you your usual hourly wage for the time."

The sports bar hadn't scheduled her for Wednesday—but a chamber of commerce meeting, representing a business she was just learning?

"I'm available, but that may be a bit out of my league. I'm too new at Eye of the Beholder to do you or the shop justice. And I'm too new in town to contribute anything to the meeting."

"I disagree. After working with you last week while you learned the ropes, I'm impressed by your intellect and insights. You'll probably be more of an asset at the meeting than I would be."

A rush of pleasure warmed Christi. How long had it been since anyone—other than Tasha—had given her a sincere compliment?

Too long to remember.

Wes certainly never had.

She erased the image of her husband from her mind. Swallowed past the sour taste in her mouth. "I appreciate the kind words."

"All of them true."

"You convinced me. I'll attend in your place—but I'll restrict my involvement to note-taking."

"Participate however feels comfortable. It starts at seven at Grace Christian. I'll text Marci to expect you, and I know she'll welcome you with open arms. As Ben said, she's a ball of fire. If she could bottle and sell her enthusiasm, she'd be a millionaire."

"I'll put it on my calendar." Christi twisted her wrist to check her watch. "I should let you rest. Are you certain you don't need a ride home tomorrow?"

"No. A friend from here in Coos Bay volunteered to pick me up. I tried to dissuade her, but she said she was craving Charley's tacos—and who am I to argue with that? I'm addicted myself."

"I can understand that. I've only had them once—but I plan to be a regular customer." On impulse, she reached over and took Beth's hand. Gave it a squeeze. "Call if there's anything I can do for you."

"I will." Beth squeezed back. "And thank you for all you're doing. Most of all, for showing up in town when you did. It would have been the answer to a prayer . . . if I still prayed." Her features hardened, and she flicked a glance at the envelope on the sheet.

So Beth had once had strong faith—and the envelope must hold a clue about why it had lagged.

Would a few words of encouragement be appropriate?

"I didn't pray much either for a number of years." Christi kept her tone conversational. "But adversity can be a road map to God."

"Or a dead end." Beth eased her fingers free, sadness oozing from her pores. "It's hard to keep believing when he deserts you."

A nurse came in, sabotaging any further discussion, so after one more "take care of yourself," Christi left the hospital room behind.

But as she walked down the hall toward the elevator, her thoughts remained on the woman who'd undergone major surgery with no one by her side.

What had caused Beth to lose her faith?

How was the letter related to that?

And why was no one standing in the wings to help her after she was released tomorrow except a few friends and an employee who hadn't even been in her life two weeks ago?

"Looking good, Beth." The nurse finished checking her vitals and positioned the call button by her hand. "If you want anything or have any concerns, though, don't hesitate to alert us."

"I won't."

As the woman left, Beth picked up the envelope Christi had delivered half an hour ago, addressed in Steve's familiar hand.

Another card. Just like the ones he'd sent every ten days or so since she'd moved out.

None of which she'd opened.

They were all in a box on the shelf in her bedroom closet, gathering dust.

Why bother to read them? There was nothing he could say to fix the damage. Jonathan was gone. Period.

And a son couldn't be replaced like a bum knee.

The familiar soul-deep grief squeezed her heart, and pressure built behind her eyes, blurring her vision.

God, why? Why?

The silent cry of anguish came from the depths of her soul. It was the same question she'd flung to the heavens over and over again in the days and weeks after they lost Jonathan.

But eventually, when God had remained mute, she'd stopped asking.

Stopped believing he cared.

Stopped trusting he was more interested in her welfare than her woe.

Stopped turning to him for comfort.

So why had the question burst out again tonight?

Had Christi's comment about adversity leading her *to* the Almighty rather than away from him prompted it?

Maybe.

But it hadn't worked like that in her situation. Her faith had been strong until God had betrayed her. How could you love a God you couldn't trust?

How could Christi?

If her new employee had been as down-and-out as she'd appeared at their first meeting, why hadn't her faith suffered?

Beth fingered the blue envelope. Her favorite color, as Steve knew. There'd been an abundance of blue envelopes these past months, each one sending a clear message that he wanted to reconnect.

Yet he'd honored her wishes for space. Respected her request to keep his distance until—or unless—she wanted to talk.

So far, that hadn't happened.

She leaned over and slid the envelope under the box of tissues on her tray. Out of sight.

Yes, she missed him. Missed the affectionate touches, the surprise carryouts he used to bring home, the impromptu outings he'd planned, the cuddling together in bed on cold, rainy nights.

But she couldn't get past the bitterness or anger or resentment. Couldn't forgive him, despite the platitudes about mercy and compassion and understanding she'd once spouted.

And until she did, this card would join all the others in the dusty box in her dark closet.

11

Jack pressed the button for the fourteenth floor, swiped his damp palms on his dress slacks, and took a steadying breath as the doors whooshed closed and the elevator began its ascent to Erica's high-rise condo.

He hadn't been this nervous since his first job interview at sixteen, when his dream of buying a used car rested on whether he could convince old man Harper he was up to long days of hefting and toting fifty- and hundred-pound bags of feed.

Only today the stakes were far higher.

Whatever happened in the next few minutes would have a huge impact on his relationship with his daughter going forward. First impressions mattered.

Big time.

The elevator doors slid open, and his pulse skittered.

This was it.

He stepped into the wide hallway, deserted on this Monday night, and took a quick inventory while he adjusted his sport coat. Wainscoting, plush runner over hardwood floors, tall window at each end fronted by a marble table holding a fresh-flower arrangement.

Erica had done all right for herself—unlike Natalie, who'd known even during that long-ago summer that she was fated to toil as a waitress all her life. That's why she'd urged him to go back to college rather than spend his working years laboring as a landscaper.

But Christi had been his top priority in those days.

Until she wasn't.

He jammed his hands into his pockets and mashed his lips together.

If nothing else, her betrayal had forced him to rethink his life. Only after he'd discovered her true character had he returned to college, determined to find a career no one would ever sneer at again. It had been the kick in the pants he'd needed to get past his grief and find his true calling.

Yet successful as he'd been in both careers, his heart had never quite recovered from her duplicity.

The elevator doors closed behind him, and he moved forward . . . slowing as he approached Erica's unit.

But delaying the inevitable wasn't going to change it. They were waiting for him inside. And perhaps, after the first few awkward minutes, this wouldn't be as hard as he feared.

Holding tight to that encouraging thought, he continued to Erica's condo and pressed the bell.

Ten seconds later, the door opened.

Though the midfortyish woman who answered was a stranger, her kinship with Natalie was apparent. The sisters shared the same high cheekbones and amber eyes. But unlike her younger sibling, Erica had acquired the kind of polish success wrought—classy clothes, a self-confident bearing, and a practiced smile designed to put business associates and clients at ease.

"Jack. Welcome." She extended her hand.

"Thank you." He returned her firm shake.

"Please come in." She moved back, and he crossed the threshold, giving the room to the right of the foyer a sweep.

Hannah was nowhere in sight.

Erica closed the door, pitching her volume low as she answered his unspoken question. "She's in the guest room. Let me get you settled and I'll bring her out." Without waiting for a reply, she led him into the spacious living room. "Make yourself comfortable. What can I get you to drink?"

"I'm fine."

Liar, liar.

But a drink wasn't going to calm his nerves—unless it contained a significant amount of alcohol. Not an option, since he'd sworn off liquor after his night with Natalie.

"Give me a minute or two." Faint creases appeared on Erica's brow. "I've laid all the groundwork for this visit, but she's quite apprehensive. You *are* a stranger to her."

"That wasn't my choice." A note of defensiveness crept into his voice.

"Understood. I won't try to defend my sister's decision . . . but she was a fine mother, from what I could tell." She swept a hand over the room again. "Please, have a seat."

Leaving him on his own, she disappeared down a hall.

Rather than sit, Jack sized up the room.

The minimalist décor was striking if not warm. A large modern art painting adorned one wall, the sole touch of color in the room's neutral palette. Nothing was out of place. No stray candy wrappers, no opened book, no purse or bag left on a chair. The room could have been lifted from one of those glossy interior design magazines that high-end clients likely found on waiting room coffee tables at places like investment firms and plastic surgeon offices. Sophisticated . . . classy . . . chic . . . those were the adjectives that came to mind.

It did *not* feel like a home.

Despite Erica's willingness to take Hannah, this wasn't where Jack wanted her to grow up.

As the minutes ticked by, he began to pace. The delay couldn't be a favorable omen. It wasn't as if he'd expected Hannah to run to him with open arms, but wasn't she at least curious about him?

Or did she regard him as simply a stranger who'd arrived to disrupt her world yet again?

Thank goodness he'd had the foresight to allow them a couple of get-acquainted days before he whisked her back to Oregon.

But what if that wasn't sufficient?

His stomach began to churn.

What would he do if she decided to—

"Sorry for the delay, Jack." Erica reappeared in the hallway, holding Hannah's hand—but the girl stayed behind her, out of sight. Like she didn't want to see him.

The roiling in his stomach intensified.

Now what?

Erica continued to tow the girl along behind her. "Come on, dear. Your dad traveled all the way from Oregon. Don't you want to say hello?"

His daughter stayed in Erica's shadow, and Natalie's sister gave him a slight, apologetic shrug.

It was clear Hannah did *not* want to say hello.

Meaning it was up to him to break the ice.

If he was still a praying man, he'd ask for God to put the right words in his mouth—but in view of the long gap since his last conversation with the Almighty, pleading for help seemed presumptuous.

Curling his fingers into his palms, he put forth the best argument he could think of for her to emerge from hiding.

"I've been looking forward to meeting you, Hannah. I can come back tomorrow if you'd rather wait until then to say hello, but your aunt will be at work—so it will be just the two of us."

Surely having a more familiar face close at hand during their initial meeting would be an incentive to get it over with tonight.

After a few beats ticked by, Hannah edged out from behind Erica—though she kept a tight grip on the woman's hand.

The photo he had was an excellent likeness. And in person, the Colby family resemblance was more pronounced than ever.

Hannah tucked her hair behind her ear as she regarded him, tugging on the huge purple sweater she wore over her leggings and sport shoes. The garment hung almost to her knees, and the sleeves had been rolled up several turns. Even for kids who favored the baggy look, this was excessive.

But hey, if she liked it, the outfit was fine with him.

He called up a smile. "Your sweater is a pretty color."

Her lips remained flat. "It was my mom's."

Wardrobe choice explained. Wearing a piece of Natalie's clothing would allow her to keep her mom close.

Somehow he managed to hold on to his smile. "I remember your mom liked that color." Sort of. Somewhere in the recesses of his mind, a memory stirred to life of a comment she'd made to a customer once about purple being her trademark color—hence the purple T-shirts she often wore to work.

"She has one exactly the same." This from Erica. "Natalie knitted them matching sweaters a few years ago, but Hannah's doesn't fit anymore." She motioned them both into the living room. "Let's sit and get acquainted."

They all claimed seats, with Hannah choosing the chair farthest from his.

The next hour was stilted, at best. He and Erica chatted, but hard as he tried to draw his daughter into the conversation, all she offered were one-syllable answers.

Erica's phone pinged, and she withdrew her cell from her pocket. Skimmed the screen. Tapped in a response. "The pizza I ordered is here." She rose, and Jack followed suit. "I have a quick errand to run tonight. You two can continue to get acquainted over dinner." Her gaze locked onto his.

This hadn't been part of the plan. It was supposed to be the three of them together all evening. She must have ordered the pizza half an hour ago, after she'd excused herself to deal with a call.

But her strategy was smart. With their get-acquainted session tanking, Erica had switched tactics to try and improve the outcome.

Probably very similar to her modus operandi in the corporate world.

He gave a tiny nod to indicate he was on board with her plan.

Hannah stood too, panic etched on her features, posture stiff. "I'm not hungry. Can I go with you, Aunt Erica?"

"It's business related, dear—but I won't be gone long." She redirected her attention to him. "Help yourself to drinks and whatever else you need. Someone from the desk will deliver the pizza." She disappeared into the kitchen for a few moments, reappeared with her purse. "I'll see you both in an hour or so."

With that, she crossed to the foyer and slipped out the door.

Silence descended.

Hannah edged behind her chair, giving him a wary once-over.

He tried not to let her caution hurt. Tried to put himself in her place. A grieving little girl, thrust upon an aunt she hardly knew, about to be passed off to a father she'd never met who was going to hustle her away to live in a place she'd never been.

That had to be super traumatic.

While there wasn't much he could do to alleviate her grief over the death of her mom, surely he could find a way to allay her fears. To communicate that he would do his best to welcome her into his life and his heart. That she didn't have to be scared, because he would do everything he could to—

"You don't have to take me." She spoke from behind the chair, her fingers gripping the back. "I could stay with Aunt Erica. She said I could. The first day, when she came down after . . . after my mom died." Her voice choked.

But that was before Erica knew there was a father waiting in the wings—which changed everything.

The bell rang.

Perfect timing. This would buy him a few minutes to figure out how to address her comment.

"That must be our pizza. Let me get it, then we'll talk. Okay?"

No response.

He walked over to the door, pulled out his wallet, and twisted the knob. A twentysomething guy wearing dark slacks and a light blue dress shirt held out a pizza box. "I ran into Ms. West in the elevator. She said you were waiting for this."

"Thanks." Jack took it and flipped open his wallet.

"No tipping allowed for staff, sir. We're happy to deliver. Enjoy." He retreated down the hall.

Jack closed the door, stowed his wallet, and returned to the living room. "Why don't we talk while we eat?" He continued to the kitchen and set the pizza box on a glass-topped table for two.

When Hannah didn't follow, he closed his eyes. Filled his lungs. Silently repeated the mantra he'd been cycling through all day.

Don't spook her. Be nice. Be approachable.

He returned to the doorway between the kitchen and living room/formal dining area. "Do you think you could help me find plates and napkins and glasses? I wouldn't have a clue where anything is."

She hesitated.

Lord, don't let her run to her room and close the door. Please. I don't know what I'll do if she refuses to talk to me.

The silent plea spilled out, despite his earlier decision not to bother praying.

But maybe God would listen to a prodigal son, even one who hadn't yet returned home.

Hannah left her barricade behind and approached the kitchen.

Thank you, God!

He ditched his jacket, backing away to give her space as she edged around to the far side of the island.

"The plates and glasses are in that cabinet." She pointed to one closer to him. "I can get the napkins. The soda's in the fridge." Also closer to him.

He retrieved the plates and glasses. Set them on the table. Opened the fridge and gave it a quick perusal.

The contents looked like an ad for Whole Foods. Every healthy item was grouped by category, each one precisely arranged. Including the organic soda.

"What would you like to drink?" He searched in vain among the black currant, passion fruit, and rhubarb—rhubarb?—flavors for a simple Diet Sprite or Dr Pepper.

Nada.

"Water."

"I'm with you." He pulled out two bottles of water and set them on the table. "Let's see what she ordered."

She sidled closer, several napkins in hand, as he opened the box.

"It's pepperoni." He folded the lid under the bottom. "Do you like this kind?"

"Better than the one with pineapple we had last week."

He wrinkled his nose. "I like pineapple, but not on pizza." He extracted two pieces, put one on each plate, and sat. "Come on. Let's eat while we talk."

She slid into her chair as he picked up the pizza he didn't want. But his last meal had been hours ago, and he was operating on fumes. He had to eat.

"Don't you say grace?"

Whoops.

He set the pizza down. "I, uh, kind of got out of the habit." And near as he could recall, Natalie hadn't been the praying type back in St. Louis.

But perhaps having kids compelled you to rethink your relationship—and theirs—with God.

"Aunt Erica doesn't pray either."

"It's a good idea, though. You want to say it?" He folded his hands.

She offered a simple prayer, and he picked up his pizza again while she peeled a piece of pepperoni off her slice.

As he started to swallow his first bite, she returned to the subject he'd promised to talk about.

"I know you came all across the country to see me, but I could stay here."

The piece of dough lodged in his windpipe, and he grabbed his bottle of water. Took a long swallow. Tried to breathe.

Like her aunt, Hannah wasn't one to beat around the bush.

Best plan was to be honest—while making a case for moving to Oregon with him.

"I know you could. Your aunt and I talked about it—and she does have a big condo. Much bigger than my apartment. But I like living by the beach."

She nibbled on a piece of crust, watching him. "There's a beach where you live?"

"Yes. I can walk to it. And it has tide pools filled with bright yellow and purple starfish—and all kinds of other creatures." That ought to appeal to a kid. "Have you ever been to a beach?"

"No."

"I think you'd like it—and you could meet Floyd and Gladys."

Her forehead puckered. "Who are they?"

"My seagull friends." Well, Charley's, actually. Personally, he couldn't tell one from another. He'd have ask the taco chef to introduce them to Hannah.

"I've never seen a seagull."

"You'll see plenty where I live. We have a lighthouse too." He proceeded to sell her on the attributes of Hope Harbor while he ate two pieces of pizza and she picked the pepperoni off her slice, eating the meat but leaving the crust almost untouched.

She didn't ask many questions—or say much, period. Her responses to his questions were confined to one or two words. Nor did she volunteer any information.

But at least she hadn't run away and locked herself in her room.

Keeping her engaged, however, was hard work. When the front door lock clicked an hour later, he was as exhausted as if he'd run a marathon.

Erica joined them in the kitchen, maintaining her smile despite the pained glance she cast at the grease smudges and fingerprints on her once-pristine glass tabletop. "How was the pizza?"

"Excellent." Jack wiped his mouth on a napkin and stood.

"Give me two minutes to put my purse in my room and freshen up." She continued down the hall.

Jack sat back down as Hannah scrubbed at the table with her napkin. "I was messy."

"No. You ate pizza. You can't be neat with pizza."

"Aunt Erica is."

Yeah, she would be.

He lowered his voice. "Does she get mad if you're messy?"

"No—but she doesn't like messes. She tries to smile, but her mouth pinches up funny."

"Let me scrounge up a dishcloth and see if we can get rid of the evidence."

He rummaged around under the sink and found glass cleaner, along with a sponge. "This ought to do the trick." He rejoined her, closed the pizza box, and had the table sparkling with a few spritzes and swipes of the sponge.

By the time Erica returned, he'd stowed the cleaning material and was slipping his arms into his jacket.

"Are you heading out?"

"Yes. It's been a long day."

"You can still claim the couch if you like."

"I appreciate the offer, but the hotel is fine. I'll be back before you leave for work tomorrow, though. Hannah, would you walk with me to the door? You can lock it behind me for your aunt."

"That would be helpful, Hannah." Erica picked up their plates from the counter. "I'll put everything in the dishwasher while you say goodbye."

She'd gotten the message that he wanted another few moments alone with his daughter. Smart woman—but clearly one whose life would be turned upside down by the permanent addition of a child.

Hannah complied but trailed him by several feet and hung back when he reached the door.

He had forty-eight hours with her before they boarded a plane for Oregon on Thursday. That wasn't much time to win her over, but he intended to give it his best shot.

"I have a whole list of things we could do together tomorrow." Fortunately Erica had arranged for a tutor who'd worked in tandem with Hannah's former school to help her finish her classwork for the year two weeks ahead of schedule. One less issue for him to deal with—and less distraction as they focused on getting acquainted.

If she *wanted* to get acquainted.

Hard to tell whether he'd made many inroads tonight, given her silence.

"Have you been to the zoo?"

She shook her head.

"Would you like to see it?"

She lifted her shoulders. Let them drop.

This was going nowhere—and leaving on such a stilted note wouldn't be wise.

Tension pulsing through him, he sat in a chair beside the front door, putting himself closer to her eye level. Clasped his hands in front of him. "Hannah, I know this is really hard for you. I know you miss your mom, and moving to a new place is always scary. Worse if you're going with someone you don't know—even if he *is* your dad. But I'm going to do all I can to be the best father any girl ever had. I don't live in a fancy place like your aunt does, and I don't eat as healthy as she does, but I'll love you forever and I'll always take care of you. That's a promise. Will you give me a chance to prove that to you?"

As she considered him, his heart thudded hard against his rib cage.

After a few eternal seconds ticked by, she gave a small, slow nod.

It wasn't much, and there was zero enthusiasm in her response, but she hadn't said no.

He could work with that.

And he'd live up to his promise to her every day for as long as he lived.

No matter how many challenges cropped up as he launched his new life as a rookie single dad.

12

"Christi! Nice to see you again."

As she hesitated inside the doorway of Grace Christian Church's fellowship hall, Charley lifted a hand in greeting and strolled toward her.

At least there was one familiar face at the special chamber of commerce meeting. Everyone else in the crowd was a stranger.

"Hi." She returned his smile. "I'm filling in for Beth from Eye of the Beholder."

"I know. Marci told me." He indicated a woman with slightly frizzy shoulder-length red hair who was in an animated conversation with a man in clerical garb on the far side of the room. "She's talking to Reverend Baker, the pastor here. Father Murphy—over there helping himself to a cookie—is his counterpart at St. Francis. If you're a churchgoer, either congregation would welcome you with open arms now that you've decided to stay. I was happy to hear that news, by the way."

"Thank you—and I do intend to check out the area churches as soon as I catch my breath."

Marci glanced their direction, had another brief exchange with the minister, and wove through the crowd to join them. "Sorry. I meant to hang out by the door and watch for you, Christi, but I got waylaid. I recognized you from Beth's description the minute you came in. Thanks for stepping in to welcome her, Charley."

"My pleasure."

"And thank *you* for representing Beth." Marci touched her arm.

"Representing may be a stretch. I'm more of a scribe. New as I am to the job and to town, I won't be able to offer much."

"Considering the pickle we're in, I'll be happy to hear ideas from anyone who has a thought or two." She twisted her wrist. "Time to get this show on the road."

Marci moved to the front of the room, picked up the mic, and asked everyone to find a chair.

Charley indicated two seats in a row near the back. "Why don't you sit next to me? I can brief you on the players—and answer any questions you have."

Perfect.

She dropped into a folding chair and opened her notebook. "I already have one for you. What did Marci mean about being in a pickle?"

"That's why this special session is being held. If she runs true to form, she'll provide a concise recap of the situation up front. If she doesn't, I'll fill in the gaps."

As soon as the attendees were seated, Marci spoke. "Good evening, everyone—and thank you for coming tonight to discuss an issue that's important to all of us. But first, let's give Reverend Baker a round of applause for offering the use of this fellowship hall. We would have strained the fire code if we'd met in the city hall conference room."

She led the ovation as the minister stood and waved at the assembly.

Once the group quieted again, Marci dived into the issue at hand, as Charley had predicted. "Most of us count on visitors for a hefty chunk of our income. As we all know, the area wildfires have been taking a toll on tourism. That's hurt many of us throughout the spring, and if the situation continues into our busy summer season, we'll all be feeling the pinch."

A murmur of assent rippled through the crowd, and Marci waited for it to subside before continuing. "The chamber board has discussed this at length, and we'd like to be proactive about the situation—but to be honest, we haven't come up with any viable ideas about how to address it. That's why we're here tonight. We want your input. The floor is open."

As Marci waited for someone to speak, Christi leaned toward Charley. "How many wildfires have you had?"

"Several over the past eight months. If the wind's blowing our direction and the fire is large, we catch an occasional whiff of smoke. That's enough to spook visitors."

"Is there any danger to the town?"

"No. The closest fire was thirty or forty miles away. But with all the beautiful towns on the Oregon coast, there are other options for visitors who have concerns." He indicated a youngish woman with long, wavy light brown hair who'd risen. "That's Jeannette Mason. Married to Logan West, the doctor in charge of our local urgent care center. She owns Bayview Lavender Farm and Tearoom."

Christi scribbled down the woman's name.

"I want to reiterate what Marci said." Jeannette motioned toward the *Herald* editor. "I'm very worried about the summer season. I'm used to being booked solid at the tearoom, but my business has been down about 25 percent since the first of the year. I agree we should try to come up with a plan to generate tourism, but I'll have to leave that to more creative minds."

Another woman rose, also midthirtyish.

Charley leaned over again. "Katherine Parker. You may have heard of her from her Hollywood acting days. She's opening a gourmet chocolate shop in town."

Christi added the woman's name to her list. Lucky for her, the taco chef had taken her under his wing tonight. He was a treasure trove of information.

"I don't have any creative suggestions about how to attract visitors either, but I *am* concerned about the drop in tourism, and I'll support whatever ideas the board thinks are worth trying. As a new business owner, I was counting on the seasonal summer revenue to help me recoup start-up costs."

Christi frowned.

Was Beth in the same boat? Her shop was relatively new too.

A tall, lanky guy rose next.

Charley leaned in. "Adam Stone. Married to our police chief. Makes custom furniture. He's a gifted craftsman."

Christi wrote down the name Charley supplied, along with a few notes.

The man shifted from one foot to the other, as if he was uncomfortable speaking in front of a crowd. "The bulk of my business comes from out-of-town commissions, but many of the visitors who stop in at my workshop do end up ordering custom pieces or buying items I have on display. Do you think we should ask for a show of hands to verify the problem is as widespread as we think it is?"

"Excellent idea." Marci gave him a thumbs-up. "Everyone who's noticed a significant decline in revenue because of the drop in tourism, please raise your hand."

Almost every person in the room did so.

"Wow." Marci surveyed the crowd. "In light of that response, I think it's urgent for us to put our heads together and come up with a plan to attract visitors." She pursed her lips. "I wonder if we could build on our farmers' market?"

As several people rose to comment on that suggestion, Charley again filled in the blanks. "The town has a farmers' market every Friday from Memorial Day through Labor Day. Most of the merchants have a booth, and there's usually live music."

"Does it draw well?"

"Always has. That's Patrick Roark." He motioned to a sandy-haired man who'd risen. "He's quite a historian. Gives talks all over the Pacific Northwest. And he's a first-class photographer too."

While the man spoke, and as several other people stood to throw out ideas or offer their thoughts, Christi continued to jot down the information Charley shared. In the lulls between writing, she reread her notes.

It was obvious Hope Harbor needed to convince tourists to visit the town—but doing business as usual wasn't the answer. Popular as the farmers' market was, those were fairly common. They needed a unique attraction. One that would draw attention and garner a ton of advance publicity, generating interest in the town as well as the event—perhaps all summer long.

Organizing something on that scale would be a massive undertaking, but it would also be an exciting challenge. Similar to the charitable fundraising affairs her dad had asked her to get involved in on his behalf whenever he, like other prominent business leaders, was asked to lend his support. But she hadn't minded helping out. It had felt good to contribute in a small way to worthwhile causes. Plus, serving on those committees had been an education in organization and planning.

She skimmed her notes again. Tearoom. Gourmet chocolates. Hand-crafted furniture.

Hmm.

Her brain began clicking.

She added renowned artist, expert historian, famous actress, and bestselling author to the list.

This town was crawling with talent.

Could they somehow harness that? Use it to showcase Hope Harbor, draw visitors in?

"That's an intriguing list."

At Charley's comment, she looked over to find him perusing her scribbles, his expression thoughtful.

"The amount of talent you have here is amazing."

"When you put it in a list, it *is* impressive. I feel honored to be included—if that's me." He indicated the renowned artist line.

"It is—unless there's another artist in town I haven't yet met."

"As a matter of fact, there is. Eric Nash. He's an attorney here who paints on the side. He's newer to the art world than I am, but his work is displayed in several prestigious galleries." Charley cocked his head and studied her. "What are you thinking?"

Warmth suffused her cheeks, and she closed her notebook. Strange how he'd picked up on her brainstorming, nebulous as it was at this point. "I was just noodling on an idea that would probably never work."

"Never say never. Most brilliant ideas begin with a random notion."

"Brilliant may be an exaggeration."

"Not if it helps the people in this room." He scanned the assembled group, concern etching his features. "I'd hate to see any of their businesses suffer—or close. That would have a huge impact on this little town all of us cherish."

The meeting continued, with more comments—but few ideas—offered. As the gathering wound down, it was clear the group wasn't any closer to finding a solution to the dilemma than it had been at the beginning. And from the worried faces and undertone of anxiety in the room, it was also apparent that a bad summer season would deal a huge blow to many of the business owners here—and to the town.

That was sad.

New as she was to Hope Harbor, the charming seaside community had already claimed a piece of her heart, and it was hard to see it hurting.

But she was still an outsider. It would be presumptuous to offer suggestions, no matter what Marci had said earlier in the evening.

The *Herald* editor ended the meeting, and Christi stood along with Charley. There was nothing she could do to help.

Yet as she walked back to her car with the notebook containing the genesis of an idea tucked in her purse, a question from her conscience niggled at her.

Are you certain of that?

Steve tossed the remains of his nuked frozen dinner in the trash, guzzled the last of his iced tea, and rinsed the glass in the kitchen sink.

The only sound in the too-quiet house was the running faucet and a pinging hot-water pipe.

Sighing, he dried the glass and returned it to the cabinet. Solitary dinners were the pits. And no prepackaged meal could compete with Beth's home cooking.

But much as he loved—and missed—her culinary talents, the lack of mealtime companionship was far worse. Beth had always believed families should gather at dinner, and she'd worked around his odd hours to carve out half an hour every day for the three of them to eat together, share a few laughs, and catch up with each other's lives.

It was a rare gift in today's world, based on the tales his co-workers told of meals caught on the run while family members scattered to their various activities—and he hadn't appreciated those golden hours with Beth and Jonathan enough.

Like he hadn't appreciated a lot of things.

And now it was too late.

Shoving his hands in his pockets, he trudged out to the back porch. From next door, the scent of grilling meat wafted his direction, along with a muffled sound of conversation between the newlywed husband and wife who'd moved in a few months back. They must be getting ready for a cozy dinner.

That didn't improve his mood.

He pivoted and returned to the house. After detouring to the counter for the latest card he'd bought for Beth, he sat again at the kitchen table. Pen poised, he stared at the blank space under the brief sentiment.

What else could he say that he hadn't already said in the twenty-plus cards he'd sent her? Sorry as he was for what had happened, he couldn't turn back the clock, alter the outcome. And so far, she hadn't been receptive to his pleas for forgiveness.

How could he convince her he'd seen the light? Persuade her to give him a second chance?

His phone began to vibrate, and he laid the pen down. Pulled out the cell. The name on the screen wasn't familiar—but it was a local number.

Let it roll—or deal with whatever this stranger wanted?

Rhetorical question. Cops always responded.

He pressed the talk button and greeted the caller.

A male voice responded. "Is this Sergeant Adams with the state police?"

Must be official business.

"Yes."

"This is Will Butler. I'm Noah Walsh's foster dad. He said you gave a presentation at his school last week and talked with him afterward."

"That's right."

"He also said you told him he could call you. He has one of your cards."

Hard to tell the guy's mood from his inflection—but finding a cop's card in your foster child's possession could create a boatload of anxiety.

"I did tell him that." Steve kept his tone conversational. "I spotted him sketching in the cafeteria as I was leaving and stopped to chat. I was impressed with his talent."

"That's what he said—but I wanted to verify there wasn't a problem. I also cleared this contact with the caseworker. May I put him on the line?"

Reassuring to know the man was following protocols designed to protect the welfare of foster children in his charge.

"Of course."

"I'll make sure this doesn't become a habit. I don't want him bothering you."

"It's no bother. I lost my son a few months back, and talking to Noah reminded me of him. I enjoyed our conversation."

"Oh, wow. I'm sorry for your loss. In that case, I'll tell Noah he can call once in a while. My wife and I aren't much into art, so I'm glad he's found someone to talk with about that kind of stuff. I'll put him on."

As the phone was handed off and a muffled conversation took place, Steve rose and walked over to the window. The sun was setting, the shadows lengthening. Nights were the hardest—and loneliest—times. The hours when it was toughest to keep grief at bay.

Noah's call couldn't have been better timed.

"Sergeant Adams?"

"Hi, Noah. How are you doing?"

"Okay. My foster dad said I shouldn't talk too long."

"Don't worry about that. I don't have anything going on tonight. We don't have to hurry."

"Awesome. I, uh, wanted to tell you I've been working on a drawing like that dragonfly you looked at real hard, and I thought you might like to see it—if you aren't too busy."

Steve followed the contrail of a high-altitude plane, tracing the long white lines against the deepening blue sky until they faded away and disappeared.

Should he ask Noah to have his foster father snap a photo of the drawing and email it to him, confine their interaction to phone—or meet with the boy?

It all depended on how involved he wanted to get in Noah's life beyond an occasional phone call.

But what else did he have to do during his off-duty hours these days? And perhaps spending a few hours nurturing and encouraging a young boy's talent would help him atone in some small way for the failure with his own son that ate at his gut and amplified his grief.

"Can you tell me about the drawing?" He turned away from

the window, buying himself a few more moments to consider the best course.

As he listened to Noah describe his close-up sketch of a tide pool, Steve's gaze fell on the small plaque with the quote from 1 Corinthians that had always graced their kitchen.

Love never fails.

Once upon a time, Beth had believed that with every fiber of her being. But her love hadn't saved Jonathan, nor had it helped her husband see the light.

No wonder she'd grown distant and bitter.

And he'd failed at love as well. Instead of being disappointed that Jonathan preferred art over athletics, he should have recognized, appreciated, and valued him for who he was and for his unique talents.

He'd learned, though. Painful as the lesson had been, he was a better person today. He'd prove that to Beth if she gave him the opportunity. And he'd keep working toward that goal.

In the meantime, why not apply the lesson he'd learned to Noah? The boy's foster parents were no doubt qualified if they'd passed the rigorous screenings required for certification, but that didn't mean Noah couldn't use another cheerleader in his section. Especially one who understood the importance of encouraging talents that weren't always valued by others.

As Noah wound down, Steve made his decision.

"That sounds wonderful. I'd like to see it—and anything else you're working on. We could get together for ice cream while you show me your latest sketches."

"Really?" Hope and excitement raised his pitch.

"Yes. Assuming you like ice cream."

"I do!"

"Why don't you put your foster dad back on the line and I'll see what we can set up?"

Noah rounded up the man fast, and in less than sixty seconds Steve had a date with an eleven-year-old for Saturday afternoon.

After pocketing the cell, he returned to the kitchen table and picked up his pen again. Beth hadn't responded to any of the notes he'd sent, nor had she acknowledged them on the few occasions the two of them had emailed about business-of-life matters like tax returns and insurance—but it was possible she'd come around if he kept trying . . . and praying.

He began to write, angling the card to catch the last rays of sun filtering in through the window. Quickened his pace to finish before it was too dark to see.

As he wrote "yours forever" at the end, as he always did above his name, the light disappeared from the room.

Like it had disappeared from his life since he'd lost Jonathan and Beth had walked out.

Maybe, though, her heart would soften in time.

And while he waited, he'd do his best to shine a bit of light and hope into a young boy's life.

13

If this kept up, Hannah was going to starve.

Jack scraped the remains of her Friday night dinner into the garbage.

No, scratch that. These weren't remains. The bulk of her take-out dinner from the Myrtle was untouched. She'd poked at the green beans, downed a few bites of the meat loaf, and swiped up a forkful or two of mashed potatoes.

He squirted dish soap into the sink and gave her a surreptitious scan. Even the brownies from Sweet Dreams Bakery hadn't sparked her appetite. They sat untouched on the plate in the center of the table.

Man, this was hard. Far harder than he'd anticipated.

But grief took many forms. In Hannah's case, it seemed to be manifesting itself through muteness and an aversion to food.

After wiping his hands on a towel, he rejoined her at the table. "Did you like the beach today?"

"I guess."

"The starfish we saw at the tide pools were colorful, weren't they?"

"Uh-huh."

So much for conversation. But maybe he could tempt her to eat. Chocolate wasn't the healthiest way to rack up calories, but desperation trumped sound nutrition at this stage.

"These are the best brownies in the world." He took a square he didn't want. "You should try one."

She regarded him with the same solemn expression she'd worn since his arrival at Erica's high-rise condo late Monday afternoon. "My mom made the best brownies in the world."

Of course she did. No store-bought version would ever compare to a treat made by a loving mother.

He set the brownie down on his paper napkin. "I wouldn't be surprised."

"Did she ever make them for you?"

"No."

Hannah took a drink of milk, leaving a white mustache above her lip, her gaze never leaving his. "Aunt Erica said my mom liked you a lot."

News to him, until he'd spoken with Natalie's sister. Yes, they'd had quite a few conversations that carried past the end of her shift during the summer he'd spent in St. Louis. She'd been a sympathetic listener, and her upbeat attitude had lifted his sprits.

But she'd never let on that her feelings went deeper than friendship.

Until that last night.

Yet as she'd said in her note, their hours together had been about comfort rather than commitment.

On his end, anyway.

"I liked her too."

"So why did you leave?"

O-kay.

This wasn't a conversation he'd expected to have so soon, after Hannah's reticence—but her sudden willingness to ask questions could be a step forward.

Now all he had to do was come up with answers.

"It's kind of complicated."

"That's what Aunt Erica said." She continued to watch him, a fat tear forming in the corner of one eye. "I miss my mom."

His gut twisted. Dealing with little-girl tears was way beyond his realm of expertise.

"I know." He rested two fingers lightly on her arm. Swallowed. "It's hard to lose your mom. Mine died when I was fifteen."

"Do you have a dad?"

Jack drew in a slow breath. He hadn't spoken to anyone in detail about his background since the summer he'd poured his heart out to Christi. Her betrayal had taught him to suppress every feeling and memory that could cause pain. Dredging them up tonight—or ever again—hadn't been in his plans.

But perhaps opening up a bit to this child who was linked to him by DNA if not yet by heartstrings would crack the door to future sharing . . . and caring.

"No." Jack moved the brownie he'd taken back to the plate with the others and wove his fingers together on the table. "He died while I was in college—six months after my older brother was killed in a car accident."

Hannah continued to watch him. "Do you have any other brothers or sisters?"

"No."

"So are you all by yourself?"

He tried to conjure up a smile, but only managed a twist of the lips. "Not anymore."

The tear spilled over her lower lash and began to track down her cheek. "It's lonely without Mom."

"Maybe we can keep each other company."

"It's not the same."

"I know."

Hannah drew her finger through a wayward drop of milk on the table. "Mom never told me anything about you, except that you were nice. Whenever I asked her why you weren't with us, she always said she'd tell me someday." Hannah looked at him, as if expecting an answer to that question.

He began to sweat.

If he said he hadn't known she existed, she might be mad at her mother for keeping the secret from him. That could complicate her grief. At this age, she wouldn't understand Natalie's rationale.

Heck, *he* didn't understand it. In fact, since the reality of his paternity had sunk in, it had been a struggle every day to deal with his growing anger over her decision to keep that knowledge a secret all these years and deprive him of the chance to be part of his daughter's early life. Yes, taking on the role of dad back then would have changed his plans—and maybe Natalie hadn't wanted to foist that obligation on him, given the state he was in the last time he'd seen her—but the choice of how to deal with his daughter should have been his.

Hannah didn't need to know any of that, though.

And he sure wasn't going to mention the one-night stand that had produced her. Besides, how much did a ten-year-old know about what went into making babies, anyway?

"You aren't going to tell me either, are you?" Another tear trailed down Hannah's face.

Not the whole story—but a few pieces of information could help smooth the troubled waters in her mind.

"I went away before you were born. Before I knew you were coming. I don't know if your mom knew how to find me. But I can tell you this. If I'd known about you sooner, I would have been part of your life from the beginning."

She continued to watch him, as if measuring his sincerity. "What if you get tired of me?"

"That will never happen. We're a team from now on. That's a promise."

After a moment, she emitted a tiny, shuddering sigh, and her taut posture relaxed a hair. "Could we see if my sweater is finished drying?"

"Sure." Not much chance it was ready yet, but at least he'd managed to convince her the garment she'd worn since he met her was overdue for a washing. Prying her away from the community laundry room long enough to eat dinner—what little she'd downed—had taken all of his negotiating skills.

She slid out of her chair, hurried to the front door, and snatched up her jacket—reinforcing the message he'd already received.

The sweater was a vital link to her mom.

Its next trip to the laundry might have to be after Hannah was asleep—if he could convince her to stop wearing it to bed.

He joined her at the door, locked it behind them, and headed down the sidewalk, shortening his stride to match hers.

Once inside the laundry room, she made a beeline for the rotating dryer.

"It's not done yet, honey." He joined her and eyed the gauge. The cycle was winding down, but it wouldn't be finished for several more minutes.

"Could we check? In case it dried faster than everything else?" She hopped from one foot to the other, her focus riveted on the machine.

"Yes—but don't get your hopes up."

He opened the door, and the rotation stopped. One sleeve of the sweater was visible among the other clothing items, and he reached in to feel it. "It's still damp."

"Can't it finish drying at your apartment?" From the set of her jaw, she wasn't leaving without her sweater.

"I don't see why not." This wasn't a battle worth waging. He could always come back in fifteen minutes to collect the rest of the laundry.

After extricating the garment from the jumble of damp clothes, he draped it over his arm and pushed the door closed.

Hannah fingered the hem of the sweater. "It's not too wet. Can I wear it home?"

"I think we should let it dry for a while first." Moisture was already seeping through the fabric of his long-sleeved shirt. "Wearing wet clothes isn't healthy. You could get a cold or—" A tug stopped him as he leaned forward to press the restart button.

Whoops.

A sleeve had gotten caught in the dryer latch when he'd shut the door.

"What's wrong?" Hannah edged closer.

"Nothing. A slight snag. I'll have it free in a jiffy." He opened the door again and exerted pressure on the sleeve.

It stretched but didn't give.

He bent down. A loop of yarn had gotten caught in the upper latch that kept the door closed. Should be easy to extricate, though.

After dropping to the balls of his feet, he tried to work the loop loose.

It refused to budge.

Geez. How hard could it be to untangle one piece of yarn?

"Is it stuck bad?" Hannah hovered at his shoulder while she monitored his progress, a thread of panic weaving through her voice.

"No. I should have it straightened out in a minute."

Except he didn't. Instead, as he fiddled with it, the loop of yarn began to separate into delicate individual strands.

Not good.

But after all his manipulation, would another small tug free it?

Worth a try at this point. He wasn't getting anywhere with his current approach.

He gave a firm but gentle pull. The loop of yarn broke—but as he drew back, the dryer maintained its grip on the severed end.

A line of stitching began to unravel.

The shriek in his right eardrum pierced his skull. "Stop! Stop! You're wrecking it! It's coming apart!"

Hannah's screech turned into a keening wail punctuated by gut-wrenching sobs as she stared in horror at the damaged garment, wrapped her arms around herself, and rocked back and forth.

Jack gingerly extracted the piece of yarn from the latch, taking care not to do any further damage.

But as he cradled the damp sweater in his arms and watched his daughter have a meltdown, he couldn't help but think what a perfect metaphor the unraveling garment was for his life.

What in the world was going on in there?

Christi slammed on her brakes as she drove away from Beth's apartment after delivering an evening meal to her recuperating boss.

The howl was from a child—and it sounded more like intense grief than a tantrum.

After a microsecond hesitation, Christi pulled into a parking space in front of the Sea Haven Apartments laundry room and slid out from behind the wheel. How could she walk away from such anguish—even at the risk of being told this wasn't any of her business?

She sped toward the door and pulled it open.

At the scene on the other side, her jaw dropped.

Jack—face stricken, a purple knitted garment draped over his arm—was watching a girl of about nine or ten sob as tears streamed down her cheeks.

Neither noticed her.

Should she back out before they—

As if sensing her presence, Jack's head swiveled toward her.

Now she was stuck. She couldn't leave *anyone* in the lurch whose taut posture communicated such a panicked SOS.

Letting the door close behind her, she took a few steps closer to the duo. Much as she wanted to ask who the child was, she settled for a question more appropriate to the immediate problem. "How can I help?"

As she spoke, the girl spun toward her and went silent. But her splotchy complexion and heaving chest suggested her distress hadn't abated.

"The sleeve of the sweater got caught in the dryer latch while I was taking it out." Jack lifted his arm to display the limp garment. "It started to unravel." He angled sideways to give her a view of the damage.

"May I take a look?"

"Please."

She crossed to him and gently lifted the damaged sleeve. About three inches of a row of stitching had unraveled. "Did you pull this?"

"Yeah. I guess that was a mistake."

She didn't bother to confirm what he already knew as she gave the damage a closer perusal. While her experience with needle and thread was limited, the skills she'd gleaned from the learn-to-knit class she'd taken to fill up her solitary evenings a couple of years ago ought to help.

"I may be able to fix this."

The girl eased closer, hope sparking in her eyes. "Would you try?"

"I'd be happy to. May I take it home and work on it?"

As renewed anxiety darkened the girl's irises, Jack spoke. "She doesn't like to let it too far from her sight. It was her mom's."

"Oh." Christi examined the unraveled section again. "Do you have any sewing supplies?"

"Other than an emergency sewing kit from a hotel I stayed in once, no."

That wouldn't be sufficient.

But Beth was into needlepoint. She'd been working on a piece a few minutes ago. Perhaps she also had sewing-related items.

It was worth asking.

"I'll tell you what. I was just visiting my boss, who lives in this apartment complex, and she may have the supplies I need. Give me a few minutes to see what I can scrounge up and I'll meet you at your apartment. Unless your friend has to go home first?"

"I live there too."

What?

Christi gaped at the girl as she tried to digest that bombshell. Refocused on Jack.

His cheeks grew ruddy, and he reached around to massage his neck. "I, uh, should have introduced you sooner. This is my daughter, Hannah."

The words registered—but didn't compute.

Jack had a daughter?

"I'll explain at the apartment." He was watching her like she was a spooked deer about to bolt.

No wonder, if she looked as shocked as she felt.

"Okay." She backed toward the door, feeling for the knob behind her. Somehow she managed to coax up the corners of her mouth as she spoke to the traumatized child. "I'll do my best to fix your sweater so it's almost as good as new."

"Thank you." Hannah gave her a tremulous smile.

Jack rattled off his apartment number, and Christi filed it away in her memory as she exited.

On the other side of the door, she paused to kick-start her lungs while the startling news continued to loop through her mind.

Jack had a daughter.

So where was her mother?

But what did it matter? Their summer of romance was long past. Life had gone on for both of them. If there was a wife in the picture that Christi's pretrip research hadn't uncovered, so what? She'd made the taxing trek up here for a loan, nothing more.

Yet as she returned to her car and drove back toward Beth's apartment, she couldn't contain her burgeoning disappointment that Jack had found someone else to love soon after they'd broken up.

Because he wasn't the only one whose heart had been tattered by their parting.

It had just taken her a lot longer to recognize all she'd lost.

And by then it had been too late.

14

This wasn't how he'd wanted Christi to find out about his daughter.

As Jack led Hannah back to his apartment, the girl in lockstep beside him mere inches from the sweater draped over his arm, the meager dinner he'd managed to choke down hardened into a lump.

Christi's shock had been almost palpable.

Not because she'd ever cared about him. The evidence proved otherwise. But his paternity wasn't consistent with her image of the honorable, fresh-off-the-farm country boy who'd dropped out of college after the back-to-back deaths of his two remaining family members upended his world.

A guy with the values he'd espoused would never choose to be a single dad.

She had to be wondering if he'd been as upright as he'd seemed back in those days, or if he'd been as disingenuous as she—

"Who is that lady?"

Forcibly shifting gears, Jack refocused on Hannah. "Her name is Christi."

"Is she your friend?"

Not even close.

"More like an acquaintance." He picked up his pace.

"She's nice." Hannah broke into a trot. "Do you think she can fix my sweater?"

Not the Christi he'd once known. She would have relegated repairs and alterations to a tailor. He'd be willing to bet a week's salary she'd never threaded a needle in her younger days.

"I hope so." He turned onto the path that led to the door of the apartment. "But if she can't, I'll find someone in town who can."

Hannah's eyebrows dipped into a V. "Would we have to leave my sweater with them?"

"Probably."

"I don't like that idea." The stubborn tilt of her chin was another familiar Colby trait.

He twisted the key in the lock and pushed the door open. "We'll let Christi try first."

"Why don't you put the sweater here?" Hannah walked over to the couch and patted the back.

He complied, draping it carefully over the upholstery. "You want to help me put away the brownies and tidy up the kitchen?"

"No. I'll wait here." She took up sentry duty beside the sweater.

Fine. He could use a few minutes to regroup—and decide how much he wanted to tell Christi about the circumstances of Hannah's birth.

Unfortunately, she gave him less than five. The bell rang before he'd done more than stow the unwanted brownies, wash the beverage glasses, and begin to formulate the framework of an explanation.

"I'll get it." Hannah jumped up and ran to the door.

He tossed the dish towel on the counter and joined them as Christi entered. She was carrying the kind of sewing box his mom used to have.

"We're in luck. Beth gave me a few pointers after I explained what happened, and she offered to help if I run into any trouble.

She also had all the supplies I need. I think I can handle this. May I?" She motioned to the couch.

"Of course."

She set the box on the floor, picked up the sweater, and turned it inside out. "Hannah, would you like to sit next to me?" She patted the seat cushion. "You can hold the bottom of the sweater while I work."

His daughter didn't wait for a second invitation. She perched on the edge of the couch beside the woman who was trying to salvage the mess he'd made.

Brilliant move by Christi.

After witnessing Hannah's meltdown, she'd realized that letting the girl maintain physical contact with the sweater during the repair process would offer her a modicum of comfort.

Jack propped a shoulder against the doorframe, folded his arms, and kept his distance while Christi chatted with Hannah, talking her through every step.

Using a hook of some sort, she worked the shredded ends of the yarn from the right side of the sweater to the inside, then threaded one piece though the eye of a large needle.

"I'm going to pull the ends through all these loops, one at a time. See?" She motioned for Hannah to lean closer as she worked. "After I do that, I'll use regular thread to close up the gap and hold the ends of the yarn in place. Once they're secure, I'll sew back and forth to give the repair extra strength. The overlapping stitches should keep it from unraveling again."

She continued to sew as she talked, handling the needle and thread like a pro.

The woman was full of surprises.

"I have one like this, but it doesn't fit me anymore." Hannah smoothed a hand over the hem of the sweater in her lap.

"I love the color."

"It was my mom's favorite."

Based on Christi's infinitesimal hesitation, Hannah's use of the past tense had registered.

He ought to explain. But how could he do that without upsetting Hannah? Whatever he decided to tell his unexpected guest would be best relayed in private.

"My mom liked purple too." Christi kept stitching. "One of her favorite dresses was a few shades lighter than this."

"Does she still have it?"

"No. She went to heaven a long time ago."

Hannah bunched the hem in her fingers. "Do you miss her?"

Christi stopped sewing and gave his daughter her full attention. "Every day. I think I always will."

"My mom went to heaven too. Last month." Hannah's response was muted and tear-laced. "I miss her a l-lot."

"Oh, sweetie." Features softening, Christi laid the sleeve in her lap and pulled Hannah into a hug. "I'm so sorry."

His daughter didn't resist the embrace—nor stiffen like she did if he got too close. On the contrary. She clung to Christi as if the two were old friends.

Easy to see why. Compassion, caring, and warmth radiated from the woman on his couch. No one who was hurting or in need of comfort would be immune to that kind of empathy.

Including him.

Which was weird.

Why would he be drawn to a woman who'd callously used him? Who'd led him on and broken his heart? Was he a masochist, or what?

When no answers came to mind, he stuffed the questions into a dark corner of his mind to think about if he ever had a few minutes to breathe.

Like that would happen anytime soon.

At last Christi drew back and smoothed the hair away from his daughter's forehead. "I know how important it is to keep something that belonged to a person you love." She pulled out the ring on the chain around her neck and held it out for Hannah to see. "This was my mom's. I always keep it close."

The girl examined the sparkling diamonds. "It's pretty."

"I agree." Christi tilted the band to let the stones catch the light. "She had other jewelry, but this was her favorite piece. All I have to do is hold it and I feel like she's with me."

"That's how I feel when I wear my mom's sweater."

"Then I'm glad I was able to fix it. Let's see how it came out." She turned it right side out and smoothed it flat.

"Wow! I can hardly tell where it was ripped." Hannah bent close to examine it, touching the spot that had unraveled. "This is awesome. Can I put it on?"

"It's kind of damp. If your, uh, dad lays it on a bed and uses a blow dryer, that would speed up the drying process." Christi addressed him for the first time since Hannah had sat beside her.

His cue to reenter the conversation.

"I can do that."

Hannah gave him a leery once-over and spoke to Christi. "Could you do it instead?"

In other words, she didn't trust him with her treasured sweater.

Understandable after the fiasco of the past half hour, but her wariness hurt nonetheless.

Christi shot him an uncertain look.

"If you can spare another few minutes, I'm fine with letting you take the lead on this." Jack pushed off from the wall and joined them.

"Please?" Hannah touched her arm.

Only someone with a heart of stone would be able to resist his daughter's earnest plea and beseeching eyes.

Christi caved. "All right. It won't take long."

"The bedroom's this way." Without waiting for a response, Jack walked down the hall, past the office that would become Hannah's room as soon as her furniture—and whatever else she and Erica had chosen to keep from Natalie's apartment—arrived. Somehow he'd cram his desk and printer and other equipment into his bedroom.

He waited at the door as Christi and Hannah followed. Christi glanced in the darkened office as she passed but didn't comment.

"I'll get the blow dryer." He detoured to the bathroom, retrieved it, and returned to find Christi smoothing the sweater flat on the comforter. He plugged in the dryer and handed it to her.

"Thanks." She smiled at Hannah as his daughter yawned. "Someone's getting tired."

"She's on central time. We flew in from Chicago yesterday." He hooked his thumbs in the pockets of his jeans and remained at the foot of the bed.

It was impossible to miss the questions in Christi's eyes—but she didn't ask them.

"In that case, I'm betting it's past your bedtime." She again directed her attention to Hannah. "I'll work fast."

"Why don't you get ready for bed while Christi dries your sweater?" Jack opened a drawer in the dresser behind him, pulled out a pair of pajamas, and held them out to her. "You can brush your teeth too."

She took the pajamas—but hesitated.

"I promise to keep your sweater safe." Christi touched her shoulder.

Hannah chewed on her lower lip for a moment, but in the end, she scurried into the master bedroom bathroom and closed the door.

Leaving him alone with Christi.

The silence between them didn't last long. She flipped on the blow dryer, and the noise eliminated the possibility of conversation.

Perfect. What he had to say to her about his daughter would keep until after Hannah was in bed and he and Christi could have a quiet, adult discussion.

Unless she took off as soon as the sweater was dry, despite her obvious curiosity.

But he'd do his best to convince her to stay for a few more minutes and hear him out. Not that it mattered to the two of them at this stage, but for reasons he hadn't yet analyzed, he didn't want her to think his feelings for her had been as insincere as hers had been for him. He wasn't proud of how Hannah had been conceived, but it hadn't happened while he and Christi were dating. That wasn't how he was wired.

Before she left his apartment tonight, he'd make that clear.

And while he was at it, he'd add a thank-you for helping him avert a crisis that could have sabotaged his efforts to connect with his daughter for the indefinite future.

"Is it dry yet?" Hannah burst through the bathroom door, a dab of toothpaste on her chin.

Christi shut off the blow dryer and felt the garment. "The front's done. I'll turn it over and do the back next. That won't take as long."

She revved up the blow dryer again while Jack dropped down to Hannah's level.

It was impossible to hear his quiet words over the racket of the dryer, but Christi watched the interchange in her peripheral vision.

Hannah kept her eyes downcast as Jack talked, one bare foot propped on top of the other, hands clasped behind her back. Near as Christi could tell, she didn't speak. Her only response was an occasional nod.

Christi gave the bedroom another discreet scan. It was a man's room, through and through. Unless her instincts were off, there wasn't a wife—or any woman—in Jack's life now. And the somewhat stilted interaction between father and daughter suggested the two of them were little more than strangers.

He'd promised an explanation while they were in the laundry room—but would he follow through? It was possible he'd have second thoughts about sharing what had to be an intensely personal story with a woman who'd hurt him deeply.

On the other hand, she *had* come to his rescue tonight. That had to count for something—didn't it?

She felt the back of the sweater and switched off the blow dryer. "You're all set, Hannah."

The girl sped over to the bed and lifted the garment as if it were spun glass. Held it to her cheek. "Thank you."

"It was my pleasure." Christi set the blow dryer on the bed.

"Will it unravel again if I sleep in it?"

"I don't think so. Want me to help you put it on?"

"Yes, please." She handed over the sweater.

Christi slipped the too-big garment over her head. "Shall I roll up the sleeves?"

"Uh-huh." The girl yawned and held out her arms.

Task accomplished, Christi eased back. "Someone's ready to sleep."

Jack moved forward. "Jump up and I'll tuck you in."

Christi frowned. "Isn't this your room?"

"He sleeps on the sofa." Hannah climbed up onto the bed with a boost from Jack.

"Only until her furniture arrives." He pulled up the covers. "It's a two-bedroom unit."

But from what she'd seen earlier in passing, the other bedroom was his office. Where would he work in the small apartment after that space became a little girl's room?

And if furniture was coming, Hannah's presence must be permanent.

"Good night, honey." Jack smoothed out the blanket. "Call me if you need anything."

"Okay. Will you leave a light on again?"

"Yep." He crossed to the bathroom, flipped the switch, and cracked the door.

Christi took Jack's place beside the bed and gave the girl's hand a squeeze. "I'm happy I got to meet you, Hannah."

"Me too. Will I see you again?"

Better not make promises Jack might not want her to keep.

"Hope Harbor is a very small town. Most people who live here see each other on occasion."

"Maybe you can come visit."

"Let's talk about that tomorrow, Hannah." Jack joined the conversation. "It's late, and Christi has to go home."

Did that mean he wasn't going to explain about Hannah after all?

Disappointment welled up inside her—but if he wanted to keep his secrets, how could she blame him? She had plenty of her own she'd never shared with anyone except Tasha. And even her dear friend didn't know them all.

"I'll wait in the living room while you finish up in here." She slipped through the door and walked back down the hall, the murmur of voices following her.

Less than a minute later, Jack joined her. "Are you in a hurry?"

"No. I'm not working tonight."

"If you want to stay for a few minutes, I can fill you in on the situation here."

Lines of fatigue radiated from the corners of his eyes, and faint smudges under his lower lashes spoke of stress and sleepless nights. He seemed a world removed from the confident, in-control cop who'd confronted her at Sea Glass Cottage a mere two weeks ago.

But the curveballs of life could take a toll—as she knew all too well.

"Are you certain you want to?" The question was out before she could stop it—prompted by empathy rather than lack of curiosity.

"Yes." His mouth was set in a grim line. "I can imagine the questions running through your mind, and it would be easy to jump to wrong conclusions. Would you like a soda or water?"

"No thanks."

"If you don't mind, let's sit on the front porch." He tipped his head toward the hall.

She got the message. Children had excellent hearing. "That's fine."

He opened the door for her, and she exited, purse in hand. "Take that." He motioned to the single patio chair and leaned back against the railing, bracing himself on his palms.

Since it was either claim the chair, stand, or sit on the steps and invite him to join her—a far too cozy arrangement—she went with the chair.

Several silent seconds ticked by in the deepening dusk. The dead-end road in front of the apartments led to Starfish Pier, according to Beth, and tonight there wasn't a car in sight. Nor were any of the apartment residents out and about.

It wasn't as isolated and private as Sea Glass Cottage, but at least Jack should be able to tell his story without any interruptions.

Yet he didn't speak.

Had he changed his mind?

If he had, she shouldn't hold him to the spur-of-the-moment promise made in the laundry room in the midst of a crisis.

"Listen, I'll let you off the hook if you'd rather not discuss this."

"No. I was just trying to organize my thoughts." He blew out a breath. "Let me give you the short version. Hannah was conceived the night I overheard you talking to Dirk Mason by the pool at your father's house—after I'd downed one too many whiskeys at the bar and grill where I often ate dinner. Over the summer I'd gotten to know one of the waitresses there who had a kind heart and sympathetic ear. By the end of the evening, I was in no condition to drive—and apparently talking crazy. She took me back to her apartment to sleep off the booze and calm down. But I was hurting, she was willing to offer consolation, and under the influence of alcohol I behaved completely out of character. That's a fact, not an excuse."

As the implications of his confession sank in, shock reverberated through Christi.

She was the reason Hannah had been conceived. If she hadn't hurt Jack badly, he wouldn't have been desperate for solace.

Her stomach knotted.

How could she have been so shallow and cavalier in those days? How could she not have realized that playing with fire was dangerous? That people would get burned? Why hadn't she seen that what had started as a lark . . . a game . . . a chance to have a bit of clandestine fun with a man outside her social circle . . . could escalate? That Jack would begin to fall in love with her?

As she'd begun to fall in love with him.

That had been the dilemma she'd been trying to solve when she'd assured Dirk that Jack meant nothing to her. A lie meant to buy her time to sort through the quandary. Figure out what to do about the kind, principled man who'd prompted her to rethink the future she'd envisioned.

"I was going to ask you to marry me that night."

At Jack's admission, her lungs stalled.

It was worse than she'd thought.

"Jack, I'm sorry." Voice choking, she pressed a hand to her chest. "I never meant to hurt you. What you heard that day . . . it wasn't true. But I wasn't ready to tell the world—or my father—about us."

It was hard to read his face. His back was to the setting sun, leaving his features in shadows.

"It doesn't matter anymore." His tone was cool. Controlled. "Like I said the day you showed up in town, it's ancient history. I didn't bring this all up to rehash it but to confirm that while I was with you that summer there wasn't anyone else. I'm not the kind of guy who would run around on someone I cared about."

"I know that. And here's a piece of the story *you* don't know. I went to your apartment that night. I also called repeatedly. When I couldn't reach you, I went back to your apartment again. You were gone. For months I kept trying to find you—but it was like you disappeared into thin air."

"That was the intent. The morning after Hannah was conceived, I returned the ring I'd bought you and left town. My goal was to start over as far away as possible from all the bad memories in the Midwest, and I didn't stop until I hit an ocean. My new life was humming along until you showed up and I found out about Hannah all in the space of forty-eight hours."

Wow.

No wonder Jack appeared shell-shocked.

"She referred to her mother in the past tense." That had to be why the girl had appeared so suddenly.

"Yeah."

Christi listened as he told her about the letter, the DNA test, his discussions with Erica, and the trip to Chicago earlier this week to pick up his daughter.

Talk about a life spinning out of control.

As he finished, she exhaled. "I can't begin to imagine the upheaval all that has caused."

"That's a gross understatement. But everyone in the PD has bent over backward to accommodate me, which has been a godsend. The chief let me take eight unscheduled vacation days, and the other officers are working extra hours so I can help Hannah settle in and finalize day care arrangements. She's not quite old enough to be by herself for extended periods, especially in a brand-new environment."

"How is this affecting your writing career?"

"I've worked ahead on my next deadline, but I'll have to establish a new routine soon." He pushed off from the railing. "Now you know the background."

Their conversation must be over.

Christi rose. "I appreciate you sharing all this with me."

"Like I said, I didn't want you coming to the wrong conclusions about my character."

"Why not?" The question spilled past her lips.

He folded his arms, adopting his intimidating cop stance again. "My dad always said a person's reputation was everything. That matters to me."

"I don't disagree—but I'm surprised you care what *I* think."

His brow crimped, and a few beats passed. "I don't so much care what you think as what you might say."

As his inference registered, she clutched her purse tighter. "You really think I'd bad-mouth you or spread insinuations?"

"You want the truth? I don't know what to think. But in light of past experience, my trust level with you isn't super high."

The knot below her rib cage tightened.

His assessment was harsh—but deserved in light of their history. Even if the woman she'd been when he'd formed his opinions had ceased to exist.

"Understood." She rummaged through her purse for her keys. "If you have any more issues with the sweater, let me know. If I can't fix it, I'll find someone who can."

She stepped off the porch and walked toward her car.

"Christi."

At his summons, she paused. Angled back.

"Thank you for your help tonight."

"No problem. I know what it's like to have your world implode."

Without waiting for a response, she continued down the walk to her car. She didn't look back until she was behind the wheel and the car was in gear.

Jack was walking in the direction of the laundry room, perhaps to reclaim the rest of his items from the dryer. He didn't give her another glance.

Spirits tanking, she pressed on the accelerator and drove away.

It was bad enough that his opinion of her hadn't budged. That no matter how contrite she was, no matter how much she'd changed, he couldn't find it in his heart to recognize that—or forgive her.

Even worse, though? If his trust level was as low as he claimed, the odds of him giving her the loan she'd pinned her hopes on were slim to none—and Tasha's dream would have to be put on hold.

All because, once again, she'd messed up back in Dallas . . . and left carnage in her wake.

15

"This is it, Noah. The studio of world-famous artist Charley Lopez." Steve drove past the modest clapboard cottage and parked by the weathered wood structure fifty yards behind that overlooked the sea, a large expanse of glass covering the top half of the outbuilding's north wall.

"Are you sure he doesn't mind us coming here?" Noah clutched his sketchbook against his chest, nervousness and excitement radiating off him. "I don't want to bother him."

"When I called him yesterday, he told me he likes to meet young artists. And he said today would be perfect if it rained, because he wouldn't be opening his taco stand." Steve swept a hand over the misty, gray setting. "Mother Nature cooperated."

"I've never met a real artist."

"You'll like Charley. Everyone does."

"Are you two friends?"

"Everyone who knows Charley is his friend. I've been eating his tacos and shooting the breeze with him for years." Though not as much lately with Beth living in town and wanting her space.

Noah fingered the edge of the sketchbook. "Is he really famous?"

"In the art world. But around here, he's just Charley. And I bet he's going to love the tide pool sketch you showed me while we had our ice cream." He leaned around to the back seat and snagged the plastic bag he'd brought along. "Why don't you put your drawings in this and we'll go in?"

After the boy complied, the two of them jogged toward the door of the studio through the intensifying rain. Before he could knock, a muffled voice called through the door.

"Come on in, Steve. It's open."

He gave the entry a quick inspection. No security cameras that he could see, but there must be one in the area. However, it was too wet to linger outside trying to spot it.

"You heard the man. Let's do this." He twisted the knob and ushered Noah through the door.

As he stepped inside, Steve gave the high-ceilinged, light-filled studio a sweep. Numerous shelves held books and painting supplies, canvases in various stages of completion were propped against the walls, and a small octagonal window on the far side offered a glimpse of the sea. A faint smell of paint and solvents hung in the air, and classical music emanated from a vintage turntable.

The room was as unique and eclectic as the man himself.

"Welcome." Charley smiled at them from his seat in front of an easel. "Did you have any trouble finding me?" He set his brush down, wiped his hands on a rag, and stood.

"No. Your directions were excellent." Steve laid a hand on Noah's shoulder and introduced him.

The boy was fairly quivering with excitement as he said hello and gave the man's lair a round-eyed survey.

"I'm happy to meet you, Noah." Charley crossed to them and extended his hand.

The boy shook it. "Th-thank you for letting us come."

"It's always a treat to meet other artists."

Color suffused the boy's cheeks. "I'm not a real artist. Drawing is a hobby."

"Well, as Ralph Waldo Emerson said, 'Every artist was first an amateur.' I didn't start out as a professional either. That happens over time. Steve tells me you're very talented."

Noah's pink hue deepened. "I try hard, and I draw whenever I can, but I don't know if I'm very good. I've never had lessons."

"Why don't you let me take a look at what you have and I'll give you my honest opinion?"

Noah caught his lower lip between his teeth and slowly pulled his drawing pad from the plastic bag. "This is my newest stuff."

"Perfect. Let's go over to that table and you can tell me about the sketches while I page through the book." Charley motioned toward the corner of the room. "Would you like a soda?"

"No thank you. I already had ice cream."

"A much better treat than soda. Steve, there's java in the pot if you'd like a cup." He indicated a coffeemaker on one of the shelves. "Not as tasty as the brew at The Perfect Blend but a decent follow-up to ice cream."

"Thanks. That would hit the spot." And provide an excellent chaser to the cloying sweetness clinging to his tongue.

He helped himself, perusing the art and philosophy books on the shelves—and eavesdropping on the conversation as Charley and Noah put their heads together.

The Hope Harbor artist was as gracious as he'd expected. He asked questions, praised certain details of the different drawings, offered a few subtle suggestions, and gave the boy his full attention, treating him like an artistic peer rather than a kid.

And Noah ate it up. He grew more and more animated as the discussion continued, his eyes bright as he hung on Charley's every word, clearly in his element in this studio and with a man who understood his compulsion to create.

A compulsion Jonathan had shared.

All at once the sip of coffee he'd taken turned bitter. Grimacing, Steve swallowed it, the acidic liquid burning a trail down his throat.

Why couldn't he have done for his son what he was doing for this boy he barely knew? Why hadn't he recognized sooner what Beth had told him all along—that he should appreciate and encourage Jonathan's unique talents instead of holding out hope that one day he'd outgrow his fascination with art and become the athletic son Steve had always hoped to have? How would he ever fill the void Jonathan's death had left in his heart? Vanquish the grief and guilt that darkened his empty days and—

"—in a hurry? Steve?"

At a touch on his arm, he recalibrated and pivoted toward Charley. "I'm sorry. I was lost in thought. What did you ask?"

"I wondered if you were in a hurry. I was going to let Noah experiment with a brush and paint."

The boy stood beside the man, eyes alight with eagerness—and hope.

"I don't want to keep you from your work." He motioned toward the easel.

"My work isn't going anywhere—and I enjoy encouraging young people with talent. Your friend here has an abundance of it." He smiled at Noah.

The boy beamed back at him.

"In that case, have at it." Steve lifted his cup. "I'll get a refill." Not that he wanted one, but it would keep his hands occupied.

Charley set Noah up with a blank canvas, gave him a few instructions, and turned him loose. Within seconds, the boy was engrossed in whatever project the artist had suggested he tackle.

After monitoring his progress for a couple of minutes, Charley rejoined him.

"He seems to be in his element here." Steve hooked a thumb toward the boy.

"I agree. He has a natural talent. One that should be nurtured." The corners of Charley's mouth rose as he watched Noah work. "He reminds me of Jonathan."

Steve stared at the man. "Did you . . . how did you know my son?"

"Beth brought him to the studio a few times." Charley cocked his head. "She didn't tell you?"

"No." Or if she had, it hadn't registered. Art had never been on his radar.

"She did mention that you weren't too interested in drawing and painting."

"I wasn't—but I should have been. Anything that was important to Jonathan should have been important to me."

"Should haves can be hard to live with." Empathy flowed from the man, the compassion in his dark irises reaching deep into Steve's soul.

"Yeah." He set the cup down on the table beside him. Kneaded the bridge of his nose. "Especially when you can't undo the damage."

A few beats ticked by, remorse hanging heavy in the room. Weighing him down.

"I was deeply saddened by your loss last summer." Charley's gentle tone was filled with kindness. "Jonathan was a fine young man, and it's hard to rationalize such heartbreak. But the minister was wise to remind us at the service that just as the heavens are higher than the earth, so are God's ways higher than ours. His plans are often beyond our understanding."

Charley had attended Jonathan's funeral?

"I'm sorry. I didn't see you there." The whole nightmare sequence of events was a blur.

"No worries. Grief has a tendency to blind us, not only during the initial period of shock but long after. I know Beth is still having a difficult go of it too."

Steve curled his fingers into tight fists. Was that an observation—or had his wife talked to Charley about the circumstances of Jonathan's death? Filled him in on more than the facts everyone knew—that he'd died from a congenital coronary artery defect on a father-son hiking trip to the bottom of the Grand Canyon, and that his grieving parents had separated eight weeks later?

Why not feel the man out, see how much he knew? Perhaps even seek a bit of advice. Charley often had a few nuggets of wisdom to offer, whatever the subject.

"I haven't talked to Beth in a while. Her choice—and I can't blame her." Steve checked on Noah. The boy was on the other side of the room, intent on his work, and the music would mask a quiet conversation. "She wanted to give Jonathan an immersive art experience for graduation. I insisted on a father-son Grand Canyon trip. A strenuous hike in the heat of summer." He shook his head in disgust.

"From what I understood, no one knew he had heart issues."

"That's true. But I knew what was *in* his heart—art, not athletics. The trip was for me, not him. Jonathan went because he always tried to make both of us proud—and happy." Steve's voice choked, and he picked up his coffee, willing his vision to clear.

"If you had it to do over, would you plan such a trip again?"

At Charley's quiet question, he looked at the man. "Of course not."

"Sometimes the most important lessons we learn are the hardest."

"But what's the point in learning them if it's too late?"

"Is it?"

"Jonathan's gone."

"Other people can benefit from your change of heart, though. Like Noah—and Beth."

Steve let out a slow breath. "I won't disagree with you about Noah. Beth's a different story. I haven't been able to breach the wall between us. Her anger and hurt and grief go too deep."

"Have you talked to her?"

"She wants space, not conversation. But I've sent notes and cards on a regular basis."

"Powerful as words can be, you know what they say about actions."

Steve gave a helpless shrug. "What else can I do? She asked me to keep my distance while she thinks about what she wants going forward, and I've tried to respect her wishes. If I show up at her door, she'll probably kick me out."

"You never know. People's perspectives can change—and she's not in a position to do any kicking right now anyway." Charley picked up a small, half-finished seascape that was leaning against the wall at his feet and examined it.

Steve frowned at the man's odd comment. "What does that mean?"

"I wish I could figure out why this painting isn't working." Charley angled the canvas toward him. "What's missing here?"

He gave it a cursory scan, still fixated on Charley's previous remark. "I'm not an artist. What did you mean about Beth not being in a position to do any kicking?"

"You don't have to be an artist to give me a reaction."

It appeared Charley wasn't going to answer his question until he offered feedback on the painting.

Fine.

Steve examined the roughed-in beach scene, storm clouds gathering on the distant horizon, whitecaps hinting at the turmoil in the restless sea. Even in this early stage, Charley had masterfully captured a relentless sense of urgency. A hint of power and danger. As for what was missing . . .

"You could put a guy in a boat out on the water. Like he's struggling to reach shore before the storm hits."

"Ah." Charley's countenance brightened. "You think I should add a human touch. Give the viewer someone to care about. To root for."

"Yeah." Not that he'd have thought to express it in those terms.

"That could do the trick. It's always more effective to convey emotions up close and personal rather than in the abstract." Charley set the painting back down. "I was referencing Beth's knee replacement."

It took Steve a moment to switch gears after the abrupt change of topic—and to process Charley's comment. The claim his insurance company had sent from the orthopedic specialist Beth saw on occasion hadn't raised any red flags. She'd been talking about having knee surgery for several years. Had she finally followed through—without telling him?

"Are you saying she had her knee replaced?"

Charley hiked up an eyebrow. "You didn't know?"

"No. She didn't tell me."

"Charley?"

At the summons from Noah, the artist rejoined the boy at the easel.

As the two conferred, questions tumbled through Steve's mind.

Why would Beth keep a major operation like that a secret?

How was she coping on her own?

Who was running her shop, supplying her with food, taking her to doctor's appointments and physical therapy?

Steve had no answers—and there was only one way to get them.

Call Beth, or visit her.

He glanced down at the painting Charley had set back against the wall, the man's comment echoing in his mind.

"It's always more effective to convey emotions up close and personal rather than in the abstract."

Maybe he should replace the cards and notes with an in-person visit—and an offer of help.

Worst case, she'd refuse to talk to him. But what did he have to lose? He couldn't get any lonelier than he already was.

Best case, she'd realize he'd seen the light and learned the hard lesson Charley had mentioned—and give him a chance to prove he was a different, better man.

An outcome he'd continue to pray for, as he had from the day she'd walked out.

But since the words he'd been writing to his wife hadn't swayed her opinion of him, it was possible Charley could be right.

It might be time for action.

16

What was poking him in the arm?

Emitting a sleepy groan, Jack tried to wriggle into a more comfortable position on the narrow couch in the living room.

Mission impossible.

The couch was fine for sitting, but it had *not* been designed to accommodate a six-foot-two, broad-shouldered frame for a full night's sleep.

Maybe he ought to—

Another jab in the arm. This one harder.

He pried open one eye.

From eighteen inches away Hannah stared at him, hair tousled, her mom's sweater slipping off one shoulder. Behind her, light seeped around the edges of the shades in the living room. Not pale morning light either.

No surprise he'd slept later than usual after tossing throughout the night—thanks to both the uncomfortable couch and his so far unsuccessful quest to find suitable day care. Who knew it would be that hard to line up an appropriate place for her?

Maybe he should have tamped down his usual deal-with-it-now MO and let Hannah stay with Erica for a while.

But that hadn't been an ideal solution either. Natalie's sister had to resume her work travel, and Hannah would have ended up in the care of strangers who shared no blood ties.

"Are you awake?" Hannah peered at him.

"I am now." He pushed himself up, swung his feet to the floor, and squinted at his watch. Almost nine.

Definitely on the late side.

"Aren't we going to church?"

Church?

Jack forked his fingers through his hair, trying to engage his sluggish brain. "I, uh, don't always go." Like never since he'd left St. Louis. After all the years he'd been a faithful follower, where had God been when his dad and brother died within months of each other? When Christi had broken his already bruised heart?

"Mom and me went every week—and Aunt Erica took me while I stayed with her."

News to him about Natalie's regular church attendance. The summer they'd known each other, Sunday services hadn't been part of her routine. She *had* plied him with questions about his faith, though. Perhaps some of his answers had resonated.

Strange how life worked. By the end of that summer, she must have connected with God just as he'd walked away from him.

But being on the outs with the Almighty didn't mean he should deprive Hannah of her Sunday visits with God—especially if that's how Natalie had raised her.

"Then I guess we're going." He stood, picked up his phone from the side table, and googled Grace Christian Church. They'd missed the early service, but they could make the later one. "Why don't you get dressed while I shower and shave?"

"Can I wear my sweater?"

He gave the baggy garment a dubious once-over. Not happening. The other members of the congregation would wonder about his competence as a caregiver if he let her show up in that.

"I think it's too casual for church. You can take the sweater, but why don't you change into something else?"

She gave him a disgruntled look. "Aunt Erica wouldn't let me wear it either." With a huff, she disappeared back down the hall.

His decision may not have won him any brownie points with his daughter, but if Erica had concurred, it wasn't off base.

After gathering up his bedding and stowing it in the hall closet, Jack followed Hannah to the bedroom, waited while she picked out a suitable outfit, and retreated to the bathroom.

Forty-five minutes later, fortified with a glass of juice and half of the bagel they'd split, he pulled into the Grace Christian parking lot.

"Do you know anyone here?" Hannah inspected the group converging on the entrance.

"I'm sure I do. I meet a lot of people because of my job."

"Look!" Hannah released her seat belt, bounced forward, and pointed toward the front of the church. "Christi's here!"

Jack followed the direction of her finger.

Sure enough, the newest Hope Harbor resident was ascending the steps to the front door.

Huh.

She must not have been exaggerating that first day when she'd mentioned praying.

Another disconnect from the woman he'd known.

"Can we talk to her?" Hannah fumbled for the door handle.

"Not before the service." And not afterward either, if he could avoid it. Every time they met, she managed to chip away at his defenses—and he wasn't ready to forgive and forget . . . or trust that she'd changed as much as it seemed. Her acting skills had been top-notch the summer she'd convinced him she was falling for him, and there was no reason to think she'd lost that talent.

"Can we talk to her later?" Hannah clutched her sweater tighter.

"We'll see."

The corners of her mouth turned down. "That's what Mom always said if she meant no."

His instinctive answer must be the natural default for all cornered parents.

"Let's go in or we'll be late." He opened his door.

She didn't press her point—but he had a feeling she wasn't going to give up either.

Hannah stayed close as they walked to the front door, and once inside, his height advantage allowed him to spot Christi faster than his daughter did.

Unfortunately, she'd chosen a seat near the back—as he'd planned to do.

But there were pews on either side of the main aisle. He didn't have to pick one close to her.

Except as he started to direct Hannah toward the aisle on the far right, Christi glanced their direction . . . and their gazes locked. Not for more than a beat or two—but that was all it took for Hannah to follow his line of sight and home in on the woman who'd saved her sweater.

"There she is!" Hannah tugged on the bottom of his sport jacket.

"I see her."

"Can we sit with her?" Hannah rose on tiptoe and waved at Christi.

She lifted a hand in acknowledgment.

"There's more room over there." Jack motioned toward the pew he'd planned to claim.

"We can fit next to her. Come on." Without waiting for him to say yea or nay, she took off that direction.

Now what?

He couldn't very well sit alone. That would raise eyebrows once people realized he and Hannah were together. And if he avoided Christi, his daughter would doubtless ask questions he didn't want to answer.

Resigned, he followed her over and claimed the aisle seat in the pew.

Thankfully the service began almost at once.

As the organ launched into a familiar melody, he pulled a hymnal from the rack on the pew in front of him. Added his voice to those around him. And all at once, a powerful sense of déjà vu—of homecoming—enveloped him.

He frowned.

Considering all the years he'd driven by this church without the least inclination to go inside, the strong reaction was odd.

Yet now that he'd crossed the threshold, the surroundings *did* feel familiar. Like the church of his youth, where his family had worshiped together—and the one he'd attended alone while away at college—this one seemed like an oasis of calm and stability in a changing world.

That feeling only intensified as the service progressed. Despite his extended absence from Sunday services—and his radio silence with God—a soul-deep contentment settled over him.

The sole blip on his otherwise tranquil radar was the woman sitting a few feet away, beside Hannah.

Hard as he tried to ignore her, he found himself sneaking frequent peeks her direction and admiring her classy black skirt, soft silk blouse, and elegant profile.

She, on the other hand, didn't appear to have any difficulty concentrating on the readings from Scripture, the sermon, or the hymns. Her focus remained front and center throughout until the organ struck up the introduction for the closing song.

Jack again joined in the familiar hymn, eyeing the exit a few rows back. If Hannah cooperated, they ought to be able to escape as soon as they said goodbye to Christi. Much as he'd like to dispense with farewells, it would be rude to leave without exchanging a word—especially after she'd come to his rescue Friday.

The organ wound down, and Jack replaced his hymnal in the pew rack as Christi spoke to Hannah.

"How did the sweater hold up?"

His daughter picked it up and showed her. "It hasn't unraveled again."

"I'm glad to hear that." She finally acknowledged him. "Hello, Jack."

"Morning."

"Are you a regular at this service?"

He hesitated.

Was that an innocuous chitchat type of query—or had she asked in order to alter her church schedule to avoid another awkward encounter?

Hannah stepped in before he could reach a conclusion—or formulate a response that wasn't too telling.

"He doesn't come every week. I had to wake him up today or we would have missed."

Surprise flashed in Christi's irises . . . and she waited. As if she expected him to explain why he was no longer a regular churchgoer.

Not happening.

"We should be going, Hannah. We didn't have much breakfast, and you must be getting—"

"Good morning, Jack."

At the greeting, he swiveled toward the aisle. Eleanor Cooper had stopped beside their pew, keeping a firm grip on her walker as other departing congregants edged around her. Despite her advanced age, the woman's eyes sparked with life.

"Good morning, Eleanor."

"I'm so pleased to see you here. For a moment when I spotted the three of you, I thought a new family had joined our congregation."

"No—but this is my daughter." Jack rested a hand on Hannah's shoulder and introduced her. "She arrived a few days ago."

If Eleanor was taken aback by the news of his fatherhood, she hid it well. "It's a pleasure to meet you, my dear. I'll have to whip up one of my chocolate fudge cakes to welcome you to town. I do that for all my new friends. Do you like chocolate?"

"I love it." Hannah returned the woman's smile.

"Excellent. I can see we'll get along fine." Eleanor patted her hand, then shifted her attention to Christi. "And who is your other lovely friend, Jack?"

Heat crept up his neck. "Actually, we're not together. We just happened to sit in the same pew."

"But we know her," Hannah chimed in.

Of all times for his taciturn daughter to get chatty.

"Christi Reece." She leaned forward and extended her hand to the woman. "I'm new in town too. I work for Beth at Eye of the Beholder."

"Ah. I heard she'd found someone to help out at the shop—and none too soon, with that knee replacement putting her out of commission for a while. I hope she's recuperating without complications."

"She is."

"Please give her my best. And as for that chocolate cake—perhaps Hannah and Jack will share it with you."

"We will," Hannah promised.

"Wonderful." Eleanor beamed at Jack. "Cake is always best enjoyed with friends. Expect a delivery soon." She gave his arm a squeeze.

As the woman continued down the aisle, Jack scanned the throng of people shuffling toward the vestibule, where the minister was greeting congregants. Short of escaping through a side door, they'd have to join the queue.

"You seem in a hurry to leave."

At Christi's comment, he angled back toward her. "Not in a hurry—but the service *is* over."

She gave the space a slow sweep, her countenance serene. If she felt as awkward as he did about their enforced pew sharing, she gave no indication of it. "I know—but it's peaceful here. I think I'll linger for a few minutes." She bent down to his daughter. "I'm glad I got to see you again, Hannah."

"Me too—and you can have a piece of our cake if that lady bakes it like she said she would."

"Thank you." She straightened up and addressed him. "Enjoy the rest of your day." With that, she picked up her purse, left the pew by the side aisle, and moved to a spot closer to the front.

He stared after her. Even in his most devout days, he'd never hung around church after a service. He was always out the door and on to—

"Are we going?" Hannah plucked at the sleeve of his jacket.

"Yes." The line was dwindling, and he maneuvered them out of the pew, keeping her in front of him.

A number of people peeled off in the vestibule rather than wait around to talk to Reverend Baker, but before he could follow their example, the minister flagged him down.

So much for an inconspicuous exit.

He guided Hannah toward the man.

"Jack! What a pleasant surprise to see you here today. I've been hoping you'd join us one of these weeks." He gave his hand a firm shake. "And who is this young lady?"

Like Eleanor, the pastor didn't show any surprise or shock as Jack introduced his daughter.

"Welcome to Grace Christian, Hannah."

"Thank you." She offered the man a tentative smile.

"Hannah's why I'm here today." Jack tucked the trailing sleeve of the purple sweater into the bundle of yarn in her arm. "Her mom took her every week."

"Ah." The minister gave a slow nod. "God works in mysterious ways, his wonders to perform."

"The services are finished for the day, Paul. You can cut the Bible quotes."

As a new voice joined the conversation, Jack turned toward the front door.

Father Murphy hustled over, his usual cheery grin in place.

"You better bone up on your Scripture, Kevin." The pastor gave his Catholic counterpart a stern look, but his eyes were twinkling.

Jack tamped down the twitch in his lips. This ought to be fun. The two clerical golfing buddies' banter was always entertaining.

"You mean that's not from the Bible?" The priest's feigned

surprise was comical. "And here I thought it was from the book of Cowper."

Reverend Baker exhaled and shook his head. "Very funny. But I'm surprised you know the composer. That's not a Catholic hymn."

"I have nonsectarian taste in music." The padre directed his attention to Hannah. "And who do we have here?"

Once again, Jack performed the introductions.

"I'm pleased to meet you, young lady." Father Murphy gave a mock bow, embellished with a theatrical hand flourish.

At Hannah's giggle, Jack did a double take. That was a first in their acquaintance—and very encouraging. Maybe she'd transition to her new life here with less difficulty than he'd expected.

"We should be getting home." Jack pulled out his keys.

"I hope to see you here again next week." Reverend Baker aimed his comment at both of them.

"But if you get tired of this fine minister's sometimes long-winded sermons, you're always welcome at St. Francis." The priest winked at them.

"Trying to steal my congregants again?" The reverend's eyebrows rose.

"No. Only your doughnuts. I want to grab a couple before we talk about that idea you had for a new Helping Hands program." The priest turned to them again. "You're staying long enough to have a doughnut, aren't you?"

"Can we?" Hannah touched his jacket, her expression hopeful.

"They're in the fellowship hall." Father Murphy waved that direction. "I'll give you my review of the selection if you want to walk over with me."

"And he'd be the person to do it. He's sampled every variety." The minister expelled an exaggerated breath. "Why don't you eat your own doughnuts? You always claim they're better than ours."

"They are. *Ours* are homemade. But this isn't doughnut Sunday at St. Francis. You've upped your game here, having doughnuts every week." Father Murphy grinned at Hannah. "Shall we go have a taste?"

It was hard to resist the priest's good humor—or his daughter's hopeful face.

"Sold." The chores waiting for him at home weren't going anywhere. "We'll stay for one doughnut."

They said their goodbyes to Reverend Baker, and Hannah fell in beside the priest, who entertained her with a humorous story about his church's first attempt to make homemade doughnuts.

Jack took up the rear, slowing as he passed the doors from the vestibule into the church.

One person remained inside.

Christi.

She was seated in the same spot, head bowed—as if in prayer.

He paused, studying her.

Was it possible she'd really changed?

And if she had, what had caused the transformation?

Could the bad marriage she'd referenced and her shaky finances have been the catalyst?

If so, why had major tribulations led her *to* God instead of away from him?

And who was the persion she was willing to go into debt for with the loan she'd requested?

So many questions—so few answers.

Which reminded him . . .

He still owed her an answer about the loan.

Now that the situation with Hannah was under control—more or less—he ought to tell her no and be done with it.

But as he hurried to catch up with the doughnut-seeking duo ahead of him, the message in one of the Scripture passages Reverend Baker had read this morning replayed in his mind. The exact wording escaped him, but it had been about letting go of bitterness and wrath and malice. About being kind and merciful—and forgiving.

Wasn't it hypocritical to attend church if he didn't intend to follow the precepts of his dormant faith?

A faint pounding began to throb in his temples, and he massaged his forehead.

The answer to that question was obvious. And the evidence he'd seen since Christi's arrival gave him little excuse to cling to his anger.

But after vilifying her for so long, could he manage to switch gears and open his mind and heart to the possibility that she'd changed . . . and deserved not only the requested loan but forgiveness—and a second chance?

17

"Christi, how can I ever thank you? I would never have been able to manage without your help." Beth touched her arm.

"No thanks necessary." Christi set the to-go container from the Myrtle on Beth's kitchen table as the woman eased into a chair. "Shall I take those?" She motioned toward the crutches.

"I can manage." Beth balanced them against the wall. "With the help of the physical therapist who's been coming, I've learned to do almost everything on my own. Not at my usual speed, however." She opened the container and leaned close to inhale the savory aroma. "No one makes meat loaf like the Myrtle."

"And look what I brought for dessert." Christi unwrapped a napkin from around a frosted doughnut, set the treat on the table, and retrieved eating utensils from a drawer.

"Did you get that at Sweet Dreams?"

"Nope. I filched it from the doughnut table after the service this morning at Grace Christian. It was my first visit to the church. Have you been there?"

"No." Beth picked up the knife and fork. "This looks delicious."

In other words, she didn't want to talk about church.

Her choice—but it was sad she wasn't able to call on God for support while she recovered.

"I know you haven't been up to hearing a report on the chamber of commerce meeting, but I have the notes in my purse if you'd like a quick recap."

"I'd love a briefing—but I hate to infringe on your Sunday any more than I already have."

"You aren't. I don't have any plans until later." Her shift at the bar and grill didn't begin until five, and while she'd rather go for a walk on the beach than wait tables—or wear that skimpy uniform—the tips were excellent. "Give me a minute to get my notebook. I left it in the living room."

Once she had it in hand, Christi took the other seat at the small round café table.

"How many merchants came?" Beth broke off a piece of meat loaf with the edge of her fork, eyebrows peaking as Christi gave her an estimate. "That's a large turnout for Hope Harbor."

"Everyone was concerned about the impact of the wildfires. Most businesses are being adversely affected, and there was a lot of discussion about the importance of increasing tourism over the summer months."

"Were any viable ideas offered?"

"Marci mentioned building on the farmers' market."

Beth's brow wrinkled. "Much as I enjoy the market, I don't think we could embellish it enough to draw the number of visitors we'd need to solve our problem."

That had been her conclusion too—but it carried more weight coming from someone who'd lived in the area longer and knew the lay of the land.

"I've never experienced the Hope Harbor market, but I've been to others. To be honest, they all tend to be similar. Charming but not distinctive."

"True." Beth poked her fork in the mashed potatoes but didn't take a bite. "I expect the waters ahead are going to get rougher.

The businesses that have been around awhile should be able to weather the downturn if it doesn't last too long, but new shops like Eye of the Beholder may not survive." She glanced out the window beside the table, irises shimmering. "I really wanted this to work. It's all I have l-left."

Christi's throat tightened at the woman's poignant admission. "I wish I could help."

Beth sniffed. "You already have. I'd be in worse straits if I'd had to close the shop while I recover."

"I mean, help at a deeper level. With whatever is making you sad." Maybe she was overstepping, but how could she ignore Beth's obvious distress?

"It's too late for that."

"It's never too late for hope. I know that firsthand." Christi caught her lower lip between her teeth. She didn't share her past with many people, but perhaps it would encourage the woman whose kindness had lifted *her* up at a particularly low moment. "Between you and me, I married a loser and lost everything. I've been as low as a person can get."

Beth fished out a tissue and studied her. "Yet you survived."

"When you hit bottom, there's nowhere to go but up unless you want to let the trials of life defeat you. It does help to have a strong faith, though."

"I used to—or thought I did—until God ignored my pleas to enlighten my husband and let my son die."

Christi's pulse stumbled.

She'd lost her son?

Tough as her own situation had been these past few years, no one she'd cared about had died.

"I'm sorry." Lame. But without knowing any of the details, what else could she say?

"Thank you." Beth dabbed at her nose with the tissue and closed the lid on her meal, as if the sight and smell of food had suddenly grown distasteful. "I don't talk much about what happened—and we're new acquaintances—but I sensed the day we met that you'd been through the fire. That we were kindred spirits and that I could trust you."

Too bad Jack hadn't felt the same at their reunion.

But it was heartening to know a new acquaintance recognized the changes in her—and realized they were genuine.

"I appreciate you saying that—and I assure you I'll keep anything you share with me in confidence."

Beth pressed a crease into the folded paper napkin beside her plate. "The bottom line is my son died because my husband pushed him to be something he could never be."

While Christi tried to absorb Beth's revelation, the woman told her in a handful of tear-laced sentences about all the years her pleas to her husband had fallen on deaf ears . . . how she'd begged him to forget about his dreams of an athletic son and instead encourage the boy's artistic talents . . . and the fateful high school graduation gift that had precipitated Jonathan's death.

"Oh, Beth." Christi laid her hand over the woman's clenched fingers. "I had no idea."

"Few people do. Steve and I always kept our disagreements about Jonathan to ourselves. In every other way he was a wonderful husband and father, but that was a constant conflict. And after Jonathan died . . ." She wadded the tissue in her fist. "I couldn't stay with him. How could I forgive him not only for what he did to our son but for ruining my life and the future I'd hoped for?"

As Beth's question hung in the air between them, Christi's stomach bottomed out.

From everything Jack had said in the past couple of weeks, he'd felt exactly the same after her betrayal—his life ruined, the future he'd hoped for in tatters.

And having heard Beth's emotional story, it was easier than ever to understand why he'd be as unwilling to forgive as her boss.

"I'm sorry. I didn't mean to dump all my troubles on you." Beth pushed her meal aside.

"Don't apologize. I'm glad you told me. I noticed your ring the day we met, and I wondered if you were a widow."

She examined the sparkling stones. "Steve's very much alive—and we're still married. For now."

"Has he tried to reconnect?"

"I asked for space, and he's respected my wishes. But he sends a card or note every week or two. None of which I've read. They're in a box in my closet."

"So you haven't thrown them away." That was telling, whether Beth was willing to acknowledge it or not.

"No. I expect I will one of these days."

"Without reading them?"

"Why bother? Nothing's changed."

"Maybe Steve has."

She pressed her lips together and shook her head. "For years, I clung to that hope—but I finally accepted the truth of the old adage. A leopard doesn't change its spots."

Another conviction Jack appeared to share with Beth.

Christi's spirits tanked.

The day that had begun on an optimistic note with the uplifting service at Grace Christian was deteriorating fast.

"I don't know, Beth." She pressed her finger against a stray crumb on the table. "Everything I went through changed *me*. I used to be spoiled and selfish and a bit of a snob." At the very least.

"That's hard to believe."

"Believe it. I wasn't a nice person. I also hurt someone very badly—a regret I'll carry with me for the rest of my life. By the grace of God, I learned from my mistakes—but it's hard to convince people who knew me in my previous life that I've changed."

"Is that why you decided to stay here? To start over? Escape the mistakes from your past?"

"Partly—but I also wanted to try and fix one of those mistakes."

"Have you?"

"It's a work in progress—and that's a story for another day."

She rose. Much as she could use a sounding board to talk out her feelings about Jack, even Tasha didn't know the details she'd always been too ashamed to verbalize. And it was doubtful Jack had shared the sordid tale with anyone either. "Would you like me to plate that and put it in the fridge for you?" She motioned toward Beth's food.

"Yes. Thank you." Her boss yawned. "Sorry. I'm not sleeping as well as usual with this leg. I'm overdue for a nap."

"Do you want a hand into the bedroom? I could let myself out."

"No. I can manage. I'll lock up behind you. The doctor encouraged me to walk."

Christi handed her the crutches, waited while she fitted them under her arms, and slowed her gait as Beth left the kitchen and hobbled to the front door.

"I'll stop by again tomorrow after work to get your mail and deliver the Myrtle special. But if you need anything sooner, give me a call."

"Thank you. And thanks for listening today—and giving me food for thought. To be honest, though, I can't imagine you were ever as self-centered and indifferent to others' feelings as you claim."

"I'll take that as validation I've changed my spots, to use your analogy—and if I have, your husband may have too."

"Even if that's true, getting past the anger and resentment is hard."

"I know. I'm dealing with a similar situation, but from the opposite side—and praying hard for a favorable resolution."

"I hope your prayers are answered better than mine were."

So did she. But unlike Beth, she had no doubt God was listening to her entreaties—whatever the ultimate outcome.

After giving the woman a quick hug, she continued to her Nissan, slipped behind the wheel, and drove down Starfish Pier Road toward 101, slowing as she passed Jack's apartment.

Like Beth, the man who'd once loved her had anger and resentment in spades—and the passage of more than a decade hadn't softened them. Nor had their interactions over the past two weeks.

Depressing.

Even more disheartening, however?

The odds of him giving her the loan that would salvage Tasha's dream continued to dwindle as the clock ticked toward its deadline.

Should she open them or not?

Beth touched the box of notes and cards from Steve that she'd set on her bed.

The wisest course would be to take the nap she'd mentioned to Christi. But ever since the younger woman had left, she'd been fidgety—and her restlessness wasn't a side effect from her pain medication.

It was caused by a sudden barrage of doubts.

Could Christi have changed as much as she claimed? And if she had, was it possible Steve had also been transformed by tragedy?

Or was that a pipe dream? Wishful thinking? The kind of misplaced hope she'd clung to for too long as she'd pleaded with God to let him see the light about his son?

Who knew?

But despite all her attempts to push thoughts of Steve from her mind, she *did* miss him. Other than her disappointment in his unwillingness—or inability—to understand how important Jonathan's art was to him, he'd never lost all the other fine qualities that had convinced her to say "I do" twenty-five years ago.

A pang echoed in her heart.

Too bad the silver on their milestone anniversary had tarnished.

She picked up the first envelope in the box, sent less than a week after she'd moved out. Weighed it in her hand.

Open—or pitch?

If she opened it—and the others—it was possible they could convince her his remorse was real and pave the way to a reconciliation. That was the upside.

The downside? If she let go of her anger, what would shield her from the debilitating grief that had sucked her into an abyss after Jonathan died? An anger that had been her salvation by giving her the strength to walk away, find a new purpose in life with Eye of the Beholder. That business had required her singular focus and devotion, forcing her to put her grief on the back burner, especially with wildfires tamping down tourism and eroding her bottom line.

Perhaps she should wait until—

Ding-dong.

As her doorbell chimed, she frowned.

Could Christi have returned?

Unlikely.

But who else would come calling on a Sunday afternoon? Solicitors were few and far between on this dead-end road.

The chime sounded again, and she reached for her crutches. It was possible one of her friends from Coos Bay had decided to drop in.

As she approached the front door, a third chime echoed through the apartment.

Whoever was on the other side was determined to see her.

She paused by the door and peeked through the peephole. Sucked in a breath. Jerked back.

What on earth was Steve doing here?

"Beth?" His muffled voice came through the wood panels. "I saw you pass by the sidelight. I know you're there. Please open the door."

Pulse racing, she gripped the crutches tighter.

How strange was it that he'd appeared on her doorstep after all these months just as she was considering reading his notes and cards?

"Please, Beth."

Oh my.

That beseeching tone was *not* typical for her husband.

From the first day they'd met, he'd presented a strong front to the world. His job demanded it, and that had carried over into his personal life. Rarely had she seen him cry—the last time at the cemetery, as they'd each placed a white rose on Jonathan's casket before it was lowered into the ground.

But unless she was mistaken, her indomitable husband was on the verge of tears.

Without second-guessing her decision, she flipped the lock, twisted the knob, and pulled the door open.

He looked good . . . so good . . . despite the dark half moons beneath his lower lashes, the new lines that creased his face, and his obvious weight loss. But his eyes, though tempered by sadness, were as blue as always—and the ever-present five-o'clock shadow she loved, which he claimed was the bane of his existence, was in evidence.

For a moment, he seemed surprised she'd complied with his request. Then he gave her a slow sweep, the hunger in his eyes matching the yearning deep inside her that refused to be throttled.

When he didn't speak, she managed to activate her vocal cords. "What are you doing here?"

His Adam's apple bobbed. "I heard about your knee replacement."

"From whom?" Had one of the Coos Bay friends who'd been keeping in touch with her shared the news with him?

"Charley—indirectly. He mentioned it, assuming I already knew. Why didn't you tell me?"

"Why would I?"

"You're my wife, Beth. I love you—and I'm here for you. Why haven't you let me help you?"

She steeled herself against the hurt in his inflection. "I can manage on my own."

"I know that—but you don't have to."

"Maybe I want to."

He scrutinized her. "Do you?"

No.

Going through the knee replacement by herself, despite the support of a few close friends and Christi, had been far more taxing than she'd expected. Steve could have relieved that burden. Would relieve it now, during the remainder of her recovery, if she let him.

But practical considerations didn't justify inviting him back into her life.

"I'm learning to like being independent." Hopefully he wouldn't call her on that hedge.

He regarded her with the discerning shrewdness that served him well in his job, and she held her breath.

Thankfully, he let her comment go. "If you won't accept my help, I hope you'll accept these."

He lifted a generous bouquet that contained all her favorite flowers, in her favorite color—Siberian iris, hydrangea, delphinium—and her heart thawed a few degrees.

Unlike some men who were stingy with tangible expressions of love once a wife was wooed and won, Steve had never stopped bringing her flowers, helping with household chores, and taking her out to intimate dinners to let her know how much he cared for her. How special she was to him.

Their life together would have been as perfect as possible in an imperfect world if they hadn't clashed on a regular basis about Jonathan.

How different it all could have turned out if Steve had seen the light.

Her vision fogged, and she dipped her chin on the pretense of fiddling with one of her crutches.

"I'll be happy to carry these in for you, since your hands are occupied."

Beth stared at the Berber carpet beneath her feet.

Letting him into her apartment wasn't wise—but she couldn't tote the flowers, and refusing them seemed petty. And unkind.

She swallowed and drew back. "You can put them on the coffee table."

He stepped around her, leaving the familiar scent of his after-shave in his wake.

Another wave of yearning swept over her.

Oh, how she'd missed that—and all the sweet memories it evoked of happier days, when she'd still clung to the hope he'd come to appreciate Jonathan's amazing talent as much as he'd always appreciated their son's kindness, intellect, and principles.

A hope that had withered after Steve insisted on the Grand Canyon trip—and died along with Jonathan on a hiking trail in the baking sun.

"I should add water to the vase first." Steve stopped at the coffee table. "I didn't want it to spill on the drive over."

She motioned toward the kitchen. "You can fill it in there."

Less than a minute later he returned and set the flowers on the table in the bland, spartan room. If he noticed the sharp contrast in décor to the lovingly decorated house they'd shared, he didn't comment on it.

She noticed it every day—but why waste any effort on a living space that would never feel like home?

Steve faced her. "I've missed you, Beth."

Keeping her distance, she shifted her weight on the crutches. No way was she going to return that sentiment—even if there were nights when darkness pressed in and a soul-deep loneliness left her aching for his touch. Even if her conversation with Christi today had made her wonder whether tragedy could have wrought a lasting change in Steve as her new clerk claimed it had in her.

"I'm sure your job keeps you busy."

"Not busy enough. Life's not the same without you and Jonathan." He shoved his fingers into the pockets of his slacks. "I've tried to tell you that in my cards and notes, but I've never been much of a writer. I wasn't born with a single creative gene—nor the ability to appreciate them in others. The latter can be cultivated, as I've learned. But as you know from my attempts to express my regrets on paper, I found that out too late."

Beth's jaw dropped.

He'd realized the mistakes he'd made with Jonathan? Acknowledged them? Written to her about his epiphany?

His squinted at her. "What's wrong?"

"Nothing." She rebalanced her crutches. "I, uh, haven't read any of the letters you sent me."

Shock flattened his features. "You threw them out?"

"No—but I've never opened them."

"Oh, Beth." He winced, as if in pain. "I knew you were angry—and you have every right to be—but I thought you'd at least . . ." His voice choked, and he swallowed. "This has been a terrible time for both of us. It would have been hard to weather together, but alone it's been . . ." Again, his words rasped. "I keep hoping we'll get back together. Is that really a lost cause?"

Pressure built in her throat at his abject misery—and her own. "I don't know. The hurt runs deep. And it would never be like it was. Not without Jonathan."

"I know that. But we could try to rebuild. I'll do whatever it takes, Beth."

Slowly she exhaled. "I'm not certain we can ever get past the heartache between us."

He let a few beats pass. "Are you ever going to read my letters?"

Part of her wanted to say yes—but fear held her back.

"I don't know."

His shoulders slumped, and he pulled his hands from his pockets, keys gripped in his fingers. "I hope you do. They may not be articulate, but they're from the heart. In the meantime, I'm here if you need help during your recovery—or with anything else."

"I appreciate that. Thank you for the flowers."

There was nothing left to say. Yet he remained where he was, gaze locked with hers, longing—and love—radiating from him.

She steeled herself against both. Steve had brought this on himself, and no matter what pretty prose he'd written in his cards, it wouldn't bring Jonathan back—or restore the life she'd once had.

At last he turned away, crossed the room, and let himself out, the apartment silent except for the quiet click of the door behind him.

Legs shaky, Beth maneuvered herself over to the couch and sat beside the overflowing vase. Touched one of the soft petals. Inhaled the fresh scent of the hydrangea. Drank in the beauty of the delicate sprays of delphinium.

The bouquet had been a thoughtful gesture, and the flowers were beautiful, each blossom perfect.

But they wouldn't last. In a few days, they'd begin to wither and die—as her feelings had for Steve.

Or so she'd told herself.

Yet after hearing Christi's story today . . . after digging out the box of cards and letters from the dark recesses of her closet . . . after looking into Steve's regret-filled eyes and feeling his remorse and sorrow . . . was that true?

Or had her love for him simply been lying dormant beneath her anger, much as flowers like these died back during the harsh winter but rebounded in spring at the first touch of warmth?

His letters—and her reaction to them—could provide a clue.

But did she have the courage to let go of her insulating anger and open her heart to Steve's message—and the possibility of a new beginning?

18

This could be a mistake.

From behind the counter, Christi flicked a glance toward the door of Eye of the Beholder. Rubbed her palms down her slacks. Checked her watch.

It wasn't too late to call Marci, tell her not to bother stopping by on her lunch hour.

Except she wanted to help. Especially after hearing the collective worry of business owners at the chamber of commerce meeting, seeing Beth's distress Sunday about the impact of declining tourism on her shop, and staying up late to flesh out the idea that had come to her during the meeting.

Her enthusiasm, however, may have warped her perspective about the practicality of what she'd intended to propose.

Perhaps she should think it through a bit more.

As Christi pulled out her phone, the bell over the door jangled to admit Marci.

Drat.

Too late to back out.

But Marci would probably shoot her idea down anyway, so no harm would be done.

"Hi, Christi!" The *Herald* editor dashed into the shop, sparks of energy pinging off her. "How's business?"

"Slow."

"I hear you." The red-haired woman grimaced and gave the empty shop a scan. "Tuesday isn't the busiest day for a business like this, but Beth told me it's been slow on weekends lately too. The same story I'm hearing from everyone." She propped a hip against the counter and folded her arms. "How's she doing?"

"Improving every day. She claims she's going to start coming in next week in the afternoons."

"Wow. Has she talked to her doctor about this?" Marci grinned. "That would be my husband, by the way."

"I know. I met him at the hospital the day of Beth's surgery. She claims he's on board with the plan—barring any complications."

"In that case, more power to her. I wouldn't want to be stuck in the house day after day either—much as I love our cozy little haven. Now what can I do for you on this beautiful spring day?"

Christi straightened a counter display of handcrafted earrings and summoned up her courage. "For whatever it's worth, I wanted to pass on an idea about how to give tourism a boost."

Marci slid onto the stool across from the jewelry display. "Lay it on me. We're still foundering after last week's meeting. I'm open to all ideas."

"It may not have much merit, and it could be too difficult to implement."

Marci's lips bowed again. "Don't get carried away or build it up too much or anything."

Her cheeks warmed. "It's just that I feel kind of awkward about offering a suggestion when I'm so new here."

"Don't. Some of the best things that have happened in this town in the past few years have come from new blood. Mine included. I'm all ears."

You're on, Christi. Spit it out. The worst she can do is give it a thumbs-down. Or laugh. After all you've been through, you can handle having an idea rejected.

"Okay." Fingers trembling, she pulled her notes from below the counter. "I sat next to Charley during the chamber meeting, and he filled me in on a number of the players. As I jotted down names and professions, it occurred to me that this town has an abundance of talent. Talent many people would travel quite a distance to tap into. That's a unique asset."

"Hmm." Marci crossed her arms on the counter, expression pensive. "I never thought of it quite like that, but I see your point. Go on."

"Well, I wondered if a sort of hands-on weekend-long arts festival might draw a crowd. An event that offered masterclasses or seminars on painting, acting, furniture making, writing, the culinary arts, area history—all taught by noted experts who happen to be residents. It could kick off with the farmers' market and run Saturday and Sunday. With sufficient advance publicity, the event would have the potential to draw a large crowd—and if press releases spotlighting our local experts were sent out in advance, pre-event media coverage could generate interest in the town in general and whet people's appetite to visit beyond the festival weekend."

"Wow! I love it!" Excitement radiated from Marci. "And I think you were the perfect person to suggest it. Those of us who've lived here awhile tend not to see the forest for the trees—but Hope Harbor does have an amazing amount of talent. This could be really big!"

Gratifying as Marci's enthusiasm was, it was only fair to mention the negatives. "It would be a huge undertaking, though—and all of the experts I mentioned would have to be willing to participate. It would be a big time commitment, and I imagine they're all busy."

"I'm not too worried about getting commitments." Marci waved aside that concern. "Everyone who lives here loves this town and wants it to prosper. Volunteers tend to come out of the woodwork if a call goes out." Her expression grew pensive. "Maybe we could even get Rose Fitzgerald to open up Edgecliff for tours. That would be quite a coup."

"Who's Rose Fitzgerald—and what's Edgecliff?"

"Rose is our resident hermit. She lives just south of town on an estate named Edgecliff that was built by her lumber-baron grandfather. Rumor says it's a showplace—but few in town have ever seen it. I tried to get her to let me interview her for the *Herald* once, but she declined."

"Tours of a private, historic estate could be a big draw."

"I'll give it a go. Putting out a feeler is a piece of cake—unlike organizing an event on this scale. That would be a huge challenge." Her forehead crinkled. "As far as I know, no one in town has any experience with that—me included. The publicity side is more my forte. Still, I'd be willing to tackle it if I didn't have two-year-old twins. As it is, I don't have a spare minute to call my own, and the learning curve for organizing an event like this would be formidable."

"I hear you. Children demand a huge amount of energy, and this would be an ambitious undertaking."

"It would put Hope Harbor on the map, though—and we have the talent to pull this off. Other towns don't." She drummed her fingers on the counter. "I suppose we could hire someone to do it—but everyone's budget is already stretched to the limit. We can get merchants to donate time, but money for an event planner in this tight market could be an issue."

Event planner?

Like the ones she'd worked with on the charitable affairs she'd volunteered for on behalf of her father?

"What are you thinking?" Marci squinted at her, a speculative gleam in her eye.

"Nothing worth mentioning." She stuck her notes back under the counter. "I do agree an event planner would help."

"Do you have any experience with this sort of project?"

Was the woman a mind reader?

"No. Not exactly. I mean, I did help plan a few large-scale events in a previous life, but that was long ago."

"I bet it's like riding a bicycle. And from what I know about the residents' backgrounds, I expect you have the best qualifications in town to organize a festival like this."

Christi stared at her. "You mean put this together by myself?"

"No, no, of course not—but we do need a leader. Someone to spearhead the effort and keep us all on track. I'd have to run the idea by the board first, but I have a feeling it will get unanimous endorsement—especially if I tell them someone's agreed to be the point person. Would you consider it? I know the town would be forever grateful."

Sweet heaven.

What had she gotten herself into?

Heart hammering, she wiped her palms on her slacks again. "It's kind of an overwhelming prospect. I don't even know that many residents."

"This would be a fantastic way to meet a boatload of them." Marci slid off the stool, as if the matter was a done deal. "I'll tell you what. Why don't I call the board members this afternoon, get their feedback? If everyone gives a thumbs-up, we'll schedule a meeting to discuss your plan and appoint committee heads. They'll do the legwork, and you can be the big-picture person. Sound reasonable?"

In theory, yes.

But from what she'd observed in the past, the person leading the effort often ended up doing the yeoman's share of the work, despite the existence of committees.

"If everyone pitches in, that could be manageable, but—"

The bell over the door jingled, and two women entered.

"Ah. Customers. I'll let you get to work." Marci was already halfway across the store—as if she was afraid her newest recruit was already getting cold feet.

Smart woman.

She was out the door with an "I'll call you soon" tossed over her shoulder before Christi could protest.

A wave of panic swept over her.

Marci was going to put her in charge of this—if the idea got the board's endorsement.

And in light of the *Herald* editor's enthusiasm, she'd be able to convince the members it had merit.

But did it?

While it had definite potential, pulling it off would require extensive planning and scheduling plus stellar pre-event publicity. Without a ton of favorable advance press, the festival—or whatever term they ended up using for it—could fall flat on its face.

And if it did, not only would everyone in this community she now called home end up with a negative impression of her, she'd have one more failure to add to her already long list.

How could it be this hard to find someone to watch a ten-year-old?

Expelling a breath, Jack jabbed the button on his cell and shoved the phone back in his pocket as two gulls soared past the porch of his apartment.

All the day care places among his rapidly dwindling options either didn't have space or catered more to younger children. The few that took older kids had long waiting lists.

So barring a miracle in the next thirty-six hours, when his Thursday morning patrol shift began, the one facility he'd found in Coos Bay that fit most of his parameters was going to have to suffice—even if the long drive was less than ideal.

Hannah may have stayed by herself while her mom worked, as she'd claimed, but that wasn't happening on his watch. At least not yet.

Yawning, he twisted his watch toward the fading light. Eight twenty. Much too early to be this tired.

Unless you were trying to befriend a daughter you hadn't known about until two weeks ago, catching up late into the night on word count for your next contracted novel, and reorganizing your life to accommodate a ten-year-old.

The transition had been stressful for Hannah too, though—and hers had been compounded by grief. It was no wonder she fell into an exhausted slumber before the sun set every night and often thrashed and cried out in her sleep until the wee hours.

He wiped a hand down his face and sighed. May as well admit the truth.

Despite his many professional credentials and competencies, he wasn't equipped to raise a child alone.

But Erica hadn't been the best choice either.

So he and Hannah would have to muddle through together and figure out—

Frowning, he peered at the vehicle approaching from the far end of the long, low apartment complex.

Was that Christi's Nissan?

Yeah, it was.

Had she stopped by to see Beth again?

Whatever the purpose of her visit, if he didn't retreat fast, she'd spot him. Perhaps stop. Attempt to engage him in conversation. Maybe ask about the loan again.

Since a visit with her wasn't on his agenda for tonight, he ought to hustle inside and shut the door.

But his feet refused to budge.

And sure enough, as she approached his unit, she slowed.

Best to ignore her if he didn't want to engage.

Instead, he lifted a hand in greeting.

Well, crud.

What was wrong with him tonight?

The car inched along . . . then swung into a spot at the end of his walkway. A few seconds later Christi got out—but she stayed by the door.

"Hi." Her tone was tentative.

"Evening. What brings you to our neck of the woods?"

"My boss lives down there. You know—Beth Adams. I've been bringing her dinner from the Myrtle and picking up her mail since she had her knee replaced."

Christi had been coming here on a mission of mercy every night?

One more chink fell out of the wall he'd created around his heart.

"I didn't know about her knee replacement."

"I don't think she wanted it announced in the *Herald*, but she told the people who needed to know."

Did that include Steve?

None of his business.

Another yawn snuck up on him, and he clapped a hand over his mouth. "Sorry."

"I expect you've had your hands full adjusting to the new normal."

Had compassion softened her features as she spoke—or was his imagination putting in overtime in the fading light?

"That would be a fair—"

A muffled cry came through the open window, and he eased back. Motioned toward the door. "Sorry. I have to go in."

Frowning, she took a step toward him. "What's wrong?"

"Hannah's been having bad dreams. Too much upheaval thrust upon her all at once, I guess." He reached for the door handle. "But I didn't see any point in waiting to take her. Her aunt was a virtual stranger too—and she had to begin traveling again for her job. That meant Hannah would have been left in the care of total strangers for days on end. I didn't think it was in her best interest to let her adjust to that routine and then upend her world again by bringing her out here."

Thankfully the family court judge had agreed with that rationale and had fast-tracked the paperwork terminating Erica's guardianship and giving him custody—and authority to take Hannah to Oregon—while he waited for the final order naming him father to wend its way through the court.

"Is there anything I can do to help?"

He hesitated.

So far nothing he'd tried had comforted his daughter during her bad dreams. It was possible Christi would have more luck. The two of them had clicked the night of the sweater disaster.

"Any assistance would be appreciated." He held the door for her, and she edged past him—but waited to let him take the lead down the hall.

"I'd hoped having her own furniture would help, but it hasn't seemed to make any difference." He continued to the twin bed in the dim room, where Hannah was curled up in a ball beneath the blanket.

"Does she ever take the sweater off?" Christi drew up beside him, her voice a whisper of warmth against his jaw.

His pulse lost its rhythm, and he curled his fingers into a tight ball. "Only in the shower—and at church. Even then, she wants it within sight. I doubt I'll ever convince her to let me take it to the laundry room again."

"Handwash it with Woolite in the sink instead. Use cold water and lay it flat to dry. She can stay close throughout that process."

"Duly noted."

Hannah let out another pathetic, gut-twisting whimper, and he leaned down to stroke her hand. "I hate to wake her up, but I don't know how else to stop the bad dreams."

"May I try?"

"Have at it." He stepped back and motioned toward the bed.

"If you have anything to do, why don't you take care of it? I'll stay for a little while." With that, she slipped off her flats and sat carefully on the mattress. After stretching out beside his daughter, she tucked herself behind the girl and smoothed her hair back.

Within half a minute, Hannah wiggled closer to her, and Christi slipped an arm around her. After a couple more minutes, his daughter's breathing evened out and she stopped thrashing.

Huh.

Christi was almost as much of a stranger to his daughter as he was. Why would her presence soothe Hannah?

Could it be that a woman's touch reminded her of her mom?

No matter. Whatever worked.

Leaving them alone, Jack wandered into the kitchen, pausing at the window. In the distance, clouds were moving in, and the last bands of gold on the horizon were tarnishing as day transitioned to night.

Just as his golden image of Christi had tarnished eleven years ago during the course of one brief, overheard conversation.

But tomorrow the sun would rise again. After the dark night, a new—and different—day would dawn.

Was it possible a new Christi had also emerged after the dark periods she'd mentioned?

And if that was the case, was it fair to hold on to old grievances? Should he give her a chance to prove she'd really changed?

To do that, though, he'd have to see more of her. But his new responsibilities with Hannah and ongoing work commitments—not to mention Christi's jobs—didn't leave much opportunity for socializing.

Unless . . .

He froze as a crazy idea began to percolate in his mind. An idea that could solve a host of problems in one fell swoop.

It did carry risk, however—to everyone involved. If he'd misjudged, there could end up being hurt all around.

Yet bottom line, it felt right.

Should he follow his inclination—or err on the side of caution and nix the idea?

As he waited for Christi, he gave the pros and cons a thorough vetting. And by the time she appeared in the kitchen doorway fifteen minutes later, he'd reached a decision.

"She's sleeping quietly now." Christi hovered on the threshold, shoes in hand.

He flicked a glance at her bare feet, fighting back an annoying surge of testosterone. He must be desperate for female companionship if exposed toes could stoke his libido.

"Thanks for helping out." He managed to maintain a neutral inflection.

"No problem." Her cheeks pinkened, as if she'd sensed his reaction and was as discombobulated by it as he was. "I didn't want my footsteps to wake her." She lifted the shoes as she offered her explanation, then bent to slip them on.

He forced himself to look away. Fiddled with the coffeemaker. "You two seem to have bonded."

"She's a sweet girl—and my heart aches for her. I know what it's like to have your world turned upside down. It was hard enough to handle as an adult. I can't imagine going through that as a child and not having someone you love to lean on. She needs a ton of TLC for the foreseeable future."

The perfect segue to the topic he wanted to discuss.

"I'd like to talk to you about that, if you have a few minutes." He pivoted back toward her and wrapped his fingers around the edge of the counter behind him.

She gave him a wary scrutiny. "There's nothing on my to-do list tonight other than unpacking the boxes the movers delivered to the cottage a couple of days ago."

"In that case, would you like a cup of coffee?"

"Depends how long our conversation is going to last."

"That's up to you. I have a proposition. If it's not to your liking, this could be a short discussion."

A beat passed as she continued to study him, curiosity warring with caution in her eyes.

Curiosity won.

"I'll take the coffee."

"Have a seat." He motioned toward the small kitchen table. "Cream and sugar?"

"Black."

"I thought you liked your beverages sweet."

"I still enjoy an occasional caramel latte—but tastes change. Like people." She locked gazes with him as she claimed a chair.

Touché—and message received.

"That makes it easy." He filled two mugs, set one on the table in her place, and slid onto the opposite chair. "I agree with you about Hannah needing TLC, and I've tried to give her that. However, I have to go back to work on Thursday, and the only day care place I've been able to find is in Coos Bay. Problem is, it doesn't meet all my criteria, it's a long drive, and Hannah is balking. She wants to stay on her own, but I'm not comfortable leaving her alone. That's where you come in."

Her brow knitted. "How?"

"Hannah likes you. I think she'd be okay with you watching her."

Christi gave a slow blink. "You want to hire me as a . . . a nanny?"

"More or less."

The indentations on her forehead deepened. "I already have a job, Jack. Two jobs—plus caretaking at the cottage."

"You could give up the waitress gig. The shop job is part-time—or it will be once your boss is back on her feet. I've already talked to the chief, and since the rest of the officers are agreeable, she's going to let me work the three-to-eleven shift for the indefinite future instead of following the usual rotation. You could spend mornings at the shop and be with Hannah in the afternoon and evening. All you'd have to do is feed her dinner, put her to bed, and hang around here until I get home. I can offer a decent salary."

At the figure he quoted, she did a double take.

Her reaction wasn't surprising. The amount had to be *way* more than she earned at the sports bar and Eye of the Beholder combined.

"That's very generous."

"I'm in a bind. I don't mind paying a premium. And I'll sweeten the pot with a bonus." He lifted his mug, watching her. "If you take the job, I'll give you your loan."

She drew in a sharp breath. "Seriously?"

"Yes—with caveats."

"Ah." Her lips tipped into a wry smile. "Why am I not surprised there's a catch? Most too-good-to-be-true offers are exactly that."

At her cynicism, his gut clenched. Whatever she'd been through had done a number on her once sunny, if shallow, disposition. Despite the old Christi's negatives, her buoyant, upbeat lightheartedness had never failed to lift his spirits. That was a regrettable casualty of the trials she'd endured.

He took a sip of his coffee. Set the mug on the table. "Not always. And my caveats are really questions. If I'm leaving my daughter in someone's care, I need to vet that person. Find out more about them."

"You know me."

"*Knew* you. To be blunt, I wouldn't leave Hannah with the Christi Reece from eleven years ago."

Her infinitesimal flinch activated his guilt complex—as did the jab from his conscience.

When she responded, her voice was softer. "She doesn't exist anymore."

"So you've told me—and the evidence I've seen supports that. Unless it's an act." Too blunt, perhaps, but she already knew how he felt about her. He'd made that crystal clear during their first two encounters.

"It's not."

"In that case, I have questions. Like, what happened to bring about such a dramatic change? Who is this person you're trying to help? What sort of obligation do you have to them?"

Her chin rose a hair, and a spark ignited in her blue irises. "I don't see how those answers are relevant to the position you've offered me."

"I don't want to leave my daughter in the care of someone who could be in trouble or is of questionable character. I'm a cop—and your desperate financial situation raises major red flags. If there's a reasonable explanation for your predicament, I'm willing to reserve judgment and listen."

Her knuckles whitened around the mug. "I'm not in trouble. My character is sounder than it's ever been. And there *is* an explanation for my situation."

He waited—but that was all she offered.

Time to play hardball.

"I need more than that—and the job offer and loan are contingent on the answers."

And not just because he wanted to ensure he was leaving Hannah with someone he could trust.

The truth was, hard as he'd tried to deny it, Christi's plight had been eating at him almost from day one.

Whether she wanted the loan badly enough to bare her soul, however, remained to be seen.

If she didn't? If she called his bluff, threatened to walk away and leave him in the lurch with Hannah?

He could be the one who caved.

The reality was that this gamble depended on who was most desperate to get what they needed.

And he wasn't placing any bets on the outcome.

19

Jack was willing to give her the loan—and a job that was far preferable to her gig at the sports bar—if she bared her soul.

A hard bargain.

Sharing her distressing secrets with this man would be the ultimate humiliation.

Yet she had to get that money.

Gripping the mug with both hands to keep the liquid from sloshing over the rim, she took a fortifying sip of the strong brew that suited the man on the other side of the table. Peeked at him over the rim.

While his impassive expression was impossible to read, one fact was clear.

She wasn't the only one who'd changed.

The cop sitting across from her was a much more mature, insular, cautious, and skeptical person than the fresh-off-the-farm, innocent young landscaper employee who'd worn his heart on his sleeve and trusted unreservedly.

Yet different as his personality was, he still exuded integrity. Should she choose to confide in him, her secrets would be safe.

Heart hammering, Christi set her mug back down. Stared into the dark depths.

If she'd driven thousands of miles to ask Jack for a favor, she ought to be able to find the courage to take this one last step to secure it—no matter how embarrassing the confession would be.

Decision made, she linked her fingers into a tight knot on the table and forced herself to begin. "The story starts after my father died of a massive heart attack."

Though his demeanor didn't change, the subtle tension in the room abated slightly. As if he was relieved she'd capitulated.

That made one of them.

"Six years ago." He sipped his coffee, his hand far steadier than hers.

"Yes." At least he'd been listening that day on the wharf. "He was all the family I had, and I was lost without him. Too lost."

Jack narrowed his eyes. "Explain that."

"With no one to turn to other than the aloof, all-business attorney who handled my dad's affairs, I was susceptible to charm and feigned affection."

A muscle in his cheek ticced, and his features hardened. "That can happen."

The coffee flavor on her tongue soured at the oblique reference to his own situation with her. He could even be thinking that turnabout was fair play.

And maybe it was. Maybe she deserved everything she'd gotten.

Yet she'd risen above the morass of her own making. Applied the lessons she'd learned. Built a new life.

Such as it was.

The small pile of boxes the movers had deposited in her living room was telling. How sad that it had taken so few to hold what was left of her life.

But feeling sorry for herself was useless. It was far more productive to focus on becoming a better person.

"I'm sorry, Jack. If I could change the past, I would."

He waved her apology aside. "Go on with your story."

A flash of lightning slashed across the dark sky out the window, followed by a low rumble of distant thunder. Both left an unsettled atmosphere in their wake.

How appropriate for this true-confessions session.

She rubbed a fingertip over a slight mar on the table and picked up her tale. "At my lowest point, Wes Powers entered my orbit. He was five years older than me and claimed to have been a business associate of my dad's. To cut to the chase, I fell hook, line, and sinker for his empathy act and his offer to oversee my affairs. We began meeting for lunch, one thing led to another, and in short order I found myself with a ring and a new name."

"I'm assuming he wasn't what he seemed."

"Not by a long shot." Christi reached for her mug. Hesitated. If she drank any more of the strong brew it would no doubt curdle in her churning stomach.

"Would you rather have a glass of water?"

Apparently he'd honed his intuitive instincts through the years.

"If it's not too much trouble."

In silence, he rose, filled a glass with ice and water, and set it beside her mug.

"How long were you married?" He retook his seat.

"Too long." She sipped the water, letting the coolness sluice down her throat. "Thirty-four eternal months, to be exact."

"How did you end up in Dallas?"

"He claimed it was a better base for his investment business. In hindsight, I think he just wanted to remove me from familiar surroundings—and people—so that I'd come to lean on him more. Give him further control over my world. It worked. Besides, I was used to letting other people handle the logistics of my life. I was an easy mark."

"The term *mark* also raises red flags for a cop. Did your money problems start with your marriage?"

"Yes. I trusted Wes and gave him full control over my inheritance.

I didn't realize he was using most of it for speculative investments that didn't pan out—and to keep a succession of mistresses happy. I was nothing more to him than a source of funding."

Jack's nostrils flared, but his tone was calm. "What tipped you off to his true character?"

"A text message. He left his cell on the kitchen counter one day while he took a shower. It wasn't password protected, and a text came in as I was passing by." She swallowed. "It was a photo of him with a woman. She was wearing one of the pieces of my mom's jewelry Wes had convinced me to keep in a safe-deposit box at the bank. The message said 'miss you.'"

Jack linked his fingers on the table. His manner remained neutral, but emotions she couldn't pinpoint smoldered beneath the surface. "That had to be tough."

"Yes—and it got worse." She massaged her temple, where a headache was beginning to throb. "I demanded answers—and he provided them without holding anything back. At that stage he had nothing to lose. The money had been spent, my mom's jewelry was gone except for the ring I always wore around my neck, our credit cards were maxed out, and we were in hock to the hilt. I told him I intended to file for divorce, packed a bag, and went to stay with a friend."

"I thought you said he died."

"He did. Before I could find an attorney to set the divorce proceedings in motion and try to reclaim my jewelry, he was critically injured in a motorcycle crash after a night of drinking. He lingered in a coma for six weeks but never regained consciousness—and as his wife, I inherited all the debt . . . including his hospital bills. The jewelry was lost forever. The police were able to track down the woman in the phone message I saw on his cell, but she claimed she'd sold the piece he'd given her."

She could almost hear the gears whirring in Jack's brain.

"Did you consider filing for bankruptcy?"

"Briefly. I knew that would eliminate a portion of my debt.

But in the end, I didn't think it was fair to penalize others for my mistakes."

"All of the mistakes weren't yours."

"I gave Wes control of my finances. Abdicated my responsibility to be a good steward of my dad's inheritance. That was the first mistake—and it led to all the others."

Silence fell between them as he regarded her. "Did you talk to an attorney after your husband died?"

"Yes. I couldn't afford to hire him, but he did give me a bit of free advice." She swiped a bead of condensation off the side of her glass. "I was able to negotiate the hospital costs down. The credit card companies wouldn't budge. Everything we didn't own outright—the house, cars, electronics—was repossessed."

Jack tapped a finger against the table. "The Christi I knew wouldn't have had a clue how to cope with that kind of catastrophe."

"No, she wouldn't have—but I'd already begun to change. I knew early on something was wrong in my marriage, and I began searching for help. I found it in God—and a church community."

He gave her a dubious once-over. "I don't recall you being interested in religion."

"I wasn't back then. After Mom died, Dad and I stopped going to church. But in my younger days we went as a family. Those memories, and hearing you talk about your faith, led me back to God—and to my best friend, who attended the church I found. Tasha stood by me through the entire mess. I could never repay her kindness. Without her and my faith, I don't know if I would have survived."

"Is the loan related to this friend?"

"Yes."

He folded his arms. "Shouldn't you take care of your own financial problems first?"

"I have—for the most part. I sold everything that wasn't repossessed to help pay off the bills, took on two serving jobs that first year, and cut living expenses to the bone. My head was almost above water when—" Her voice faltered.

This was the hardest part.

Mortifying as it was to admit being duped, the blame for that was as much on Wes as on her. The fault for what happened next was hers alone. And once Jack heard this part of the story, her loan could be toast.

"When what?"

At his prompt, she twisted her fingers together. Sugarcoating what had happened would help her save face, but she was done misleading people. She had to be honest—whatever the outcome.

"When I made a terrible mistake." She moistened her lips. Forced herself to continue. "Three months ago, once I could see the light at the end of the tunnel, I invited Tasha out to dinner. I had a couple glasses of wine, which was out of pattern—but I was feeling upbeat that night and in the mood to celebrate. On the drive home, the car slid on slick pavement. I didn't get hurt, but the car was totaled—and Tasha ended up with a compound fracture in her leg that sidelined her for weeks. Plus, her insurance didn't cover all of her medical bills."

He studied her. "You blame yourself for what happened to her."

"Of course. It was my fault. I was driving—and I'd been drinking."

"Two glasses of wine shouldn't have put you over the BAC limit."

"They didn't—but I was feeling the effects of the alcohol. I doubt my reflexes were functioning at optimal levels."

She girded, prepared to insist on her culpability—but after a moment he switched gears.

"If she had any insurance at all, she shouldn't have racked up the kind of dollar amount in medical bills you asked me to loan you."

"The money isn't for medical bills." Christi took another sip of water. "It's to replenish her dream fund. She's had to tap into it for living expenses and medical bill balances."

He arched an eyebrow. "Dream fund?"

"Tasha wants to open a restaurant. She's a fabulous chef, and she's worked hard to save money for that dream. A few months ago she found the perfect spot and signed a contingency lease. She also paid for the remodel design. But two weeks from now, all the money she's spent will be lost—along with the opportunity—unless I get that loan."

"Isn't there anyone else who can help her?"

"No. She comes from a hard-working, lower-middle-class family. Her brother has four kids, one of them with Down syndrome. Her sister's in graduate school. Her parents are on Social Security. There's no spare money to fund dreams." She leaned forward, posture taut. "I owe her this, Jack—and not just because of the accident. She was there for me when my life spiraled out of control."

A few beats of silence ticked by before he responded. "Your inclinations are admirable."

Gratifying as his praise was, what mattered was helping Tasha.

She twined her fingers together again. Braced. "So what's your verdict on the loan?"

He didn't hesitate. "It's a go."

Pressure built behind her eyes, and she exhaled. "Thank you."

"You're welcome." He finished his coffee and set the mug aside. "Are you willing to sign an agreement for the loan?"

"Yes. How soon can your attorney have it ready?"

"I don't want to use my attorney. He lives in Hope Harbor, and while I have total confidence in his discretion, I'd prefer to keep this matter private. An agreement like this could raise questions—and speculation—given the timing of your arrival with Hannah's."

"Oh." She hadn't thought of that. "I see how that could be awkward. How would you like to handle this?"

"I'll find a boilerplate agreement online, if that's acceptable."

"Fine by me. How soon can we do this?"

"Tomorrow?"

"That works. The sooner the better for Tasha."

"I do have one more question." His businesslike manner softened a hair. "Does your friend know you came here to ask me for a loan?"

"No. She would *not* have been happy."

"What if she won't accept it?"

"She will. I'm not letting her lose her chance to realize her dream."

"What about *your* dreams?"

At his gentle question, her breathing hitched.

The Jack who'd turned her world upside down that long-ago summer *was* still there. He'd simply learned to hide his softer side under a no-nonsense, hard-nosed exterior.

Around her, anyway.

"I've given up on dreams." She pushed her chair back and stood, resting her fingertips on the table to steady herself as her shaky legs balked. "I'll be satisfied to help Tasha find *her* happy ending. Can we discuss specifics about Hannah's schedule tomorrow, after I sign the loan papers?"

He stood more slowly. "Sure."

"I should go."

Without waiting for a reply, she hurried toward the living room, snatched up her purse from the couch where she'd dropped it, and continued to the door.

He beat her to it, leaning around her to twist the knob, his breath a warm caress against her temple. "Are you stopping in to see Beth again tomorrow?"

"Y-yes."

If he noticed the revealing hitch in her voice, he didn't comment on it.

"Come by afterward and we'll take care of the paperwork and discuss scheduling. I'll wire transfer the funds to your account Thursday morning." He pulled the door open.

"Thank you again." She eased past him, onto the small porch, just as the skies opened.

"Wow." Jack surveyed the pelting rain. "Let me get an umbrella."

"I can make a run for it."

"You'll be soaked." He disappeared back into the house before she could protest.

Less than half a minute later he joined her outside, opened a large golf umbrella, and took her arm.

She held back as he tried to guide her toward the edge of the porch. "Why don't I take the umbrella and return it tomorrow?"

"It tends to be unwieldy in the wind. I can hold it while you get in your car. No sense trying to juggle the door and keys too."

Hard to argue with his logic—even if the right side of her brain was sending out a red alert.

He tugged again, and she gave up. What could happen on a fifteen-second dash to her car—even if his touch was reawakening old feelings best left in mothballs? Feelings so strong she'd been on the verge of ditching her rich-girl lifestyle, defying her father's wishes for a match he deemed suitable, and running off with a man who worked in the dirt with his hands but whose heart was pure gold.

Until she'd sabotaged that future with a few ill-chosen, overheard words.

"Didn't you unlock your doors?" Jack stopped beside her car and tried the handle.

"It's an older-model car, and the auto locks didn't work when I bought it. The convenience wasn't worth the cost of the repair." But why hadn't she had her keys out and ready?

You know why, Christi. Distraction was always your middle name around Jack.

Too true.

She found the keys at last and fumbled for the right one. But when she tried to fit it in the lock, it slipped from her trembling fingers and fell to the wet pavement.

"Sorry." She started to bend down, but he stopped her with a touch on her shoulder.

"Let me."

He scooped the keys up in one smooth motion, unlocked the door, and handed them back, his fingers brushing hers.

Her respiration shorted out.

Good grief.

She was acting like an adolescent on her first date.

And she had to get over it. Fast. Whatever lingering feelings she harbored for Jack, any attraction he'd felt for her had died long ago.

She clutched the keys tight in her fist and tried to keep breathing. "Thanks again—for everything."

"My pleasure." His response came out husky.

She risked a peek at him—and at his tender expression, she grabbed the edge of the door and held on tight.

Unless her instincts were experiencing a major malfunction, he was feeling the same zing that was making her fingertips tingle.

Was it possible she'd finally convinced him she'd changed? That he was not only letting go of his animosity toward her but exchanging it for affection? Attraction, even?

As if he'd read her mind, he canted the umbrella to shield them from the wind and driving rain. Slowly lifted his hand. Traced the line of her jaw with a fingertip that didn't feel any too steady.

Surrounded by darkness, under the shadow of the umbrella, his features were fuzzy. But his almost palpable yearning was crystal clear.

He wanted to touch her. Hold her. Kiss her.

And she wanted him to, God help her.

With the rain pummeling the earth and the distant cry of a gull in search of a safe roost providing the soundtrack to their insular world, she licked the salty tang of the nearby sea from her lips.

His gaze dropped to her mouth, and the yearning in his eyes morphed to a visceral hunger.

A shiver rippled through her that had nothing to do with the chill of the cool mist wafting around the edges of the umbrella. It was all about longing.

Because his hunger became hers . . . and it tantalized. Tempted.

How many years had passed since she'd felt so wanted? So cherished? So loved?

Except Jack didn't love her. Loathing couldn't transition to love this fast. The magnetism between them had to be hormones, nothing more.

So before either of them made a mistake they regretted, someone had to end this dangerous interlude.

Since Jack didn't seem inclined to break the spell, it was up to her.

Summoning up every ounce of her willpower, she pulled back, fumbled for the edge of the door, and slid behind the wheel. "You should g-go in or you'll be soaked. The umbrella won't protect you for long."

He didn't move.

"Jack." She clasped the door handle. Gave a tiny tug.

At the nudge, he lurched back. "Drive safe." His words rasped—and her willpower wavered.

Get out of here, Christi.

Smart advice.

Somehow she managed to twist the key in the ignition. Put the car in reverse. Back out of the spot and aim the Nissan toward Sea Glass Cottage.

Only after she was a safe distance away did she venture a glance in the rearview mirror.

Jack remained standing where she'd left him. Watching her.

Was he as flummoxed as she was?

Was he wondering what would have happened if they'd followed through on the electrical impulses zipping between them?

Was he thinking that would have been a mistake—or regretting her sudden departure?

Who knew?

As he faded into the night, only one thing was certain. Risking the loan by muddying up the agreement with an amorous encounter would have been foolish. It would also complicate the arrangements for Hannah. How would she face Jack every day if they'd succumbed to the kiss that had been a whisper away?

For now, it was smarter to maintain an arm's-length distance from the man who'd once stolen her heart—even if she'd much rather be *in* his arms.

As for what tonight's emotional parting portended for the long term?

Time would tell.

20

Charley had come to visit her?

As Beth peeked through the peephole in her front door, the taco-making artist smiled and lifted a brown bag.

She frowned.

How could he know she was on the other side? After Steve had spotted her through the sidelights, she'd learned to approach the door with stealth—in case any other unwelcome visitors showed up.

Yet Charley had never been anything but friendly—and if that bag held his famous tacos, he was more than welcome.

She flipped the lock and opened the door. "Hi, Charley. This is an unexpected pleasure."

"Glad to hear it. I'm always cautious about calling on people who are under the weather—but I hoped an order of tacos would hasten the healing process."

"Better than any medicine the doctor could order. Would you like to come in?"

"If I'm not intruding."

"Not at all. I'm used to talking with customers at the shop. It can get lonely here all by myself." She pulled the door wide.

"No other visitors?" He stepped past her, into the apartment.

"A few friends from Coos Bay have dropped in—and Christi gets my mail and brings me takeout from the Myrtle." She closed the door. "I hired her to help at the shop, not be a nurse—or a food delivery service. She's been a godsend."

"The perfect word." He lifted the bag. "Shall I put these somewhere for you, since your hands are occupied?"

An echo of what Steve had said on Sunday.

"If you don't mind. The kitchen's straight ahead, through the living room."

Charley took the lead, slowing to touch a blossom as he passed the bouquet of flowers. "Pretty."

He didn't ask who'd sent them—and she didn't fill him in as he continued to the kitchen.

"I put a bottle of water in the bag, but I'll be happy to get you a different beverage if you like." He set the food on the table.

"Water is fine."

"You should eat these while they're hot—unless you've already had lunch."

"No. Your timing was providential."

"I won't argue with that. A mighty hand governs the eternal clock."

Interesting observation from a man who often spouted thought-provoking statements—and radiated a certain spiritual aura—but who'd never referenced God during her many visits to his taco truck.

"You seem surprised by my comment." He offered her a smile.

She shifted her weight on the crutches. "I am—a little. I guess I've never thought of you as that religious."

"Depends how you define religious, I suppose." He motioned to the bag of tacos. "If you'd like company while you enjoy those, I'd be happy to discuss the subject."

While religion hadn't been on her lunch menu, it would be rude to dismiss him after he'd gone to the trouble of bringing her this unexpected treat.

"I wouldn't mind a bit of conversation. Solitary meals get old. Please, have a seat. There's soda in the fridge if you'd like one."

"I'm fine, thanks." He sat as she set her crutches aside, lowered herself into her chair, and opened the bag.

"These smell divine. Was it busy at the stand today?" Maybe if she changed the subject, he'd forget about religion.

"No. The traffic was much lighter than usual. The drop in tourism is hurting us all. But Christi's plan to attract visitors is promising."

"You know about that?" Beth unwrapped her first taco. The younger woman had only mentioned it to her last night.

"Marci hasn't wasted any time getting input from the merchants in town. From what I've heard, the response has been very favorable. And that brings me back to my comment about timing. Isn't it remarkable that she showed up in town now—out of the blue—with such a clever idea to help us increase business?"

"Could be coincidence."

His lips curved up again. "As my abuela used to say when I was a boy in Mexico, coincidence is nothing more than a small miracle in which God chooses to remain anonymous."

Another reference to God.

Rather than follow up on that comment, she continued to eat. If she didn't respond, he might change the subject.

No such luck.

"You mentioned you'd never thought of me as religious. May I ask why that is?"

She finished chewing the bite of taco as she pondered that question. "Well, you never talk much about God or going to church or reading the Bible."

"Reading the Bible is easy. Living it is hard. Besides, putting God's words into action can change hearts faster than spouting verses—don't you think?"

Couched like that . . .

"I suppose you're right." And by that definition, Charley was *very* religious. He lived the Good Book. The tacos she was enjoying today were tangible proof of that—and his kindness and empathy were legendary in town.

"My abuela, in her great wisdom, taught me to live my faith rather than talk about it. Don't preach, she said. Do. Feed the hungry. Give drink to the thirsty. Visit the sick. Be compassionate. Forgive."

The bite of taco stuck in her throat, and Beth washed it down with a swig of water. "I haven't done the best job at a few of those. Worse, after my faith faltered."

As the admission spilled out, she frowned. Her lapsed relationship with the Almighty wasn't a subject she'd talked about with anyone except Christi—and then, only in passing.

Why had she brought it up to this man, whose beliefs were obviously strong?

And what would he think of her now that he knew she didn't share his rock-solid trust in God?

She looked across the table as she unwrapped her second taco—and her breath caught.

Understanding and acceptance radiated from him, enveloping her in warmth.

"Everyone stumbles, Beth." His voice was gentle, his demeanor nonjudgmental. "But even when people give up on God, his love never wavers. He just opens his arms and waits to welcome his children back, with all their faults. Reconciliations in the human realm can be difficult, but with God there's no risk of failure or rejection."

She tucked a stray piece of red onion back into her taco. "Can I be honest?"

"Please."

"I'm not sure I want a relationship with a God who doesn't answer prayers."

"You mean in the way that you want them answered." His tone remained benign. Conversational.

"Yes."

"What we want isn't always part of God's bigger plan, though.

We see the back of the tapestry, with all its loose threads, while he sees the beautiful, intricate pattern on top. That's where trust comes in." He rested his elbows on the table and interlaced his fingers. "But I do agree it's difficult to trust—or love—someone who disappoints us."

A subtle change in his inflection put her on alert.

He was talking about Steve.

Beth continued to eat, despite the sudden disappearance of her appetite—but chewing bought her a few moments to think.

While everyone who knew her and Steve was aware of their split, she'd never shared the background with anyone other than Christi. Yet Charley, with his keen intuitive abilities, had probably discerned more than most people about what had prompted it—and he'd opened the door for her to talk about it, if she chose.

In light of his compassion and empathy, it could be helpful to get his take on the situation.

She wadded the white paper from the second taco into a tight ball. "If you're referring to Steve, that's true. And it's more than disappointment. I'm angry and disillusioned. I know the Bible says to forgive—but the hurt runs too deep. I can't get past it."

"Even if he's repented—and changed?"

"How can I be certain he has?"

His lips flexed. "As that clever philosopher Benjamin Franklin said, the only certainty in this world is death and taxes. However, when it comes to people, listening with the heart can improve our odds of arriving at a sound conclusion."

Hard to dispute—but first you had to hear the words being spoken.

Like the ones she'd never read in all the cards and letters Steve had written.

But if she pulled out the box she'd shoved back in her closet and opened his notes, the insulating anger could evaporate, leaving her vulnerable once again to grief and pain.

What a quandary.

And it wasn't one Charley could solve for her—even if he'd given her food for thought as well as for lunch. This decision was hers alone.

"I think I'll save my last taco for later." She tapped the bag. "I've reached my limit." With food—and unsettling questions.

"In that case, it's back to the studio for me." He stood.

"I'll walk you to the door." She reached for her crutches.

"Don't bother. Stay here and enjoy the concert." He motioned toward her open window and paused to listen as a goldfinch trilled. "He's giving quite a performance. I'd say he's in full courting mode. Enjoy the rest of your day, Beth."

"Thank you. And thanks for the lunch treat."

"It was my pleasure. As my abuela also said, we may not be able to fix everyone's problems—but it *is* within our power to give everyone we meet a moment of joy. Take care of yourself."

He exited the kitchen, and half a minute later the door clicked shut behind him.

Beth remained at the table, sipping her water for several more minutes, the song of the courting finch filling her kitchen with music—and hope—as she replayed her visit with Charley.

Odd.

During all the years she'd frequented his taco stand, they'd never had such a serious one-on-one conversation. Yes, Charley always listened and offered his typical sage comments, but she'd never given his diplomatic advice much consideration. Perhaps because she'd been shutting out his gentle guidance all along.

As she was shutting out Steve's attempts to reconnect.

Beth pushed herself to her feet, fitted her crutches under her arms, and maneuvered herself over to the window.

On a nearby limb, the goldfinch continued to sing. Searching for companionship, if Charley's comment about courting was correct.

Even birds got lonely, it seemed.

Yet they didn't have the kind of baggage humans carried around when relationships went awry. A mere song wouldn't be sufficient to smooth out the tangles in a situation like hers.

But written words could—if they came from the heart.

Did Steve's?

Reading his notes would help her determine that. Only after she listened to what he had to say could she know if giving him a second chance was worth the risk.

And thanks to Christi and Charley, she was getting closer to taking that step every day.

Yes!

Tasha was finally returning her call.

Christi slid onto a stool behind the counter at Eye of the Beholder and pushed the talk button. "It's about time."

"Hey, girlfriend. My phone died at the restaurant last night, and I slept in this morning." A yawn came over the line. "What's up?"

"I have news."

"Yeah?" A banging pot reverberated in the background. "Good or bad?"

"Good."

"Lay it on me. I could use an injection of optimism to get me through my double shift at the restaurant today. My boss has been on a tear lately. Another incentive to escape and open my own place."

"Your escape is at hand."

A few beats of silence ticked by.

"What does that mean?"

Christi smiled. "Hang on to the pot you're holding. Your dream fund is on the cusp of being replenished. The restaurant is yours."

Three seconds passed.

Four.

Five.

"Hey—are you still there?" Christi glanced at a couple strolling by the display window, but they continued past the front door.

Good. Hopefully the store would remain empty during this private conversation.

"Yeah. I'm here. Just trying to process your bombshell. It's not computing."

"The money will be in your account by Monday at the latest. All you have to do is give me the wire transfer instructions."

"Okay. Wait a minute. I'm sitting down." A chair scraped against the floor. "Now back up. Start over."

"The restaurant is yours."

"I heard *that* part—which is why I think I'm in an alternate universe."

"Nope. This is for real. Getting the money for you was why I made this trip. I didn't say anything because I knew it was a long shot—but my gamble paid off."

"Still not computing. You didn't have a spare dime when you left here three weeks ago. I want details. Where did you get the big bucks I need?"

"Someone from my past loaned it to me."

"Male or female?"

"Male."

"What sort of strings are attached?" Suspicion underscored her question.

"There aren't any. Or not the kind you're referring to."

"What does that mean?"

"It means the so-called strings are all in my favor. The loan came with a job offer as a nanny. I can also keep my part-time job at Eye of the Beholder and dump the sports bar gig you told me I shouldn't take anyway." No way was she telling Tasha that one of the strings had been a requirement to bare her soul.

"So who is this guy?"

"Someone I knew long ago."

"How come you've never mentioned him?"

"It's ancient history." Same words Jack had used—and the veracity of her response was as questionable as his had been.

"If you haven't kept in touch, why would he loan you such a large sum of money?"

"I caught him at a vulnerable moment. He needed a nanny fast and I needed a loan. We were able to help each other out. My timing was perfect." For once in her life.

Tasha gave a long sigh. "I appreciate the offer, Christi—but I can't take your money."

"It's not *my* money. It's *yours*. A small repayment for all you've done for me—and for being my friend."

"You don't owe me anything. Friendship doesn't come with a price tag."

"Maybe not—but I *do* owe you. Not only have you been my lifeline these past few years, but I was behind the wheel in the accident that wiped out your dream."

"That wasn't your fault."

"I'm not going to debate that again. However, I *will* get down on my knees and plead with you to accept this gift if I have to. Otherwise my marathon drive will have been in vain." Not quite accurate, in light of all the beneficial outcomes so far—but true in terms of her original purpose.

She held her breath as she waited for Tasha to respond, prepared to continue this fight if necessary.

"I'm paying it back, you know."

The tension in Christi's shoulders eased. She wasn't going to have to strong-arm Tasha after all.

"We'll talk about that down the road. In the meantime, can you text me the wire transfer information?"

"I'm on it. You know, it may be spring, but it suddenly feels like Christmas." Tasha's growing elation and excitement crackled through the connection. "I can't believe this. It's like . . . like a miracle."

"For me too. The best I hoped for from this trip was a loan—but I found a new home in a beautiful place I already love. It's a win-win all around."

Not to mention all her progress toward making peace with Jack—an unexpected and gratifying bonus.

"In that case, I'm glad you went—even if I miss seeing you."

"But you'll be moving to KC anyway, with your restaurant about to become a reality."

"That's why phones, video-chat apps, and other technology were invented. However—one of these days, I'd like to come out and see Hope Harbor and that beautiful house in person. The virtual tour you gave me whetted my appetite for a visit."

"You're welcome anytime. But unless my mysterious landlord agrees to renew the agreement, I may have to give up Sea Glass Cottage come the end of October."

"I better hustle getting my place up and running, then. And thank you for—everything. I'd pretty much given up hope. You'll never know how much this means to me. Not just the loan but our friendship." Her voice choked.

"The feeling is mutual." A customer came in, and Christi stood. "I have to go. Stay in touch."

"Always."

As the line went dead, she slipped the cell back in her pocket and welcomed the woman who'd entered, Tasha's comment about miracles playing through her mind.

So many of the things that had happened since she'd arrived in Hope Harbor fell into that category. Not at a dramatic parting-of-the-sea level but on a quieter, smaller scale. Like the beautiful cottage, rent-free. Beth's job offer. Charley's kindness. The softening of Jack's heart.

Gratitude bubbled up inside her for all the wonders this trip had wrought.

And while she didn't feel at all equipped to spearhead the interactive masterclass festival the chamber of commerce had endorsed, she would do everything in her power to help the town that had restored her own hope weather its current crisis and emerge stronger than ever.

21

Man, he'd missed this place.

Steve picked up his vanilla latte from the serving counter at The Perfect Blend and claimed a table by the picture window overlooking Main Street—and Eye of the Beholder. With Beth laid up, he wouldn't have to worry about running into her at their favorite coffee shop and breaking his promise to keep his distance.

He took a sip of the steaming brew.

Bliss.

The treat didn't smooth out the kinks in his world, but small pleasures like this did add a touch of brightness to his days.

As he savored his java, Charley appeared across the street, a folded newspaper under his arm. The taco chef waved at someone out of view, then headed for the coffee shop as the morning sun began to chase away the lingering wisps of fog.

Less than a minute later, he entered, scanned the interior, and homed in on the table Steve had picked.

Lifting a hand in greeting, he strolled across the shop and stopped a few feet away. "You look happy this morning, my friend."

Did he?

Must be the coffee.

"No one makes lattes like The Perfect Blend." He lifted the disposable cup.

"The café de olla is also exceptional. Mexican coffee was nowhere to be found in our serene little hamlet until Zach opened. Have you ever tried it?"

"No. I'm a latte guy. Why switch from the tried and true?"

"Because you never know what you could be missing if you don't occasionally venture outside your comfort zone—whether in coffee or in life." As usual, his words of wisdom were tempered with a good-natured grin.

"I'll take that under advisement. What are you up to today?"

"Painting. As soon as I get my coffee fix, I'll be hunkering down in the studio. But I'm glad I ran into you. I saw an article in our local paper I thought might interest you." He pulled a copy of the *Herald* from beneath his arm and flipped it open. "I bet Noah would enjoy this." He set the paper on the table and pointed to one of the listings under a column of area activities.

Steve skimmed the item about a series of six Saturday-morning art classes for middle-school-age students that would introduce them to a variety of mediums. It was being taught at the Hope Harbor high school by an art instructor from one of the colleges in Coos Bay—and it started in two days.

He pulled out his phone and snapped a photo of the write-up. "Thanks for passing this on. It *does* sound right up Noah's alley. It's kind of last-minute, though. The class may be full." And who knew whether Noah's foster parents would have the time—or inclination—to shuttle him back and forth, especially on such short notice?

"Couldn't hurt to ask." Charley refolded the paper and slid it back under his arm. "Beth appears to be recovering well from her surgery, don't you think?"

Steve squinted at him. Had Charley forgotten their conversation at the studio—or had the man somehow gotten wind of Sunday's visit?

"Have you seen her?" He sipped his latte. One handy deflection skill he'd learned as a cop was to answer a question with a question.

"I stopped by yesterday. We had a most pleasant chat."

About what? And had Beth mentioned his visit?

"I'm sure she appreciated the company."

"That was my impression. I noticed the beautiful flowers, by the way. I assume they were from you."

Ah. That helped explain Charley's earlier question. While one of Beth's friends could have sent the flowers, the sort of lavish bouquet he'd brought would be more apt to come from someone who cared deeply—like a husband.

But that didn't mean he'd hand-delivered them.

"Yes." Nothing wrong with admitting he was the sender.

"A thoughtful gesture—and flowers communicate a powerful message."

"If the receiver is receptive. She didn't seem to be."

As his response spilled out, Steve cringed. That was more or less an admission he'd been there.

"You may be surprised."

What did *that* mean? Did Charley have inside information?

"Why? Did she say something to you to suggest that?" Since Charley had already picked up on his visit, why not see what more he could learn from the man?

"Actions speak louder than words." He motioned toward the growing line at the counter. "If I don't join the queue, my muse will get antsy. Talk to you soon."

He took off before Steve could follow up on his actions comment.

Geez.

Charley was as adept at evading questions as a hardened criminal—but without the guile.

He tapped his cell and gave the photo he'd snapped of the art program offering another read.

Being stuck in a holding pattern with Beth was the pits, but at least with Noah he could be proactive. All he had to do was confirm a spot was available in the class and call the boy's foster dad. See if Will Butler or his wife could shuttle the boy to the class for six Saturdays.

He had his first answer in less than a minute. There was room in the class for Noah.

His second call was more problematic. While Butler didn't give the suggestion a thumbs-down, there were logistical issues.

"I know he loves art, and I'd like to support that interest, but we also have a special needs foster child who demands a lot of our attention. Plus, my wife often works weekends." The man sighed. "I don't see how we could commit to every Saturday for six weeks."

It was difficult to fault Butler's excuse.

So much for that idea.

Unless he volunteered for chauffeur duty.

Phone pressed to his ear, Steve stared out the window, toward Eye of the Beholder. It wasn't as if he had any other obligations on Saturdays—or anytime else, except for work—and six weeks wasn't all that long. It would also fit with his current shift schedule. And it would mean the world to that little boy.

He could do this.

Maybe he *ought* to do this.

For Noah—and for Jonathan.

Quashing a wave of all-too-familiar melancholy, he refocused on the interior. Charley lifted his Mexican coffee in salute as he sauntered toward the door, vibes of encouragement and support flowing from him.

"Sergeant Adams? I wish I could agree to this, but with everything—"

"I'll tell you what." Steve took a deep breath—and took the plunge. "If it's okay with you, I'll run him back and forth. I'll also pick up the tab for the class."

A beat ticked by.

"Seriously?"

"Yes."

"If you're certain it's not too much of an imposition, I'll take you up on the offer to drive him. But we can swing the fee."

"Why don't you let me take care of it?" If the man had a special needs foster child too, funds could be tight—no matter how much the state provided in assistance. "I'd like to play a role in helping Noah develop his talent."

"In that case, I accept. Thank you. Wait until he hears this. He'll be over the moon. Do you want me to round him up so you can tell him? He's in the yard somewhere sketching."

"No. You can have him call me later, after he comes in."

They finalized arrangements for the first pickup, and Steve ended the call. Went online to register Noah for the class. Finished off the latte that had brightened his morning.

But as he left The Perfect Blend to begin his workday, it wasn't the boost of energy from the caffeine flowing through his veins that lightened his step.

It was a healthy dose of optimism—and a sudden sense that somehow today he'd turned a corner. That life was about to take an upswing.

While there was no rational basis for that feeling, it stayed with him as he returned to his car—and was reinforced by the thumbs-up Charley gave him as he passed the bench where the man was enjoying his coffee a few minutes later. Almost as if the resident artist knew the seed he'd planted this morning had taken root and sprouted.

Was it possible that Charley's hint about Beth being more receptive to his overture than he'd thought had also been prompted by the man's uncanny sixth sense?

Perhaps. After all, she'd kept his letters, even if she hadn't opened them. That had to be a positive sign—didn't it?

Or was he fooling himself? Grasping at straws?

No way to know.

But as he swung onto 101 and shifted into work mode, he refused to let doubts undermine his buoyed spirits. His life would improve.

It had to.

In the meantime, he'd focus on adding a touch of joy to the life of a little boy who'd already endured too many hard knocks in his young history.

The loan papers were signed, all her belongings had arrived at Sea Glass Cottage, she was officially in charge of the masterclass festival, and Jack would be delivering Hannah to Eye of the Beholder any minute en route to work.

Whew.

Christi propped her elbow on the sales counter and scrubbed at her forehead.

Who could have guessed when she rode into town three weeks ago that her life would change so dramatically?

But all for the better—not counting the festival. Clerking and nannying she could handle. Running an event on which the merchants in town were pinning their hopes?

Big-time scary.

The bell over the door jingled, and Hannah entered, a uniformed Jack on her heels.

Christi summoned up a smile for the little girl whose life had been upended far more than her own in the past month and stood. "Hi, Hannah."

The girl tugged on the purple sweater that had become *her* uniform, lips bowing. "Hi."

"I brought a few things to keep her busy until you close for the day." Jack crossed to the counter and held out a tote bag. "Also a snack in case she gets hungry."

"Thanks." She took the bag, her fingers brushing his for a mere second—but long enough to disrupt her equilibrium.

If the slight contact had any impact on the man across from her, he gave no indication of it. Instead, faint creases appeared on his forehead. "Are you certain you don't want to take her straight to the apartment after you close and pick up dinner to have there?"

So he was going to play this all business, as he had last night at the contract signing, despite their near-kiss on Tuesday. The one she'd put a damper on.

Smart move—even if the right side of her brain didn't agree.

"No. Let's stick with the plan we discussed last night. Takeout gets old—and the cottage has more outside play area." She tipped her head toward Hannah, who was examining the colorful jewelry in the display case.

"As long as that works best for you. Do whatever's easiest. And remember to keep a running tab of whatever groceries you buy for dinner. I'll reimburse you every week."

"I have to eat anyway—and I don't think Hannah's going to chow down like a sumo wrestler."

He didn't respond to her teasing tone. Instead, the indentations on his forehead deepened. "I thought we settled this last night."

Not quite. She'd managed to sidestep a commitment. He was paying her a more-than-fair salary, and nickel-and-diming him for Hannah's dinner would be petty.

"Christi?"

At his more insistent tone, Hannah bit her lip and darted him a worried glance.

Uh-oh. Stress alert—and his daughter did *not* need any more tension in her life.

"We did talk about it." And there would be a round two some night after Hannah was asleep. Perhaps even later this evening. But for now she'd appease him. "I'll keep a running total of her share."

"You have the key to the apartment, right?"

She patted her slacks. "In my pocket. We'll be fine, Jack. Don't worry."

He hesitated, as if he wasn't certain about that, then dropped down on one knee beside his daughter. "I'll be home tonight, after you're asleep, but Christi will stay with you until I get there. Okay?"

"Yes. You already told me that last night."

"I just want to make sure you know you won't be by yourself."

"I'm fine."

But she wasn't. If she didn't loosen her fierce grip on that sweater soon, more repairs would be in the offing.

After scrutinizing her, Jack stood. "Call me if anything comes up."

"I will—but I doubt that will happen."

He smoothed a hand over his daughter's hair. "Christi will take good care of you, honey."

"I know."

Hannah eased closer, and Christi put an arm around her thin shoulders. "I'll see you tonight at your apartment."

"Right." After a moment, he gave her a parting nod and strode toward the exit.

As the door shut behind him, Christi peeked into the tote bag. Books, a drawing pad and colored pencils, peanut butter crackers. Not bad for a bachelor father.

"Looks like your dad has you covered, sweetie."

"I helped him pick everything out."

That explained it.

"I have a table set up for you over there." Christi indicated a quiet, out-of-the-way spot in the back corner. "But let me give you a tour of the shop first. We have all kinds of pretty things here."

As they completed a walk-through, several customers in succession came through the door and she left Hannah at the table.

For the next two hours, until closing time, the girl kept herself occupied while Christi took care of business. It wasn't an ideal setup—but it was only for two days, assuming Beth was able to return for half days next week, as planned.

Once the last customer of the day departed with her purchases, Hannah wandered over. "Should I leave my bag here until tomorrow?"

"Yes. Good idea." Christi locked the display case and pocketed the key. "Are you getting hungry?"

The girl shrugged.

Not unexpected, after Jack's warning last night that getting Hannah to eat more than a few mouthfuls was a challenge. And she wasn't the world's best—or most experienced—cook. Thank heavens Tasha had taught her a few tricks and shared several easy recipes.

Another reason she was in her friend's debt.

"What have you been having for dinner?" Christi guided Hannah toward the front door.

"He gets takeout at a restaurant in town."

He—not "my dad."

Ouch.

Jack was going to have an uphill battle winning this child's heart.

He may have told Hannah he'd been unaware of her existence—as he'd relayed last night during the contract signing—but it would be hard for a child of ten to grasp the nuances of why he'd been an absentee father.

"I don't get much takeout." Thanks to her shaky finances. "Do you like spaghetti? I thought we'd have that tonight—and chocolate chip cookies." Two foolproof recipes, courtesy of Tasha.

Hannah's eyes lit up as they exited and Christi locked the shop door. "I like both of those. My mom used to make them."

Well, shoot. Tasha's recipes were excellent, but they'd never be able to compete with the memory of a favorite dish made by a mother.

Somehow Christi held on to her smile as they continued toward her car. "Mine will probably be different than hers—but I hope you like them anyway." Best to tamp down any unrealistic expectations before they could take root.

"I bet I'll like them better than what *he* gets."

More animosity.

Hannah's discontent wasn't about the quality of the food, though. Jack had to be frequenting the Myrtle. It was the only game in town for a meal, other than Charley's stand. And it was hard to fault their cooking, based on the two tasty meals she'd enjoyed there.

The girl's downer attitude had more to do with her father—and the whole new situation she'd found herself in.

In light of that, tonight's pasta and cookies might pass muster after all. Judging by her behavior to date, Hannah was more receptive to a relationship with her than to one with Jack.

She opened the front passenger door, waited while Hannah buckled her seat belt, and circled around to the driver side—all the while mulling over Jack's situation.

Her plate was already full, but in addition to her babysitting duties—and planning a masterclass festival that could be the last hope for many of the town's merchants who were as much at risk from the area wildfires as the flora, fauna, and man-made structures in their direct paths—maybe in the coming weeks she could also help the novice father and reluctant daughter bridge the yawning gap between them.

No pressure there.

She rolled her eyes as she slid behind the wheel and twisted the key in the ignition.

With prayer and hard work, it was possible she'd succeed at both.

But if she'd overextended, she could be setting herself up for an epic fail that would have long-lasting repercussions not only for Jack and Hannah but for the entire town.

22

Coming home to find Christi in his apartment at eleven thirty at night was going to be dangerous.

Jack swung the Jeep into his parking spot, shut off the engine, and stared at the light spilling through the living room window in his unit—which was always dark . . . and safe . . . when he returned from an evening shift.

Not tonight.

Not with Christi inside.

Not after what had happened in this parking lot on Tuesday.

He massaged the bridge of his nose and rolled down his window. Filled his lungs with the salt-laced air. Exhaled.

Hiring Christi may have been a mistake. Yes, he'd been desperate to find childcare, but using that as an excuse to tap her for the nanny job was disingenuous.

The truth was, her plight had touched him, and he'd wanted to relieve her burden—especially after the tale of woe she'd told him that had cinched the loan.

Meaning he was now more susceptible than ever to the charms of the woman he'd once loved who, based on the evidence, appeared to have reinvented herself into a new and much-improved version.

So being with her in the house at this late hour wasn't wise. Despite his daughter's proximity, Hannah would be asleep—giving him every opportunity to pick up where he'd left off Tuesday night if he wanted to.

And heaven help him, he did. Even if it was too soon. Even if the possibility of making another mistake scared him senseless. Even if he was wary of the green light his usually trustworthy instincts were giving him.

Thank goodness Christi had had the wisdom—and fortitude—to back off from their almost-kiss.

But would she again?

And if she didn't, would he once more find the temptation to taste her lips too strong to ignore?

No way to know.

So he'd go with the game plan he'd developed tonight during his patrol rounds—ask Christi to brief him on her hours with Hannah, thank her, and show her to the door. Fast.

If he stuck with that strategy, nothing inappropriate could happen.

Shoring up his resolve, he left the car behind, hit the autolock button, and strode toward the apartment.

After fitting his key in the lock, he entered, closed the door behind him—and froze as he turned to scan the living room.

Christi was on the couch, head resting against the back, papers scattered around her, eyes closed, her breathing slow and even.

She was out cold.

Not surprising. After putting in a full day at Eye of the Beholder and another eight hours with Hannah, she had to be exhausted. At least her schedule would be less demanding next week if Beth spent afternoons at the shop, as planned.

He propped his fists on his hips as he traced her slumbering profile and kept his distance. How best to rouse her without moving within touching range?

Keys. That would work.

He pulled them out and jingled them.

No reaction.

He took a step closer and tried again. Louder.

At last she stirred, and after a moment her eyelids fluttered. The instant his presence registered, she straightened up and shoved her hair back, a rosy hue blooming on her cheeks. “Sorry. I didn’t mean to fall asleep on the job.”

“I sleep while Hannah sleeps. That’s not against the rules.”

“It’s against *my* rules.” She began to gather up the papers strewn around her. “You’re not paying me to sleep.”

“Staying awake until I get home wasn’t part of the agreement. I don’t care if you rack out on the couch after you put Hannah to bed.”

She continued to collect the papers. “I’ll concede that—if you’ll forget about repaying me for the food Hannah eats at my house. The salary you’re paying me is more than sufficient to cover a few groceries.”

They were back to that.

“If I say no?”

“I’ll do whatever it takes to stay awake in the future after she goes to bed.”

He could argue the point—or he could just build in a salary bonus down the road.

Problem solved.

“I can live with that.”

She stopped gathering up the papers and inspected him, as if his concession surprised her. “You can?”

“Yes.”

She gave him a wary look. “Why do I think there’s a devious motive behind your quick capitulation?”

“Because you’ve become a cynic?” He tried for a casual tone, but a touch of tenderness crept into his voice.

Her color surged again—and she changed the subject, adopting a brisk, businesslike manner. “Would you like a report on my afternoon and evening with Hannah?”

"Yes."

She shuffled the papers into a pile and set them on her lap. "Thanks to the material you provided, she kept herself occupied at the shop. After I closed, we went back to the cottage, and while I fixed dinner she explored the yard—but I kept her in sight from the kitchen window. She not only ate her whole meal, she asked for more. After we cleaned up and came back here, she was ready for bed."

Jack gaped at her. "She ate all her dinner?"

"Yes."

"What did you feed her?"

"Spaghetti. Tasha gave me a fabulous recipe for sauce."

Recipe?

"You mean—you cook? The sauce wasn't from a jar?" The kind he used, on the rare occasion he fixed dinner for himself at the apartment.

"No, it wasn't from a jar, and yes, I cook—a little. Thanks to Tasha." She stood and settled the stack of papers in the crook of her arm. "I should go."

Yeah, she should—and he should let her. A fast exit dovetailed with his safety plan.

Instead, he found himself motioning toward the papers. "What's all that?"

Bad move.

The longer she stayed, the more trouble he could get into.

But he could handle a slight delay.

Maybe.

Her brow creased. "It's for a project I'm working on. I was going to talk to you about it—but it's getting late."

"I'm wide awake. Will it take long?"

"No. But I'm not as awake as you are—and I want to be able to put forth a convincing argument." The corners of her lips rose, but indecision clouded her irises.

"Now you have me intrigued."

She regarded him for several seconds. Exhaled. "If you want to sit for a few minutes, I guess we can talk about it tonight. I'll leave the choice up to you."

He should let her go. Pick this up in daylight—or by phone.

Again, he throttled the voice of logic and claimed the closest chair. "Let's do it tonight."

After a moment, she retook her seat on the couch. "Have you heard anything about the masterclass festival being planned in town for June?"

"The what?" He usually picked up on news during his patrols, but this nugget of intel had escaped him.

"I'll take that as a no." She tucked her hair behind her ear, much like Hannah did when she was nervous. "Let me try to give you the condensed version."

He listened without interrupting while she filled him in—and as the scale of the task she'd taken on began to register, he frowned. Impressive as her idea was, it would require a huge amount of time and energy to pull off—and she already had multiple jobs. Plus, she was new in town and still learning about both Hope Harbor and its residents. She didn't have the connections to pull this off, despite her admirable intent.

As she finished, he gave a slow nod. "I like the idea." Somewhere along the road of life he'd learned to lead with a positive if you were about to be critical.

She saw straight through his attempt to soften her up for the concerns to come, however.

"I hear a but in there." She linked her fingers into a tight knot, and her chin tipped up a hair. "If you're thinking this is beyond the organizational abilities of an airhead like me, I do have—"

"Whoa." He held up a hand. "Wrong conclusion. I do have a few misgivings, but not about your aptitude for coordinating this. I know you used to get involved in charitable events on behalf of your dad. But the scope of this one would be a challenge even for a longtime resident who knows the terrain and the players—and you're already stretched thin. Putting this together would be very taxing."

She offered him the facsimile of a smile. "Taxing is working two full-time jobs as a restaurant server and hefting heavy trays for hours. Taxing is discovering your husband's been cheating on you and finding yourself penniless. Taxing is learning to stand on your own two feet after a lifetime of being coddled. Compared to all that, working at Eye of the Beholder is a piece of cake—and watching Hannah is a joy. As for being new in town—Marci assures me scads of people will volunteer to help with the project. It won't be a one-person operation."

He stifled a groan.

In one fell swoop, she'd demolished his reservations.

"I can't dispute any of that." But the idea of watching her wear herself out twisted his gut—not that he could admit *that* concern to her.

"Good." She clutched the papers tighter against her. "Then we can move on to the convincing argument I mentioned."

He braced. After hearing her spiel, it wasn't hard to predict what was coming.

He was about to be recruited as a presenter for one of the masterclass sessions.

She confirmed that before he could marshal his defenses.

"I'm sure, after listening to me describe the festival, you know I'd like to tap you as one of our experts."

He stifled a groan.

Why hadn't he listened to his inner voice and followed the fast-exit plan tonight? Let her leave rather than detain her? After eight hours on patrol, he wasn't up for a debate.

And that's where this was heading. Because difficult as it was to admit for a man who liked to present an in-control, in-charge image to the world, the prospect of getting up in front of an audience to talk about his writing scared the daylights out of him.

He flicked a piece of lint off his uniform slacks.

The truth was, while he had confidence in his cop credentials, as a novelist he still felt like an imposter. Despite the critical praise and stellar sales his first book had garnered, he couldn't get past the fear it had been a fluke. That his subsequent efforts would tank.

So how could he weasel out of her request without losing face?

He crossed an ankle over a knee and offered the first excuse that came to mind. "I try to keep a low profile with my writing in Hope Harbor. That's one of the reasons I use a pseudonym."

"Charley doesn't make a big deal out of his painting either—but everyone knows about it, and they respect both his careers. Being a taco chef doesn't take anything away from his work as an artist, and vice versa. I don't see why it would be any different with you."

Checkmate.

He'd have to try a different argument.

"I'm not a teacher, Christi."

"No one who's presenting is. Marci told me it was a tough sell with Adam Stone too. You know him, right?"

"Yeah." The ex-con married to the police chief avoided the limelight like the plague—for understandable reasons.

"But he finally agreed. Marci can be very persuasive, as you may know." A touch of wry humor glinted in her irises for a nanosecond before she leaned forward, posture intent. As if she was poised for battle. "If Adam can do it, you can too."

No, he couldn't. He'd feel like a fraud, offering wannabe novelists advice. Heck, he wasn't certain his *own* career would survive after his next book released. The mere thought of standing up in front of a roomful of people and pretending to be an expert was worse than an altercation with an armed criminal.

He couldn't say any of that to Christi, though. It would be too embarrassing to admit being that insecure.

"Adam is a renowned furniture maker." He folded his arms. "His work is well-known."

"So is yours. You're a *New York Times* bestseller."

"For one book. I don't have a track record like the other folks you mentioned."

"No—but you've achieved a milestone I suspect most novelists would kill for. Pardon the pun, given the nature of the books you write."

Her attempt at levity didn't ease his tension.

"I wouldn't know what to say."

"All you have to do is talk about your career and how you work on a book—your routine, your research, tips you've learned. You could do a long Q&A. Critique samples the audience members bring or send beforehand. Do a writing exercise. We can structure this however you like."

She was making it hard to say no.

"I think you missed your calling." He tried to coax up the corners of his mouth. "You should have gone into sales."

"Is that a yes?"

"It's a maybe."

Actually, it was a punt. Same as the day she'd pressed him for a loan at Sea Glass Cottage. And his ultimate intent was the same now as it had been then. To say no. But not tonight. He had to decide how best to frame it first.

Of course, that was the strategy he'd planned to follow with the loan request too—and look how that had turned out.

A wave of queasiness swept over him.

As if sensing that further pushing tonight would be unwise, Christi rose. "How soon do you think you could give me your answer?"

"By the weekend?" That would buy him two or three days to come up with a more solid excuse to refuse.

"There's a meeting Sunday afternoon for all the participants and committee chairs Marci's rounded up. I'm going to present my fleshed-out plan." She waved the sheaf of papers in her hand.

"I can let you know before that."

"Great." She slung her purse over her shoulder. "See you tomorrow, same time, same place."

"Let me walk you out."

"No!" She scuttled toward the door, papers crackling as she crimped them in her fingers, a hint of panic in her eyes. "My, uh, car's close. I won't get lost." She flashed him a smile that seemed shaky around the edges.

Her message was clear.

She didn't want a repeat of Tuesday night's parting.

Neither did he.

"I'll go as far as the porch."

"That works." She slipped out and hightailed it toward her car.

By the time he reached the threshold, she was already sliding behind the wheel of her Nissan.

He waited while she pulled out, watched until her taillights disappeared, then wandered to the kitchen for a glass of water.

A plate of what appeared to be homemade cookies sat on his counter beside the window over the sink.

Christi also baked?

That was definitely not a skill she'd had in St. Louis.

He crossed to the plate, worked the plastic wrap free, and pulled out a cookie. Sank his teeth into the crumbly richness, savoring the flavor as a chocolate chip dissolved on his tongue.

When had he last had homemade cookies—not counting the ones from Sweet Dreams that were as close to home baked as you could get?

Too long ago to remember. The only ones he could recall were his mom's gooey butter cookies. They'd always been his favorite.

But these were a close second. Tender and delectable and tempting, with just the right amount of sweetness.

Like the woman who'd made them.

Jack finished off the cookie in two bites, brushed his hands over the sink, and surveyed the moon that cast a luminous glow on the landscape, mitigating the darkness.

Again, like Christi had done for his world since her arrival.

Determined as he'd been to hold on to the bitterness and wrath and indignation Reverend Baker had referenced from Ephesians last Sunday, that task was becoming more difficult by the day.

Was it time to let them go and do as that passage instructed? Be kind and merciful and forgiving?

He wrapped his fingers around the edge of the sink and held on tight.

That wasn't a place he'd ever expected to reach with Christi—but life had thrown him more than a few curves lately.

Yet if evidence of her transformation continued to mount, one of these days the temptation to kiss her would sweep over him again—perhaps too strong to resist.

And while the ramifications of such a development were a bit daunting, the pros of stepping over that line were definitely beginning to outweigh the cons.

23

Oh my.

Beth let out a slow breath, lowered Steve's most recent letter, and surveyed the empty envelopes on the couch to her left and the box on her right containing the rest of the notes and cards he'd sent. The ones she'd spent the past hour and a half reading—and rereading—on this Saturday morning.

So many words.

So many regrets and apologies.

So much heart.

And following Charley's counsel, she'd listened with *her* heart wide open as she'd read.

Conclusion? It appeared Steve had repented—and changed.

She lifted the last card again. Once more read the words she'd longed to hear through all the years she'd beseeched him to stop trying to push Jonathan into sports and instead appreciate and encourage his son's artistic talent.

> *You were right all along, Beth. I put food on the table for Jonathan, but I neglected to feed his soul. While you recognized his talent early on as a special gift, for me it was*

a disappointment. And that was the crux of the problem. It was always about me. My selfish desires. I wanted to coach Little League. Cheer Jonathan on from the stands in whatever sport he chose. Brag to friends about his athletic abilities.

I'll carry the shame of this profound failure to my grave—along with the grief we share over the loss of the son who added such joy to our days.

If I could change the past, I would. I'd send Jonathan to the art camp you suggested as a graduation gift instead of taking him to the Grand Canyon. I'd seek opportunities for him to develop and showcase his talent. I'd give more than lip service praise to the drawings he showed me. Art isn't my forte, but it was important to him—and I owed him my enthusiasm and support. I should have respected him for who he was instead of trying to squeeze him into the ill-fitting mold I'd created.

As for how I failed you, there are too many ways to mention. I know there is much to forgive. Perhaps too much.

But I'm asking for your pardon anyway—because I love you. I always have, and I always will. Life without you is empty and lonely and bleak. Please give me the opportunity to prove I've seen the light, and that I've changed. All I ask is a chance.

Fingers quivering, she lowered the letter to her lap. Touched the petal of a hydrangea in the bouquet Steve had delivered. The flowers were beginning to wither . . . as her love for her husband had withered in those final months as they argued nonstop over the graduation gift—the apex of their years-long dispute. And it had dried up after Jonathan died, crumbling like an autumn leaf after a hard freeze.

But unlike the flowers in this bouquet, their love had roots—and roots could harbor life, despite a parched landscape.

In fact, wasn't there a Scripture verse about that? In Job, appropriately enough?

Beth pushed herself to her feet, fitted her crutches under her arms, and hobbled to the bedroom. Dug through a drawer in her dresser. Pulled the Bible from beneath a stack of scarves she never wore.

She clamped it under her arm and moved on to the kitchen. After setting it on the table, she lowered herself into a chair and flipped through to Job.

A quick skim brought her to the verse she was seeking.

"For a tree there is hope; if it is cut down, it will sprout again, its tender shoots will not cease. Even though its root grow old in the earth and its stump die in the dust, yet at the first whiff of water it sprouts and puts forth branches like a young plant."

She read through the passage again as a goldfinch launched into its courting song outside the window. Closed the book.

Strange.

She hadn't been praying for guidance. She hadn't been praying period since she'd walked away from God. But it seemed he'd provided it anyway. Through Christi, and Charley's visit, and her sudden recollection of this somewhat obscure but hope-filled verse that spoke of second chances.

For Charley was right about the Almighty. He didn't hold grudges—unlike his sons and daughters, who not only often rejected *him* but harbored resentments against each other.

She sat back in her chair as she listened to the finch's lyrical warble.

Maybe she needed to trust, as Charley had said, that her prayers hadn't gone unheard. That God had, indeed, listened with compassion from his clear view above the human tapestry. A tapestry his children saw from the ragged, messy underside, and who prayed without knowing the big-picture consequence of a positive response to their pleas.

What good, if any, could possibly come of Jonathan's death and her estrangement from Steve was impossible to fathom. But perhaps it was time to put such futile ponderings aside, give her anger and resentment and despair to God, and begin living in the present instead of dwelling on the past.

Outside, a delivery van rumbled by—and all at once her stomach joined in the chorus.

She checked her watch. No wonder. It was lunchtime. And for once, she was hungry rather than merely empty. Her recovery must be progressing—from more than a physical standpoint, considering the little surge of hope lifting her spirits.

So why not leave this confining apartment behind for an hour or two? Her doctor had given his blessing for driving and a return to work on Monday—a mere two days away. A dry run would be reasonable, as would a change of scene.

And she knew just where she wanted to go.

The wharf.

If Charley was cooking today, his tacos would be a perfect lunch. She could sit on a bench near his stand and enjoy the fresh air and sea view.

After running a finger over the embossed cross on the front of the Bible, she stood and maneuvered herself over to the counter to get her purse.

Outside, the finch continued to sing, trying to convince the female who'd become the center of his world to give him a chance.

Sort of like Steve had done with his letters and notes, plus his recent visit and bouquet.

And maybe, while she enjoyed her lunch, she'd find the courage to put aside the protective anger that had kept grief—and Steve—at arm's length. To accept the truth of what the medical examiner had told them after the tragedy—that while the majority of deaths like Jonathan's occurred during extreme exertion, the condition he'd had could also have taken him even in sleep. To admit that putting all the blame on Steve had been wrong.

Perhaps it was time to reach deep inside and open the door to an in-person dialogue. Not today. But soon.

Fifteen minutes later, Charley lifted a hand in greeting as she approached his stand after managing the drive to town without any glitches.

"Now this is a pleasant surprise. You must be on the mend if you ventured into town alone."

"I am. As a matter of fact, I'm going back to work part-time on Monday." She stopped in front of the serving window and sniffed. "Those smell like heaven."

"Not quite—but close. One order?"

"Please."

He set to work, pulling out fish fillets, corn tortillas, and a handful of chopped red onion that he tossed on the griddle. "You picked a beautiful day for your foray back into the world. Are you planning to enjoy your lunch here on the wharf, or take it home?"

Home didn't come anywhere close to describing the apartment where she'd been eating and sleeping for the past eight months.

"I think I'll eat them here." She surveyed the benches along the wharf. All but the farthest one were occupied, and the hike would be too taxing in her current state of recuperation. Her spirits deflated. "Or not, unless someone leaves before my order is ready."

"You could try the park." Charley flipped the fish on the grill.

If the benches were full, the picnic table in the gazebo that graced the tiny park behind the stand wasn't likely available. That was prime veg-out property.

"I suppose I can check." Worst case, she could eat on the small front porch of her unit. Anywhere outside would be an improvement over her minuscule kitchen.

"Couldn't hurt." Charley set the tortillas on the grill and picked up the bottle of his special sauce. "You want to pay me for these on your next visit? It may be tricky to get to your wallet while you're juggling those crutches."

"I came prepared." She balanced one crutch against the side of the stand, pulled several bills from the pocket of her slacks, and laid them on the counter. "I have the tab memorized—but it would be easier if you took credit cards." She tipped her head toward the "cash only" sign taped inside the serving window.

He began assembling the tacos and wrapping them in white paper. "Would it?"

"Of course. Paying with plastic is quick and less messy."

"Also less transparent—and less immediate. Plastic gets a host of people into trouble. Handing over cold, hard cash helps shoppers appreciate the value of what they're buying—or the lack of value. If you ask me, there's too much plastic in the world already . . . in merchandise and in people." He slid the tacos into a bag, along with a bottle of water.

"I didn't pay for the water, Charley."

"On the house. You'll need it to wash down the tacos if you end up staying on the wharf to eat."

"I doubt there's a spot in the park."

"You never know." He lifted the bag. "Can you manage this?"

"Yes." She took it, crimped the top in her fingers, and repositioned her crutch. "Thanks for lunch—and your thoughts on plastic."

"My nugget of wisdom for the day." He gave her another one of his radiant smiles. "I believe in authenticity—in art, in food, in relationships. Being real can make you vulnerable, but the rewards are great." After holding her glance for a moment, he indicated an approaching family group. "More customers in search of a taco fix. Enjoy your lunch, Beth."

As the newcomers took her place at the counter, she navigated to the end of the truck, turned the corner—and jolted to a stop.

The picnic table was occupied, as she'd expected.

What she *hadn't* expected was to see Steve there—with a young boy she didn't recognize.

Her pulse skittered.

Charley had to know her husband was in the park. Steve and the boy were eating tacos. The resident taco maker would have seen them circle the truck toward the gazebo.

Conclusion? He'd set her up. This—along with the wisdom he'd dispensed about the rewards of risking vulnerability—was his attempt to nudge them together.

Hard to fault his benevolent intentions.

But was she ready to initiate the dialogue she'd been mulling over less than half an hour ago?

The decision was taken out of her hands when Steve angled toward her, as if he'd sensed her presence.

Shock flattened his features, and he froze. But a moment later he vaulted to his feet.

The boy beside him looked up, followed Steve's line of sight to her, and spoke.

After a brief, inaudible response, Steve left the gazebo and walked toward her. Slowly, as if he was afraid of scaring her off.

Smart man. If she wasn't tethered to these crutches, she'd be halfway back to her car already.

But thanks to her condition, there was no fast—or graceful—way to exit.

So she waited for him, legs trembling, heart pounding, lungs balking.

He stopped a few feet away. "What are you doing here? Are you alone?"

"Yes." Her response came out shaky, and she took a breath. "My doctor and therapist are happy with my progress, and they've given me the green light to go back to the shop half days starting Monday. I was in the mood for tacos today and decided to venture out. Who's your friend?" She nodded toward the boy.

"A foster kid I met at a school presentation earlier this month. I, uh, kind of took an interest in him. His name's Noah." He shoved his hands in his pockets. "Would you like to join us while you eat?"

Eat lunch with Steve?

No. She couldn't do that.

Or could she? A threesome would break the ice, help ease them into the new territory they were about to explore without the pressures of a one-on-one encounter.

Perhaps this opportunity was a literal godsend.

She tightened her grip on the crutches. Moistened her lips. "If I'm not intruding."

The tension in Steve's features diminished. "Not at all. Let me take that bag for you."

He tugged it from her fingers and stayed within touching distance while she navigated the path to the gazebo.

As she approached the table, the boy ducked his head and gave her a shy smile.

Her step faltered.

Oh, mercy!

With his strawberry blond hair and the sprinkling of freckles across his nose, Noah didn't resemble Jonathan at all at that age—yet there was a quality about him reminiscent of her son. A shyness, an insecurity, a quiet studiousness. Some subtle nuance she couldn't quite pinpoint. The similarity was uncanny.

Was that what had drawn Steve to the boy too?

All at once, Noah's smile dimmed.

Way to go, Beth. Make him more *self-conscious.*

Somehow she managed to coax up the corners of her mouth and resume her trek toward the table. As a foster kid, he could already be dealing with a ton of baggage. She couldn't add to that. "Hi, Noah." She swallowed past the slight tremor in her voice. "Steve invited me to sit with you while I have my lunch. Is that okay?"

"Sure. I guess." He pushed his own meal aside, along with what appeared to be a sketchbook, and slid down the bench.

"This is Noah's first visit to Charley's." Steve took her crutches, rested them against the end of the table, and sat across from her.

"Your first visit? Don't you live around here?" She opened her bag and pulled out a taco.

"No. I live in Coos Bay."

"That's a long drive. Was it worth the trip for Charley's tacos?"

"Uh-huh. But that's not why I came. I'm taking a class at the high school."

"What kind of class?"

"Art. Sergeant Adams signed me up."

Beth transferred her attention to her husband, who wadded up the wrapping paper from his tacos and stuffed it into the bag.

"Charley told me about it. I thought Noah would enjoy it."

"And you're taking him back and forth?"

"Yeah." Noah chimed back in. "We went out for ice cream once too." A dribble of Charley's secret sauce began to track down his chin.

Without stopping to think, Beth picked up a napkin and reached over to wipe it away.

Alarm flared in Noah's eyes, and he jerked back.

She did the math—and her lungs froze. There was abuse somewhere in this boy's background. The faint furrows creasing Steve's forehead suggested he'd come to the same conclusion.

But drawing attention to his behavior would make the boy more uncomfortable.

To lighten the atmosphere, Beth winked at the boy and waved the napkin. "Sorry, Noah. My mom always used to wipe stuff off my face, and I never liked it either." She tapped her chin. "Some of Charley's secret sauce is dripping down here."

Noah's taut posture relaxed, and he picked up his own napkin. Swiped off the sauce. But he kept his distance.

It was clear the boy had trust issues.

"Noah, why don't you show Beth your sketchbook? She likes art. I think she'd especially enjoy seeing the dragonfly and tide pool." Steve used his calm voice. The one he employed on the job whenever someone he was dealing with got spooked.

The boy cast her an uncertain look.

"I'd love to see them, Noah. Please?"

A few beats passed, and then he sidled nearer to her on the bench, sliding the sketchbook along with him. "I'm not real good."

"That's not what Charley said." Steve took a swig of his water.

"Charley's seen your drawings?" Beth waited while Noah flipped the book open to the first page.

"Uh-huh. Sergeant Adams took me to his studio and I showed him my book. It was awesome!"

Again, Beth scrutinized Steve.

Why had he done for this boy what he'd never done for their son?

Or had he homed in on Noah *because* he'd recognized his mistakes with Jonathan and was trying to make amends?

That was a question worth contemplating.

But for now, she gave Noah her full attention while she ate her tacos. Praised his work, offered encouragement, savored his shy smiles and the enthusiasm that sparked in his eyes. Like it once had in Jonathan's.

And as the boy began to respond to her attention, the hope she'd experienced earlier resurged.

Maybe the sudden uptick in her attitude was due to the bright blue sky above, or the inspiring Pelican Point lighthouse visible on the soaring headland in the distance, or the warmth of the sun soaking into her skin, or the expansive view of the cerulean sea and limitless horizon.

Or maybe it came from the uplifting sense that today could be a new beginning—if she found the courage to open her heart to the possibilities ahead.

Steve gave his watch a surreptitious scan. Much as he hated to break up their impromptu picnic, they had to leave.

But Noah would be disappointed. He was having a blast. The boy was completely relaxed now, chatting away with Beth, responding to her genuine interest—as did everyone who entered his wife's orbit. While she claimed to be an introvert, her quiet sincerity was like a magnet for people of all ages. Noah was no exception.

And his reaction earlier when she'd reached toward him was evidence he needed Beth's tender, caring empathy more than most.

Steve uncapped his water, watching the boy. Unless he'd misread that cue, there was abuse somewhere in his background. He'd have to do a bit of digging, see what he could find in the records.

One thing for certain. He hadn't had a mother like Beth.

Steve finished off his water and pulled out his keys.

Noah stopped talking midsentence and shot him a crestfallen look. "Do we have to go?"

"Yes. Your foster dad will be worried if we're late."

He heaved a sigh. Squeezed the wrapper from his last taco into a tight ball. "I guess."

"But don't forget we have a date next Saturday too." Steve stood and gathered up their trash.

"Could we come for tacos again?"

"I don't see why not." He tossed the debris into the receptacle on the edge of the park.

Noah turned to Beth. "Could you come too?"

Rather than respond, his wife took a sip of water.

Fighting back a wave of disappointment, Steve forced up the corners of his mouth. If she was trying to think of a diplomatic way to decline, he ought to help her out. After all, he'd put her in this awkward situation by inviting her to join them. "It appears someone has a new fan. But if you want to play this by ear, see how your knee is, we could—"

"No." She set her empty bottle down. "I can come. I have to be at work by one, though. What time does the class end?"

"Noon." Steve supplied the answer. "We could be here by twelve fifteen. Does that work?"

"Yes."

"Then it seems we have a date."

A flush washed over her cheeks. He could have picked a less-loaded term, but he viewed their meeting as a date. If she saw it as simply an act of charity for a little boy who'd had too many hard knocks, may as well find out.

"Yes. We have a date." She held his gaze.

Thank you, God.

"Awesome!"

The boy's exuberance altered the mood—but Steve could relate to the boy's elation on a different, more personal level.

"We'll walk you back to your car." He handed Beth her crutches and pitched her water bottle.

As they passed the taco stand, he glanced at the counter. At Charley's grin and thumbs-up, he gave the man a small salute.

They slowly traversed the walkway toward Beth's car, Noah beside her while he followed in their wake.

"Did you hurt your leg?" The boy gave her a once-over.

"No. I had to get a new knee—but it will be better soon and I won't have to use these crutches anymore."

"I guess it's lucky you have Sergeant Adams to help you then, huh?"

Whoops.

This was sticky.

"I'm, uh, living by myself now. Here in Hope Harbor." Beth spoke before he could come up with an appropriate response. "I have a shop in town, and it's more convenient to be nearby."

Noah skirted two seagulls sitting on the edge of the path that were watching them with an odd intentness.

Strange that they didn't fly away.

"My mom and dad didn't live together either." Noah hugged his sketchbook tight against his chest. "And my mom . . . she was kind of mad all the time. At first I thought it was because my dad wasn't there. But then I wondered if it could be . . ." His volume dropped, and he kicked at a rock. "If it was my fault."

Another clue that could suggest abuse.

Anger nipped at Steve's composure.

"I'm sure it wasn't, Noah." Beth's voice was gentle—and filled with compassion. "Sometimes moms and dads disagree about certain things, and it's hard for them to live together. Usually it has nothing to do with their child."

But sometimes it did.

The tacos Steve had ingested turned into a hard lump in his stomach.

"Do you want to know what I think?" Beth stopped beside her car, waiting until Noah lifted his chin to continue. "I think your mom was blessed to have a son like you. A child is a precious gift from God. And even though we just met, I can tell you're a very special—and talented—young man. You remind me of someone I loved very much."

"Jonathan?"

Beth telegraphed a question over Noah's shoulder.

"I told him about Jonathan." Steve gave her the short version of the discussion he and Noah had had while driving home from Charley's studio the day of their visit. "How he had a bad heart we never knew about, and that God called him home last summer."

Beth's irises began to glisten, and she gave a small nod. Refocused on Noah. "Yes. He was a wonderful young man. He liked to draw too."

"I know. Sergeant Adams told me. He said you both miss him a bunch."

"Yes, we do."

"I'm sorry he died—but he was lucky to have you guys. I know he didn't live very long, but shorter might be worth it to have a mom and dad who love you." Noah shuffled his toe against the pavement.

Beth's breath caught.

She was trying not to cry.

Steve could relate. The scene around him had blurred as well.

"Noah—would it be all right if I give you a hug before I go?" Beth's question came out choked.

"I guess."

She balanced the crutches against the car and held out her arms, letting the boy come to her. When he did, she drew him to her and held on tight.

Noah didn't seem in any hurry to let go.

At last, however, he stepped back.

"Thank you." Beth touched his arm. "I haven't had a hug like that in a long time."

"I've *never* had one like that."

At the boy's soft admission, pressure built again in Steve's throat.

"We'll do it again next time too. Okay?" Beth managed to give him a shaky smile.

"Okay."

She moved to open her door, but Steve beat her to it, stowing her crutches on the passenger side and shifting aside to let her ease behind the wheel.

"May I call you this week?" He leaned close so she alone was privy to the question. Close enough to touch her. But he didn't. Even if Noah wasn't the only one who could use a hug.

"Yes."

That was all she said—but it was sufficient. It was the opening he'd prayed for.

"Drive safe." He backed away and shut the door.

He rejoined Noah, and they watched while she backed out and drove away.

"She's nice." There was a wistful note in Noah's tone.

"Yes, she is."

"How come she lives here and you live in Coos Bay? Aren't married people supposed to live together?"

"Usually. But sometimes people need a bit of . . . space." He started down the wharf, toward his car.

Noah fell in beside him. "My mom used to say she needed space a *lot*. I think she got tired of having me around. I bet Mrs. Adams never got tired of having Jonathan around."

"No, she didn't."

"And I bet she misses you too."

About that, he was less certain.

"I don't know. She has plenty to keep her busy."

"Busy isn't the same as happy, though. And I think it's better for people in a family to stick together. Then no one would ever get lonely."

Out of the mouths of babes.

Too bad Beth hadn't heard Noah's words of wisdom.

But perhaps in the weeks ahead, with the help of a young boy wise beyond his years, he could prove to her they were true— and convince her to give up her self-imposed isolation and come home at last.

24

Didn't all kids like macaroni and cheese?

Jack surveyed Hannah's half-eaten dinner.

Apparently not.

Or maybe his effort just hadn't passed muster. The instructions on the box had sounded easy—but the cheese shouldn't be this gummy. Nor should the carrots he'd prepared as a side dish require chomping.

Verdict?

His Saturday dinner foray into the kitchen was a bust.

But Hannah didn't like his usual go-to fare from the Myrtle either.

Jack forced down another bite of macaroni.

Sunday dinner tomorrow could end up being takeout from Frank's. The rustic eatery near Bandon was a hole in the wall, but the man made the best pizza this side of the Rockies. Surely his daughter would like that.

He could hope, anyway.

"Are you finished?" He gave up on the macaroni and laid his fork down.

"Uh-huh." She pushed her plate away.

"It wasn't too good, was it?" Avoiding the truth wouldn't change it.

"No." His daughter wrinkled her nose. "The macaroni stuck to my teeth, and the carrots were too crunchy. Christi cooks better than you."

That wouldn't be hard.

"What did you have for dinner last night?" He rose and picked up their plates.

"Fried chicken—'cept she made it in the oven. It was real crunchy and yummy. And she cut up potatoes and made french fries in the oven too."

His mouth began to water. "That would definitely be an improvement over this." He tried to scrape their leftover macaroni and cheese into the trash, but it was glued to the plates.

"A *big* improvement. Why can't she cook for us every day?"

"Because she isn't a cook. I only pay her to stay with you while I'm at work. She doesn't have to cook at all. That was her idea."

"I'm glad she wants to. She said on Monday she'd fix us—"

The doorbell rang, and they both turned toward the living room.

"Do you think that might be Christi?" Hannah jumped to her feet, anticipation brightening her features.

"No." At least he hoped not. He still owed her an answer about the masterclass festival, and he hadn't yet come up with a way to gracefully decline. "But let's find out who it is." He rinsed his hands and strode toward the front of the apartment, Hannah on his heels.

Luis Dominguez was waiting on the other side of the door, one of Eleanor Cooper's legendary fudge cakes in hand. "Good evening. Eleanor asked me to deliver this welcome gift to our newest resident." The Cuban immigrant who was Eleanor's right-hand man smiled at Hannah. "I think that would be you, yes?"

"Yes." Hannah's focus remained fixed on the cake. "Is this from the lady we met at church?"

"The very one." Luis held out the cake, and Jack took it. "She sends her best wishes and hopes you will enjoy it."

"That goes without saying." Jack had sampled the woman's

specialty only twice, but both occasions had been memorable. "Please thank her for us."

"It will be my pleasure. Have a wonderful evening." He gave a slight bow and returned to his car.

"Wow." Hannah continued to ogle the cake as Jack shut the door. "That's awesome."

"I agree. Shall we sample it?"

Hannah caught her lower lip between her teeth. "I think we should invite Christi to have a piece too. That lady told us to share."

Now that was an appealing prospect.

Except she'd expect him to also serve up an answer about the masterclass festival.

"I don't know if we should bother her tonight."

"Why not? I bet she's all by herself. She could be lonesome." Hannah planted her hands on her hips. "Don't you like her?"

Yeah, he did. Too much.

That was the problem.

"I like her."

"Then how come we can't call her and ask if she wants cake? She loves chocolate. We had Hershey's Kisses for dessert last night, and she ate five."

"She worked at the shop all day. She may be tired."

"You could ask her, couldn't you?"

He was out of arguments.

"Fine. I'll give her a call—after I put this in the kitchen."

Resigned, he retraced his steps through the living room. It was probably for the best that the arrival of Eleanor's cake had forced his hand. He'd dragged his feet long enough, and he owed Christi an answer.

So before she arrived, he'd come up with a way to turn her down that would be clear and definitive.

And he would *not* let her undermine his resolve to refuse, as he had with the loan that morning he'd found her sleeping at Sea Glass Cottage.

The *Hope Harbor Herald* editor had outdone herself signing up talent for the masterclass festival.

Christi nibbled on her omelet and perused the list of presenters. There would be sessions offered on photography, painting, furniture making, research and genealogy, chocolate making, acting, lavender crafts, fishing tips, the art of coffee, and gardening. All taught by qualified experts, many with national renown. Quite a few would be concurrent, so several people had agreed to teach duplicate sessions to accommodate the hoped-for demand.

It was a full weekend roster.

There was just one slot yet to fill on the tentative schedule she'd drawn up.

Writing.

Because she had yet to deliver on the one presenter she'd promised to solicit.

Christi poked at her eggs.

Why hadn't Jack called?

And what if he said no?

She sighed and stabbed a bite of omelet. The world wouldn't end if he declined, not with all the talent already committed—but failing to deliver the one presenter she'd promised to ask would be embarrassing.

Should she call him?

But what if—

Her cell began to vibrate, and she picked it up off the table.

Speak of the devil.

Pulse picking up, she pushed talk. "Hi, Jack. Your timing is impeccable. I'm working on material for tomorrow's masterclass festival meeting while I eat dinner." That must be why he'd called, so why pussyfoot around?

"I don't want to interrupt your dinner or your work, but Eleanor

Cooper—the woman who stopped by our pew last Sunday at church—followed through on her promise and sent over one of her famous fudge cakes. Hannah and I wondered if you'd like to join us for dessert."

Huh.

That had come out of nowhere.

Yet sharing a sweet treat with Jack and Hannah would be the highlight of her day.

She inspected the ratty fleece jogging suit she'd donned after work and her stockinged feet. Sighed. Much as she wanted an answer on the masterclass tonight, the thought of changing clothes again and leaving her cozy cottage held zero appeal. After putting in a full week and juggling both of her paying jobs the past two days, the spirit was willing—but the flesh was weak.

However, she could plead her case about the masterclass more effectively in person.

If a change of clothes and a short drive were what it took to get him to commit, so be it.

She marshaled her waning energy and tried for a cheery tone. "I appreciate the invitation. I'll be finished with dinner in a few minutes, and as soon as I change, I can come over."

Several silent seconds ticked by.

"You sound tired."

Her eyebrows rose.

How had Jack picked up on her fatigue?

"I'm fine."

More silence.

"Would you rather we bring the cake to you—assuming you're in the mood for chocolate?"

Yes!

"I'm always in the mood for chocolate."

"I'll take that as an affirmative. Would half an hour work?"

"Are you certain you don't mind driving over?"

"It's not much of a trip. Everything is close in Hope Harbor."

"In that case, let's aim for twenty minutes. I'm almost finished with dinner, and you've whetted my appetite for cake."

"Twenty minutes it is. See you then."

As soon as the line went dead, Christi gobbled down the rest of her omelet, took care of her dishes, gathered up her notes, and pulled a folding chair from the closet to accommodate a third person at the small café table in the bay window. It would be tight—but manageable.

She also detoured to the master bath upstairs. Changing her clothes was too much of an effort, but touching up her mascara and lipstick? Putting on shoes? No problem.

The crunch of gravel on the drive announced the arrival of her guests as she came back down the stairs with three of the twenty minutes to spare. She continued to the door, peeking through the clear glass edge of one of the sea glass mosaic sidelights as Hannah bounded toward the porch while Jack retrieved the cake from the back seat.

As her young charge reached the steps, she opened the door. "This is a lovely surprise."

"It was my idea to share the cake. Well, mine and the lady's who baked it." She continued into the living room, already at home in the cottage where she'd spent the past two evenings. "But *he* was the one who decided we should come here. And I'm glad. This is a happy house."

Happy?

She'd never thought of it in quite those terms—especially after Jack had relayed its history. Yet she did feel safe and contented and at home here. Had from the instant she'd stepped over the threshold that first foggy night. It wouldn't take much to make it a happy place. Just a little love to fill the empty corners.

"Cake delivery." Jack hefted the plate as he approached. "You're in for a treat."

"I can't wait to try it." She closed the door behind him and motioned toward the back of the house. "Let's cut it in the kitchen."

After giving the empty room to the left of the front door a sweep, he took the lead through her sparse living room.

Christi followed as he surveyed the interior.

If he wanted proof she no longer lived the high life, the barebones space offered irrefutable evidence. There hadn't been room for more than a few pieces of furniture in her tiny efficiency in Dallas, and the small couch, upholstered chair, side table, and lamp had been adequate.

Here, they seemed lost.

But they served her needs. And it wasn't as if she was trying to impress anyone.

Never again.

While Hannah busied herself getting plates, forks, and paper napkins, Jack set the cake on the counter, watching his daughter. "You're very at home here."

"I help Christi fix dinner and set the table." She continued with her task, folding the napkins in half diagonally and placing them on the small table.

"She's an excellent helper." Christi stopped a few feet away from the counter. "I put on coffee, if you'd like a cup. And I have milk in the fridge for Hannah."

"Sold. Why don't I pour us each a cup and get Hannah's milk while you cut the cake?"

"You don't want to do the honors?"

He snorted. "After tonight's dinner fiasco, I don't want to get anywhere near food for the rest of the day—except to eat it."

"What happened with dinner?" She opened a drawer and removed a large knife.

"It was yucky." Hannah made a face. "The macaroni was gloppy and the carrots were hard."

Christi arched an eyebrow at Jack.

"Hey. What can I say? I'm a stereotypical bachelor. For the most part I live on cereal, takeout from the Myrtle, and frequent visits to Charley's. But in light of recent developments, I decided to try to up my game. So far I'm striking out."

"Practice makes perfect."

"If you survive the practice. Where are the mugs and glasses?"

"Cabinet to your right."

He opened it, no doubt wondering about the sparse interior. But why buy more than two or three of anything? Tasha had been her only guest the past couple of years.

"This looks delicious." Christi cut into the cake, served up three generous wedges, and leaned close to inhale. "The chocolate aroma alone would make this a bestseller in any bakery."

"Do you want me to carry those to the table?" Hannah was almost licking her lips.

"Yes. Thank you."

She set the knife in the sink and joined the duo in the bay window. Hannah had already claimed the seat in the middle, facing outside, but Jack remained standing.

"Did I forget something?" She hesitated at her chair.

"No. I was waiting for you."

It took a moment for his comment to register.

He didn't intend to sit until she did.

Pressure built in her throat at the courtesy that had been long absent from her life.

Keeping her gaze down, she took her place across from him. "Thank you."

"Can we start?" Hannah was poised to attack, fork in hand.

"By all means." Christi picked up her own fork, broke off a tender bite, and slid it into her mouth. The thick frosting and fudgy cake did a tango on her tongue, dissolving into a delectable, intense, oh-so-satisfying burst of lingering chocolate flavor.

"Wow." Hannah's hushed conclusion said it all.

"I agree." She closed her eyes, savoring the decadent richness. "Have I died and gone to heaven?"

"If you have, I'm right there with you. This is as amazing as I remember." Jack broke off another large bite.

Silence fell as they devoted themselves to the scrumptious cake and splurged on smaller second helpings.

As they scraped their plates clean, Christi leaned back. "I'll have to go on a diet for a week after this."

Jack shook his head. "I don't think that will be necessary. You were always thin, and you've lost weight over the years. Too much."

While she tried to think of a response, Hannah's gaze darted between them. "Did you guys know each other somewhere else? Like when you were kids or something?"

Christi passed the ball to Jack with a glance. Hannah was his daughter, and she'd follow his lead on whatever explanation he wanted to offer.

"I met Christi while I lived in St. Louis." Jack wrapped his fingers around his mug. "But we lost touch until she moved here last month."

"So you were friends once?"

"Yes. We were."

Emphasis on the past tense.

Christi's stomach bottomed out. Perhaps her hopes that she'd repaired some of the damage between them had been in vain.

"How come you didn't stay friends?"

Jack swiped a chocolate crumb off the table with his index finger. "I moved away—and Christi got married."

Hannah's eyes rounded, and the girl turned to her. "You're married?"

Thanks a lot, Jack.

"Not anymore. My husband died."

"Oh, wow." Hannah stared at her. "Like my mom."

Not quite. As far as she knew, no one had mourned—or missed—the cheating liar who'd squandered her inheritance.

Jack must have sensed her train of thought, because he jumped back in. "So Christi came here to start over. Like you did."

Hannah regarded her, face solemn. "It's hard, isn't it?"

"Yes. Very." Christi covered the girl's hand with her own. "But you and I are strong. We'll be okay. Especially since we have people who care about us. That makes all the difference."

"I have Aunt Erica—and him." She slid a peek toward Jack. "But who do *you* have?"

"A very dear friend named Tasha. She lives in Dallas. And I have you now too." She forced up the corners of her lips.

"He can be your friend again too, can't he?" She indicated Jack.

Before she could respond Jack spoke. "Yes."

At the warmth in his eyes, her breath hitched.

Maybe they'd made progress after all.

"Oh, goody! Harpo's here." Hannah pushed her chair back and jumped to her feet.

"Who?" Jack's head swiveled to the window that overlooked the lawn and offered a view of the sea.

"The resident pelican." Christi inspected the large white bird with the oversized orange beak. "Marci lives down the road, and she introduced me to him one day while I was at her house dropping off festival material. He's been hanging out here the past few days, and he and Hannah have struck up an acquaintance."

"Can I go out and see him?" Hannah bounced from one foot to the other.

"Fine by me, as long as Christi approves." Jack deferred to her.

"No objection." This would give her an opportunity to ask for his decision about the masterclass—and do her best to convince him to change his mind if he said no.

Hannah dashed toward the kitchen door, clattered down the steps on the deck, and approached the pelican.

"Won't he fly away?" Jack watched the bird.

"Only if he feels threatened." She exhaled. "Too bad humans don't have such reliable instincts."

He refocused on her. "If they did, I would never have gotten to know you."

Ouch—but fair.

Thank goodness she'd changed.

"The same is true for me, with Wes." She swirled the dregs in her mug.

"*My* instincts are better now." Jack's expression was impossible to interpret.

Curious as she was about what that meant in terms of the two of them, tonight wasn't the time to launch into such a personal discussion. Not when Hannah could come in at any moment. Not when she had to face the chamber of commerce and the town merchants tomorrow and present her plan. A plan that still had a hole in the programming she wanted to fill.

She finished off the last of her cooling coffee and set the mug on the table in front of her. "Can we switch subjects? I know you said you'd get back to me this weekend about the masterclass, but the meeting is—"

His phone pinged, and he held up a finger as he pulled it out. Two parallel grooves appeared on his forehead as he scanned the screen. "I need a minute. Do you mind if I step outside?"

"Not at all. I'll clean up our snack."

They both rose, and he headed for the front door. Let himself out.

Christi carried their dishes to the sink, pausing to watch Hannah interact with the taciturn pelican. He wasn't flying away, but he wasn't getting any chummier either.

A metaphor for Jack.

She wasn't going anywhere, though—and once they had the masterclass situation resolved, she would do her best to convince him once and for all she was worthy to be his friend.

If not much, much more.

25

Cell in hand, Jack left Christi's porch behind, strode to his Jeep, and slid behind the wheel—where he'd be less exposed if she decided to check on him.

Because he wasn't going to respond to the text, despite his implication. It wasn't urgent. But the timing had been providential, giving him an excuse to get away from a situation he wasn't ready to address.

Same strategy he'd used to buy himself a few minutes to decide what to do the morning he'd found her trespassing here.

He tightened his grip on his phone and expelled a breath.

Running away was getting to be a bad habit.

If he didn't want to participate in the festival, he should say so. He didn't have to explain why, no matter how hard she pushed. He was a cop, for crying out loud. Used to taking control of high-pressure situations. Dealing with this should be a piece of cake.

Too bad it wasn't going down as easily as Eleanor's fudge cake had.

He tapped a finger against the steering wheel and watched two seagulls circle over the cottage.

The truth was, he was no more confident of his resolve to say no than he was of his ability to teach paying customers how to write a book.

But he couldn't hide out here forever—much as he wanted to.

Psyching himself up to deal with whatever recruitment persuasion she employed, he left the Jeep and returned to the house.

Christi was still tidying up in the kitchen, and she offered him a tentative smile. "Everything okay?"

"Yeah."

"Would you like a refill?" She indicated his mug on the counter.

"Sure." Another shot of caffeine couldn't hurt.

She crossed to the coffeemaker. "I expect Saturday-night calls aren't all that unusual in a job like yours."

She'd assumed the call was work-related.

No reason to tell her otherwise.

"More unusual than not in a town the size of Hope Harbor—but they can happen."

"How did you end up in law enforcement, anyway? I wouldn't have pegged you for that sort of career." She filled the mug and handed it over.

"I took a class in criminal justice at Western Oregon University after I went back to college. I was already working on a book, I had an elective open, and I thought the subject matter would give me useful background. It did—but it also sucked me in. I took a few more classes, realized the job would be a fit, and ended up changing my major."

"Did you come here straight after graduation?"

"No. My first job was in Coos Bay. I found Hope Harbor while tooling around the area in my free time and knew this was where I wanted to settle. As soon as there was an opening, I applied. There's something special about this place."

"I hear you." She took a sip of her coffee. "I imagine your career gives you valuable insights and inside information for your novels."

"A side benefit."

"So how's the next book coming?"

He appraised her over the rim of his mug. Was she trying to segue back into the discussion about the festival—or was she genuinely interested in his writing?

The silence lengthened, and soft color stole over her cheeks. "Sorry. I didn't mean to pry. But I imagine it would be difficult to concentrate on a creative project when your world's been disrupted."

"It has been." There was no downside to admitting that. In fact, there *might* be an upside. Maybe he could use the need to make up time as an excuse to decline her request about the festival. "I try to work every night for a couple of hours after my shift ends, but it's been a slow slog. I'm losing ground on my deadline."

Her features softened. "More pressure you don't need right now." She motioned toward the back door. "Why don't we sit on the deck? The space is kind of tight, but it's relaxing out there—and the view is world-class."

"Fine by me." Anything that could help him chill was worth a try.

She took the lead, claiming one of the two folding chairs tucked close together on the tiny deck.

Too close.

She hadn't been kidding about the tight quarters.

This may not have been the best idea after all.

"I won't bite, Jack." She cradled her mug in her fingers, a teasing glint flashing in her irises.

"That's what you said the day we met at your dad's house." When she'd stopped to talk to the newest landscaping employee—and put him in her sights.

"Oh." Her amusement faded. Shoulders drooping, she swirled the dark liquid in her mug. "I guess my past behavior will haunt me forever—no matter how hard I try to atone for my mistakes." She let out a slow breath and looked up at him. "You aren't going to do the masterclass, are you?"

He claimed the chair beside her, keeping as much distance as possible between them in the confined space—and pushed out the word. "No. But it has nothing to do with our history. Bottom line, I don't have a spare minute to put together a class—especially on a subject I'm not qualified to teach."

"You're successful. That's a decent credential."

"I'm not an expert on writing, Christi. I don't have any formal training. I was just a guy who wanted to write a thriller, and after a number of false starts, the stars happened to align. My success is due as much to luck as talent—maybe weighted more toward luck. On top of that, the subject matter in my book ended up coinciding with world events. The timing of the release worked to my advantage."

"You think your success was a fluke?"

"It's possible."

She shook her head. "No, it's not. I read your book. It blew me away. All the critical accolades were spot-on."

A rush of pleasure washed over him at her praise, even if he wasn't convinced any of the acclaim he'd received was warranted. "I appreciate the vote of confidence—but a stellar debut doesn't guarantee future success."

"Which translates to more pressure."

"Yeah."

She studied him, and her sharp, insightful perusal suggested she was peeking behind the curtain. Seeing more than he wanted her to see.

Her next question confirmed that. "Are you struggling with the second book?"

He shrugged, watching Hannah attempt to cozy up to Harpo. So far, the bird was playing hard to get. "Trying to write late at night after working a full shift isn't ideal. And I don't think it's fair to leave Hannah on her own for long stretches while I write. At least not until she settles in."

"Hmm." Christi sipped her coffee. "Would it help if I picked her up after Beth relieves me at Eye of the Beholder instead of you dropping her off here on your way to work? That would give you ninety minutes to write before your shift. You'd be fresher, and you wouldn't have to worry about her being on her own."

That was an unexpected—and tempting—offer. An hour and a half a day of focused writing could produce a fair number of pages every week, relieve some of the pressure of the fast-approaching deadline.

But it didn't seem fair to Christi.

"You already spend eight hours a day with her."

She glanced at his daughter, and the corners of her lips flexed. "Can I tell you the truth? It doesn't seem like work. I almost feel guilty for taking your money."

"Don't. I was at my wit's end trying to find suitable day care. It was a win-win."

"I think I got the better part of the deal—but in any case, my offer stands. And in the interest of full disclosure, I do have an ulterior motive."

He took a sip from his mug. "Such as?"

"First, let me be clear that my offer about Hannah isn't contingent on this—but it did occur to me that if I could free up your time a bit, you might be able to squeeze in the necessary prep for a masterclass."

He stifled a groan.

Despite his no, she wasn't giving up.

And she'd deflated his argument about being stretched too thin by offering a solution.

However, despite her insistence that his bestseller status was a sufficient credential, she hadn't solved his insecurity issues.

It appeared he'd have to reveal a tad more than he'd prefer about his deeper-seated reservations.

"To tell you the truth, Christi, I wouldn't know where to start."

"I could help you." She leaned closer, the setting sun gilding her classic profile as she rested her slender fingers on his forearm. "Not with the technical part. I have no writing talent. But in terms of content and organization. I'm sure we could find a structure that would be a comfortable fit."

Too bad he wasn't.

"Is that your intuition talking?" He hitched up one side of his mouth, trying to ignore the warmth seeping into his skin from her hand.

"Yes. And *my* instincts have improved with age too." Her generous lips curved up again. Soft. Appealing. Tempting.

His resolve began to slip.

Blast.

Better deflect until he could shore up his defenses.

"Let me ask you this." He cleared his throat and lifted his mug, forcing her to retract her hand. "Why is my participation such a big deal?"

She sat back in her chair and waved a hand over the peaceful panorama. "Because I've fallen in love with Hope Harbor. When I heard at the chamber of commerce meeting how the drop in tourism was hurting the merchants, I felt compelled to do everything I could to help support the town—including lining up talent that will sell tickets for the festival."

In the quiet that followed, his conscience rumbled to life.

He loved this town too.

And while his livelihood didn't depend on tourism, his patrols put him in contact with many merchants who *did* rely on visitors to keep them afloat.

If Christi, as a brand-new resident, was willing to spearhead a project to help the town, shouldn't he at least agree to play a minor role? Even if that meant he had to step outside his comfort zone? Pump up his self-confidence? Pretend he knew more than he did?

You know the answer, Colby.

Yeah, he did. Unfortunately.

He squirmed as the distant, doleful blare of the foghorn in town wafted through the air, suggesting visibility-reducing fog had rolled in and obscured the safe harbor.

Maybe he ought to reconsider. After all, there was no guarantee anyone would want to hear what he had to say. Perhaps only a handful of people would sign up for his session. If that was the case—and he fell flat on his face—there would be few witnesses.

In addition, beyond doing his part—however small—to help the town, there was another upside to volunteering. It would appease the publicity folks at his publishing house who were always after him to raise his profile and make public appearances.

He squeezed his mug as his resolve to stay the course began to slip. “Your altruism is giving me a major guilt trip.”

“That wasn’t my intent.”

“Nevertheless, it worked. I’ll take you up on your offer with Hannah, and . . .” He gritted his teeth. *Just do it, man.* “And you can sign me up for a slot.”

Sparks of excitement lit up her blue irises. “Seriously?”

“Yes—but don’t expect an overwhelming response.” Best to dampen expectations—for both their sakes. “Hope Harbor is off the beaten path, and I doubt there are many people in the area who’ve read my book.”

“You may be surprised. With the roster of talent we have, I’m hopeful we’ll attract people from all over the state—and beyond. Plus a ton of media, if the publicity Marci has planned does its job.”

That did *not* add to his comfort level.

“So what do I have to do in the immediate future?”

“Come to the kickoff meeting tomorrow, if you can. It’s at four o’clock at Grace Christian.”

“I’d have to bring Hannah.”

“No problem. The more the merrier.”

Merry was pushing it. His daughter would no doubt be bored—and he’d be battling second thoughts.

“You’re not going to bail on me already, are you?” She squinted at him.

Weird how she could read his mind.

“I said I’d do it—and I keep my promises.”

The tension around her eyes relaxed. “I know that. You were always a man of honor.”

As their gazes connected—and held—electricity began arcing between them.

An alert started beeping in his mind.

He had to get out of here. Now.

Straightening up in his chair, he twisted his wrist and scanned his watch. "We should be going."

"You'll miss the sunset if you leave now. It's quite a view from here." She sank back in her seat and motioned toward the western sky, where the golden orb was dipping toward the horizon through the trees on the headland. "I don't have time to enjoy it often, but it's always a treat. God was definitely watching out for me the night I stumbled onto this place in the fog."

"And almost got cited for trespassing."

A dimple appeared in her cheek. "But a certain police officer took pity on me."

"I wasn't the only one. How did you convince the owner of this place to give it to you rent-free, anyway?" There had to be more background to the arrangement than she'd shared.

"Like I said weeks ago, I didn't initiate the rental. The offer came out of the blue."

She was sticking with her story. And unless he was misreading her, it was the truth.

"Have you had any contact with the owner since you moved in?"

"No."

"Strange."

She cocked her head. "I agree—but I'm sensing there's a deeper meaning to that comment."

Her people-reading skills were formidable.

Why not tell her the truth about his interest? It wasn't as if *she* was in a position to buy the place if it ever came on the market.

"I tried to rent the cottage myself. More than once. I also tried to buy it. No go."

"Do *you* know who owns it?"

"No. The person's identity is shrouded in layers of secrecy."

Her forehead wrinkled. "If the owner was concerned about security, as the management company claimed, why would he or she offer it to me instead of a cop?"

Bingo.

"I don't have that answer."

"The plot thickens—but we'll have to solve that mystery another day. The bonding session appears to be over." Christi nodded toward the lawn as Harpo flapped his wings and took off, leaving Hannah to watch as he soared toward the sunset. A few seconds later, his daughter trotted toward them.

Once she joined them, the electricity subsided to a manageable thrum, so he stayed for the sunset. But after the glowing sphere dipped below the horizon, there was no excuse to linger—especially after Hannah let loose with a huge yawn.

"Someone's getting tired." He picked up the mug he'd set on the deck beside his chair.

"No, I'm not." She regarded him from her seat on the steps.

"Well, I am." He stood.

His daughter sighed. "I don't want to go. I like it here."

Better than at your apartment.

She didn't have to say the words for the message to come through loud and clear.

"You'll be back Monday. And you'll see Christi tomorrow. We have to go to a meeting for a project she's in charge of."

"The festival?"

He looked at Christi.

"I told her about it yesterday. No personalities mentioned." Christi stood too.

"Yes. It's for the festival." He emptied the remains of his coffee over the side of the railing.

"How come you have to go?"

"Christi thinks people may want to hear me talk about the books I write."

"Why?"

Excellent question.

"Your dad is kind of famous in the book world, Hannah." Christi stepped in. "People all over the country have bought his novel."

Actually, all over the world. But that didn't mean anything in terms of attracting a crowd to the Hope Harbor festival.

"I thought you were a policeman." Hannah regarded him.

"I am. That's my main job. I write my books before or after my shift."

"Is that what you do late at night?"

"Yes. How did you know about that?"

She fingered the edge of her sweater. "Sometimes I wake up. I heard tapping one night, so I looked in your room and saw you at the computer."

"That won't happen from now on. Christi's going to pick you up after lunch and I'll write before I go to work instead of at night."

Hannah considered him. "How come you write books, anyway?"

Because he'd been graced with the gift of words. Because he liked using that talent to entertain and uplift people. Because he enjoyed writing tales where the good guys won and justice prevailed. Because the stories inside him clamored to get out.

But he said none of that.

"I like to tell stories."

"Hmph." She seemed unimpressed. "Will the meeting last long?"

"Not if I have anything to say about it." Christi smiled and laid a hand on the girl's shoulder. "No one wants to spend their Sunday afternoon in a conference room. Now let's go collect your cake and then you two can be off."

Jack insisted she keep a couple of generous pieces for herself, and after a half-hearted protest, she capitulated.

Juggling the remains of the cake in his hand, he followed her to the front door, Hannah trailing behind.

"Thanks for the treat tonight—and for agreeing to do a masterclass." She twisted the knob and pulled the door open.

"You made it hard to say no."

"I wish my persuasive powers had been as effective with a few of my creditors in the past two years." Her mouth contorted into a wry twist. "Drive safe going home. Good night, Hannah." She pulled the girl into a warm hug.

Nice send-off.

Too bad he wasn't next in line.

But if she got that close to him, the chocolate on the cake he was holding would probably melt. Because a hug with Christi wouldn't just be warm. It would sizzle.

And it was too soon for that.

Way too soon.

Every scrap of evidence suggested her days of artifice and manipulation and self-centeredness were over—but there was no need to rush into a deeper relationship. If they were meant to have any sort of future, that would be revealed to them in time.

He lifted a hand in farewell, then walked back to the Jeep beside Hannah.

After securing what was left of the cake in the back seat, he slid behind the wheel, put the car in gear, and crunched down the gravel drive toward Pelican Point Road.

"Christi's nice."

"Yep." But he didn't want to discuss her with his daughter. "You and Harpo seemed to be getting along well tonight."

"He's letting me come closer—but if I move too fast, he flies away. Christi says I have to be patient and wait until he's ready to be my friend."

Wise counsel.

And perhaps she was following her own advice with the wary man who'd fallen hard for her long ago. Waiting patiently for him to accept that the Christi Reece who lived in Hope Harbor wasn't anything like the socialite who'd dazzled—and deceived—him eleven years ago.

He pulled onto the paved road and hung a right, the lights from

Sea Glass Cottage twinkling through the trees in his rearview mirror as he drove away.

If that was the case, it was possible her patience would be sorely tested.

For he wasn't about to venture into what could be an emotional minefield until he was as certain as possible that this go-round, his heart wouldn't take a devastating hit.

26

Once again, the turnout was huge for the chamber of commerce meeting—and the butterflies in Christi's stomach were becoming more frenetic by the minute as the clock inched toward four o'clock.

Five minutes and counting.

She searched the room from beside the seat Marci had saved for her in the front row. No sign of Jack yet—but he'd show. He wasn't the type of guy who let people down.

"Afternoon, Christi."

At Reverend Baker's greeting, she swiveled around.

He held out his hand as he approached. "You zipped out after the service this morning—understandable in light of today's meeting—but I wanted to express my appreciation for the splendid idea you brought forward to generate more business in our charming town."

She returned his warm clasp. "I just hope it does the job."

"I have every confidence it will. God works in wondrous ways. He brought a newcomer into our midst who recognized the incredible talent we have right under our noses and showed us how to tap into that. Your suggestion was inspired."

"If you're seeking inspiration, I'm at your service." Father Murphy hustled over, beaming a smile their direction. "What can I help you with, my son?" He nudged the minister with his elbow.

"Very funny." Reverend Baker planted his fists on his hips. "What are *you* doing here?"

"Volunteering. The business of saving souls is also affected by Hope Harbor's current economic crisis. Money worries can distract people from other priorities. I intend to do my part to alleviate those so the good people of this town can focus on spiritual, rather than temporal, matters."

"And what part might that be? This festival is supposed to feature masters in their fields. Please don't tell me they signed you up to lead a session on Scripture studies—or, heaven forbid, plumbing." He gave an exaggerated shudder.

Christi did her best to contain the tug on her lips. The banter between these two was just what she needed to dispel her nerves.

"May I remind you which congregation is the reigning champion of our annual Bible trivia contest? And my plumbing fix worked fine at the rectory. Who knew it would unleash Niagara Falls at *your* house? You have weird pipes." The priest gave a dismissive wave. "As for my role in the festival—I'm going to assist Pete Wallace with his class on gardening."

"Ah. An assistant. I suppose that's safe. Less chance to do serious damage." The minister refocused on her. "Pete owned a landscaping company before he retired and moved to Hope Harbor. And I have to admit, my Catholic counterpart here"—he hooked a thumb toward the priest—"does have a beautiful meditation garden at St. Francis. You should stop in if you're passing by."

"Yes, please do, Christi. As the sign over the entrance says, all are welcome." Father Murphy transferred his attention to his fellow cleric. "Now that we've established I have a legitimate reason to be part of this talented crowd, why are *you* here?"

A tap sounded on the microphone, and Marci called the meeting to order.

"Saved by the rhetorical bell. Aren't you lucky?" Father Murphy grinned at the minister. "Where are you sitting?"

"In the back." He motioned toward the rear.

"I'll join you."

The two clerics switched to a discussion about golf as they wandered off, and Christi gave the room one last sweep.

Still no sign of Jack.

Odd.

But she couldn't dwell on his absence. She had to psych herself up to run this meeting once Marci introduced the committee heads.

Which the *Herald* editor did with alacrity.

"And now, please welcome the woman who came up with this phenomenal plan—our fearless leader . . . Christi Reece."

Fearless?

Ha.

She was shaking inside and out.

Yet when she stood and faced the assembled group from behind the mic, she saw only encouraging—and grateful—smiles. Marci had assured her she wouldn't be in this alone, and the one-for-all, all-for-one vibe wafting toward her was heartening.

Jack had also arrived and claimed a seat off to the side, with Hannah. The thumbs-up he gave her, along with Hannah's wave, also helped quiet her nerves.

Okay.

She could do this.

After setting her notes in front of her, she laid out her vision for the structure of the festival. They'd launch with the usual farmers' market, spiced up with free entertainment and enhanced by a ticketed sample-of-Hope-Harbor food tent. Concurrent masterclass sessions would be scheduled on Saturday, if demand warranted. More entertainment was on the roster for Saturday night. The schedule would be open on Sunday morning, giving those who were inclined an opportunity to attend church or visit the lighthouse. The last round of sessions would begin at noon and wrap up by three o'clock so attendees could return home and be ready for the workweek.

"In terms of programming—we have a stellar lineup, as you already know. We'll have to find venues for all the sessions, but possibilities include the church halls, the special event facility at the lighthouse, and local schools. We're open to other suggestions. Like Marci said, we do have to fast-track our planning. A five-week start-to-finish schedule is ambitious—but necessary if we want to salvage the summer tourist season."

And she intended to hammer out as many details as possible in the meeting with committee heads on Tuesday night so they could announce a detailed agenda over the weekend and begin taking ticket orders next week.

"Before I turn this back over to Marci to wrap up, I'd like to open the floor to any comments or questions." Christi positioned her notebook in front of her and picked up her pen.

Beth raised her hand, and as Christi acknowledged her, the woman maneuvered herself to her feet. "I do have one thought. Many of the people we hope to attract may be parents. I wonder if we should add a few classes for the children who attend. That could be an added draw."

"Excellent suggestion, Beth. Do you have any specific ideas?"

"Well, in keeping with the theme, I could see an art class of some sort. There's one being held now at the high school, taught by an instructor from a college in Coos Bay. I'm certain we could find qualified local people to teach those kinds of sessions."

Several other youth-centered ideas followed, from asking a state park ranger to do a hands-on tide pool session for kids at Starfish Pier to a tutorial on sandcastle building. The local first-grade teacher also offered to recruit her coworkers to provide supervised day care for parents with children too young to participate in the other activities.

Christi furiously scribbled notes as the discussion took on a life of its own, ranging from venues and ticket prices to a myriad of other subjects.

By the time Marci came back to the podium and adjourned the meeting, the excitement in the room was almost tangible.

"I am *so* pumped." Marci joined Christi in the front row as the noise level in the hall grew and attendees began to mingle or depart. "This is going to be phenomenal! I can feel it."

"There's a ton of enthusiasm, that's for sure. Did you ever manage to connect with Rose Fitzgerald about opening up her estate to tours?"

Marci made a face. "Just an hour before this meeting. No go on the tours."

"That's a shame."

"I know—but she did promise to make a generous contribution to help offset the cost of the event. I'm still bummed, though. A unique opportunity to see a historic home usually closed to the public would have been a coup. I'll let the committee know Tuesday night at our meeting that she declined."

"Speaking of the meeting—would you mind if I bring Jack's daughter?" She'd have to clear that with him, but it was doubtful he'd object. Especially in light of his participation in the festival.

"Not at all. She was quiet as a mouse today." Marci peered through the crowd toward the father-daughter duo. "I do need a bio and headshot from Jack ASAP for my publicity campaign. I want to launch the festival Facebook page Tuesday with teasers and speaker bios to spark interest. Could you catch him before he leaves and ask him to send those to me? I have to grab Reverend Baker and confirm the hall for a few more meeting dates."

"Sure. But I'll have to move fast." She rose on tiptoe to see over the crowd. "I think he's about to escape."

"Have at it. Email is fine for the info." Marci sped off toward the minister.

Christi snatched her purse from the chair and wove through the crowd, keeping Jack in sight as she paused to respond to greetings, thanks, and questions.

Fortunately, Charley had waylaid him near the door.

As she approached, all three of them looked her direction.

"Wonderful meeting, Christi." Charley touched the brim of his Ducks cap in salute. "I predict this event will be a great success."

"From your mouth to God's ears."

"Don't rule that out." His eyes began to twinkle. "Now I'm off to paint. Enjoy the rest of this beautiful Sunday." He winked at Hannah and strolled toward the exit.

Jack pulled out his keys, suggesting he was ready to leave too.

Shoot. He must not be in the mood to chitchat—or linger.

"I don't want to detain you, but I have a message from Marci." She passed it on, along with the woman's email address, then spoke to Hannah. "How are you today, sweetie?"

"Okay, I guess. But he spilled tomato sauce on my sweater." Glaring at Jack, she held out the bottom of the garment, where a very faint stain was visible.

"That's why we were a few minutes late." He frowned at the sweater. "I was trying to get it out."

"I can still see it." Tears welled on Hannah's lower lashes.

"Why don't we work on it again tomorrow afternoon?" Christi smoothed a hand over the girl's hair. "I bet we can fix this. Your dad was in a hurry today because of the meeting." She looked at Jack. "What did you use?"

"Dish detergent and water."

"Not laundry stain remover?" His blank expression gave her the answer. "Never mind. I'll try that tomorrow." She transferred her attention back to Hannah—and switched to a less-charged subject. "What did you think of the meeting?"

"I liked the part about classes for kids. I've been to the tide pools, but the other ones would be fun." She sidled closer. "We're gonna get a pizza for dinner. Do you want to come with us? We could have more cake too."

The sudden grooves that appeared on Jack's forehead indicated he hadn't been consulted about—nor was he receptive to—that suggestion.

She quashed a surge of disappointment.

It wasn't as if her evening would be idle, after all. Between festival planning and a scheduled call with Tasha to get an update on her moving plans to KC and the restaurant, she'd be busy until she went to bed.

"Thank you for thinking of me, but I—"

"Christi, do you have a minute?"

At the question, she pivoted. Tried to call up the name of the woman who was going to run the lavender session. Jeannette. That was it. And the interruption couldn't be more perfectly timed—from Jack's perspective. He was off the hook about the invitation.

"Sure." She angled back toward the father-daughter duo. "Would you two excuse me?"

"No problem. We'll see you tomorrow." Jack hustled a protesting Hannah toward the door.

Although Christi tried to give Jeannette her full attention, she couldn't quite mute the distracting question that kept looping through her mind.

What would it take to convince Jack once and for all that the shallow girl who'd dazzled him almost a dozen years ago had become a responsible woman who was worthy of his love?

Her knee was throbbing tonight. Bad. But the painkillers made her loopy.

Maybe she could muscle through.

Beth shifted in the chair on the front porch of her apartment, grimacing as she adjusted the leg she'd propped on the lower rung of the railing. She may have overdone it the past two days, trekking to the meeting this afternoon at Grace Christian and to Charley's yesterday.

Yet both trips had been worthwhile. Christi's festival idea was mobilizing the merchants, and the impromptu lunch on the wharf had been a solid first step toward a reconciliation with Steve.

A Jeep pulled into a parking spot farther up in the apartment complex, catching her attention. Seconds later, Jack and his daughter emerged. He didn't notice her in her tucked-away spot as he reached into the back seat and withdrew a pizza box—and that was fine. She wasn't in the mood for conversation.

At least not with a neighbor.

Steve?

Different story.

She eyed the cell she'd set on the railing—within easy reaching distance. Where it had been ever since their meeting in the park yesterday, when he'd asked if he could call and she'd said yes.

". . . Christi eat with us?"

The young girl's voice floated toward her on the breeze, and she looked back toward Jack's unit again.

His response was inaudible.

But one thing was clear.

The mistake Christi had come to Hope Harbor to address was somehow connected to Jack. She hadn't mentioned him by name—but he had to be the person she'd claimed to have hurt very badly. How else would she have known him well enough after her brief tenure to step in and help with his daughter's unraveling sweater? Why else would her glance have strayed his direction so often at the meeting today? What other explanation could there be for her obvious disappointment when he'd hurried out the door afterward, leaving her to talk with Jeannette?

Those two had a history, no question about it.

And Christi claimed the problems in their past had been her fault. That she hadn't been a nice person.

Hard to believe, in view of the woman she was now.

Yet if what she alleged was true, she'd undergone a dramatic transformation. While Jack may not yet be convinced of that, it was obvious to anyone without his judgment-clouding history that she was a fine person.

Proving people could change.

As Steve had, from all appearances.

Beth watched the man and girl ascend the steps and disappear inside with their pizza—sans Christi, despite his daughter's entreaties. Meaning the rift between them hadn't been repaired. He was holding on to his grudge.

She could relate.

Hurts that ran deep were hard to heal.

But if people changed . . . if remorse was real . . . didn't withholding forgiveness end up hurting the victim as much as the offender?

The answer was obvious.

Yes.

Resentment and rancor could also turn rancid, leading to a lens of bitterness that distorted a person's view of the world—as she'd discovered during these past months of solitary living.

That wasn't how she wanted to spend the rest of her life.

Beth scanned the sky to her right, where the sun was descending toward the sea that was hidden from view, tinting the billowy clouds pink and gold. It was the kind of view she and Steve had often enjoyed together as the day wound down.

And would again, if she went home.

That wasn't a decision she had to make tonight, though. The two of them would have to talk first. Listen. Reconnect. Recommit.

Then, if they agreed to give it another go, perhaps the Almighty would temper their grief and help them embrace new opportunities that would grace their marriage for all the years to come.

27

She was asleep again. Third night this week.

As the clock ticked toward midnight, Jack closed the front door with a quiet click and surveyed the scene in his living room.

Christi was on the couch, head tipped back against the upholstery, laptop on one side, papers strewn across the cushion on the other. Much like the first night he'd found her there. A lined tablet rested in her lap, and her pen lay on the floor where it must have fallen after she'd nodded off.

His prediction had come true. Working two paying jobs plus spearheading the ambitious festival project was taking a toll.

He moved a few steps closer and extracted his keys—his usual wake-up call.

But he didn't jingle them.

Instead, he studied the face that had haunted his dreams for years. More seasoned now but still beautiful despite fine lines at the corners of her eyes and faint, permanent creases in her brow.

At this range, there was also clear evidence of fatigue. Pale blue shadows beneath her lower lashes. A slight pallor unrelated to her fair complexion. Too-prominent cheekbones that suggested weight loss.

In light of everything he'd been hearing from the various merchants he'd encountered during his rounds this week, her exhaustion was warranted. Apparently she'd been barreling full speed ahead on the festival since Tuesday night's committee-head meeting.

In fact, according to Beth—who'd summoned law enforcement this afternoon to investigate a suspicious vehicle parked across from her shop that was gone by the time he arrived—Christi was giving Marci a run for her money in the dynamo department. Steve's wife had regaled him with a litany of her new clerk's many fine attributes.

Cementing his initial hunch that he'd been summoned to the shop on spurious grounds.

He tightened his grip on the keys. Ran the pad of his thumb over one bumpy edge.

In light of the sweater disaster she'd been recruited to help with—and the smiling reference she'd made to a dinner date with Steve the prior night—Beth may have realized he and Christi had a history and had morphed into matchmaker mode. As his mother had told him long ago when his best friend in high school kept trying to fix him up with his girlfriend's sister, people in the throes of romance liked to spread the wealth.

Trouble was, he didn't need any encouragement with Christi. It was getting harder and harder to resist her charms.

Like now, as he watched her slumber—her features relaxed, at peace, unguarded.

However, she would *not* appreciate being gawked at while in such a vulnerable state. Nor was that his style.

He lifted his hand and jingled the keys.

She stirred at once, sending another sheet of paper wafting toward the floor. Knuckling her eyes, she righted herself. "What time is it?"

"Eleven twenty-five." He cleared the huskiness from his voice.

"Shoot. I lost an hour." She powered down the laptop and began to gather up her papers. "I'll have to finish after I get home."

"You ought to sleep instead."

She dismissed that suggestion with a flip of her hand. "A highly overrated luxury. I'll catch up on my z's after the festival." She tapped the papers into a neat pile and grinned at him, animation erasing the last vestiges of sleep from her features. "I have big news."

"Must be positive." He retreated a few feet and sat in the chair across from her.

"Yep. Marci emailed me earlier this evening. The teasers she's been putting out have been generating a huge amount of interest and questions. Area media have been calling her, and she's even heard from two outlets in Portland that want to do stories—including a TV station. Isn't that awesome?"

Yes—but not as awesome as the flush of excitement that had chased away Christi's pallor and added exponentially to her appeal.

Not thoughts he should be entertaining at this hour of the night, with their chaperone asleep.

He pushed them aside and concentrated on her question. "To be honest, I'm not surprised. Marci knows how to get attention in the press. She saved the lighthouse on Pelican Point."

"I know. I've heard that story from multiple people. She's legendary in these parts."

"She's also a savvy marketer. But without unique material, it's hard to get noticed—and you provided that. The masterclass festival is a one-of-a-kind event. For this area, anyway. Far more noteworthy than the standard farmers' markets and sandcastle contests found all along the coast. I expected the press to eat it up."

"I wasn't as confident—but I'm glad you were right. And there's more. People are clamoring for the registration information she's going to post on Monday. If the initial response is any indication, it appears we'll be doing quite a few duplicate, concurrent sessions." A dimple dented her cheek. "Guess which presenter is drawing the most interest?"

Uh-oh.

"I don't think I'm going to like this."

"You aren't—but facts are facts. Your bio has gotten the most hits and comments. *You* may be worried about your credentials, but it's clear readers have no such qualms. That should reassure you."

No, it didn't. Just the opposite. It added to the pressure to come up with a memorable and worthwhile session.

"I guess I better get to work on my presentation."

"My offer to help you organize it stands. I bet we could have the framework done in one session."

"And when would you shoehorn that into your already-packed schedule?"

"We could do it on a Saturday or Sunday afternoon."

"That's your only downtime."

"If I'm not helping you, I'll be working on the festival. I could squeeze in a brainstorming session for a worthy cause."

"I'll tell you what. Let me take a stab at it. If I hit a roadblock, I'll keep your offer as a backup plan."

She hesitated, as if she was thinking about pursuing the subject, but after a few moments she stacked her papers on top of her laptop, pulled her keys from her purse, and stood. "I should go. Eight o'clock will roll around all too fast."

"It *is* getting late." For her, not for him. Now that he didn't have to work on his book into the wee hours, he was getting a decent amount of sleep—unlike the woman across from him.

"I know—and there are a couple of tasks I want to finish tonight. I also owe our facilities chair a follow-up email."

"Couldn't all that wait until tomorrow? I'm sure Beth wouldn't mind if you worked on the project at the shop. There must be lulls between customers—and everything you're doing will benefit her too."

"She's 100 percent supportive. But after the Facebook page went live, there was an uptick in customers, which has kept me busy. Marci predicted that would happen. She said once you raise a town's visibility, interest grows in general—and people begin to visit. I don't think anyone expected a perceptible impact this fast, but there seems to be more traffic on Main Street in the past two days. Or that could be wishful thinking."

No, it wasn't. There *were* more cars on the streets—but he hadn't attributed the busyness to the festival project.

Maybe he ought to take a look at that Facebook page Marci had created.

"It's not your imagination. I noticed it too. It didn't register, because that's typical during the summer season, especially around weekends. But it's a significant increase over what we've been seeing this May."

"Good to know—and I'll take it as a hopeful omen for the future too." She resettled the material in the crook of her arm. "Let me know if you decide you want to toss around presentation ideas."

"I will." He crossed to the door and opened it for her. "Drive safe."

Again, she hesitated. As if she was hoping he'd offer to walk her to the car.

Not happening.

She might have decided *she* was ready to test the waters of a new relationship, but he wasn't there yet—even if the thought of a kiss in the dark by her car was tempting.

Very tempting.

However, he wasn't a naïve, bedazzled country boy with unruly hormones anymore. He could summon up the willpower to remain hands-off for a while. Wait-and-see was the safest strategy.

But if no red flags went up over the next few weeks—and he survived his presentation?

All bets were off.

"How come you keep looking toward the street?"

At Noah's question, Steve refocused on the boy seated across from him at the picnic table in the park.

"I'm watching for Beth."

"Are you afraid she won't come?" Noah gathered up a few stray pieces of purple cabbage from the white butcher paper that served as his plate and put them back in his taco.

"No." Not after their dinner Thursday night at the upscale restaurant in Coos Bay that had long been their favorite special occasion place.

An appropriate choice for their date—because Thursday *had* been a special occasion.

No, Beth hadn't yet agreed to come home—and the closest they'd gotten to a kiss was his peck on the cheek after he took her back to her apartment.

But they'd talked. Really talked. Heart to heart. And unless his gut was failing him, the road to reconciliation would be short from this point forward.

Two seagulls fluttered to the ground beside the table and waddled up to Noah.

"Can I give them a piece of fish?" The boy watched as the two birds cuddled feather to feather.

"Sure—but be prepared for a tussle. It's survival of the fittest in the natural world."

Noah broke off a chunk and tossed it to them.

The bird with a nicked beak stretched its neck and snatched it midair.

"See? That will be gone faster than—"

The gull set it on the ground, pecked it apart, and pushed half toward his companion.

Steve did a double take.

That was a first.

"Ah. I see Floyd and Gladys have dropped in for a visit." Charley sauntered over, a brown bag in hand.

"Are they your pets?" Noah stared at the man.

"No. They're old friends." He set the bag on the table. "Here's the order you placed for Beth."

Steve frowned. Cold tacos wouldn't be very appetizing. Charley was supposed to wait until she got here to make them. "Would they stay warmer in the—"

Beth's car turned the corner.

Huh.

How could the taco chef have predicted her arrival with such precision?

"My timing was perfect." The man watched Beth's car roll down Dockside Drive. "I ran into her this week at The Perfect Blend, and she mentioned she was meeting you here today at twelve fifteen. I've never known her to be anything but punctual."

Question answered.

Steve rose. "I'll walk her to the table."

"Very considerate." Charley claimed a seat on the bench. "I'll keep Noah company while you're gone, since there's no one in line for my fine fare at the moment."

Steve jogged toward his wife, arriving at the car as she eased her left leg out. "Sergeant Adams, state police. May I help you, ma'am?"

Her smile was genuine, not forced like it had been during their last meeting at the wharf. "This gives new meaning to the term curb service."

"We aim to please."

She passed him her crutches. "If you could hold these for me, that would help—and I'd appreciate it if you could carry this too." She picked up a bag from the seat beside her and handed it to him.

"I'll be happy to."

He waited while she stood, closed the door, and walked beside her as they traversed the path to the park.

"Sorry to slow you down." She sent him an apologetic glance.

"I can adjust my pace to yours. No worries." He met her gaze, willing her to recognize the deeper significance of his response—that it was a reinforcement of his promise Thursday night to let her set the pace for their reconciliation . . . and his vow to be patient, however long it took.

The faint flush on her cheeks said his message had been received.

As they entered the tiny park, Charley rose from his seat beside Noah. "I'll leave you three to enjoy your lunch. Keep up the good work, Noah."

"I'll try. The class is awesome. The teacher says I have a lot of potential."

"I'd have to agree—on many fronts." Charley encompassed all of them in his response, lifted a hand in farewell, and wandered back toward the stand.

"Hello, Noah." Beth stopped beside the table. "May I sit by you again?"

"Sure." He moved his bottle of water aside but didn't scoot to the far end of the bench as he had last week. "Is your knee getting better?"

"Yes, it is—and I have some news for you." She settled onto the bench, and Steve took her crutches. "There's going to be a festival here in town next month I think you'd enjoy."

As she proceeded to tell him about the event, Steve tuned in too.

Noah became so engrossed that he stopped eating. "That sounds epic!"

"Best of all, there will be sessions for younger folks too—including one on art and another on sandcastle building."

"Wow. I hope I can come."

"If your foster dad approves, maybe Steve and I could bring you."

Steve's breath hitched.

Beth wanted to commit to an event for the three of them four weeks down the road?

Hallelujah!

"I'll ask him. I don't think he'll mind, as long as I give him advance notice." He pulled one of the wrapped bundles out of the bag and set it in front of her. "You should eat, or your tacos will get cold."

"I've been waiting all morning for these." She sniffed the savory aroma as she unwrapped the package. "And I brought dessert too. Chocolate chip oatmeal cookies."

"My favorite?" Another encouraging development.

"Yes." Her color deepened again, and she made a project out of tucking a piece of red onion back into her taco.

"Noah, you're in for a treat. Beth bakes the best cookies in the whole world."

"I *love* cookies!" The boy beamed at both of them, dived back into his taco, and chattered away for the rest of the meal as he responded to Beth's interest and attention.

A rush of tenderness washed over Steve at the transformation in his young friend. The boy sitting in the park today was one-eighty from the subdued, beleaguered child in the school cafeteria.

Amazing how warmth and kindness could transform a life.

And this boy needed a heaping dose of both, based on the information in his file. A father who'd disappeared, a mother who'd died from a drug overdose, three foster homes in the space of as many years—and a possible history of abuse. Despite the attempts of the social worker to ferret out the truth, Noah had never admitted to being ill-treated by his mother—but his malnourished condition and suspicious bruises when he'd been taken under the wing of the child welfare folks were telling.

Those had healed—but who knew what other, less-visible wounds remained?

Beth would help heal those, though. For however long their lives continued to intersect, the boy would blossom under his wife's caring touch. She had a way of bringing out the best in people—even if her husband had been a slow learner.

That, however, would change going forward. He was a different man now. And he'd prove it to her every day for the rest of his life, if she gave him that chance.

As if she'd tuned in to his thoughts, she glanced toward him while Noah scarfed down a third cookie.

And then she slid her hand across the table.

Throat tightening, he wrapped her fingers in his. Gave them a squeeze.

She squeezed back, only breaking eye contact after Noah reclaimed her attention. But she left her hand in his.

Where it belonged.

The two gulls took flight while Noah and Beth continued to chat, winging toward the open sea. And as they soared toward the sun, against the deep blue backdrop of the heavens, Steve gave thanks.

For here in this little town with the perfect name, his prayers had at last been answered.

He and Beth were going to be okay.

28

The masterclass festival had been a smashing success.

And she was exhausted. Elated, but exhausted.

Christi picked up the bulging file that had kept her organized over the past five weeks, shoved it into the tote bag that did double duty as her purse, and waved to the volunteer cleanup crew putting the parish center at St. Francis back in order after the final Sunday session.

Next stop? The deck at Sea Glass Cottage, where she intended to put her feet up, enjoy a glass of lemonade, and—

Her phone began to vibrate in her pocket.

Heaving a sigh, she set the tote on a folding chair and pulled out the cell. Thank goodness the chamber of commerce was reimbursing her for festival-related calls on her pay-by-the-minute phone. The bill she'd racked up over the past month would have put a hefty dent in her budget.

But all those calls had paid off with a sold-out event.

She glanced at the screen—and her weariness evaporated.

Jack.

Smiling, she put the cell to her ear. "How did your second class go?"

As if she had to ask. Every seat had been snatched up in both of his sessions, and from what she'd observed after popping in for part of his presentation yesterday, his concerns about satisfying customers had been groundless. He was a natural, engaging speaker, and the audience had eaten up all his tips and stories.

"It was fine. But can I admit I'm glad it's over?"

"You can—and that makes two of us. I think I'll sleep for a week . . . at least while I'm not working."

"Where are you?"

"St. Francis—but I'm getting ready to head home and crash."

"Could I interest you in a celebration later? You deserve it after the work you put into this."

A spurt of reserve energy zipped through her. "What did you have in mind?"

"How about a picnic on the beach?"

Her pulse picked up. All these weeks, he'd kept his distance—despite the occasional, if brief, glimpses of banked fire she'd caught in his eyes when his guard slipped—but this sounded kind of like a date.

Getting her hopes up would be foolish, though. This wasn't a romantic rendezvous. How cozy could a beach picnic get with a child in tow?

Spirits deflating, she sank into one of the folding chairs. "Hannah will like that."

"Hannah won't be there."

What?

She vaulted to her feet again. "I thought you didn't like to leave her alone."

"I don't. She and that boy Beth and Steve brought to the festival hit it off at the sandcastle session yesterday. They invited her to join them for a pizza party tonight. I planned to have a threesome for our celebration, but I didn't want to tell her no. She could use a friend her own age."

Oh.

He hadn't intended for this to be a date.

Her spirits plummeted again.

On the bright side, though, a date by default was better than no date at all, right?

And one of these days, if she stayed the course, Jack would come around.

At least she hoped so.

Because as she'd realized over the past few weeks, she'd never stopped loving him. She may have convinced herself she'd moved on after he left, that she hadn't cared as much as she thought she had, but that had been denial, pure and simple. Deep in her heart—even in her self-centered days—she'd recognized goodness and grace when it had crossed her path.

And after all that had happened during the intervening years, she not only appreciated it even more—she was finally worthy of it.

Perhaps in time, if she continued to earn his trust, Jack would recognize that.

"Christi?"

"Yes." She refocused. "I'm here."

"So what do you think?"

"I'm glad Hannah connected with Noah. Beth's brought him to the shop on a couple of occasions. He seems like a nice boy."

"I meant about the picnic."

Did he sound a bit anxious? Like he was glad to have an opportunity to get her alone and hoped she'd say yes?

She rolled her eyes. You'd think she'd sat in on the acting masterclass Katherine Parker had taught, with all this melodramatic musing.

The wise course was to take his invitation at face value and see where it led.

"I could be persuaded—as long as you won't be insulted if I doze off while we're eating." Like that would happen. The electricity in the air whenever they were together would keep sleep at bay.

But better to be lighthearted about this or he might think she was reading more into the invite than he intended.

"No offense will be taken. Why don't I swing by the cottage around six and pick you up?"

Two hours. That would give her breathing space to chill for a while and take care of a few important matters—like redoing her hair and touching up her makeup.

"That works. What can I bring?"

"Nothing. I've got it covered. See you then."

He severed the connection, and she slid her cell back into her pocket as a delicious tingle raced through her.

A picnic on the beach with Jack.

What an unexpected end to the festival weekend—even if no romance was involved.

She hefted her tote bag and resumed her trek toward the door.

Charley pushed through as she approached. "Ah. The woman of the hour—or should I say the weekend? Kudos on a job well done."

"Thank you. I have to admit I'm thrilled with the results."

"You should be. And I'm even more impressed by the ripple effect. Tourism has been higher than usual all month—and I predict the residual effect will last all summer."

"I hope you're right. It would be the answer to a prayer."

"To many prayers."

"So what are you doing here?" She swept a hand over the room. "Between holding two painting classes and manning the taco stand in between, you have to be operating on fumes."

"On the contrary. The whole experience was energizing. I volunteered for the St. Francis cleanup crew too."

She grimaced. "I feel like a slacker, cutting out already."

"That's misplaced guilt. You've worked harder than anyone on this. You deserve a healthy dose of R&R. May I recommend a walk on the beach?"

"As a matter of fact, I *am* going to the beach."

"Wonderful. By the way, if you happen to run into Jack, would you let him know I sat in on part of his presentation yesterday and thought it was excellent? I didn't get to talk with him afterward."

Odd that he'd bring up Jack—and in the context of a beach.

Had to be a coincidence.

But she didn't intend to mention that. Until—or unless—Jack decided to ramp up their relationship, why fuel speculation in town?

"I'll do that."

"Enjoy your evening. And thank you again. Hope Harbor is in your debt."

He strolled off before she could respond—but Charley was wrong.

Coming to this tiny seaside town had changed her life—and she would always be in *its* debt. For her, Hope Harbor was a little piece of paradise.

The only thing that could make it better would be Jack's forgiveness and trust—and an opportunity to prove to him every day for the rest of her life that this time around, her love was here to stay.

Tonight was the night.

Jack hung a left onto Starfish Pier Road and picked up speed toward the beach as Christi told him a funny anecdote about the sandcastle class. Something to do with a harbor seal that had watched the proceedings from a close-in rock while belching his approval, which had sent the young participants into gales of laughter.

He was listening. He really was.

Sort of.

But it was hard to concentrate while trying to formulate a game plan. After all, until three hours ago, this celebration had included Hannah. It was supposed to be a simple, quick trip to the beach for brownies and a sunset show, not a one-on-one date.

Yet the impromptu invitation from Beth and Steve had seemed like a heaven-sent opportunity to take the next step with Christi after dragging his feet for weeks.

Not that his prudence and restraint hadn't been warranted, in light of their history. Who wanted to put their heart at risk twice?

An excess of caution, however, could immobilize. The time had come to break his self-imposed holding pattern and set a course for a new destination.

As Christi finished her harbor seal tale, he pulled onto the shoulder at the end of the road that led to Starfish Pier beach and set the brake.

"I guess I'm not a very engaging storyteller." She released her seat belt.

"What do you mean?"

"You didn't laugh at my punch line."

There'd been a punch line?

He must not have been listening as well as he'd thought.

"Will you buy the excuse that my brain is still fried from my two presentations and not operating at full capacity?"

A teasing glint sparked in her eyes. "It depends on what you're going to feed me. I didn't have lunch, and I'm starving. An excellent picnic will earn you great forbearance."

"I think the food will pass muster—but we'll see. Sit tight while I grab it from the trunk and get your door."

He circled the Jeep, stopping at the back to retrieve a throw and the large white shopping bag that held their dinner. He'd had to scramble to cobble together an impressive picnic after the last-minute change of plans, but the gourmet shop in Coos Bay had come through.

After pulling open her door, he held out his hand. "Let's claim a dune."

She didn't hesitate to tuck her fingers in his. "I haven't been to this beach yet."

"It's not the prettiest one in Hope Harbor—but the tide pools are world-class. They're at the far end of the beach, past what little remains of the namesake pier." He nodded to his right as they crested one of the small dunes that buffered the beach from the road. "Tide's in, though. We'll have to explore them another day and content ourselves with sand, sea, and seclusion tonight."

She surveyed the scene as he released her hand to shake out the throw. "It may not be the prettiest beach in the area—but for someone from the landlocked Midwest, this is spectacular."

"You're easy to please."

"Comes with maturity—and perspective." She angled toward him, holding his gaze for an instant before she snagged the end of the throw that was flapping in the breeze. "We should tag team this." After helping him spread their makeshift seat on top of the sand, she claimed one side. "Bring on the food."

He unpacked the bag, and as they dined on French bread, pâté, cheeses, chicken salad tucked in miniature croissants, and an assortment of desserts, they chatted about the festival.

"That was incredible." Christi picked up a bite-sized cheesecake. "The perfect ending to a perfect weekend." She lifted the sweet treat, as if in toast, and popped it in her mouth, leaving a smidgen of the filling on her lower lip.

Speaking of perfect . . . this was a tailor-made mood-changing opportunity.

Pulse accelerating, Jack reached over and gently swiped off the dab with his finger.

She stopped chewing.

He put his finger in his mouth and dispensed with the creamy confection.

Her breath hitched.

Mood change complete.

"We should talk."

A pulse began to throb in the hollow of her throat as she searched his face. "Okay."

"You've convinced me."

"Of what?" Caution warred with hope in her eyes, and she squeezed a handful of the sand beside her.

"That you've changed. That trusting you isn't a risk. That maybe the future I once thought we had didn't die eleven years ago. That God, in his wisdom, just pressed the hold button until we grew up and he was certain we were both ready for everything a serious relationship involves."

Her breath caught again, and her irises began to shimmer. "So how do we . . . where do we go from here?"

"Forward—if you're willing. To a proper courtship. I'd like to take you out in a style I couldn't afford the summer we met."

"I don't need that kind of courting." A tear welled on her lower lash. "Picnics on the beach are more my style now."

"We'll do that too." The tear spilled out and trailed down her cheek. "Hey." He gently swiped it away. "I didn't mean to make you cry."

"I just . . . I can't believe my prayers have finally been answered. It seems like more than I deserve."

Jack scooted closer and touched her cheek with none-too-steady fingers. "That's not true. Despite all the tough breaks you've had, you persevered. You walked through fire—and instead of letting it destroy you, you used it to forge a new life. From this point forward, you deserve the best life has to offer."

"I don't know about that—but I do know that all the bad breaks I've lamented did have an upside. They not only made me stronger and wiser, they brought me back to you. Which proves that good can come out of bad."

"I suppose the same is true for me, in hindsight. If I'd stayed in St. Louis, I might never have followed my dream to write a book. Or found Hope Harbor. Or discovered that law enforcement offered the perfect opportunity for me to deliver justice in real life the way I do in fiction." He exhaled. "It's been a long and winding road, though."

"Yet it led us here." She wove her fingers through his. Squeezed. "Back to each other."

He returned the squeeze. "Do you have any idea how hard it's been to keep from touching you these past few weeks?"

"Do you have any idea how much I *wanted* you to touch me these past few weeks?" Her response came out shaky. Breathless.

"Touching isn't all I wanted to do." He let his gaze drop to her lips.

"Touching isn't all I wanted you to do either."

The breeze picked up, ruffling her hair.

Too tempting to ignore.

He lifted his hand. Ran his fingers through the strands. The color was different than it had been eleven years ago, but it was as soft and silky as it had been during that bright St. Louis summer.

Her eyelids drifted closed, and she gave a quiet sigh. One that captured exactly how he felt.

Content.

As if his whole life had been a journey, and the destination was at last in sight.

A wave of yearning swept over him, too strong to ignore—so he did what he'd been wanting to do for weeks.

He leaned over and captured her mouth with his.

The kiss started out tender and sedate. A let's-get-reacquainted, welcome home, exploratory melding of lips.

But as Christi responded with a hunger that confirmed she was as ready for this moment as he was, it morphed into a Fourth-of-July fireworks finale, Tchaikovsky's 1812 Overture, and the Hallelujah Chorus all rolled into one.

By the time they separated, Jack's heart was pounding as hard as if he'd run a hundred-meter dash.

Arms looped around her neck, he rested his forehead against hers, their choppy breath mingling in puffs of warmth. "Maybe we need—" His voice rasped, and he cleared his throat. "Maybe we need a chaperone."

"We'll have one going forward. Don't forget about Hannah."

Hannah.

Right.

That was a subject they should discuss, if he could get his brain to cooperate.

He backed off far enough to see her face. "How do you feel about the idea of a ready-made family?"

Her lips curved up. "What's not to like? A wonderful guy plus a charming daughter equals a terrific package deal."

"But her presence does change the dynamics. And it may put a crimp in romance."

"Life's taught me to improvise and go with the flow. I expect those skills will come in handy with romance too. The bigger question is how you think Hannah will feel about this."

"Elated. I think her reaction will be, 'It's about time.'"

"I'll second that. As for romance—I suppose we'll have to work it in when the opportunity presents itself."

"Like now?" He brushed a kiss over her forehead. Trailed his lips down her temple.

"Uh-huh. I hope you . . ." Her voice squeaked. "I hope you don't anticipate a long courtship."

"Eight or ten months?" Fat chance, if he had anything to say about it.

Her groan confirmed they were on the same page. "You're killing me here."

"Three or four may suffice."

She eased back a tad to study him, the setting sun casting a golden glow on her skin. "We can take this slower if you prefer."

"Nope. I'm tired of slow—and I'm tired of waiting." He played with another lock of her hair. "I say we shift into high gear. Any objections?"

"Not a one."

"Then let's pick up the pace." He leaned forward—but jerked to a stop at a sudden, high-pitched squeak.

Up in the gold-and-orange-streaked sky, two gulls wheeled and dipped, putting on an exuberant aerial display.

"I'll say this for you, Jack Colby. You know how to throw a world-class picnic. Not only gourmet food but after-dinner entertainment."

He gave her a slow grin. "That's just the preshow. Are you ready to move on to the main act?"

Her eyes warmed. Sizzled. Beckoned. "I'll let actions speak louder than words." She tugged his head down.

And as the gulls continued their joyful noise overhead, he gave her a performance to remember.

Epilogue

"Good morning, Mrs. Colby."

At the warm nuzzle on her neck, Christi came slowly, deliciously awake.

Mrs. Colby.

Could there be any sweeter sound?

Smiling, she stretched and rolled over—toward her new husband of some eighteen hours. "I'll have to get used to that title."

"Take your time." He propped himself up on one elbow and began playing with her hair. "I'm not going anywhere."

"Neither am I."

"Best news I've had all day." He trailed a kiss across her forehead. "You hungry?"

"Are you referring to breakfast?" She slid her arms around his neck and wiggled closer.

His eyes darkened. "I *was*. Before we went to bed last night, I peeked at the gourmet fare your maid of honor prepared for us. But I could be persuaded to postpone that indulgence. I've learned to delay gratification—by eleven years in one particular case."

"Was it worth the wait?" She grazed her fingertips over the morning stubble on his chin, the nubby bristles creating a tantalizing friction against her fingertips.

"I think you already know the answer to that." He growled deep in his throat as she brushed the pad of her thumb over his mouth. "Keep that up, we may have to forget about breakfast altogether and focus on other priorities." He captured her hand and pressed his lips to her palm.

"Works for me—but speaking of priorities, don't you think we should call Hannah, make sure she's okay?"

"Later." He rested his hand on her hip, the possessive weight of it sending a shiver of delight through her. "Steve and Beth will take excellent care of her, and she was excited about spending a few days with them—and all the activities they have planned for her and Noah. They'll call if any issues arise. And it's not like we're going to Tahiti for a three-week tropical honeymoon—unfortunately."

"But we'll make the most of our four days in the San Juan Islands. Though I don't know how that could be any nicer than here." She glanced toward the late October view framed by the window in the master bedroom of Sea Glass Cottage. Towering spruce and pine trees, blue sky studded with billowy alabaster clouds, and the very top of the white tent where their small group of guests had shared hors d'oeuvres and cake yesterday afternoon after witnessing the exchange of vows on the secluded bluff high above the sea.

What more fitting place to begin their life together than in the cottage that had offered her a haven when she'd needed it most—and opened the door to a wondrous reunion? That had hosted family-style dinners and laughter and love these past four months—and become, for all three of them, the happy house Hannah had christened it during one of her earliest visits.

"I won't argue with that." He gently traced the curve of her jaw with his knuckles. "I love this place as much as you do. There's something special about—"

At the sudden rumble from her stomach, warmth flooded her cheeks. "Sorry. That is *so* not romantic."

He grinned. "But it moves food to the top of our priority list.

Let's check out what Tasha left us and save dessert for later." He winked, swung his feet to the floor, and stood. "Sit tight and I'll round it up. I think we deserve breakfast in bed today."

"Why don't I help you carry it up?"

"Nope. I can handle it." He pulled on a black T-shirt and padded over to the door. Paused beside the simple but elegant sleeveless white lace sheath she'd worn as they'd exchanged vows. "In case I forgot to tell you yesterday, that's a stunning dress."

"You didn't forget—and I'm glad you liked it."

"I like the stunning woman who wore it even more."

Pleasure rippled through her at the unbridled love in his eyes. "You could turn a girl's head with that kind of talk."

"I plan to do more than that after breakfast." His lips rose in a slow smile.

"Promises, promises."

"Give me five minutes."

He disappeared out the door—and was back so fast she barely had time to run a brush through her hair and stack pillows for them to lean against while they enjoyed their breakfast in bed.

"That was quick." She sat cross-legged as he approached with the loaded tray, a white-wrapped square package under his arm.

"Every minute away from you felt like an hour." He eased the tray onto the bed.

"You have a silver tongue."

"Nope. *You* inspire eloquence." He set the three-inch-thick package next to the tray and gave her a short but potent kiss.

"Another gift?" She lifted her hand and touched the flat platinum choker with the sapphire in the center that he claimed matched her eyes—and which she'd insisted on wearing to bed.

"Not from me. I caught a glimpse of this through the front window on my way to the kitchen. It was on the porch, leaning against the railing."

"It must be a wedding present."

"Why would someone leave it there?"

"We did ask people not to bring gifts. Maybe they didn't want to call attention to it."

"Could be. You want to open it now? The food won't get cold, and it will take a few minutes for the coffee to brew."

She surveyed the continental breakfast Tasha had somehow found time to put together during her whirlwind visit to act as maid of honor in the midst of getting ready for her restaurant grand opening. The croissants, jam, cheese, fresh fruit, pastries, and juice were tempting but why not wait until the coffee was ready and their feast was complete?

"Let's open it. I'm curious."

"It's on the heavy side, considering the size." He handed her the fourteen-by-fourteen-inch package.

She weighed it in her hands. "You're right. Want me to do the honors?" She indicated the business-size envelope taped to the top that was addressed to both of them.

"Have at it." He scooted beside her on the bed.

She pulled the envelope off, slit the flap, and removed two sheets of paper folded together. After opening them, she positioned the short cover note so they could both read it.

Mr. & Mrs. Colby:

My client has instructed me to pass this package along to you. It was discovered in a closet after the house was purchased from the estate of the original owner, John Wright.

My client has also instructed me to offer you the opportunity to buy the cottage. The price and a few other details are listed on page two and are nonnegotiable. I look forward to hearing from you.

All my best wishes on your marriage.

It was typed on company stationery and signed by the man who'd contacted her about leasing the cottage, his cell number jotted underneath.

Christi blinked.

Could this be for real?

She turned to Jack, who appeared as puzzled as she was. "What do you think?"

"The letterhead seems legit—but it's an odd approach to selling a house. And why now? I tried for months to convince the owner to talk to me and got nowhere."

"I have no idea—but all the dealings I've had with my mystery landlord have been unorthodox. This follows that pattern." A rush of excitement swept over her. "Wouldn't it be wonderful if Sea Glass Cottage was actually ours?"

"Yes. But much as I love this place, the nonnegotiable caveat raises a red flag. This person could be asking a gouge price. Not unheard of for desirable coastal property."

"You want to peek at page two—or have breakfast first?"

"At the risk of indigestion if the amount is sky-high, let's pull back the curtain."

She held out the two sheets of paper. "You do it."

"Chicken."

"Guilty."

He took the papers from her . . . took a breath . . . and switched the sheets back to front.

Christi curled her fingers around the edge of the package in her lap as he read, heart flip-flopping when twin creases appeared on his brow. "It's too high, isn't it?"

The grooves deepened. "This has to be a typo."

Shoot.

"How bad is it?"

After a moment, he held the paper out to her.

Bracing, she searched for the price. Did a double take after she found it.

"That can't be right—can it? I mean . . . I'm no real estate expert, and I'm too new here to have a feel for this market, but isn't this way low?"

"Yes."

"Do you think we should call the guy from the management company?"

"Yeah." Jack grabbed the cell he'd left on the nightstand, powered it up, and tapped in the number on the letter, switching to speaker as it rang.

The man answered at once. "Good morning, Mr. Colby. I've been expecting your call."

Jack took her hand. "I'm here with my wife, and we have you on speaker."

"You opened the package."

"Not yet. Only the letter attached to it."

"And you want to know if the sale price is a mistake."

"Yes."

"No, it's not. We advised the law firm representing the owner's interests that the property had been undervalued, but the owner didn't wish to change the price. As I told your wife when we discussed her lease arrangement in April, we're dealing with someone who appears to be rather eccentric. I would assume you're interested in pursuing a purchase."

"Yes." Christi and Jack spoke in unison, and he grinned at her.

"I'll let the law firm know and we'll begin the paperwork. In the meantime, enjoy your honeymoon, and best wishes to you both."

The line went dead, and Jack slowly set the phone back on the nightstand. "This is surreal."

"I agree. Who *is* this person—and why would they give us such a deal?"

"I haven't a clue. But what a wedding present."

Pressure built behind Christi's eyes. "Oh, Jack. I can't believe this place is going to be ours. Forever."

"It seems too good to be true—but I feel the same way about you and me being together for always too . . . and that says it's real." He touched the diamond-encrusted band on the fourth finger of her left hand.

"And *that* says the house deal is too." She nodded toward the letter, then smoothed a hand over the white wrapping paper on the package in her lap. "I wonder what this is?"

"Let's find out."

She worked the tape loose and pulled the paper and bubble wrap free to reveal a sea glass mosaic heart set on a clear glass background in a hexagon driftwood frame.

"Ohhhh." Christi traced a finger over the pieces of colorful glass, similar to the ones in the front door sidelights but even more translucent. "This is beautiful."

"There's a note." Jack pulled an envelope from the wrapping paper. "And it's been opened." He bowed it, and the top gapped. "Look how it's addressed." He held it up.

To the future owners of this cottage.

She took it and removed the handwritten note inside, angling sideways so Jack could see it too.

If you're reading this, you've purchased the home where I'd hoped to live out my retirement with my beloved wife, Kristen. But that was not in God's plan. He called her home before the cottage was finished, and I had no heart to complete the job—or live here without her by my side. Yet I couldn't part with this property, which was filled with our dreams. So I locked the door and walked away.

I made this suncatcher for Kristen and planned to give it to her the day we moved into the house. On my last visit, I left it here, with this note—where it belongs.

I gift this now to you. Not to make you sad but to encourage you to love this house as much as we did. To fill it with dreams. And to cherish each day you spend in this special place with the people who add sweetness and light and warmth to your days.

God bless you and keep you—always.

John Wright's signature was at the bottom.

"Check out the date." Jack's voice was hushed.

Christi fluttered her lashes to clear her tear-misted vision. Sucked in a breath as the date registered.

Different year, but the same month and day she and Jack had broken up. The day he'd intended to propose.

"That is so strange." She continued to stare at the date. "Not to mention their names. Versions of ours."

"It's almost like you and I were meant to be here together."

"And to have this." She ran a finger over the heart made of sea glass that had been tumbled and tossed by storms and waves until all the pieces had landed safely on this shore, the sharp edges and imperfections scoured away. "And also to have the happy ending they never had." She motioned toward the small dormer window at the front of the house that looked out over the forest. "This would be perfect in the east window."

"I agree." He took it from her, set it against the wall beside the bed, and rejoined her. "We have much to be grateful for today."

"I agree."

And not only for themselves. There were happy endings all around.

Beth and Steve had begun adoption proceedings for Noah. Jack's latest novel was finished and turned in. Hannah had settled into her new life here—even to the point of calling Jack "Dad." Tasha had her restaurant. The chamber of commerce had created a part-time special events coordinator position for her, and Beth was talking about a partnership in Eye of the Beholder.

Best of all, she had Jack.

Today and for always.

Life didn't get any better than this.

"So do you want to eat—or delay that gratification a bit while we celebrate our latest blessing?" The gold flecks in Jack's dark brown irises turned molten.

No contest.

"Why don't you move the tray and we'll discuss it?"

He whisked their breakfast away, returned in a flash, and tugged her close as a yellow-rumped warbler outside the window welcomed the new day in song and sunbeams danced across the sheets.

She went to him willingly, no longer in the least hungry. Because she was satisfied at the deepest possible level—in her heart and her soul.

And as he wrapped her in his arms and told her with every lingering touch, every gentle stroke, every tender caress, how much she meant to him, she gave thanks.

For despite the long and winding road they'd both traveled to find each other again in this tiny town on the Oregon coast, they'd at last reached their destination.

It was called home.

Read On for a Special Sneak Peek of the Triple Threat Series Conclusion!

Coming Soon

Someone was in the mortuary prep room.

Someone besides her and the body in the cooler, awaiting tomorrow's autopsy.

Someone who shouldn't be here.

Forensic pathologist Grace Reilly set aside the police report on seventy-six-year-old Mavis Templeton and cocked her ear.

Silence.

She waited, straining to pick up another out-of-place sound.

Only the drip of the leaky faucet, the hum of refrigeration from the cooler, and the squeak of the desk chair as she leaned forward broke the stillness.

There was no one here.

And she shouldn't be either.

There were better places for a thirty-year-old single woman to hang out at nine o'clock on Friday night than a funeral home in rural Missouri.

Unless you were a thirty-year-old single woman whose last hot date had been three months ago. A date that had cooled off fast after the guy asked about your day—and you'd told him in perhaps a *tad* too much detail while the two of you were chowing down on barbecue.

Grace sighed and slumped back in the chair.

As soon as the color began leeching from her companion's complexion, she'd changed the subject—but not fast enough to salvage the evening or win herself another dinner invitation. He'd dumped most of his meal into a takeout container, hustled her home as fast as he could, and never called again.

So with nothing more interesting to do on *this* Friday night, she'd swung by the mortuary to review the paperwork and medical records for tomorrow's autopsy.

Pathetic.

Huffing out a breath, she pushed the chair back and stood. She was out of here. Watching a movie by herself from her collection of oldies wasn't her first choice of activity for a date night, but it was preferable to—

She froze.

There it was again. A muffled, metallic tapping noise. Faint but discernible.

And it was coming from the cooler.

A shiver snaked down her spine.

The only person in there was Mavis—and she wasn't doing any tapping.

Sidling around the desk, she eyed the refrigeration unit. There had to be a logical explanation for the noise.

Of course there did.

Nevertheless, she opened her purse and pulled out the compact Beretta she'd carried ever since—

No.

She was *not* going there.

That was then, this was now—and lightning didn't often strike twice. She was overreacting.

Even so, she kept her pistol at the ready as she approached the cooler.

The faint tap sounded again, more to the right—and muffled. Like it was outside the building.

Exhaling, she lowered the gun. A noise on the other side of the wall was nothing to worry about. For all she knew, a carful of teenagers had pulled into the parking lot of the funeral home and decided to down a few illegal beers where no one was likely to disturb them.

This out-of-proportion response to a stray noise wasn't like her.

But she *was* tired. It had been a long week, and she was stretched thin. Doing autopsies for six adjacent rural counties—not to mention the occasional private job she picked up—kept her on the move.

Add in that weird noise she'd heard outside the window of her rental house last night, and it was no surprise her usual calm was a mite wobbly.

Time to call it a night, go home, watch that old movie—and chill.

She returned to the desk, picked up her purse, and started to tuck her Beretta inside. Hesitated. Shook her head in annoyance.

This was farm country, for pity's sake. Two and a half hours away from St. Louis and the types of crime that plagued all big cities. In the three years she'd been doing autopsies for the county coroners, homicides had been few and far between.

After all, if you couldn't be safe deep in the heartland, where could you be safe?

Despite that little pep talk, she kept her weapon in hand—where it would stay until she was behind the wheel of her car and locked inside. It never hurt to be careful . . . as she'd learned the hard way.

She exited through the wide back door in the small foyer off the work area, filling her lungs with the warm June air as she gave the dim parking lot a swift perusal.

No beer-drinking teens in sight.

So much for that theory.

Nor was anyone else about. Whatever the source of the noise she'd heard from inside, it was gone.

More proof that letting her imagination give her a case of the shakes had been silly.

She closed the door behind her, tested it to make certain it was locked, and strode toward her Civic.

Six feet away, she came to an abrupt halt, stomach lurching.

Apparently the noise she'd heard hadn't been innocent after all.

And despite her original suspicion that it had come from inside the cooler, this had been done by someone very much alive.

Backing up, she groped in her purse for her cell. Punched in 911.

And kept her finger on the trigger of her Beretta.

Sheriff Nate Cox hung a right into the parking lot of Larktree Mortuary and circled around to the back.

First call he'd ever gotten to a funeral home—but there'd been a ton of firsts since he'd been elected to the job four months ago.

A Larktree cruiser came into sight, and Nate pulled up beside it. Thank goodness local police were willing to respond to 911 calls until he or one of his deputies could arrive. With only seven of them providing 24/7 coverage for more than 750 square miles of territory, it wasn't unusual to be twenty minutes away from a crime scene, even with sirens blaring and a heavy foot on the gas pedal.

But despite the courtesy response, the mortuary was beyond the town limits—and therefore outside the jurisdiction of the local cops. Meaning this case was going to land on his desk.

He slid out of his patrol car as the officer walked toward him from the shadows of the protective roof that shielded the back door of the building. Over the man's shoulder, Nate squinted at the victim, who remained near the exit, purse gripped in front of her, posture taut. Though he couldn't distinguish any features in the dim light, she appeared to be on the young side.

"Matt Jackson." The fiftyish officer stuck out his hand.

Nate gave him a firm shake and returned the introduction. "Thanks for responding. I got here as fast as I could."

"No worries. It's a quiet night in town."

"What do we have?"

The man gave him a cursory overview. "I poked around after I got here, but I didn't see anything helpful."

"Thanks. I'll take another look. Two sets of eyes can't hurt. Who's the victim?"

"Grace Reilly."

It took no more than a second for her name to click into place. He'd seen it on a few autopsy reports—including one that had struck too close to home—but their paths had never crossed.

"What was she doing here at this hour?"

"Paperwork."

"On a Friday night?"

The man shrugged. "To each his own. Said she was prepping for an autopsy tomorrow."

Must be the one for Mavis Templeton. He'd responded to that call yesterday morning—and there'd been no other suspicious deaths in the past few days.

"Anyone else here?"

"No."

She'd been alone in a mortuary with a dead body after dark—by choice.

He suppressed a shudder. After all the death he'd seen during military missions overseas, the idea of spending an evening in the company of a lifeless body shouldn't spook him.

But it did.

Having death thrust upon you was one thing. Seeking it out? Altogether different.

"Thanks again for swinging by and hanging out until I got here."

"Happy to do it. Good luck."

As the officer returned to his cruiser, Nate circled Grace's car, giving it a cursory scan. It had been keyed on all door panels and sported several small, deep, round dents—as if someone had hammered the end of a pipe against the frame.

Circuit complete, he walked over to her, extending his hand as a low rumble of thunder reverberated in the distance. "Nate Cox. I've read quite a few of your reports. Sorry we have to meet under these circumstances."

"Likewise."

Her fingers were cold as she returned his firm squeeze, and he gave her a quick assessment.

Early thirties, at most. Five-four, give or take an inch, using his six-foot frame as reference. Wavy, longish hair the color of the spicy ginger cookies his mom used to make. A strong chin that could suggest a personality to match. Hazel eyes that were big—and appealing.

He frowned at that last, inappropriate thought. Cataloging a victim's features was part of the job. Reacting to them wasn't.

Switching mental gears, he refocused. "I know you told Officer Jackson what happened tonight, but I'd appreciate it if you'd run through it again."

She complied, her report straightforward, precise, and detailed. No less than he'd expect from a forensic pathologist. They were trained to tune in to the tiniest details.

"And that's what I found when I came outside." She motioned toward her car as she concluded.

"Any idea who may have done this?"

"No."

"Any known enemies?"

"No."

"Does anyone have a grudge against you?"

"Not that I'm aware of."

"Have you received any recent threatening communication?"

She hesitated . . . and a blip appeared on his radar.

"Not communication in the sense you mean it."

"Explain that."

She exhaled and tucked her hair behind her ear. "I'm probably being paranoid."

"Or not—considering the state of your car."

She conceded the point with a nod. "Last night, about one in the morning, I heard a noise that sounded like someone was rattling the knob on my back door."

"Did you call the police?"

"No. It was windy, and I wasn't certain anyone was out there. I also have excellent locks, a security system, and my Beretta was on the nightstand. I didn't think there was any real danger. But it was rather unnerving."

The lady kept a weapon close at hand while she slept?

The blip got bigger.

Author's Note

Welcome back to Hope Harbor—where hearts heal . . . and love blooms.

For those who've lost count, this is book #8—with at least three more to come! I hope you're as thrilled as I am that more books are on the horizon. From day one, I hoped this would become a long-running series loved by readers the world over, and I'm so grateful my wish has come true. Hope Harbor books consistently make bestseller lists in the United States, and they've been translated into multiple languages. The series has become especially popular in Germany and the Netherlands.

Thank you, readers, for embracing this special town—and loving it as much as I do.

I also want to thank my husband, Tom, who is always front and center in my cheering section, celebrating my successes . . . and encouraging me on days when I need a boost. In addition to Tom, I owe a huge debt of gratitude to my parents, my faithful and earliest cheerleaders. Until four months ago, when my dad's life ended in a handful of days after a devastating diagnosis, I could count on him to tell everyone he met about his "famous" novelist daughter—as my mom did before I lost her six years ago. I can never thank these three special people enough for all the love and support they've given me through the years.

Finally, I want to offer special thanks to The Honorable Maureen A. Gottlieb, Circuit Court Judge in the Family Division in Kent County, Michigan, for her invaluable insights into the world of family law and guardianship issues.

So what's next for me? In October, watch for the final book in my Triple Threat series, *Body of Evidence*. This one features forensic pathologist Grace Reilly, who finds herself in the line of fire after she discovers a disturbing pattern in the autopsies of older rural residents. And in April 2023, I'll take you back to Hope Harbor with a story about a reclusive man, an isolated estate, and a woman who's taken a leap of faith.

Until then, enjoy *Sea Glass Cottage*!

Irene Hannon is the bestselling, award-winning author of more than sixty contemporary romance and romantic suspense novels. She is also a three-time winner of the RITA award—the "Oscar" of romance fiction—from Romance Writers of America and is a member of that organization's elite Hall of Fame.

Her many other awards include National Readers' Choice, Daphne du Maurier, Retailers' Choice, Booksellers' Best, Carol, and Reviewers' Choice from *RT Book Reviews* magazine, which also honored her with a Career Achievement award for her entire body of work. In addition, she is a two-time Christy award finalist.

Millions of her books have been sold worldwide, and her novels have been translated into multiple languages.

Irene, who holds a BA in psychology and an MA in journalism, juggled two careers for many years until she gave up her executive corporate communications position with a Fortune 500 company to write full-time. She is happy to say she has no regrets.

A trained vocalist, Irene has sung the leading role in numerous community musical theater productions and is also a soloist at her church. She and her husband enjoy traveling, long hikes, coffee shop outings, and spending time with family. They make their home in Missouri.

To learn more about Irene and her books, visit www.irenehannon.com. She posts on Twitter and Instagram but is most active on Facebook, where she loves to chat with readers.

Meet

IRENE HANNON

at www.IreneHannon.com

Learn news, sign up for her mailing list,

and more!

Find her on